THE NIGHTMARE'S EDGE

MATTEA LORETTA

PublishAmerica
Baltimore

© 2004 by Mattea Loretta.
All rights reserved. No part of this book may be reproduced, stored in a retrieval system or transmitted in any form or by any means without the prior written permission of the publishers, except by a reviewer who may quote brief passages in a review to be printed in a newspaper, magazine or journal.

First printing

ISBN: 1-4137-3224-0
PUBLISHED BY PUBLISHAMERICA, LLLP
www.publishamerica.com
Baltimore

Printed in the United States of America

DEDICATED TO MY SISTER, CECILIA, WHO DIED BEFORE SHE COULD LIVE HER DREAMS.

CHAPTER ONE

Cruising through the narrow streets of Rome in the rented sports car, Andrew felt like a young man once more. Though the seriousness of his visit should have made him more cautious, he was savoring every moment of the adventure. The sense of freedom surging through him with each hairpin curve he took in his attempt to lose the figure behind him, was like a breath of fresh air and he never wanted the feeling to end.

His life normally consumed by the painful memories of his beloved wife's murder, of knowing the car bomb responsible for her death was meant for him left little room for anything but solitude and guilt. Withdrawing from the world and the things that reminded him of Sophia, including their son, was the only way he knew to safeguard his heart from ever feeling such pain again.

Yet, as he raced through the streets of Rome, the instincts which once made him a top agent stirred widely within his soul. Driven not only by his passion for the mission and what it meant to his future but also by his last encounter with his son, Andrew felt something coming alive inside he thought was long dead.

The events surrounding him as he continued the game were like an adrenaline high growing more exciting with each obstacle he encountered despite the risk to the mission. Whether those obstacles were manmade, like the dozens of tourists rushing across his path as they tried to maneuver through the busy streets of Rome, or those responsible for making the city famous, the vast pillars and ancient churches every street corner, Andrew never missed a beat as he drove through the narrow streets. As if the majesty and magic of the Holy City with its grand splendor and mystic powers were affecting even him.

Looking through the rear view mirror at the red car tailing him, Andrew found himself intrigued by the man inside. Was he working under orders from the president or was the agency his employer? Was he there to help or hinder him in his mission? Or maybe it was the folder and the contents he was after? Whatever the reason, the man appeared to be just as caught up in the game with his dogged pursuit of his prey and Andrew was pleased to see this.

Racing through a red light, hoping the driver behind him would do the same, Andrew realized his behavior could cost him a lot more than a few speeding tickets from the local constabulary if he were not careful. If anyone got hold of the file and the facts inside, then the fate of an entire country and its people would be altered forever.

Glancing over at the envelope lying next to him, even as he debated the fool hardiness of his actions, Andrew realized the loss to him personally was minor in comparison to what the people of San Sebastian could lose if things did not work out for them, and he prayed he would not regret his decision to keep the folder a secret from everyone involved. He was at a crossroad in his life and each action he took from now on was going to cost him dearly if he wasn't careful.

Turning down a small street leading away from the main road, he watched with humor as his shadow struggled to keep up with him. Though amused by the driver and his efforts to remain in the game, Andrew found his thoughts drifting from the events surrounding him to the past. He made so many mistakes in his road to self-discovery, and he hoped it was not too late for him to finally make things right. He spent nearly ten years filled with such rage over the cards fate dealt him that it cost him not only a career he loved but a son too, and Andrew knew even as he fought to return to the world and start over, he could never get those years back.

For a little while he thought to himself; he had everything a man could want. Sharing both a professional and personal life with the woman he loved and having a son they adored was like living the American dream. For seven years he had it all, until the fateful day Sophia was taken from him, killed by an assassin's bomb. Her death destroyed not only the dreams they shared for each other but turned his life into a nightmare he could not escape from.

Unable to cope with her death or with the boy who bore a striking resemblance to her, Andrew closed his heart to everything that reminded him of his wife including the son they shared. Shipping him off to boarding school, allowing his best friend to become Stephen's surrogate father was the only way he could handle the grief he felt, and in the end his actions cost him more than he ever imagined. Steven was a stranger to him, like a distant relative he saw on holidays or weekends, and even when they were together, the pain was so great it blinded them to what the other was feeling.

"Sorry," Andrew shouted out the window, his thoughts returning to the present and the taxi cab he almost hit. "The same to you," he replied, the hand gesture from the driver causing him to laugh as he drove past the cab.

Funny, he thought he spent so much time avoiding life over the years he never realized just how much of it he missed. Even the simplest of things like the taxi driver's unflattering gesture reminded him of all he wanted back in his life. It took him a long time to see the world again as a place he wanted to be a part of, and he hoped it was not too late to show his son just how much he really loved him. No longer the little boy who witnessed his mother's murder, Steven had grown in to a strong young man who was about to graduate from high school, and Andrew wanted to be apart of his life.

"If only I wasn't so weak after she died," he whispered as he continued to think about the mistakes of the past. If he hadn't allowed his thirst for revenge to consume his soul, then maybe he would not be on the threshold of making a decision now which could alter the fates, not only his life but Stephen's too. He was in too deep to back out and prayed the actions he was about to take would not cost him the last chance he might ever have to make things right with his son.

"Still there I see," he mumbled, checking the mirror for his shadow, the sound of a horn blowing returning his focus to the problem at hand. Relieved to see the car was still behind him, Andrew realized he did not want the chase to end too soon. If he was going to figure out why he was under surveillance, he needed the driver to play an important part in the next step of the game.

Turning down a small dirt road and moving cautiously up the hillside as he kept an eye on his prey, Andrew decided to get as far away from the public eye as possible before he made his move. If forced to confront his adversary, the last thing he needed was a street filled with witnesses to tell the police what they saw.

Staring at a father and son walking along the roadway, Andrew's thoughts drifted back to his son and the hand of forgiveness Steven extended out of the blue a few months earlier. The simple act of inviting his father on a fishing trip helped to reopen the lines of communication between them and gave him hope they could finally put things right between them. The trip a yearly father and son event sponsored by the school was normally reserved for Mark, and Steven's actions meant more to Andrew than he ever imagined. For the first time in years, they sat down together and really listened to each other, really talked like they never had before, and though there were still things to work out, scars in need of healing, Andrew knew they were finally getting their lives back on track. Recalling how good he felt after the trip and the encouragement he received from his son, Andrew knew his latest actions could cost him everything they worked so hard to achieve if he was not careful. Agreeing to this latest mission in Rome, leaving without talking to his son first might be the final act of betrayal that could tear them apart forever. As much as he wanted to tell Steven why he was leaving, he could not put his son at risk again, and he had to believe in the end the boy would understand his reasoning and forgive him.

Looking in the rear view mirror to see if the vehicle was still following him, Andrew thought about what brought him to Rome in the first place, and whatever recriminations he was feeling would have to take a back seat until those reasons were resolved. He needed to focus on the mission and the man in the car if he wanted to come out of this mess not only alive but a free man too.

"There you are," he whispered, spotting the sedan coming up from behind as it passed another car."Thought I lost you on the last turn," Andrew said sarcastically as the car continued to follow him.

Though he appeared a little green, the driver was good, though not quite up to Andrew's standards, he still managed to stay with the more experienced agent and hold his own. It was apparent he did not want the game to end either with his persistence, and this impressed Andrew as they continued up the mountain pass.

"Ready for the next move?" Andrew asked as if talking directly to the man in the other car. "Ok, then let's go." He continued shifting the gears once more as he sped up. "Time to see just how good you really are," he mumbled, setting his plan into motion.

Andrew McCormick, just a few months shy of his fiftieth birthday joined the agency while still in college. Recruited by Stewart Gibbs, the man who would later become both his boss and his friend, he found the excitement of the agency everything he ever wanted in life and more.

A man of high moral standards, he could be both a deadly adversary and a loyal friend without going against the ethics his parents taught him as a child. A quick learner he moved quickly through the agency ranks. First as a field officer and then as head of an elite squad, his natural abilities and leadership qualities made him the perfect leader. The team was part of a splinter group working outside of the agency's normal parameters and was so top-secret only a few members of government knew of its existence. The missions, many of which could not be publicly sanctioned by the government, often forced his team to cross the line to protect the safety of the country he fought for.

Skilled in the martial arts as well as a top marksmanship Andrew could also speak several languages including French, German, and Italian.

A man whose life was filled with heartache, Andrew buried not one but two wives in a matter of ten years. His first wife, a young rebel girl he married while assigned to San Sebastian, died during a gun battle with the opposing forces. While his second wife, Sophia, fell victim of an assassin's bomb. Devastated by her death, he found he could no longer handle the responsibilities of working in the field and accepting a job as an negotiator for the agency was the only way he could remain in the only world he knew. Becoming a man who found the solutions to the problems with words instead of with death and violence gave him a sense of security and solitude he sought as he mourned for his lost loves.

Handsome in his own right, he bore the scar of battle over his left eyebrow from a mission that went wrong. Though it did not hinder his good looks in any way, it was a consent reminder of how violent his world once was.

His deep blue piercing eyes and sandy brown hair with just a hint of gray around the temples helped to enhance the image of a suave spy often seen in dime store novels.

A natural athlete who jogged and skied to keep in shape, Andrew tried not to let the passages of time destroy the few pleasures in life he enjoyed. His strict regiment not only worked as a means of therapy but held him to remain both physically and mentally fit for any challenge he might encounter at the negotiation table.

"Let's just see how good you are." He began speeding up once more as the driver continued to follow him. "Come on, kid, try to keep up, I can't do this all day," he remarked as the driver appeared to be have problems staying on the road.

Slowing down, the sight of a truck a few feet ahead of him gave him an idea, Andrew decided it was time to put the game to an end. Moving closer as he waited for just the right moment, he followed the truck down a small hill before speeding up in time to pass it as they finally reached the end of path. Veering to the left barely missing the mountain's ledge as his tires whirled for a moment caught in the gravel beneath it, Andrew realized just how risky his actions were.

"Maybe next time."Hhe laughed as the driver of the red car attempted the same maneuver and failed. "Great," he mumbled, looking at the narrow path they were now on as he drove in front of the truck. As long as the driver remained on the road, his purser could not pass him and that would give him more time to find the one thing he needed to end the game.

"Come on," the driver of the other car snapped angrily as he tried several times to get around the truck. He came too far to lose his prey because of a one lane dirt road and a lead foot driver. "Hello, this is Scott." He began taking the time to contact his employer over his cell phone as he waited for another opportunity to pass the truck. "That's what I said," he shouted, swerving several times to keep from going off the mountain's edge.

"He's on to me and he's turned the damned surveillance into a game," he explained, pulling the phone away from his ear as the voice on the other end continued to yell loudly at him. He knew going up against the legendary Andrew McCormick was not going to be easy, but he never figured it would be such a pain in the ass either. The man who was almost fifty and out of the field for over ten years was as good as the rumors of the past implied he was, and this surprised the young agent.

"Look damn it, I am doing the best I can," Scott argued. "No, I haven't lost him, and I don't intend to either," he snapped. "But this bastard isn't acting like the burnt out agent you said he was. He is behaving just like the Andrew McCormick we learned about at the academy," he confessed, pausing as the person on the phone began to ask questions. "What! Of course I can keep up with him," he stated, trying not to let the tone in his voice reveal the doubts he possessed. If he wanted to prove to the agency that he was a good field operative, then he could not let his superiors know how unsure he was of his ability to outwit the man he was assigned to follow.

"Are you sure about the information we have on him?" he questioned as they continued their conversation. The in-tel on Andrew was the main reason he took the assignment in the first place. If the data on him was true and he was a rogue, then nailing him would be a feather in any agent's cap let alone someone fresh from the academy.

"I know," Scott argued as the person on the other end reminded him of the importance of the mission. "I don't care what you say, if my ass is going to be on the line, there better not be any doubt about what you told me," he shouted, dropping the phone before he could finish his sentence as he nearly missed yet another curve. "Yes, I am still here," he uttered, grabbing the phone after regaining control of his car. "No, it is this damned truck in front of me, I have been stuck behind it for nearly a mile now," he explained. "What? Of course I have tried to get around him, but it's a small mountain road, and there's no room to maneuver," he uttered, angrily. "What? Yes, I remember my training," he snapped. "All right I will try," he replied before hanging up the phone. "I'll show you who is an amateur" he mumbled under his breath, the words from his employer still stinging even as he prepared to take his next dangerous step.

Shifting the car into gear, Scott moved towards the mountain's edge as he tried to find just enough leeway to get past the obstacle which kept him from his prey.

"Easy kid, watch that turn," Andrew shouted as the driver of the car tried to get around the truck. "Come on, kid, you're too close to the ledge. Don't try to overtake him now, wait till he hits the hill," he yelled, though he was too far away for the driver to hear him. "Slow down," his warning coming too late as the driver lost his battle with the mountainside.

Watching as the events unfolding before him grew more dire, Andrew rushed back to the spot where the driver went over the mountain.

"Damn it," Andrew mumbled, standing by the ledge with the truck driver as they both let out a sigh of relieve to see the car had not gone completely over the cliff but instead sat perched along a small ravine. "Call the police," he ordered before slowly making his way down the path, the smell of burning rubber and steel growing stronger with each step he took.

What am I doing? Andrew wondered as he struggled to make his way down the mountain side. The mere fact he was being followed meant someone was on to him and whether it was a member of the Vega contingency he came to negotiate with or Gibbs himself, he was wasting valuable time trying to reach the wreckage. If he was smart, he would get back in his car and drive away before things got any worse then they already were. The truck driver was getting help so leaving the man in the car until they arrived would be all right.

"I'm coming," he shouted, the sounds of the injured man's cries for help belaying any doubts of remaining there to help. Whatever the risk, he could not desert the young man trapped inside the car. Already smoking from the small fire beneath its frame, the car would not remain on the ledge much longer, and if he did not help get the man out in time, he would have to live with yet another death on his hands. Pausing for a moment as he heard the driver cry out again, Andrew tried to reassure the terrified man he was not alone.

"Hang on, kid, I'm coming," he yelled as the strong odor of gasoline filling the air made it harder for him to breathe. "Don't move. I'll be there in a second," Andrew repeated, afraid even the slightest motion from the man would send them all over the edge. Staggering to his feet, a missed step in a sinkhole nearly cost his own life; Andrew found himself gasping for air as he finally reached the car.

"Take it easy, kid. I'm here to help you," he whispered to the driver as the terrified man stared at him.

"Andrew, you came to help me," Scott replied, finding it difficult to breath.

"Of course I came," Andrew said as he looked around. "I hate leaving a game before the final play," he joked as he continued to assess the damages surrounding him.

"How bad is it?" Scott asked.

"Relax, kid. I've got it covered," Andrew said, hoping his doubts would not seem as apparent to Scott as they were to him. "Ok," he began after looking around. "Here is the situation. The car is on fire, and if we don't get out of here soon, then both of us will end up at the bottom of this mountain," he explained, hoping the honesty of his words would give the boy the strength he needed to follow his orders without question. "Can you move?" he asked, looking at the injuries to the driver's left leg. "Good," he said after Scott indicated he could. "I have to pull you out of the car, and I can't take the time to be gentle about it," Andrew revealed, coughing with each breath he took as the air around him continued to fill up with smoke. "It's going to hurt like hell," he explained, looking at the blood pouring from the gash on his leg.

"Just do it," Scott yelled, fighting his own fears.

"Are you ready?"

"Yes! No wait," the man screamed before Andrew could get him out.

"What is it?"

"I want you to know what my name is," he began.

"We can save the introductions for later," Andrew replied.

"Please. My name is Scott Simpson, and I am from South Florida," he said as he stared into Andrew's eyes. "I want you to know that in case I don't make it," he uttered, gasping once more as the pain grew worse. "Promise me that you will make sure my parents are allowed to bury me and I won't get lost in the bureaucracy."

"You'll make it, kid. Don't worry," Andrew said, trying to reassure the young man as he moved towards him.

"Promise me," Scott cried.

THE NIGHTMARE'S EDGE

"Ok, I promise," Andrew vowed before pulling him from the car, ignoring his screams of pain as he did. "Hang on, kid," he yelled, placing him on the ground just a few feet from the burning car as he looked around. "Damn," Andrew snapped. He'd been so wrapped up in getting the boy out of the car he never noticed the fire or the path it now took. Moving quickly around them, the flames totally engulfed the escape route he planned to use. The fire made its way up the mountain ledge.

"What's wrong?" Scott mumbled, barely able to talk.

"Relax kid, I am just taking a moment to enjoy the view," Andrew joked as he looked around for another avenue of escape. It was obvious from the amount of blood Scott was losing that the leg injury was critical and every second he delayed in getting him medical treatment was bringing the boy closer to death.

"What?" he shouted as the truck driver yelled down to him, trying to signal there was another trail just a few feet away from them. "Thanks," Andrew replied, moving closer to the trail to check it out before taking another chance at moving his patient. Not the best escape route, with its tall weeds and hidden hazards would have to do if he were going to get them off the ravine in time.

Grabbing Scott once more, Andrew began his trek up the mountain, the weight of his patient and the smoke from the fire causing him to stumble several times.

"I am just going to put you down here for a minute," he said, placing him down in an attempt to catch his breath. "Everything is fine," he assured him.

Though the delay was risky for the young man, Andrew knew if he did not stop, even for a second, neither one of them would make it up the mountain. "Now you just relax and we will be back on the roadside in no time."

"Andrew," Scott began.

"Don't talk, kid. You need to rest."

"Please, you have to listen to me."

"Later, kid, we'll talk later," Andrew promised.

"No now," Scott screamed, grabbing him by the shirt as he pulled his rescuer closer.

"Ok, kid. What is it?" Andrew replied, hoping if he let the distraught young man talk, he would calm down and relax before his actions injured him.

"I was sent here to watch you because of that file; they know you have it," Scott began.

"I figured that," Andrew replied. "It's ok, kid. You were only doing your job."

"No listen," Scott moaned, finding it more difficult to talk. "I was told you committed treason and murder to get those files, and you were a rogue agent trying to sell them to the highest bidder."

"What?" a stunned Andrew replied. "I never sold out to anyone."

"I never believed it, but I had to find out for sure," Scott confessed. "You're not a rogue agent; if you were, you never would have come back for me," the dying man said as Andrew continued to listen to him. "I don't know what is going on, but until you learn the truth, don't trust anyone," he ordered. "Especially anyone at the agency."

"The agency?" Andrew questioned, surprised once more by the man's words.

"The orders on you came from the agency itself," Scott explained. "If you didn't steal those files to sell to the highest bidder, then someone is trying to set you up, and you can't trust any of them."

"Ok, kid, I won't," Andrew replied, more concerned with getting his patient to the roadside than with the news he gave him. Whatever was going on he would figure it out later; he needed to get the boy medical help before it was too late

"You have to return the file before it is too late," Scott cried.

"I can't," Andrew mumbled. He gone too far to turn back now and nothing could change what he already did. "Come on, kid, let's get you up the mountain," Andrew said, turning his attentions back to the injured man.

"Don't you understand?" Scott cried, grabbing Andrew by the shirt as he tried to fight his rescuer. "They're after you and you can't trust any of them." The words of warning were his last.

"Damn, don't you die on me," Andrew yelled angrily at the young man.

"Don't you die on me, not now, not when we are almost home free," Andrew screamed, shaking the lifeless body of the man he just rescued. "Damn you! Do not die now."

"Hey, what are you doing?" the driver of the truck shouted, seeing the strange behavior of the man below.

"What?" Andrew replied, looking up for a moment as the sound of the driver's voice distracted him from his actions "I'm sorry, kid," he whispered, turning back to the dead man laying on the ground. He never wanted this to happen, never meant for the game to turn deadly.

"Is he dead?" the driver asked as Andrew finally made his way to the road with the body of the dead agent.

"Yes," he replied, looking at the boy who barely had a chance to become a man.

Walking towards his car without saying another word, Andrew got inside to leave. There was nothing left for him to do and the last thing he wanted was to face any questions from the local police. He knew the local constable responsible for the mountain region they were in and did not want to come face to face with him just yet. Friends for nearly fifteen years, Hans was not the type of man who could be easily fooled and answering his questions could only jeopardize the mission further. For now his involvement in the young man's death would have to remain a secret. When the mission was over, talking not only to Hans, but keeping his word to the young agent would be his top priority.

"You can not leave," the truck driver yelled at him in Italian as he got into his car. "What about the police?"

"You saw what happened, didn't you? He tried to get around your truck and lost control of his car and crashed," Andrew remarked. "So tell the police that."

"But you risked your life to save him," the driver protested.

"And I failed, didn't I?" Andrew replied as he started the engine. "Tell them a good Samaritan came by and leave it at that," he remarked before driving off.

Turning back to see the driver writing down the plate number from his car, Andrew smiled slightly. "That won't help," he whispered to himself as the driver jotted down the numbers. The rental car was registered under one of his aliases, and by the time the police found the abandoned car, he would be long gone. There was nothing to connect him with the accident, and he intended to keep it that way.

Heading back to the hotel after taking care of the car, Andrew sat quietly in the lobby for a few minutes as the warnings from the dead agent continued to haunt him. He was so careful not to let anyone except Mark know what was going on, not even his superiors, yet if the last words Scott spoke were true, then all his precautions were for nothing. What did he mean by his warnings? What did he know that Andrew didn't?

Though his mind was filled with questions about the young agent and his warnings, Andrew found himself intrigued by the entire matter. Not only did he have to deal with the Vega brothers and the reasons behind his trip but now he had another mystery on his hands as well. Was he being set up by someone in the agency to look like a traitor? Was someone really killed back home as

Scott implied, or were his dying words simply a ploy to throw the agent off the scent? Maybe the dead man worked for one of the Vega brothers, maybe Phillip or Antonio was setting him up to take a fall so he could not vote at the counsel meeting? Whatever was happening, he would enjoy figuring it out. Like the old days, he was deep within the game and eager to begin the search for answers.

Stopping at the desk long enough to retrieve his keys, Andrew retreated to the safety of his room so he could formulate his next move in the mystery which now surrounded him.

Tossing the folder, which seemed to be costing him more then he bargained for with each step he took, on the nearby table Andrew fixed himself a drink as he took a few minutes to regain his composure. Despite what most people believed because of television and movies, seeing someone die, even an enemy, was not an easy thing, and Andrew could not get the sight of the young man out of his mind. It seemed no matter what he did to put the violence behind him, there was always something pulling him back. His hands were never free from the blood he spilled and today was no different.

"Here's to you," he uttered as he downed another scotch. "Here's to your ability to royally screw things up."

Looking over at the file responsible for the mess he found himself in, Andrew placed his glass down on the table as he began to sift through the contents inside.

Though in his possession for nearly ten days, he avoided looking inside, afraid it would tell him something about his friends he did not want to know. The Vega family, more than just men and women he fought along side, was family, a part of his past filled with fond memories. If the contents of the file did in fact hold information which could destroy the family he remembered, he wanted no part of it. But if what Scott told him was true and the theft of the file from the agency resulted in him being accused of both murder and treason, things were far more complicated than he imagined and the contents might be his only way out. He needed to know everything about the Vegas and what the last twenty years in power did to them. He needed to know if the men he came to negotiate with were the same two men he fought along side of so long ago, if they were worthy of him risking everything including betraying his country by stealing the file for the contents inside.

Opening the folder, Andrew looked surprisingly at the lack of paperwork inside. Under surveillance by the agency since they helped the Vegas win the revolution twenty years earlier, he expected it to be much thicker in content.

This isn't going to take long, he thought to himself as he held not more than fifteen pieces of paper in his hand. Whatever was in the file it didn't appear to be as important as he thought. "Guess I missed the boat on this one," he said to himself, thinking about the risks he took breaking into the file room after hours to obtain it. He'd gone to his superiors in hopes they would give him what he needed but instead found himself at odds with them over their refusal to help. Now as he looked at the limited information available to him, he knew all the risks were for nothing. Even if there was something inside he could use, it would not be enough, somehow he already sensed this without even reading the papers lying before him. "Maybe I will read it later," he mumbled aloud before closing the file once more.

Still bothered by Scott's words of warning, Andrew grabbed the phone as he quickly called a friend in the States he knew he could trust. Protecting his son from the fallout of his actions was his top priority and there was no time to waste. If there was a mole in the agency, someone who wanted the finger of guilt pointed in his directions, then Steven could be next on their list.

"Of course I trust you," he replied sarcastically after revealing what he been told by Scott. "And thanks," Andrew said, grateful not only for Templeton's help but also for his discretion in not asking any too many questions. "Templeton, take care of my son and keep him safe," he uttered before hanging up with his friend, relieved there would be someone watching his son's back should things go badly for him in Rome. If he could not make a deal with the Vegas and clear his name, he could end up spending the rest of his life in a prison cell.

Feeling a little guilty after hanging up the phone with Templeton, Andrew wished he could have contacted Mark with such an important assignment but he knew that was impossible. Though they were best friends since they were children, Andrew knew he could not entrust Steven's safety to Mark this time. Mark's erratic behavior since his last mission made him too much of a loose cannon to leave Steven in his care should things start to get tricky. Taking care of him on a day-to-day basis was not a problem, but should things heat up, Andrew was not sure Mark could handle the stress, and he was not going to take any chances with his son's life. He would deal with the repercussions of his actions later. Certainly when his friend learned the truth, he would understand why he chose Templeton over him.

Taking a deep breath and feeling a little more relaxed after speaking to Templeton, Andrew suddenly realized not only was he exhausted from the day's events but very hungry as well. His last meal was breakfast; he found his thoughts focused on a large plate filled with steak and eggs smothered in mushrooms and peppers.

Calling room service, he ordered a pot of coffee as well. His long day was far from over, and he would need every ounce of caffeine he could get. Instructing the waiter to send a bottle of wine as well, Andrew decided to take a quick shower before his meal arrived. Still reeking from the smell of gasoline and burnt brush, he wanted to wash as much of the day's events away as possible before tackling both his meal and the file.

"Coming," he shouted, running from the shower in only a towel as he heard the door. "Thanks," he remarked, taking the tray from the waiter as he handed him a wet five-dollar tip before returning to the bedroom long enough to finish dressing.

"Just what the doctor ordered," he mumbled, taking a bite from his steak as he made himself comfortable on the couch and began sifting through the file.

"Damn it," Andrew snapped, tossing the papers to the floor. The file was useless, just as he was afraid of after seeing just how little there was inside it. The contents consisted of nothing he could use; nothing to help him explain how two brothers who were once closer than most men turned into such deadly enemies. The file was filled with events from the past, filled with pictures of both Antonio and Phillip as he remembered them, loving brothers always standing at each other's side. Yet here they were united again in battle, this time with each other as they both stood alone accusing the other of betraying the very people and nation they once fought for, and Andrew was still stuck in the middle. There was nothing in the file to help him choose which brother to believe in, to figure out which one was telling the truth. His hands were tied, and he knew if he didn't find some answers soon, he would be forced by a promise from the past, to do something he prayed he never would have to do.

"How do you get yourself in these messes?" he said before finishing the bottle of wine.

Pacing around the room, trying not only to digest his food but also to come up with his next course of action, Andrew suddenly turned towards his laptop computer.

"You better have answered me this time," he uttered as he took his computer from the desk and began typing his code word in. Trying for days to reach an old contact in San Sebastian in hopes of learning something of value, his e-mails continued to go unanswered. No matter how many messages he sent, there was no response of from his friend, and until now, Andrew was not worried about it. His friend was a nomad, a man constantly on the move, and he just assumed he hadn't retrieved his messages yet, but the latest developments facing him, Andrew feared for his friend's safety and hoped he too wasn't a causality of war.

"Still nothing," he said before typing in another message, this time leaving a code word only the two of them knew about. "I hope you are all right my old friend," he whispered before checking to see if there was any other e-mail waiting for him.

"Damn," he mumbled, disappointed to see nothing waiting. Despite the risks he was taking by communicating with his son, he sent him two messages in hopes of at least leaving the lines of communication open between them. He prayed if Steven realized his father was trying, he too would give it a shot until they were able to meet and discuss everything in person. It was apparent from the silence, the boy was still angry with him for leaving and was not ready to communicate with him even over the computer. Wishing he could phone him directly, Andrew knew that was impossible.

"Damn," he uttered as the preset alarm on his cell phone went off without warning. He sent himself a reminder weeks ago, and now as the date flashed before him, Andrew wondered how he could have been so heartless. The message designed to reminded him of an important day served only as a reminder of the kind of man he'd become. So wrapped up in his own world and the problems he was facing, he'd forgotten what date was coming up and how hard it would be for his son. Not realizing that when he agreed to meet with the others in Rome, his trip would coincide with such an important time. Andrew berated himself for being so insensitive towards his sons needs.

The 8th of August just a few days away was not only the anniversary date of Sophia's death, it was also Steven's eighteenth birthday as well. His mother was killed on his seventh birthday and each year was just a horrible reminder, a nightmare of what he lost on that dreadful day.

"How could you be so stupid?" Andrew said, berating himself for what he had done. Deserting Steven was bad enough, but leaving him to face his birthday and the memories of his mother's death without him was unforgivable. "I'm sorry, son," he whispered, struggling with his conscience as he grabbed the phone. Could he take the risk and call his son in hopes of making things better for him, or should he let him to believe his father deserted him again and in the end keep him safe from what was about to happen? Throwing the wine glass across the room, Andrew realized no matter what he did, his son would lose in the end. Despite his own pain, he would have to let his son believe the worst about him and pray that when everything was over, he could make things right between them.

CHAPTER TWO

The shadow of darkness wrapped itself around Steven like a blanket as he sat alone in his dorm room oblivious to the fact the sun had gone down for the day. His mind cluttered with thoughts of his father and the trouble he was in made every second he waited for his uncle to call back with more news seem like an eternity. Despite the strained relationship he shared with his father, Steven still loved him, and if only a small part of the information Mark told him earlier was true, then Andrew was in serious danger because of it.

Why didn't Mark call as he promised? Steven wondered, staring at the clock on the wall. Nearly four hours passed since they spoke, he should have learned something else from the officials in Washington by now. *Why hadn't his father called either?* He tried to fight the other questions filling his mind. *What if he couldn't call? What if he were already on the run or in jail? What if he were dead?*

"How can they believe such lies?" he shouted aloud this time, jumping from his chair angry with his father's friends for betraying Andrew with their doubts. There was no way his father could have committed the crimes he was accused of, not his father, not the man he knew.

Pacing like a caged animal, Steven laughed slightly as he thought about the irony of what he was facing. He spent the last ten years trying to avoid his father's lifestyle, trying to keep himself as far away as possible from the world Andrew chose to live in, and now as he sat in the dark like a frightened child, he would give his very soul to find someone from that world willing to give him answers.

"Damn," he mumbled, berating himself for the years wasted between them because of the anger he felt for so long, years they could never get back. If only he could have found another way to channel his grief when his mother died, things might be different between them. Only a child when she was murdered, the anger he felt towards his father for his part in her death engulfed him so fully he never realized how much Andrew suffered too.

Blaming him for her death was wrong, and it took Steven ten years to work through the pain and realize the truth.

"You blew it big time," he uttered to himself. The only person responsible for killing his mother was the coward who put the bomb in his father's car in the first place.

He hoped it wasn't too late to make things up to Andrew. Shivering, a sense of dread coming over him, Steven fought back the tears. He was not going to lose his father, not when they were just staring to work through their problems.

"Who can I call?" he wondered, picking up the phone in a desperate bid to find some answers. Though Mark warned him against trusting anyone back home, there had to be at least one person in Washington he could trust. One friend who did not believe his father was guilty. But who?

"I know who." Steven began thinking about his roommate's father. Stewart Gibbs was not only Andrew's boss but a friend, and he would never turn his back on him despite what Mark said.

Dialing Stewart's cell phone, Steven quickly hung up when he heard his voice. *What if I am wrong and Stewart does believe the charges against my father? What if the phone lines are tapped and the call only made things worse?* Steven could not take the chance no matter how desperate he was. Slamming his fist several times against the desk, he knew his hands were tied whether he liked it or not, heeding his uncle's warnings and waiting at school until he called was the only option open to him.

Steven McCormick, a complicated young man, seemed much older than his eighteen years. Burdened with the memory of his mother's death on his seventh birthday, he seldom let anyone see the real person inside, afraid if he did, he would lose them too. His friends limited to a few schoolmates and man who was more like a father to him than his own, Steven used practical jokes as a way of keeping people at arm's length.

Born in France while his mother worked at the embassy, the first six years of his life was like a whirlwind, an adventure his parents made sure he enjoyed every step of the way. His father who also worked for the government, though he never knew exactly what it was he did, was always a hero to him.

A smart child for his age, Steven learned to speak both French and English before he was five. An avid reader whose quest for knowledge made him very inquisitive, he lost the thirst for life he possessed as a child after his mother's death.

THE NIGHTMARE'S EDGE

Thin built, Steven bore a striking resemblance to Sophia with his golden hair and blue eyes, though the resemblance to his mother was not limited to just his physical appearance but to his gentle soul. Despite what he endured in his short lifetime Steven's trust in his small circle of friends was unshakable.

"Ring, damn it, ring," the boy snapped at the phone as if ordering the inane object to comply with his orders would make it so. "Ring, please," he repeated but to no avail.

"Why is Mark taking so long to call back?" he mumbled, growing more upset with each second that went by without word from him. "Damn it," he repeated, this time the anger directed at himself for promising to remain at school until his uncle called back. All he wanted to do was hop on his motorcycle and head to Washington. There were answers back home, he was certain of it, and he needed to find them.

A sense of panic coming over him, Steven tried to fight the fear growing stronger. *What if Mark did not call back because something horrible happened to my father?* Andrew was not a fighter, someone with the skills needed to defend himself and if things got out of hand. He was nothing more than a paper pusher who sat at the negotiation table working as a mediator between opposing factions. *What if my father is already dead and Mark does not know how to break the news?* There were so many questions raging through his mind, questions that could not be answered if he remained at school.

"Damn you," Steven snapped, staring at a picture of his father as he spoke. "Why did you come back into my life just to leave me again?" He demanded to know. "Why didn't you just stay the hell away if you were going to do this to me all over again?" The sound of the phone ringing disrupted his outburst as he ran to answer it.

"Hello? Dad, is it you?" he bellowed out without waiting for the person on the other end to say anything. "What? No, Rick is not here," he replied, disappointed to find the person on the other end was only his roommate's girlfriend. "Yes, I'll tell him you called," he promised before hanging up the phone.

"Damn you, Dad, you promised this time it would be different," Steven whispered before returning to his vigil.

"You promised," he repeated, looking a the picture of the two of them on a recent fishing trip. The first trip taken together in years. Andrew vowed during that time never to allow the horrors of his world to touch them again.

Just like in the past, the violence he lived through once before was occurring again, and Steven felt as if he would never awaken from the nightmares surrounding Andrew at every turn.

"How did you get yourself into this mess?" he questioned aloud, thinking about the trouble his father was in. *Murder! Treason!* Even the thought of those words connected to Andrew in any way were impossible for him to comprehend. Steven did not know a lot about his father because of the walls they put up in the past, but he did know was an honorable man. He would never betray his country by stealing classified files yet alone kill someone to obtain them despite the evidence the government claimed to have.

Glancing over at the picture again, he smiled slightly as he thought about the fishing trip. More than just a father and son weekend the school provided at the end of each term, it became the first step in healing process for both of them.

"It was a good trip, wasn't it, Dad?" Steven whispered, recalling the many things they shared during the days spent together including the victory of catching a largemouth bass. It didn't matter it took them nearly two days to reel him in or that they both ended up in the water on the first day, what did matter was the sense of accomplishment they felt when they finally caught him working together as a team.

"We did it, didn't we, Dad?" Steven said as he touched the picture of the two of them with their prize. "Tell me what I should do," he begged, staring at his father's face. "What if I stay here waiting for Uncle Mark to call, and you need me? But if I go home, I may end up making things worse for you," he rambled as if the man staring back at him in the photograph could answer his questions. "I don't know what the right thing is," he continued, putting the picture back on the desk. He hated being put in this situation, hated feeling so helpless, and he was going to do something about it.

"Enough," Steven declared, grabbing his backpack from the closet. He was tired of waiting, tired of sitting around feeling sorry for the cards he was being dealt. It was time to act like a McCormick, like both his father and mother would have, and that meant going home. He would figure out the rest later, but he was going to face his father's accusers and get the answers he sought.

He grabbed his passport and placed it in the bag. Steven looked around the room. The boarding school was more of a home to him than the apartment in Washington, and if things did not go well, he might never be able to return.

THE NIGHTMARE'S EDGE

Nestled deep within the mountains of Pennsylvania, the boarding school housed the children of many important people, from diplomats to dignitaries. Its forty-two acre estate filled with the high-tech security made it one of the safest places in the world. Just miles away from many of the main stream activities surrounding the area including a national park and inner harbor. Created nearly eighty years earlier by one of the local residents whose own child was kidnaped and killed because of the work he did, the school not only provided a safe haven for the children, but an educational basis surpassed by very few other learning establishments.

"I'll miss this place," Steven remarked sadly. But it didn't matter how much the school and his friends meant to him, Andrew was the top priority, and if going on the run with him, leaving behind the only real home he ever knew was the only way to protect his father, he would do it.

"What the?" Steven uttered, the sound of laughter coming from the window distracting him from his packing. Smiling as he looked down at the courtyard below, he watched several of his friends engaged in a friendly game of basketball. A nightly ritual for the members of his dorm, it was one of the few times he enjoyed the company of others. Cheering aloud as Rick sunk a long shot, Steven waved to his friends after his uproar caught their attention.

"No thanks, not tonight," he replied after an offer to join them came next. "I'm a little tired is all, but that was a great shot," he declared, wishing his outburst had not alerted them to his presences. "No really, I'm a fine," he insisted as Rick continued to question him about his refusal to join them. "Really, I'm fine, just tired," he insisted before returning to the solace of his room and the darkness surrounding it.

Laughing as he thought about his friends, Steven recalled the look on their faces earlier when he pulled one of his pranks on the class. Like most mornings, this one started the same, with him running late for first period. It seemed no matter how hard he tried to get to his 7 a.m. biology class, he was always running five minutes late. Though his teacher Mr. Brooks took it in stride and never pursued it beyond a few lectures and extra credit courses, the headmaster was not as forgiving and trying to keep his tardiness a secret from him was not always easy, and this was one of those times.

Running later than normal for class after he failed to heed his alarm clock, Steven knew even Mr. Brooks would have to discipline him if he didn't want the other students to think they could get away with anything they wanted in his class. So Steven decided to make the punishment fit the crime and set his teacher up big time.

Showing up for class dressed only in a pair of jockey shorts and a football cap, Steven knew Mr. Brooks would see the humor in his actions before giving him any punishment. But the joke was on him. Instead of finding Mr. Brooks standing in front of the class when he walked in, he found the headmaster. He forgotten his teacher was away for the day on a personal trip and Mr. Astor was taking over his classes for him.

The look on his face was priceless, Steven thought to himself laughing as he recalled how red the man's face got as yelled at him for hours in his office. Grateful that the lecture and twenty hours cleaning the student union was his only punishment, Steven realized how lucky he was. Only weeks away from graduation, he could have suspended him during finals or even forbad him from graduating, so scrubbing toilets was not so bad.

"Hello! Who's there?" he said, startled by a noise coming from the door. "Is someone there?" he asked, checking the hallway outside his room. "Hello? Is there someone there?" he repeated again, looking around.

Great, he thought closing the door, *you're losing your mind*. There was no one at the door, and he was just letting his imagination get the better of him.

Grabbing the money he was saving for graduation week, Steven counted the bills before placing them in his pocket. It wasn't much, but it would have to do until he could find a way to get more. If he were going to search for his father, he would need a lot more than a few hundred dollars in his pocket.

"Steven, are you still here?" Rick shouted, racing into the dorm room with the look of victory still on his face.

"Rick, were you just at the door?" Steven asked, curious if it might have been his friend he heard a few minutes before.

"Wasn't me. Why?" Rick replied, catching the strange look on his friend's face. "Is everything all right?"

"It's fine," Steven lied, afraid if he told him anything, it would put him in danger as well.

"Steven, what's wrong?" Rick asked again, certain his friend was not telling him everything. They'd been friends since the first grade, and he could always tell when Steven was hiding something from him.

"Nothing's wrong," Steven repeated, fighting the urge to tell Rick everything.

"Is your dad or Mark in some kind of trouble?" he asked, not quite ready to give up his inquiry. Like Steven, he too grew up with a member of the family in the agency and knew the inherent risk which went along with it. Mark and Andrew were the only real family Steven had, if either one of them were in trouble, he would be devastated.

"I wish I could tell you, Rick, but I don't know what's going on," Steven finally confessed. "I got a strange call from Uncle Mark several hours ago, and I've been waiting for him to call back with more information but he hasn't."

"Then it's your dad who is in trouble?"

"Yes," Steven replied as he continued to put few clothes in his backpack.

"Is there anything I can do to help?" asked Rick.

"No thanks," Steven replied. "I don't want you in the middle of this mess until I figure it out."

"Ok, when you're ready to tell me, I'll be here," Rick promised, staring at the bag in his friend's hand. "Do you want me to tell the dean anything, with graduation only a few weeks away he will have a lot of questions."

"Tell him I am sorry for everything and I will try to contact him about my diploma when I can," Steven began as he walked over to the window where the others were still playing. "Tell the guys I said good-bye."

"You're really leaving?" Rick questioned, though he already knew the answer.

"I have too." Steven explained, "I tried sitting around here waiting, but it's driving me nuts. I have to do something."

"I understand. I guess if my dad were in trouble, I would do the same thing," Rick admitted. "Do you need anything, money, anything?"

"No thanks, I have it covered," Steven said as he walked up to his friend. "Look Rick, I'm not sure if or when I will be back but I promise to…"

"Just promise to call me when it's safe," Rick instructed his friend as they shook hands.

"I promise," Steven vowed.

"Good," Rick replied, trying not to get too emotional. "I better get back outside before those idiots come in here and start bugging you," he remarked as he headed for the door.

"Thanks," was all Steven said as he watched his friend leave the room.

Waiting a few minutes to be sure Rick was successful in keeping the others at bay, Steven rushed to the parking lot as he wondered what his next move would be once he arrived in Washington. Not only would he have to face Mark and his anger for disobeying the orders to remain at school, but also his father's accusers. Whatever he did next might get him into more trouble, and he needed to be very careful.

Checking his bike to make sure there was even fuel to get him home, Steven didn't notice the two men sitting in the car across the road as he headed for the highway.

"What have we here?" the passenger remarked sarcastically, reminding his partner of the bet they made earlier. "I told you if we rattled his chain long enough, he would make a move." He laughed, pleased his ploy to scare the boy into action by making noises at the door worked.

"Yea, yea," the driver said handing him the twenty-dollar that went with the bet. Unlike his friend, he was not pleased to see Steven react so quickly in his bid to help his father and in the process turn himself into their unwitting pawn in the game. He was just a kid and using him to get to Andrew was not sitting well with him despite what it meant to the mission. The boy was too much like his father, and Kirk still admired the man who was once his mentor.

"He has guts, I'll give him that," Kirk remarked as they pulled away from the curve and began following their prey.

"That will play in our favor," Henry remarked.

"Right," sneered Kirk. The mission would be difficult enough going up against both Andrew and Mark, having a headstrong kid on their hands was the last thing they needed.

"Don't lose him," Henry snapped as he took his cell phone from his jacket and phoned their employer. He wanted an account of everything Steven did and the sooner Henry filled him in on the latest, the sooner the conversation with him would be over.

"Hello, it's Henry," he began as he lit a cigar. "That is why I'm calling, the kid is on the move. He's heading back to Washington even as we speak," he reported. "Yes, we should be there in about four or five hours depending on the traffic. It's about 7 now," he continued looking at his watch, "you can expect us around midnight if there are no problems on the road." He assured the man on the other end. "What, don't worry about the kid, he's so wrapped up in his own world he wouldn't notice a heard of elephants running behind him," Henry insisted, angry his abilities to follow a frighten teenage boy were being questioned.

"Look Henry, just let the man know we're on the way and leave it at that," Kirk instructed, certain his partner was getting ready to get into another argument with their employer. The constant squabbling was becoming very old and the last thing he wanted to hear was another round between them over the way the mission was being handled.

Putting his hand over the phone for a second as he looked over at Kirk, Henry smiled. "You've got to be kidding," he said, before returning to conversation with their employer and the debate over the mission. "I still think it's a bad idea to involve the kid in our plans to nail his father, and this crazy plan of yours is never going to work," he insisted, his words sending the man on the other end into a tantrum. "I love it when he goes off, don't you?" Henry whispered to Kirk while he turned the phone away from his ear.

"Why do you keep doing this?" Kirk asked. His partner seemed to enjoy harassing their employer with his comments as much as he enjoyed the game and if he weren't careful, eventually his actions were going to come back to haunt him.

"Because he is a fool and I love pulling his chain," Henry confessed. "Besides, if I keep bugging him, maybe he will give up on this insane plan and do things my way," Henry announced. He had no problem with going after Andrew McCormick and bringing him down, but he believed the mission would go much easier if they followed his plan. Drugging the boy and securing him in a safe house until they could draw Andrew out was the best way to insure the success of the mission, and if their employer wasn't so bent on revenge against the man they sought, he would see that too.

"Just let it alone," Kirk barked as he continued to follow the boy.

"As far as I am concerned, this idiot is a fool fledged manic and I have no intentions of leaving anything alone until the mission is over."

"Personally, I think you are both insane," Kirk said.

"Thanks," Henry said sarcastically before turning his attention back to the phone. "You just make sure everything is ready at your end when we get the boy to the location and we will handle the rest," he ordered, looking over at Kirk as he whispered to him once more. "You know we could handle this mission alone without this man," he insisted as Kirk listened to his words. "We can take control of the kid right now and make sure neither Andrew McCormick or Mark Sinclair never get in our way again."

"Sure we can," Kirk said. "Except for one thing. The man on the other end of the phone is paying bills and without him we won't get the rest of our money."

"That is the only reason I haven't taken over this mission," Henry insisted.

"And taking on both Mark and Andrew at the same time has nothing to do with it?" Kirk asked, teasing his partner as he spoke. Facing one of the two renowned agents would be difficult enough but trying to take them both on at the same time would be nearly impossible.

"Oh, I will take care of them at the right time," Henry balked, refusing to concede to the dangers of such a deadly risk. "For now he can run the show the way he wants to, but I am warning you," Henry began as he kept his hand over the phone to keep the man on the other end from hearing his words, "he is nuts and his obsession with Andrew and that boy is going to get us all killed if we don't take care of him ourselves."

"I know," Kirk replied. As much as he hated to admit it, Henry words made a lot of sense. The boy was an innocent, including him in on the mission just to make life more unbearable for his father was an unnecessary risk, and if their employer were not so obsessed with making Andrew suffer, he would see that too.

"What!" Henry snapped, returning to the phone conversation and the man still ranting on the other end. "Don't worry about a thing, sooner or later the kid will be right where we want him, and Andrew will take the fall to save him."

"Just tell him we'll contact him later when we have more to report," Kirk interrupted, growing tired of the conversation.

"All right," Henry replied before hanging up. "God, I hate that man almost as much as I hate Andrew McCormick," he announced as they continued to follow the boy.

"I understand why our employer hates Andrew, but why do you?" Kirk asked, curious as to what was motivating his partner's venomous feelings towards the man.

"Because the bastard cost me my career," Henry stated. "He was on the evaluation committee and his vote against me ruined everything I planned," he continued as he lit another cigar. "I was up for promotion and would have gotten a sweet gig in Rome but the high and mighty Andrew McCormick decided I was too much of a rogue and giving me a leadership position was not good for the agency," the man explained as the thoughts of what Andrew's vote did to his life caused him to grow angry once again. "He told the committee I was too much of a hot shot who didn't obey orders and I had no regard for the innocent people who got caught in the cross fire."

"Imagine that," Kirk echoed.

"I deserved that promotion, " Henry snapped, "and if it weren't for that bastard, I would be sitting in a nice villa in Rome with a beautiful lady who could satisfy my every need, instead of being stuck in this car with you waiting for that kid to fall into our trap."

"So you blame Andrew for your miserable life and bad decisions in the field and because of this, you're willing to go after his son."

"My life was not miserable until Andrew stuck his nose in it," Henry balked. "As for his kid, why not use him if it will help the mission? He's expendable and the five million dollars a piece we are getting for this job will make everything including burying both father and son a lot easier."

"Just make sure you don't do anything stupid just to get back at Andrew." Kirk warned him. "My life depends on you watching my back and I don't intend to go down because you can't keep your emotions in check."

"Have I ever let you down, partner?" Henry uttered with a sense of confidence in his voice.

"Just don't start now."

"Don't get so close to the kid," Henry yelled, his outburst changing the conversation between them as the continued to follow their prey.

"What did we sudden become a herd of elephants?" Kirk laughed, reminding his friend of the earlier comment.

"Just shut up and stay with the kid, we should be at the apartment building in about ten minutes and I don't want you to screw things up by getting too close," Henry snapped as they pulled off the highway towards the final destination.

"Aye, aye captain." Kirk laughed, following Steven into the apartment complex and the next leg of their mission.

Arriving at his father's place shortly before midnight, Steven rushed into the lobby surprised to find Leroy, the day man standing there to greet him.

"Hey, what are you doing here at this hour?" Leroy asked.

"I could ask you the same question," Steven replied.

"The kid who normally works nights needed a few days off. His wife had a baby and they are still getting their sleeping habits settled," Leroy answered "What about you? Is something up with your dad?"

"That is what I intend to find out," Steven shouted as he raced towards the elevator. "Can you take care of my bike?" he asked, throwing Leroy the keys. "I left it parked on the sidewalk."

"What else is new?" Leroy joked. Steven insisted on leaving his bike on the sidewalk ever since he got it for his 16th birthday and it was usually up to Leroy to find a safe place for it before someone else complained. "You must be the only person I know who is not afraid to let me on a motorcycle."

"I trust you with my bike, and if I were you, I wouldn't listen to what those old fogies say, you're still one of the best riders I've ever seen and you always will be no matter how old you get," Steven insisted as he jumped into the elevator.

"Thanks, kid, I needed that," Leroy yelled. He was feeling every ache and pain of his sixty–five year old body and hearing Steven's words of encouragement helped to pick his spirits up.

Exiting the elevator on the eleventh floor, Steven realized as he reached into his pocket he not only gave Leroy the key to his bike but his house key as well.

"Oh well," he whispered, reaching behind the fire extinguisher to get the spare key his father kept there for such an occasion. "Some things never change," he mumbled as he replaced the key after unlocking the door.

"Dad! Dad, are you here?" he shouted, looking around for a response he knew in his heart would never come. His father would never take such a risk by returning to his own home, but Steven could not help but hope here might be an answer anyway. It was obvious from the moment he stepped inside the place was empty. There were no signs of life in the apartment, no music playing in the background, no aroma left from a late dinner still filling the house with exotic smells, nothing to indicate his father or anyone else was inside.

Walking quietly through the living room, looking for something which might give him a lead on his father whereabouts, Steven started searching the desk drawer. There had to be something he left behind, a note, an airline schedule, something he could use to find his father.

"Damn it," he snapped. No matter where he looked, the drawers, cabinets, shelves there was nothing to find. His father hadn't left anything behind and Steven was as much in the dark as before.

Funny, he thought touching several items on the fireplace, *the apartment always seemed more like a vacation spot then a home.* A place he came to visit a few times each school year and a month during summer vacation, yet as he looked through the apartment, the place didn't feel the same. It was his home and everything inside made him feel closer to his father.

"Ok, Dad, I won't give up if you don't," he whispered softly before continuing his search on the second floor, walking into his bedroom next. Sitting down at the computer Steven prayed his father hid a message for him there. "Ok, what code word would I use if I were you, Dad?" he questioned, typing in several words in an effort to find the right one.

ACCESS DENIED

The computer continued to flash with each word he tried.

"McCormick, think, you know password, just think. It has to be a word only the two of you know about, a simple word only the two of you…" he whispered to himself. "That's it," he yelled, typing in the word he knew would give him access to the computer. Waiting impatiently while the computer moved through several security levels, Steven sighed with relief as it finally let him in.

"I knew it." He began recalling the conversation he shared with his father on the fishing trip and the secret nickname his mother use to call him when they were alone.

"Thanks, Dad," he said. "I guess you knew one day I would need to know Mom used to call you Mickey," Steven mumbled before returning to the problem at hand. Sifting through the menu file until he found the one with the same name as the code word, Steven pulled it up crossing his fingers as he did there would indeed be a message waiting for him.

Steven, my son, if you are reading this message, then what I have always feared has finally come true. Something has happened at the agency, and I was forced to leave the country without you. My work has always been risky, and at times, dangerous, but I always knew I had the agency to fall back on. If you are reading this, then that too has changed. Steven, I don't know what we are facing or who we can trust, but I do know there is only one person you can trust. Your Uncle Mark has been by my side since we were children, and he will protect you until we can be together. I don't know when that will be, but I promise you will find a way for us to be reunited again no matter how long it takes. Until that time, trust your uncle to take care of you and remember no matter what you see or hear, I love you and always have. I wish I could tell you more but you might not understand at this time why I had to leave, so until we can be together again, remember I love you.

Dad

Reading the words several times hoping he missed something, Steven realized he hadn't. His father's message, though important, did not tell him anything he could use and he was right back where he started, with no leads on how to help him.

"Dad, why couldn't you trust me enough to leave me more?" he cried before turning off the computer. "Why couldn't you just let me help?"

Walking out of his bedroom feeling defeated, Steven sat down on the top of the stairs trying to regain his thoughts. He was certain he would find something on the computer and the fact that he didn't, only frightened him more than he cared to admit.

His father was saying good-bye to him in his message and Steven wasn't ready to hear those words.

"The plants," he uttered. Sitting on the top of the stairs, he noticed the pots sitting along the steps. He hadn't noticed when he arrived, but as he sat there staring at them, Steven finally realized what was wrong. They were dead, every one of them. It was apparent they had not been watered for some time.

That doesn't make sense, Steven thought to himself, *Mark said the trouble Dad was in began only twenty-four hours earlier.* So if that were true, why were the plants dead? Andrew was a avid gardener with a green thumb who loved to tend to his plants. There was no way he would have let them get so bad if he were at the apartment till the trouble started as Mark indicated.

What's going on? he wondered, pulling the dead leaves from the pot sitting next to him. Why did Mark lie about how long his father was missing and what did it mean as far as his father was concerned? There was more going on then he was being told, and Steven could not shake the feeling his father was in a lot more trouble than even he imagined possible.

"The bag!" Steven blurted out, running to his father's bedroom as he began tearing up the closet. His father taught him to keep a backpack handy at all times in case of emergencies. A small bag hidden in the back of the closet filled with various things, like a razor, money and passport, was Andrew's way of always being ready for any contingency. If the bag was still in the apartment, then it meant Andrew was in the country, maybe in hiding but still nearby, if it were gone...

"Where is it?" he demanded to know, throwing boxes of shoes and other items from the closet in a desperate search for the one item he could not locate. "It's gone, the bag is gone." The words were almost too hard for him to say.

Looking up at the night stand, Steven's eyes filled with tears as he noticed the picture of his mother gone as well. Andrew never traveled anywhere without it and the fact it too was missing from its normal spot only made things worse.

"I'm scared, Mom, I don't know what to do next," he said, praying to the only person he believed would hear his cries. "I'm scared," he echoed, wrapping his arms around a pillow as he curled up in his father's bed. Lying there for a while trying to sort things out, Steven felt himself fighting the sleep his body so desperately needed until he finally gave in.

A MOTHER LOST

Looking over at his mother as she worked diligently in the kitchen to prepare his birthday feast, Steven thought about how wonderful she was. Not only was she making their new home perfect for them all, but she was giving a birthday party in his honor as well. His seventh one, it would be the first time he could celebrate with kids his own age. Normally living in an embassy estate with nothing but adults around, his birthdays had not been much fun in the past, and Steven was looking forward to having his new friends from school at the house.

"Mommy, is Uncle Mark going to get here in time?" he asked as his mother threw him a candy bar to snack on while they waited for the kids to arrive.

"Don't worry, honey, he will be here soon," Sophia promised, looking at her watch. He was already fifteen minutes late, and if he didn't arrive soon, her promise to her precious son would turn into a lie.

"Did he call and say he would be late?" Steven asked. Mark was in charge of the birthday cake, and without it, he could not have a party.

"No, honey, he didn't call, but I am sure he is just tied up in traffic and will be here any minute," she replied, growing angrier with Mark with each breath she took. The other kids would be arriving soon, and if he messed things up for her son, she would never forgive him.

"But Mommy, I can't have a party without a cake," Steven protested.

"I know, honey," she said, grabbing the cell phone as she tried to reach Mark and see what was the reason behind his delay. "Great," she mumbled. The phone was turned off, and there was no way to contact Mark.

"Now what do we do?" Steven asked, seeing there was no answer by phone.

"We wait for your uncle," Sophia informed him, hoping those words would not come back to haunt her.

"But Mommy—"

"Enough, Steven. He will be here in time," she snapped.

"What about Dad? Can't he go for the cake?" Steven asked, not ready to give up on his cake.

"My, you are full of ideas, aren't you?" Sophia joked thickly to him as the two sat by the kitchen table. "Daddy is on the phone, and I don't think he can get away right now," she explained. On the phone long distance for nearly two hours, the last time she checked on him, things did not sound as if anything was getting resolved. "Besides," Sophia began, "what happens if Daddy does go out for another cake and Mark shows up with the one, he promised to bring? The last thing I need in this house is two cakes with all those calories for me to finish."

"But what if he doesn't come?" Steven cried. He didn't want his party ruined, and if he didn't have a cake, everything would be.

"I know," Sophia answered, her anger at Mark intensifying. He was doing this on purpose, she was sure of it. They argued the night before about his behavior towards her, and now he was getting back at her for what she said. Unlike her husband, she did not see Mark as a good friend but instead as a common liar who tricked his boyhood friend into believing he was still a good man. She never trusted Mark like her husband did, and only her love for Andrew kept her from revealing her true feelings. Andrew trusted his best friend without doubt, and she did not want to destroy that bond with only her suspicions to back her up.

"Mom, what will can we do?"

"I know what to do," Sophia answered as she grabbed Andrew's car keys.

Her own car in the shop, she would have to drive his to the local bakery if she wanted to get the cake in time for the party. Though she hated using the stick shift, it would have to do for now.

"Bye Mommy. Hurry back," Steven shouted, standing by the door waving as his mother made herself comfortable in the car.

"Bye, my darling. I'll be back in a few minutes," she promised before turning her attentions to the problem of driving a car she was not familiar with. Waving at her son once more before starting the engine, Sophia nervously put the vehicle into reverse.

"Mommy!" Steven screamed, staring at the car bursting into a ball of fire before his eyes. "Mommy!" he repeated several times, unable to move, to do anything but stand there.

"Mrs. Hill get him out of here," Andrew ordered the housekeeper as the two of them came running from the house to see what had happened.

"No Mommy!" Steven tried to yell as he pointed towards the car, his words barely audible drowned by the tears flowing down his face.

"Get him out of here," Andrew repeated, picking up his son as Steven started to fight with him. "Steven, what is it?"

"Mommy!" Steven shouted again, pointing to the car.

"Mom! What…oh my god!" Andrew cried out as Mrs. Hill grabbed the child. "Your mother is inside the car." The words hitting him like a sledgehammer as he tried to comprehend what his son was saying. "Your mother is in the car," he repeated before running towards the burning vehicle. "Sophia! My god, Sophia, are you in there?" he yelled, trying to reach the car, as the flames grew stronger.

"No, Mr. McCormick, it's too late," the gardener shouted, trying to pull the man away as the flames ignited the sleeve of his shirt. "You can't save her, it's too late," the gardener repeated as he helped Andrew put out the fire before he was seriously injured.

"I have to." Andrew wept looking at the gardener. "She is inside. I have to help her."

"I'm sorry, sir, but it is too late; she is gone," the man repeated for a third time before another explosion sent them both reeling towards the ground.

Holding onto Mrs. Hill as he watched his father struggling to his feet, Steven tried to free himself from her grip as both men finally reached the safety of the porch step.

"Daddy!" he cried out, running towards his father.

"Steven." The distraught man began taking his son in his arms as they both cried for the loved one they lost.

"Daddy, you have to get mommy out, you have to," Steven cried, pointing to the car. He wanted his mother and only his father could get her for him.

"She's gone," were the only words Andrew could say before his son started fighting with him for not helping his mother. "She's gone," he repeated, holding the boy tightly, his words drowned out by the sound of the fire department responding to the house.

Sitting quietly as the firefighters worked to put the fire out, Andrew handed his son back to the housekeeper as the fire chief moved closer to speak to him.

"Sir, I am sorry, but there was nothing we could to for your wife," he explained as his men continued to work on the fire.

"I know," Andrew answered.

"As soon as the fire inspector gets here, we will start our investigation into the cause of the fire," the chief promised, glancing over at the little boy standing once more by his father.

"Don't bother. I know what caused it," Andrew insisted. "I've heard enough explosive devices to know what a bomb sounds like."

"A bomb?" the chief repeated, looking over at the boy. "Are you sure you want him to hear this?" he asked.

"He did not hear anything and neither did you," Mark said, walking up behind the chief as he pulled out his ID. "Just make sure the fire is out, and we will handle everything else."

"Yes, sir," the chief responded. He'd worked in Washington long enough to know when someone started flashing a government badge, it was better to walk way than to get into a debate about it. "Sir, I am sorry for your loss," he remarked to Andrew before returning to his men.

"So what kind of trouble did you get into while I was away?" Mark pokily asked as he turned his attention back to Andrew. "I can't leave you alone for two minutes and you start the fun without me."

"Fun, you call this fun?" Andrew balked as he threw a punch. "Where the hell were you?" he demanded to know.

"Hey, so I was a little late. Is that any reason to hit me?" Mark said, still unaware of the events, which had just occurred. "I will explain everything to Sophia, I promise," he vowed as he looked around. "So where is she, in the house hiding from all this excitement?"

"Don't you understand?" Andrew screamed. "She was in the car. She was in the car."

"What!" the stunned man said looking back a the car, nothing more than a few charred remains. "No, Sophia wasn't in the car; she couldn't have been."

"She was," Andrew answered.

"Mommy was going for my cake because you never came," Steven yelled, hitting his uncle as he spoke. "She was going for my cake."

"Steven," Andrew whispered, taking his son in his arms.

"I didn't know," the only words Mark could say as he stared at the car.

Despite the strain in their relationship over the last several years, he loved Sophia from the first time he laid eyes on her, and her death was just as hard for him as it was for the others.

"No, I want my mommy," the words echoing through the house as Andrew carried his son back inside. "I want my mommy."

~

"Mom!" Steven blurted, awakening from the nightmare of the past, his heart beating as quickly as it did on that day. "Mom," he whispered, realizing where he was again and what he just endured. He hadn't dreamt of that day in a long time, and it felt just so real to him again. Shivering, Steven prayed the return of the nightmare was not a sign something happened to his father.

"Help me, Mom. I can't lose Dad too," he cried, curling up once more as he asked his mother for guidance. "I am so scared, Mom. Please help me do the right thing."

CHAPTER THREE

Aroused from sleep, startled by the sound of the front door slamming shut, Steven raced towards the corridor. *Maybe,* he thought running down the spiral steps, *maybe it was Dad.*

"Dad," Steven cried out, nearly losing his balance as he missed the last step. "Dad, is that you?" he repeated, looking around for his father. "Hello? Dad?" he whispered this time, growing a little uneasy with the thought that the person he heard might not be his father after all. "Dad, are you here?" he asked once more as he began walking towards the front door. "Great, here I go again," he uttered, angry at himself for letting his imagination to get the better of him again. There was no one at the door at school when he thought he heard something, and it was apparent there was no one at the door now either

"It's opened," Steven whispered after finding the door was slightly a jarred. It wasn't his imagination after all, someone was in the apartment.

Standing by the open door trying to decide if he should leave before it was too late, Steven rejected the idea of running. If he was going to find out the truth about his father, then confronting the intruder might be the only way he could get any answers. Despite the risks, he knew he didn't have a choice as he began moving cautiously towards the kitchen, the sounds of someone moving around growing louder with each step he took. Grabbing a nearby vase before pushing the door open, the sounds of a glass shattering startling him, Steven rushed through the door ready to face whomever was on the other side.

"Mark!" he shouted, a combination of both shock and relieve resonating from him as he found his Uncle cleaning up the mess he made. "What are you doing here?"

"I could ask you the same question?" Mark replied, looking up at the boy. "I thought you were supposed to be at school."

"I know," Steven began, "but it wasn't fair of you to expect me to remain at school without knowing what was going on with Dad."

"So your promise to let me handle this mess meant nothing?" Mark said, the tone in his voice revealing the agitation he felt towards the boy for disobeying his orders.

"Damn it, Mark, he's my father," Steven protested. "If half of what you told me is true, then I have the right to be here," he continued. "I need to do something to help Dad."

"Help!" Mark giggled, amused by his young friend. "Just how do you plan on helping? With that thing?" he asked, pointing at the vase still in Steven's hand.

"By doing whatever is necessary," Steven declared, disappointed his uncle felt his behavior was something to joke about.

"Listen, kid," Mark began, slurring his words a little as he spoke. "I know you want to help your old man, but all you've managed to do is make things worse."

"Worse but how?"

"At school you were under the protection of the security force assigned there, but here you're a target. Who is going to protect you here?"

"You of course," Steven interrupted, "and I couldn't be safer. Right?"

"Right," Mark uttered, finishing his drink before turning his attentions back to his unwelcome guest. "Alright kid, if I let you stay, then there a few rules you have to agree to first."

"Rules? What rules?"

"That's right, rules." Mark began, "First, you have to promise to follow my orders no matter how strange they might seem to you."

"I promise."

"And if things get too dangerous, you have to agree to go back to school till I send for you."

"But—"

"No *but*'s, Steven, if you want to stay, you have to give me your word about that."

"All right, I agree," Steven finally replied, though he had no intentions of following through.

"Ok, kid, you can stay," Mark declared, "for now."

"Thanks," Steven began, hesitating for a moment as Mark poured himself a drink from the whiskey bottle sitting on a nearby coffee table. "What are you doing?" he asked, curious as to why there was an open bottle in front of him. He known Mark his entire life and never saw him take a drink before. Mark's father was an alcoholic and he was always determined never to be like him in any way.

"You mean this?" the man joked, downing the contents with one swallow before continuing his conversation. "I just needed something to get the chill out of my bones."

"When did you start needing whiskey to do that?" Steven asked.

"Let me see, I guess it was when I realized I wasn't superman and needed something to help me get through this mess I call my life," Mark announced as he finished another drink.

"Your life? Uncle Mark, what are you talking about?" the confused boy asked. As far as he was aware, nothing happened to his uncle to make him so cynical about the world he lived in.

"What am I talking about?" Mark rambled. "I am talking about a single moment in life. That defining moment when everything you believe in is destroyed and you find yourself unable to cope with life any more," he continued, "and everything changes forever."

"What moment? What are you talking about?" Steven repeated, still trying to make sense of his uncle's words.

"I am trying to tell you," Mark replied, the effects of the numerous drinks he finished starting to become more apparent with each word he spoke. "Everyone has a moment when they make a decision about their life that they wish they could take back," he continued, "and my moment was eight months ago. One little mission that changed everything for me, and I have been trying to forget what happened ever since."

"Eight months ago. What happened eight months ago?" Steven asked. He hadn't heard about anything happening to his uncle and wondered what it was he was referring to now.

"Nevermind," Mark said, signally for Steven to be quiet as a noise from the living room caught his attention.

"What is it?" Steven asked.

"Quiet," Mark snapped, pulling a gun from his jacket. "Stay here and don't make a sound," he ordered the boy before heading towards the kitchen door.

"But Uncle Mark—"

"Stay here!" Mark repeated.

Waiting nervously by the door, Steven wondered what it was his uncle heard and why he missed it. He promised not to be a hindrance in his uncle's search for Andrew if he allowed him to stay, and if this was any indication as to what kind of help he would be, Steven knew his uncle would have no choice but to send him back to school.

"Mark!" he whispered slightly after several minutes passed without a word from him. "Mark, are you ok?" he repeated, moving towards the door as he opened it slightly.

"Damn it, Mark, answer me," he began, grabbing the fire poker this time as he went in search of his uncle. He waited long enough, if everything were all right, Mark would have returned by now.

Moving towards the living room, Steven stopped for a few minutes in hopes he could hear something, anything to help him determine where to begin his search. Yet, as he stood by the couch listening for his uncle, there was nothing to hear. No sounds of an argument, a fight or struggle, nothing.

"Uncle Mark, where are you?" he whispered, afraid to speak any louder in case, there was someone else there. "What the—" he uttered, looking over at the open veranda door. It was closed earlier and the fact it now wasn't, scared Steven even more. "Uncle Mark," he said, walking through the door, praying he would not find him as he moved towards the balcony edge. Nearly ten floors up, he sighed with relief to see no sign of anyone there, "Thank god."

Closing the door as he returned to his quest, Steven started up the stairs to the second floor growing more anxious with each step he took. *What is going on?* he wondered as each room he checked failed to yield any sign of his friend. First his father's bedroom, then the spare and finally his own bedroom, the outcome was always the same. There was no sign of Mark anywhere.

Standing at the door of the only room he still needed to check, Steven slowly turned the doorknob leading to Andrew's office. Mark had to be in this room; there was nowhere else left he could be.

"Mark," Steven whispered, "are you here?"

"Boo!" Mark laughed, startling his young friend as he jumped from behind the door.

"What the—" Steven shouted, catching his breath and staring angrily at his uncle.

"What the hell is the matter with you?"

"Easy kid," he said, continuing to tease the boy as he spoke, "everything is fine."

"Fine!" Steven protested, "I've been calling you, why didn't you answer me?" The irate boy began shouting, "What about the noise you heard? Did you find something?"

"Not to worry," Mark uttered, "I took care of it."

"Took care of it? Took care of what?"

"Nothing much," Mark began, as he lit a cigar up, "just some guy trying to break into the apartment. I found him on the veranda and took care of the problem."

"On the veranda? But how? We are ten floors up," the boy asked.

"As far as I can figure, he must have propelled down from the roof, and I surprised him when he came through the door," Mark concluded, motioning the boy to follow him to the living room so they could talk there.

"Where is he now?" Steven blurted out, stunned by what he heard. If someone broke into the apartment as his uncle said, then why didn't he see him when he searched the place.

"He's dead," Mark announced, showing no reaction to the words he was saying.

"He's what? But how? Where is he?"

"He's dead," Mark repeated, heading straight for the bottle of whiskey he left on the bar earlier. "We struggled on the veranda and he fell," he continued, taking a drink.

"Struggled?" Steven repeated. "What struggle? I didn't hear anything."

"Can't blame that on me," Mark declared.

"Why didn't you call for help," the boy asked, "or answer me when I called you?"

"Because, my naive friend, I didn't know if he was alone or if he had company, and I didn't want to tip my hand too soon."

"Did he? Have any friends with him, I mean?"

"Nope."

"What about the man who fell?" Steven asked, curious about the intruder. "Did you know him? Was he looking for Dad?"

"For the third time, he's dead. No and yes. In that order," Mark responded, noticing his young friend's agitation as he joked with him further. "All right, kid, let me lay it out for you in simple terms. I found the guy trying to break in, we struggled, and he fell. I have no idea who he was or who he worked for, and yes, I believe he was here because of your father," Mark said sarcastically. "I doubt he expected to find your father here, but he was probably looking for some evidence he could use."

"Like what?" Steven asked.

"Oh, I don't know maybe a clue as to where Andrew is." Mark laughed looking at the poker in Steven's hand. "So tell just what were you going to do with that?" he asked, teasing the boy who'd forgotten he was still holding the weapon.

"I don't know," Steven admitted before putting it back from the spot he'd retrieved it from.

Walking towards the veranda without saying a word to his uncle, Steven looked down towards the street as he thought about what he'd been told. He could barely make out what he was staring at but knew from the flashing lights and sirens coming from the street, what Mark told him was the truth. There was a dead man down there. A man who broke into the apartment and now he was dead.

"Uncle Mark," Steven blurted out as he walked back into the living room. "If you hadn't been here, I could be the one…"

"Who took a swan dive." Mark laughed.

Nodding, Steven realized how close he came to being killed. He was asleep in his father's room, unaware of anything going on around him, and if Mark hadn't come over when he did, Steven would have been at the mercy of the intruder.

"Now you know why I wanted you to stay at school," Mark replied, as Steven reluctantly acknowledged his words.

"I'm sorry, Uncle Mark. I know it was a dumb move, but I had to come."

"You still don't get it, do you, Steven?" Mark snapped angrily. "What if that guy wasn't here looking for evidence on your father? What if he was looking for something or someone else?"

"Me," Steven answered. "Why would anyone be after me?"

"Come on, kid, you're not that stupid," Mark began. "To get to your father."

"To get to Dad. What good would it do for the police or anyone else to go after me?" he asked, still not making the connection.

"The police wouldn't go after you like this, but the agency would."

"The agency?"

"Steven, you must have suspected something over the years about what your father really did for a living," Mark said, walking closer to the boy as he spoke.

"Suspect what?" Steven uttered, growing increasing nervous about the direction the conversation was taking.

"That your father was involved in a lot more then he led you to believe."

"My father works for a special branch of the United Nations as a negotiator," he replied, getting more frustrated as they spoke. "I know that already."

"That, my dear boy, is your father's cover story," Mark announced as he continued to watch the look on Steven's face "He might be a negotiator, but he is not part of the U.N.," Mark announced.

"What do you mean, he is not part of the UN, of course he is, that's how he met Mom."

"Steven, your father works as operative for a top level agency within the government," Mark explained. "He is a negotiator for the agency, and his job is to try and work things out verbally between the parties involved before they present a threat to the United States, and if he fails, the agency steps in and takes over before it is too late."

"Takes over," Steven blurted out. "What do you mean takes over?"

"Come on, Steven, you know exactly what I mean."

"No, I don't," the boy insisted, not wanting to admit he did.

"We step in and, if necessary, take care of the problem by whatever means necessary."

"And you're telling me, Dad was a part of this."

"Was and is," Mark declared without showing any remorse for revealing Andrew's secret life to his son. "And that, my young friend, is why the agency would send someone to the apartment to find you. Having something to hold over your father's head right now would give them the edge they need to control the situation." Mark continued as he fixed himself another drink, "They can't let your father be questioned by the local police, and if kidnaping you assures your father's cooperation, then the hunt is on."

"And I am the bait?" Steven asked.

"Hook, line and sinker!"

"Okay," Steven began, "if they get hold of me, what happens next with Dad?"

"What do you think?"

'They would arrest and charge him with treason."

"Wrong!" Mark sneered.

"Would they try to silence him for good?" was Steven's next question, though he was not sure he wanted to hear the answer.

"In a heart beat."

"But if dad is only a suspect, wouldn't the people he works with wait to learn the truth before they did anything?"

"Steven, you have to know how the game works. Once the local police got involved, the rules changed. The agency can't risk your father talking to the police or even having them investigate the crime, so if he turns up dead, it will put everything to rest," Mark explained. "Besides things are a lot more complicated now then they were when we first spoke."

"Complicated? But how?" Steven asked, curious as to how things could get any worse.

"There's a video tape from the crime, and the agency bosses feel they have enough evidence to take Andrew out of the picture."

"Video tape?" Steven repeated hesitantly.

"Seems the records center recent upgrades included its security system and a surveillance camera no one else but the head of security knew about. So when the thief broke in, he was unaware his very move was being recorded."

"The video showed Dad?"

"In all his glory." Mark laughed, a very sarcastic laugh. "It shows him breaking into the records room, stealing the files and killing the guard."

"You're lying," Steven shouted, grabbing his uncle by the shirt collar. "The video tape has to be wrong, Dad would never betray his country, let alone kill someone. He is not that kind of man," he argued. "No matter what you say, my father is not a killer."

"Yea right," Mark said, pushing Steven away. "You still don't get it. You have no idea what kind of man your father is and what he is capable of."

"What is that supposed to mean?" Steven protested. "You can't seriously believe he could kill someone just because of that tape."

"The tape has nothing to do with it," Mark snapped, growing angry with the young man for his absolute faith in his father.

"Then what are you saying?" Steven yelled. "What else do you know about my father that I don't?"

"Forget it, kid," Mark uttered as he moved away from the boy. "You couldn't handle the rest of it."

"Damn it, Uncle Mark, tell me. What other secret our you keeping from me?"

"All right, kid, you asked for it," Mark declared as he made himself comfortable on the nearby couch, "but don't blame me when you hear the truth."

"Just tell me."

"Ok, if you're sure."

"Damn it, Uncle Mark, tell me."

"Your father is more connected to the agency then you realize."

"Look you already told me about the work he does, but that only proves he is not a killer," Steven protested. "You said my father tried to stop the agency from hurting people by working through the problems at the negotiation table."

"True, but he didn't always work behind the scenes."

"What...What did he used to do?" Steven asked hesitantly.

"Your father used to be the one who carried out the orders when things failed at the negotiation table."

"Carry out what orders?" the frightened boy asked, though he already knew the answer.

"He carried out the orders to eliminate the threat if all else failed," Mark announced, staring at the boy as he spoke. "He was one of the best sharp shooters we ever had and could kill a target from 300 feet away without breaking a sweat."

"A what?" Steven said, trying to make sense of what he was hearing. "You're lying. My father is a not a killer," he shouted angrily. "Why would you tell these lies about your best friend?"

"I'm not making these things up," Mark declared as he took a small bottle filled with pills from his pocket. "I told you learning the truth would be too much for you to handle," Mark said as Steven drew closer. "Your father is a cold blooded killer."

"You're lying," Steven cried again, striking out at his uncle.

"I'm sorry, kid," Mark said, grabbing the young man before he could hit him.

"But you wanted to know the truth about your father, so now you have to deal with it."

"He can't be a killer, not my father," Steven said, struggling to face the truth as he spoke.

"I'm sorry, kid, but it is true," Mark began. "After your mother's death, your father decided to take the easy way out and left the team to become a negotiator, but for years he was the leader of the squad and handled all of the agency's dirty work."

"Then he could have been capable of killing the man in the records room?" Steven asked not sure if he wanted to hear the answer.

"Yes, he could have."

"We have to do something to help Dad before it's too late," Steven declared realizing the implications of what he just learned. If his father were now a liability to the agency, they had to find him before the order to kill him was initiated.

"No kidding," Mark balked, he already figured that out.

"But what can we do to help him?"

"First, we have to find him, and then we have to prove he is not guilty."

"But what good will that do?" asked Steven. "You said it didn't matter what the outcome was, the agency would have to cover their tracks and kill Dad."

"True, but once we find your father and prove he didn't commit the crimes he is being accused of, we can worry about the rest later. I am sure Andrew will figure out a way to get out of this mess and probably in the end come out looking like a hero."

"Do you really think he can do that?"

"The great Andrew McCormick can do anything he sets his mind too." Mark laughed.

"I hope so," Steven said sitting by the fireplace his mind reeling with questions about his father. "Do you think Dad is guilty?" Steven asked, feeling guilty even as he spoke the words.

"Don't know," Mark replied.

"Do you think he fled the country to get away?"

"That I don't know, but he did leave the country from what I've learned," Mark revealed to the boy.

"Do you know where he is?"

"He is in Rome even as we speak."

"Rome, Italy?" Steven uttered.

"The one and only."

"Why would he go there?"

"Well, the agency believes your father went to Rome to sell the contents of the file to the highest bidder, but I am sure there is a lot more going on than we know."

"Are you saying the agency knows where he is too?"

"Not exactly." Mark explained, "They know he's in Italy, but they still don't know what part of the country he's in. Your father covered his tracks up pretty good and the agency boobs haven't figured it out yet."

"How did you find him?"

"One of my contacts in Rome found your father for me."

"So our next move is to go to Rome and find Dad before the agency does," Steven declared, ready to jump into action.

"We?"

"Yes," Steven replied. "I don't care if Dad is guilty or not, I won't let the agency take another parent away from me no matter what I have to do to stop it."

"Ok, if you say so." Mark laughed, remarking how much Steven reminded him of his father. "And you are sure you're willing to do anything."

"Yes!"

"Even break the law?"

"Anything."

"Then what would you do about the tape the agency has?"

"The tape," Steven blurted out. The tape needed to be destroyed before it could be used against his father but he wasn't sure how to accomplish the feat.

"Don't worry kid, it is being handled even as we speak," Mark assured him.

"Handled?"

"Don't ask," Mark ordered. The less Steven knew of the details the better.

"I can't believe this is happening," Steven began, pacing around the room. "Less than twenty-four hours ago I was preparing for graduation and my eighteenth birthday, and now it is like some damned nightmare I can't wake up from."

"Welcome to my world," Mark joked.

"Thanks," Steven replied sarcastically. He never wanted to be a part of this world and wished he didn't have to be involved with it now.

"Before we head for Rome we have another problem to deal with," Mark announced.

"What?" Steven asked.

"We have to get out of this apartment without being seen by the police," Mark said, reminding the boy of the dead man and the police on the street below.

"How?"

"That, my boy, is all part of the game."

"Whatever you say," Steven replied. "You're in charge."

"You better believe it." Mark laughed as they headed for the elevator door.

"Why are we stopping here?" Steven asked as they got off on the third floor instead of the lobby.

"Because, my young friend, contrary to popular belief, cops aren't stupid. They will have someone watching the lobby for anyone trying to leave the building, and the last thing we want is to run into some flatfoot asking a lot questions about the dead man."

"So how are we going to get out of here?" asked Steven.

"We are going to use our own exit."

"Our own exit? Where?" the confused boy inquired. They were on the third floor of the apartment building, and as far as he knew, there was no way out of the building.

"By going out this way," Mark announced moving the statue sitting on a the mantel next to the elevator.

"What the—"

"Follow me," Mark ordered as his actions revealed a hidden elevator.

"How? Where did that come from?" the stunned boy asked as he followed his uncle into the elevator.

"Your father installed it ten years ago after you moved in."

"Dad installed this elevator, but why?"

"After your mother's murder, Andrew became very cautious about your safety and wanted to make sure there was always an escape route should he ever needed one in a hurry."

"But this is a twelve floor apartment building, what about the other tenants?" Steven asked, still finding the idea of a hidden elevator hard to believe.

"Easy, your father bought the building and had it remodeled," Mark explained.

"The tenants were taken to a hotel while he remodeled the building, and he took care of all the details himself.

"They just left their homes without questioning it?" the boy asked.

"Your father bought the apartment under an assumed name and told the tenants the remodeling was part of the upgrade ordered by the new owners."

"Where did he get the money?"

"Your father got paid very well for his special talents, and he invested the money over the years and before he knew it, he was a very wealthy man," Mark announced, revealing yet another secret to the boy.

"Another secret I didn't know about," Steven remarked as he looked at his uncle. "Is there anything else?"

"Time will tell." Mark joked.

"Great!"

"Don't worry, kid, I will cover your back no matter what happens." Mark laughed as the elevator finally stopped at the lower level of the parking garage. "See, every problem has a solution to it including this one," Mark declared before they headed out of the building from the back of the garage, away from the eyes of the nearby police.

Looking back at the apartment building as they sat in Mark's car, Steven could not help but think of the dead man lying on the ground. *Was this just the start of the body count?* he wondered. *Were things only going to get worse before everything was over?*

"What are you doing?" he blurted out angrily at his uncle. "Are you crazy? There are cops everywhere and the last thing we need is for one of them to see you with that bottle and arrest us for DUI," Steven protested, watching as Mark took a flask from his pocket and took a drink.

"A job well done deserves a reward," Mark replied, taking another drink.

"And your idea of a reward is to get blind drunk?"

"If only I could be so lucky."

"What's the matter, you can't really believe that stuff is going to help you in any way."

"Nothing helps, but for a little while, it makes it easier to forget."

"Forget what?" Steven asked. "What are you trying to get over?"

"None of your business," Mark snapped angrily.

"Mark, you have to stop this before it's too late." The boy pleaded with his uncle.

"If I want a lecture about the dangers of booze or my soul rotting in hell, I will go to a damned shrink," Mark snapped.

"Uncle Mark, please listen to me!"

"Enough," Mark ordered before driving away.

Mark Sinclair, though not biologically related to Steven McCormick, shared a friendship with Andrew that made them as close as family.

A well-built man in his mid-fifties, Mark was a complicated man with many facets to him. A brilliant man who felt he was above most he encountered, his circle of friends was few, including Andrew. Best friends for over forty years, the two men were like brothers as they shared everything in their lives including raising Andrew's young son after the death of his mother.

The eldest of four kids, his stepfather never let Mark forget he was not his biological son with his constant intimidation of the boy. A local merchant whose violence towards Mark was often cruel and painful.

A fragile sickly child who grew up with his dysfunctional family, Mark turned his hatred towards his parents into his inspiration as he overcame the frailties of youth to become a force to be reckoned with.

"Uncle Mark, please put that stuff away," Steven pleaded with his friend.

"Ok, kid, I'll put it away for now," he replied. "Besides I have much better stuff in my apartment." Mark laughed pulling away from the apartment building.

"What are we going to do next?" Steven asked, trying to change the subject from his uncle's drinking to the problem of finding his father. It was obvious he did not want to discuss it with him and Steven would let it go.

"We get ready to take a trip," Mark replied.

Arriving at the house without any more problems, Mark typed in his security code as the garage door slowly began to open.

"We're home, kid," he remarked pulling the car into the safety of the garage before securing the code once more.

Walking into the home Mark lived in for several years, Steven smiled at the familiarity of it. The same old carpet with its faded colors, the furniture that looked as if it came from a secondhand store and the shelves filled with books, gave him a sense of security he hadn't felt since he arrived in Washington.

"How's Charlie doing?" Steven asked, poking the tank with a large iguana inside.

"He's doing fine. Still trying to take over the house," Mark replied. "That's why I got a bigger tank. The old one was getting a little uncomfortable for him, and every time I came home, I found him wondering through the house."

"I'm sure your housekeeper loves that," Steven joked.

"Not to mention the ladies." Mark laughed as he tossed some food into the tank for his salty friend. "Would you like a drink?"

"Ok, Uncle Mark, I've put this off long enough," Steven began. "I want to know what is going on with you? Why did you start drinking so much?"

"*So much*, hell, kid, this is not so much," Mark protested. "You should have seen me the other night at the local club, now that was a lot of booze," he revealed, recalling the binge ending with him spending the night in the local drunk tank.

"You think this is funny, don't you? Well I don't," Steven snapped. "How are you supposed to find Dad and help him if all you want to do is sit around doing nothing but drink that crap?"

"First off, kid, I am not sitting around doing nothing," Mark said angrily. "And secondly, I can do my job no matter what shape I am in, do you understand?"

"I hope so," Steven snapped, still not convinced by his uncle's words.

"Steven," Mark uttered, grabbing the boy by the arm as he spoke. "You mean more to me than my own life, and I love you as if you were my own son. I would never do anything to hurt you in any way." Mark rambled on, "I promise you I will find your father and nothing or no one will stop me."

"I love you too, Uncle Mark," Steven replied, struggling to free himself from the man, as his grip became increasingly painful. "You're hurting me!" he finally said, his efforts to escape Mark's hold unsuccessful.

"Oh, god, I am sorry," Mark replied. His words slurred as he spoke. Stepping away from the boy, Mark let out a laugh as he fell into the couch, "I guess maybe I should have eaten something this morning. I am feeling a little light headed."

"Yea, food will help," Steven said sarcastically. "Why are you behaving like this? Please tell me what happened to change you?"

"I told you earlier, life is what happened and sometimes it is easier to deal with it after I have had a little help from my friends. The booze and the pills are the only things that help me get through it."

"Pills! What pills?" was the next question coming from the boy. It was difficult enough to see his uncle drinking but to be taking pills too.

"Why these pills," Mark answered, taking one from the bottle he held as he answered the question.

"What are they for?"

"I told you they are for the pain," Mark yelled. "The pain of life."

"Pain, what pain? You're not making any sense. The pain of life, what is going on with you?" Steven demanded to know, grabbing the glass in an attempt to keep the man from taking any more.

"Give me that!" Mark shouted, slapping Steven across the face without warning as he took the glass from him.

Stunned by what happened, Steven stared at his uncle without saying a word. No one—not his father or mother— no one ever struck him in anger before, and the last person he ever expected to strike him was Mark.

"I'm sorry." The man apologized but with no sign of remorse in his voice. "There are just certain things you don't do and taking a man's medicine from him is one of them," Mark explained as his behavior became more and more bizarre.

"Medicine! Is that what you call that crap?" Steven protested. "Uncle Mark, can't you see that stuff is no good for you and you need help?"

Moving towards the boy without saying a word, Mark hesitated as the memory of his earlier behavior caused the boy to back away in fear.

"Steven, are you afraid of me?" Mark asked, surprised by Steven's reaction.

"I'm not sure what I am," he confessed. The man before him was not behaving like the uncle he knew, and for a moment as he drew closer, Steven felt like he was staring at an enemy instead of a friend.

"Steven, I am sorry I hit you, but you gave me no choice," Mark explained taking him by the arm again. "I love you like a son, and I would never hurt you, but there are so many things you do not know about me and one of them is how much I need this stuff for the headaches," he continued. "Sometimes the pain is so bad I can't fight it."

"Let me go," Steven ordered, struggling to free himself. Whatever was going on with his uncle, the man wasn't going to manhandle him just to prove his point.

"Steven," Mark cried, turning away from the boy. He was just as confused about his behavior and didn't want the anger he felt inside to touch the boy in anyway.

"Are you alright?" Steven reluctantly asked, staring at him as the man moved back towards the couch.

"I'm fine."

"I wish you were," Steven replied. "Please just tell me what happened to change you. What turned you from a man who would never touch alcohol to a man who can't seem to stop."

Watching quietly while Mark moved towards the fireplace, Steven hoped this time he would finally open up to him and answer his questions.

"Please, Mark, tell me?"

"The last time you wanted to hear the truth," Mark declared, "you weren't too happy with what I told you, and I don't think my secrets will make things any easier for you."

"You're right, learning my father used to be an assassin did not sit too well with me, but it doesn't change the way I feel about him. He is my father and I love him, the same way I love you, no matter what you tell me, that will not change."

"Are you sure?" Mark asked.

"Yes, I am sure."

Pausing as he tried not to let his fears keep him from telling Steven the truth, Mark finished his drink before revealing his story. He had tried several times in the last couple of months to tell him what happened, but the memories were too painful and the shame he felt for his failure too strong.

"I was on an assignment and the entire mission fell through. Everything that could go wrong did," Mark finally blurted out.

"What happened ?"

"If you give me a minute, I will tell you," Mark snapped, his mood swings becoming erratic once more as he spoke about the mission. "My squad was sent on a simple rescue mission," Mark continued, "It was something we did dozens of times in the past. Go in, retrieve the objective and get out. It was supposed to be a cake walk for my unit."

"Your unit?" Steven repeated, suddenly realizing he never knew what Mark did for the agency either. He just assumed it was some type of security work, since he was a MP when he was in the Army.

"Yes, my unit. I am a field agent, and I have a squad I am in charge of," Mark snapped. "I went on some of the most dangerous missions imaginable. Assignments no one else wanted or could handle, well, I did them all," Mark insisted. "Successfully, too, I might add, until," he paused for a moment, "until that last mission."

"What happened?" Steven asked.

"I'm trying to explain it to you," Mark protested, upset the boy interrupted his thoughts. "Bet you'd be surprised to find out who rescued me from the mission," Mark uttered. "It was your father."

"Dad rescued you?" asked Steven. "Rescued you from what?"

"Yup, good old Dad came to the rescue and got me out of that hell hole," Mark replied.

"Will you just tell me what happened?" Steven yelled, growing upset with his uncle and the game he was playing.

"All right kid, don't freak out on me," Mark began. "The simple mission I thought would be a piece of cake turned into a nightmare. Everything that could go wrong did, and in the end we walked into a trap."

"A trap!"

"Yea! My men and I parachuted into a LZ we thought was secured, but before we knew it, we found ourselves in the middle a rebel camp." Mark continued as he took a drink from his glass to help calm his nerves, "It was like a damned Chuck Norris movie with the bad guys coming out of everywhere, guns firing, people screaming. But unlike in the movies, the good guys did not win in the end. By the time the smoke cleared, my men were dead and I was a prisoner of the rebels."

"A prisoner?" the shocked boy echoed. "Why wasn't I ever told about this?"

"At the time, it was a security matter," Mark explained, hoping his words would be enough of an explanation.

"Ok, I get that but what about later? When you came home? What then, why wasn't I told about what happened then?"

"Well excuse me," Mark snapped. "I guess I had a few more important things to deal with like the families of my dead men and the last thing I wanted to do was re-live the nightmare over again by telling you or anyone else about it."

"Ok, Uncle Mark, it's all right," Steven remarked, trying to calm the man down before his temper got the better of him again and something else happened between them. "If you're up to talking about it now, I'll listen."

"I don't know if I can," Mark confessed. "I wanted to tell you the truth, but it is so hard."

"Whatever happened to you wasn't your fault," Steven began, trying to reassure his uncle he would stand by him no matter what he told him.

"I wish that was true," Mark replied. "They were my men, I was responsible for them and I let them down."

"But you said yourself it was a trap," Steven protested. "There was no way you could have been prepared for what happened."

Thanking Steven for his words, Mark continued to tell him what happened and the aftermath of the disastrous mission.

"After I was taken prisoner, the rebels enjoyed tormenting me with the fact my men were dead and I'd led them to their deaths," he said, taking a drink. "And when they weren't torturing me with their words, they were physically abusing me," he explained, fighting back the tears as he spoke, recalling the horrors he lived through. "Days and nights of beatings, drugs being forced in to my body as they tried to get me to talk. I was forced to live like an animal, and by the time your father found me, I was behaving like one too," Mark admitted.

"How did Dad rescue you? Did he negotiate your freedom?"

"No, there weren't any negotiations going on. The agency could not admit one of its people had been captured, and as far as the rebels were concerned, they did not have anything worth trading for. They wanted me to publicly denounce the United States and the agency, that was all they wanted."

"So how did he get you out?' Steven asked with curiosity.

"He came in and got me out," Mark replied, the irritation in his voice becoming more apparent as the recalled how it was Andrew who came to his rescue.

"But how?"

"Your father led a team into the rebel territory and rescued not only me but the diplomat I was send into retrieve in the first place."

"My father did that!" Steven replied, still finding the information he'd learned about his, father difficult to believe.

"Yup, your dad did that!" Mark uttered, another drink in hand.

"Please, Uncle Mark," Steven began, pleading with him once more to put the drink down.

"I told you I need this for the pain," Mark protested.

"The pain you feel is not going to go away with drugs and booze," Steven tried to explain.

"You think I'm nuts like everyone else does, don't you?" Mark snapped. "Well, I'm not. The pain I feel is real not imaginary," he protested, tired of everyone he knew telling him it was all in his mind. "Those bastardy tortured me, beat me so bad there are days my head feels like it is going to explode. The pills are the only things which helps make them bearable."

"I'm sorry," Steven replied. He didn't want his uncle to feel he was abandoning him. "All that matters is you made it home safely, and as soon as we find Dad, the three of us will work on getting your life back together again"

"Of course we will," he replied sarcastically. "We can't do anything till we find Andrew. Only Andrew can do the job right. Only he can fix the mistakes I am making, and there is nothing else to do until we find him. Right."

Not sure what to say to Mark's words, Steven did not understand why he spoke with such venom whenever he mentioned his father. It was as if he hated Andrew for some reason, and this made no sense to the boy at all. They were the best of friends and nothing, not even the torture he endured at the hands of the rebels, should have changed that.

"To Andrew, the world's best agent." Mark saluted and poured himself another drink as he offered one to his young friend.

No longer able to contain himself, Steven finally confronted his uncle about his remarks.

"Why are you so angry with Dad?" Steven demanded to know.

"Angry with my best friend?" Mark laughed. "Of course I'm not angry with my best friend. I am simply making a toast to the best man I know. He is one of the few heroes left in the world. Hell, even your mother thought Andrew was the better man, that's why she married him instead of me so long ago."

"My mother?" Steven uttered. "What the hell does she have to do with this?"

Staring at the boy wondering if he was saying too much, Mark quickly covered his words. The last thing he wanted was for Steven to turn against him when he needed him so much.

"I'm sorry, kid," he said. " I guess the booze is getting to me more then I realized. I didn't mean to upset you about either of your parents," he assured him. "Maybe we should just get back to the subject of your father and helping him out of this mess he's in."

"Fine with me," Steven replied. He would save the conversation about his parents and the remarks his uncle was making for later time. "What about Dad and the people he works with?" Steven began. "There has to be someone at the agency we can trust, someone who believes my dad is innocent?" He continued, "He's worked for them for over twenty years, they can't all have turned on him?"

"Well, besides Gibbs, there might be a hand full of agents we can trust, but most of the people who worked with your father in his hay days have retired or moved on to other departments," Mark explained. "There's a new crop of spies taking over and their sense of loyalty extends to how it will benefit them in the end."

"What about Rick's father? Is he going to do something to help?"

"Yes but not out in public," Mark explained. "He is going to be working behind the scenes to try to figure out what is going on."

"What are we going to do to help Dad?"

"First we find your father, then we bring him home and prove he didn't commit the crimes he has been accused of," replied Mark

"And just how do you expect us to do that?"

"I told you my sources learned your father is in Rome so I am heading there in a few hours, and from there I will play it by ear."

"You mean we. Remember?" Steven echoed.

"You still want to come?"

"Yes."

"And you intend to keep your promise to do whatever I say."

"I promise," Steven assured him.

"No matter what?"

"Yes, I promise to do whatever you say no matter what."

"Good! Then as soon as I finish making the arrangements we can head for the airport," Mark said to his young friend. "Why don't you go freshen up a little while I make some calls and finalize the details of our trip."

"You promise not to leave without me?" Steven said, afraid once he retreated to the bathroom to shower, his uncle would leave.

"I promise, kid," Mark assured him before the boy disappeared up the stairs.

Waiting a few minutes to make sure Steven did not return, Mark picked up his cell phone from the table.

"Hello, it's me," he began, watching the stairs as he spoke to the person on the other end. The last thing he wanted was for the boy to hear the conversation.

"Yes, everything is set," he continued, "we'll be in Rome within the next twenty four hours. No! I haven't told anyone at the agency about the trip, I am not that stupid," he snapped angrily at his tormentor on the other end. "Listen to me, I don't intend to screw this up so stop worrying…What? Yes, I found two men I can trust, men who have worked with Andrew in the past: Kirk Ventura, and Henry Storm…What? No, I trust them, they're good agents. They are going to meet us in Rome and stay with the boy at the hotel. "What? Damn it, I don't like it either, but if we are going to prove to the world what is really going on, we need them. There is no one else I can trust at the agency," he said. Mark did not like using anyone from the agency for this mission, for fear their loyalties would be tested, but he had no choice. The two agents went wrong. "I'll talk to you later," he whispered, hearing Steven at the top of the stairs.

"Uncle Mark, is everything ready?" Steven said, running towards him.

"I thought you were going to take a shower."

"I will but I wanted to make sure we were set to go."

"We will be," he assured him.

"Is that who you were talking to, the airport?" Steven asked.

"I was making the arrangements for our trip and that is all you need to know," Mark assured him. "Now go take a shower," he began looking over at the pack back lying near the door. "I see you are already packed so as soon as it's time to go we can head out."

"Ok," Steven replied. "What about your bag?"

"In my car," Mark answered. "Now go get ready, we'll be heading for the airport in about an hour."

"Do you think we will find Dad?" Steven asked, standing on the stairs as he started back up to the second floor.

"Don't worry, kid, we will find your father and by the time this mess is over everything will be taken care of and finally put to rest."

"Thanks, Uncle Mark," Steven replied. "Thanks for letting me come along to help Dad," he said before disappearing up the stairs.

"You're welcome," Mark whispered before taking another drink. He hated involving the boy in anyway, but the circumstances left no choice. If he was going to find Andrew and make things right, Steven would play a very important part. More important than he knew.

CHAPTER FOUR

Placing the file on the table next to him before turning his attentions to his meal, Andrew took a moment to regain his thoughts. His head already pounding from the events of the day, the last thing he wanted to do was ruin the fine dinner sitting before by reading the contents of the file before he had a chance to enjoy it.

Walking towards the veranda, a glass of wine in hand, Andrew stood by the balcony as he took in the sights. The beauty of Rome, like a breath of fresh air, seemed to ease the tension he felt as he continued to watch the busy city around him.

One of his favorite places, he always felt like he was coming home each time he stepped off the plane into the welcoming hands of the Italian people.

Smiling, as he listened to the sounds of children singing in a nearby schoolyard, Andrew thought about the tiny church his family visited long ago and the children's choir they heard that day. Nearly twelve years earlier, it was the last trip they took together and one of his fondest memories. Though Steven was only six at the time, the excitement in his eyes as he joined the choir in song was something Andrew always cherished.

How long ago that was, he thought to himself turning away from the window and the children singing below. "Nearly a lifetime," he mumbled aloud. He lost Sophia shortly after the trip and nothing was ever the same.

Stirring uncomfortably, Andrew hoped the mission that brought him back to Rome would not end up being his last trip there. Trapped between conscious and duty, right and wrong, he knew in the end whatever decisions were made someone he cared for could end up paying the ultimate price.

Grabbing the phone, Andrew decided to call his son before returning to the file and mission at hand. Once the next step began, things would move very quickly and despite the risks, he needed to hear Steven's voice. Needed to be assured they could still work things out when the mission was over.

Tapping his foot impatiently while he listened to the phone ringing numerous times without a response, Andrew grew increasing nervous as it continued to go unanswered.

Ok kid, where are you? he wondered as the phone continued to ring. Normally not concerned about his son's safety with the security at the school being so tight, the warning from the agent he encountered on the road earlier only fueled his fears for Steven's safety. "Come on, Steven, answer," he snapped out loud, re-dialing the number. It had been a long day and he was very tired, perhaps he called the wrong one on his first try. "Damn it kid, Where are you?" he remarked, still receiving no response "Why did I leave without talking to him first?" Andrew snapped angry with himself for his actions. He should have told Steven about leaving the country, should have taken the time to explain things to him but instead let the fear of endangering the boy overshadow his better judgment. "Why did I listen to you?" he mumbled, recalling Mark's reasons for keeping Steven out of the loop. At the time the explanations sounded plausible but now he wasn't so sure.

If the mission was compromised as the dead man implied, then the likelihood he would have to cross the line again to fulfill his promise was high. Leaving without talking to his son first might be the worst mistake of his life.

"Damn it," he uttered angrily.

Already on edge from the earlier encounter on the road, his nerves were stretched to the limit as he began to worry about Steven's safety. Only the fact someone was watching over him now kept Andrew from completely losing it and abandoning his mission. He never left an assignment uncompleted before, and though this one held a personal meaning to him, he would not hesitate to turn his back on it if it meant losing Steven in the process.

"Now, where the hell are you at?" he mumbled. The next attempt to reach the friend he asked to guard Steven yielded the same results. "How can I be sure my son is safe if you don't answer the damned phone?" he snapped. The sense something was wrong grew stronger with each second that passed.

Checking his watch, Andrew decided to make a few more calls before sounding the panic button and calling in the troops. It was nearly eight in the morning back home and there was at least one person whose loyalty could never be in question, one person who could fill in the blanks and help him out.

"Hello Annie," he began, the sound of Stewart Gibbs' secretary greeting him on the other end like a breath of fresh air. If there was anyone in the world he could trust, it was Annie. "Hi, darling. It's Andrew," he continued. "Can't say," he replied, her first question concerning his whereabouts. "Just checking in to see if everything is ok back home," he started. "You haven't heard about any problems at the school I need to know about, have you?"

"Nope, everything's fine," she replied. "What were you expecting to be wrong?"she asked, curious as to why her friend was making such a strange phone call.

"Annie, my darling, you can read me like a book." Andrew laughed. "I was just wondering if there was anything going on at Steven's school I should know about."

"With the kids?" she said, surprised by the question. "I haven't heard anything, and as far as I know they're fine, getting ready for graduation." She continued trying to reassure her friend as she spoke, "I'm sure if there were a problem at the school, someone from security would have notified me by now so stop worrying about him."

"I'm sure they would have too," Andrew concurred. Annie was the heart and soul of the agency and anyone associated with it always turned to her in times of trouble.

With them for nearly 40 years, she knew everything there was to know about the agency. From the past administration to the present, her information was always reliable.

"Have you spoken to Steven in the last couple of days?" Andrew asked, still feeling uneasy about his inability to contact his son.

"I talked to him last week about graduation, but I haven't talked to him since then," she replied. "Is there something going on with him I should know about?"

"Nothing that I know," Andrew answered. " I'm just having a little trouble reaching him."

"Well what do you expect?" Annie laughed. "He is graduating from high school in a matter of days. He is probably out celebrating with his friends, getting last minute gifts and…"

"I get it," Andrew interrupted. "My son is out doing normal teenage things."

"Exactly," she concurred. "Now relax, will you."

"I'll try," Andrew remarked.

"Maybe you're feeling guilty about missing his graduation because of this trip you are on and that is making you a little more on edge then normal," Annie remarked bluntly.

"You are probably right," Andrew replied. He did feel guilty about the fact he had forgotten both the graduation and Steven's eighteenth birthday coming up in a few days when he accepted the mission.

"So why don't you keep trying to reach him, and when you do, take the time to tell him how sorry you are." She continued, "I'm sure he will understand."

"I hope so," Andrew said. "Well thanks, Annie, I guess I better go."

"Wait," she interrupted. "Since neither you nor Stewart chose to tell me what assignment you are on, can I at least ask if you are reachable through your e-mail?" she inquired. "In case there is an emergency."

"Yes," Andrew answered.

"And you're not going to tell me where you are?"

"Sorry love, I can't," Andrew explained.

"And if you need backup, do you have anyone you can rely on?"

"Just myself," he replied.

"I hope that is enough," Annie said, worried her friend might get in over his head.

"Me too."

"You know I hate it when one of my boys goes off to play without the proper toys," Annie protested.

"Don't worry, Momma, I can take care of myself," Andrew laughed.

"Well, just be careful and when I hear from Stewart, I'll let him know about your concerns and have him double check with Rick to make sure everything is ok."

"Listen, do me a favor and don't tell Stewart anything about the call or the fact I can be reached by e-mail," Andrew asked. Despite what Annie thought, Stewart did not authorize the mission he was on and if he got wind of what his friend was doing he might try to interfere with what had to be done.

"Stewart doesn't know about the mission either?" Annie remarked, realizing by the response she just received Stewart was not aware of what Andrew up too. "Then who is your contact, someone from the tower?"

"Don't worry, Annie, it's covered."

"Andrew, if you are riding blind on this mission, I want to know about it," she argued. Though it were not unusual for the tower to send agents on missions which kept the local agency out of the loop, Annie was normally notified by them of such a case and she hadn't been this time.

"Annie, honey, I'm sorry but I can't tell you anything right now," Andrew began. "Just promise me you will keep an eye on things for me and keep your fingers crossed this won't turn out to be my last job."

"That's not funny," she balked angrily.

"Sorry," he replied. "Guess not. I promise to get back to you when I can, so don't worry," he assured her.

"All right," she said, whatever he was involved with would have to remain a secret for now and she would have to wait for the answers when it was safe for him to give them to her. "I will keep out of it for now if you promise to get back to me as soon as you can."

"I promise," Andrew replied. "Annie, are you sure there is nothing going on I should know about?" Andrew asked one more time, curious as to whether the theft of the files were discovered yet.

"Andrew my love, just be careful out there and don't worry about things here at the agency," Annie ordered her friend.

"Annie, what is it? " Andrew said. "Tell me!"

"It's Peter," she said.

"Peter, the kid who works in records?" Andrew asked, surprised by her words.

"Yea, he's dead."

"Dead! How? When?"

"He was killed about a week ago in the file room. Looks like he walked in on someone stealing some files and got a knife in the back for his troubles."

"He was what?" Andrew blurted out, stunned by what he was hearing. "Does anyone know what happened?" Andrew asked. He was the thief who broke into the records center and Peter was not there when he did.

"Like I said, it looks like he interrupted someone inside and they killed him," Annie repeated.

"Do they know who is responsible?" Andrew asked once more.

"They have their suspicions but nothing solid," Annie replied. "You know the guys from internal affairs always with the cloak and danger." She continued, "The intruder got in and took several valuable files and the only piece of evidence we have so far is the surveillance video stationed outside in the hallway. It was running at the time and should show everyone who entered the file room during the time frame of Pete's death."

A videotape, Andrew thought, *that is impossible*. One of the few people who knew about the new security system installed in the records center, he secured the system before entering the file room and the tape should have been blank.

"How many people do they show on the tape?" he asked trying to figure out if the existence of the tape was possible.

"From what I could find out there are at least five possibilities. The boys were running them down, but had to put it on hold because of a top priority mission that came up," Annie explained.

"Five!" Andrew repeated, relieved if there was a tape, he wasn't the only one on it. "What was the urgent mission?"

"One of the need to know type missions," she replied, unable to give her friend anymore details about it.

"So no one is working on Peter's murder right now?" Andrew asked, finding it extremely unusual for the agency to allow such a security breach to go without a full investigation.

"I didn't exactly say that," Annie mumbled.

"Annie, what is going on? What aren't you telling me?"

"Well, Stewart wanted to keep the investigation going, but with everyone tied up he didn't have much of a choice, so he put Mark on the case until the other assignment was completed."

"What! Mark Sinclair? Is he nuts?" Andrew blurted out, stunned to learn his friend was allowed to work in the field again. "Was he taken off medical leave since I left?"

"Not really but Stewart did not want anyone else involved in the break-in other than the agents from internal affairs, so he figured giving it to Mark would be the safest thing to do. He could keep the investigation going without to much fanfare."

"But using Mark, isn't Stewart afraid he might have another breakdown?" Andrew asked. Mark was not up to fieldwork since his last mission and putting him on such a case did not make any sense.

"Guess not," Annie replied

"Well, if you say so," Andrew continued, still not convinced using Mark for such a high priority case was a good idea. "Look, Annie, I have to go but thanks for the information about Pete and Mark," Andrew said, eager to get off the phone before the conversation got more complex. "Can you contact me if you hear anything else?"

"Sure thing, I'll let you know through your e-mail, since I don't know where you are or how to reach you."

"Annie."

"Can't blame a girl for trying," she joked. "All right I will send you anything I get. Anything else I can do for you while I'm being so generous?"

"Yes, can you run a background check on the Guillermo family?"

"The Guillermos! Well that's a name I haven't heard in years."

"I know," Andrew said. He too thought they were out of the picture but with the mission he was on and the strange events surrounding it, Andrew couldn't take the chance they came out of hiding. Once a fermentable enemy, if they were back in the picture, he needed to protect the Vega brothers from their revenge.

"Ok, I'll see what I can find. Do you want me to e-mail the information to you?"

"No, I'll call you," Andrew replied. "And, Annie, don't tell anyone about this ok?"

"Who me?" She laughed. "I still haven't told anyone where Jimmy Hoffa is buried remember."

"Thanks," he replied before hanging up.

Fixing himself a drink as he thought about both agents who been killed since he started the mission. First the man on the road who died trying to outwit him in the game and now Peter. Both men were only doing their jobs, only following orders and both men were young enough to be his son. He hated the world he lived in, a world where life was so easily dismissed and after this mission was over, no matter what the outcome, it would be his last. It was time to call it quits before he ended up in a place he could never return from, a place where he seen other burn out agents end up.

"I hope you are not going to regret taking this mission," he whispered as he thought about his son and his inability to reach him. Despite Annie's assurances there was nothing wrong, knowing two men were already dead made Andrew very uneasy about Steven and his whereabouts.

"Damn! Still no answer," he snapped, slamming the phone down in frustration after another failed attempt to reach his son. As much as he wanted to call out the calvary, Andrew could not to let his fears get the better of him, not yet. As far as he knew Steven was simply too preoccupied with graduation and the parties surrounding it to answer the phone. He would give it a little more time before he did anything drastic and if that didn't work, then he would call Mark and have him check to make sure everything was all right.

Turning his attention back to the file and the notes inside in hopes of distracting his thoughts for a little while, Andrew began sifting through the pages. *Maybe*, he thought, *I can find something missed earlier, something to help figure out who is telling the truth and who is lying.* He hated feeling at odds over the mission, but relying on his instincts alone this time would not be enough. Not only were his old friends personally involved in the mission, making anything he did more difficult, but the position of power he was given so long ago by Jose Vega made every choice he made a life and death issue. "I knew some day that damned promise would come back to haunt me," he uttered as he thought about the committee formed so long ago and the promises he made when he became a member of the group. Despite his misgivings, he did not fail his old friend then or now. The safety of the people of San Sebastian was the most important thing in the world to Jose, even at the sacrifice of his own sons, and letting a man of such honor down was not an option Andrew could ever consider.

Called together for the first time since its inceptions, Andrew prayed the urgent pleas by Philippe to meet with the other members of the committee was nothing more than a simple misunderstanding on the part of the two brothers. He did not want to face the possibility that one or both of Jose's sons had turned against the people and the principles their father died for. Nor did he want to follow through on the promise he made to their father should the time ever come when his sons proved to be more of a hindrance to the people than an asset. It seemed no matter where he turned he was caught in the middle, forced to choose which of the brothers he would believe in.

Flipping through the files in a desperate attempt to find a clue, anything to support Philippe's accusations, Andrew grew more frustrated with each word he read. Years of surveillance by the agency, who helped with the original coupe against the Guillermo, only served to bring up more questions than answers. There was no prove either way that he could find in the files and this frustrated him even more.

Easing into the nearby chair, as he put a pillow behind his head, Andrew closed his eyes for a second trying to get a better perspective of what he was facing. He had traveled half way around the world, committed crimes against his own company, just to watch old friends tear each other apart. What he saw so far only made him realize the battle was far more personal than he thought, as if something or someone turned the once close brothers against each other. Torn by his loyalties, Andrew hoped the repercussions of the battle would not force him back into the world he struggled so hard to escape. It was a long and difficult journey pulling away from the lifestyle he once loved, and now after all these years, the lure of that life was surging through him again with each breath he took as he stepped back into its very soul. The violence, intrigue, danger, all the things he did for the agency so long ago were like drugs to a junkie and he was slowing getting hooked again.

Staring at an old picture he found in the file, Andrew thought about the assignment that changed his life forever. Sent to San Sebastian as an observer only, it was not long before he found himself not only a part of the fight for freedom but a member of the rebel family as well when he married Paulina Vega.

While looking at the picture of himself standing along side Jose and the family, he realized it was the only photograph he ever seen with all of them together.

Jose Vega, a farmer by trade, was a quiet man who believed in family and loyalty to his country above all else. The father of three girls and two boys, he loved all his children equally as he raised them to be true to their heart and soul no matter the consequences.

A quiet man whose reserve hid the strength and patience within him, he allowed himself the indignities of dictatorship as he waited for the right time to put his sons to work. Certain they had been chosen to free the people of San Sebastian, he taught them how to rule with honor and prepared them for the day they would overthrow the Guillermo family.

Philippe, the oldest, a strong willed but inapt man was picked to help groom his younger brother Antonio, for leadership as the next president of San Sebastian as he worked along side his father on the farm. A soldier at heart, he possessed the skills to be a great warrior and used those skills to make sure his father's dreams of freedom were fulfilled.

While Antonio, with his charismatic ways was sent away to school to be certain when the time came he had both the knowledge and the skills needed to a great leader. Together they were a quite team who could not be beat.

Recalling yet another memory as he stared at the photograph, Andrew realized he had not thought of Paulina in years. The younger sister she became more than just another member of the team to him. One of the most beautiful women he would ever encounter, she lit up the room whenever she walked in. Her coal black hair, nearly waist length, was always tied behind her head with a blue ribbon. She could fire a weapon like any experienced soldier he had seen.

Gently touching the photograph, her smile staring back at him, Andrew realized just how lucky he had been to know her. Married only six weeks, they were not only lovers but also the best of friends.

Killed while in a battle between Guillermo's man and her own troops, Paulina died doing what she believed in and Andrew never regretted the short time they shared.

"I still miss you and the family," he whispered. He hadn't spoken or seen anyone from San Sebastian in over twenty years, and now as he met with the

Vega brothers once again, Andrew regretted his actions. A coward even then, when it came to dealing with the emotions, he cut himself off from the family after he was re-assigned to Paris and never looked back.

How lucky I was, he thought to himself, placing the picture back in the folder. He loved not one but two exceptional woman in his short lifetime. Women, whose own self-confidence in themselves and their lives together made him a better man. Though both were taken from him too soon, he would never forget how much they touched not only his heart, but his soul as well.

Tossing the file across the table, frustrated by the lack of answers he found no matter where he looked, Andrew knew it was time to take a break. The mission which brought him there in the first place, was only one of the things weighing on him, and if he did not take time to think, time to rest, he knew he would miss something important. Was he allowing his own fears and guilts of the past to confuse the issues and letting the memories of a family he once loved keep him from seeing the truth, there was no way he could learn what he needed to know. No way for him to distinguish which of the two men he once called brother was the real traitor of his country.

"Now what," he questioned, a knock on the door disrupting his thoughts.

He was not expecting anyone and the last thing he needed was another crisis.

"Francisco," Andrew said, surprised to see Antonio's aide standing at the door holding a small box.

"Good morning, sir," the man replied, handing him a package. "The president wanted you to have this to express his delight in having you in his life again even under these circumstances." The man explained, "He knows this week has not been easy for you, and despite what you must do, he wants to you to know he still regards you as family."

"Francisco," Andrew began, afraid whatever was in the box might be considered a bribe.

"Do not worry, senor, the others know of this gift and do not object," the man assured him as he handed the package over to the man standing before him. "The president does apologize for taking so long in getting the package to you, but he had to have the items brought in from home."

"Thanks," Andrew replied, as the man turned and walked away without saying another word. "Nice talking to you too, Francisco." He laughed, at least some things had not changed. Francisco was the same young man he was when he fought in the revolution. Never one to say much, he did what he had to and moved on. He had delivered his message from the president now and there was no need for any other conversation between them.

Returning to the solace of his room Andrew sat down at the table and opened the package. Bursting into laughter as he looked inside at the contents and the note attached.

My dear friend,
  I know our meeting here in Rome for the first time since you left San Sebastian has not been what either one of us expected, but I want to assure you away from the negotiation table that we still consider you our brother. You found a place in our home and in our hearts when you married Paulina, and nothing, even time, will ever change that. So I am sending you a few memories of our time, of a past life you once had, and I hope you enjoy them.
  Your friend always,
  Antonio

Examining each item as he took them from the box, Andrew reveled in the treats he found as the smell alone brought back fond memories. A loaf of homemade bread, some goat cheese, and olives filled with sweet peppers and a jug of wine, though simple things to many, they meant the world to him. He'd shared these delicacies in the middle of a war with his future wife's family the night before their wedding. They were a proud family who had little, but whose heart and soul made up for what they lacked in monetary means and that night he felt like one of them.

"Thank you, old friend, I needed this," he whispered as he poured himself a glass of wine and fixed a plate filled with the treats he now possessed.

Finishing his snack shortly after eleven, Andrew realized he had gone several hours without talking to one of the diplomats he had come to see. In the last week alone it seemed as if one or all of them stopped by his room at least several times a day to continue the talks and he had gotten used to listening to the arguing as he tried to explain he would not make a decision without the proper evidence to back it up. Whatever the reason for the absences, Andrew was relieved to have some time to himself. Time to figure how what to do not only about the counsel members but the mysterious video tape as well. If he did exist, he was in a lot more trouble then he ever imagined.

Looking at his watch, Andrew knew no matter how relieved he was for the respite from his friends, he could not totally relax until he spoke to his son.

Dialing the dorm this time and not the cell phone Steven normally carried with him, Andrew waited for someone at the other end to answer.

"Hello, Rick. Is that you?" he began, relieved to finally reach someone. "Where's Steven? Is he out studying somewhere or at some party? What am I saying? It's still morning there, right? Is he there?" he questioned talking too fast for the boy to reply.

"Mr. McCormick," Rick finally interrupted. "Steven's not here. He left yesterday and I haven't heard from him since."

"What! Left? Left for where?" Andrew demanded to know.

"I think he went home, sir," Rick answered. "He had some kind of family emergency."

"What do you mean family emergency?" Andrew repeated, horrified at the thought his son left the school nearly twenty-fours earlier and had not been heard from by his friend since then. "Rick! There is no emergency," he shouted back at the boy.

"But Steven said there was," Rick repeated, his own concerns for his friend growing stronger with each word they spoke.

"Damn it, Rick, I'm telling you I checked with Annie earlier, and she said there was nothing going on. There was no emergency at home, nothing to make Steven leave school."

"Then why did he go?" Rick asked.

"I don't know," Andrew replied. "What did he tell you?"

"Mr. McCormick, Steven didn't tell me anything," Rick began, "I found him in the dorm all upset about something but he didn't want to talk about it. He said he couldn't." He continued, "When I checked on him later, I found a note telling me he was going home and he would contact me when he could."

"Upset about what?" Andrew repeated several times.

"I do not know, sir, but," Rick started.

"But what, Rick, tell me."

"Mr. McCormick, he made it sound like the problem was with you."

"With me?"

"Yes, sir, with you. He made it seem like you were hurt or…"

"Dead."

"Yes, sir," Rick said.

"What about your father? Did you call him after Steven disappeared? Does he know what's going on?" Andrew asked, forgetting for a moment what Annie had told him earlier about Stewart.

"No, sir, my father is away. He has been out the country and I haven't talked to him. He's due here sometime today."

"Ok, are you all right?" Andrew asked, concerned for the boy's safety as well. Whatever was going on could somehow involve him too and Andrew did not want to face his son later and tell him he allowed anything to happen to his best friend.

"Yes, sir, I'm fine, but what about Steven?" Rick asked.

"Don't worry about him, I'll find Steven," Andrew assured the boy. "Just notify security to have someone stay with you till you're father arrives."

"I promise, sir."

"Good, tell your father I will contact him when I can and not to call me, it might just make things worse."

"Yes, sir." Rick began, "Sir…"

"Don't worry, son, I will find Steven and bring him home safety."

"I hope so, sir," the boy replied before ending their conversation.

Picking up the phone, Andrew dialed his friend back home, praying the lack of contact with him did not mean both the agent and Steven were in trouble.

"Hello!" he uttered with relief as someone finally picked up after his third attempt to reach his friend. "Who is this?" he demanded to know realizing the voice on the other end was unfamiliar to him.

"This is inspector Strum from Washington metro police. Who is this?"

Slamming the phone down without replying, Andrew knew something happened to his friend.

"Damn," he uttered. If something happened to the man he sent to watch over Steven, then Steven could be in danger as well.

"Hello Annie, it's me again," Andrew said, calling Stewart's secretary once more. "Do you know where Templeton is?"

"Well, hello again to you too," she began.

"Annie, Templeton, where is he?"

"Templeton is dead," she said hesitantly

"What!" the distraught father shouted. He couldn't be dead, he was supposed to protect his son; and if he were dead, then Steven was in trouble too.

"The locals aren't talking about it, all we know for sure is he was killed after a fall earlier today," Annie explained.

"Come on, Annie, the agency always knows what's going on," Andrew protested. He needed some answers and not the standard run around.

"We are trying to keep a low profile on this because it doesn't appear to be agency related," she explained.

"He was one of our guys, how is that not agency related?" Andrew snapped. The man was his friend and he didn't like the idea of the local police handling his death. The agency security force should be involved to make sure nothing was missed during the investigation.

"I am sure we will look into it too, but for now the police are handling it as a local homicide. If it turns out it had something to do with his work, you know as well as I do the boys will not let it go."

"You said he fell, how did it happen?"

"I told you Andrew, we don't have much to go on, only that he fell from his apartment building," she explained.

"His apartment?" Andrew replied. *What was he doing there?* he wondered, listening to Annie as she spoke. *Templeton was supposed to be watching Steven, why was he at the apartment complex?*

"Isn't that where you live too?" she questioned.

"Yes, I got him a place there about a year ago," Andrew replied. Templeton was a good friend as well as a fellow agent, and when he left his wife, Andrew helped him with a new place to live.

"Strange, isn't it?" Annie began. "You are on a mission you can't talk about and someone living in the same building as you, falls from his balcony," she continued. Having worked for the agency most of her adult life, Annie knew there were no coincidences when it came to unusual events happening with their people.

"Was anyone else hurt?" Andrew asked without replying to her earlier comment.

"Nope, why should someone else have been hurt?" she asked, curious as to why Andrew would inquire about other injuries.

"No reason just asking! Thanks Annie, I have to go," Andrew said before hanging up. There wasn't any time to explain things to her or go into more details about Templeton, he needed to get in touch with Mark before anything else happened. Despite his hesitance in using his friend because of his recent problems, Andrew knew he didn't have any choice. Three men were dead now, three men who were somehow connected to him and his mission, and he needed someone to cover his back.

"Hello! Mark, is that you?" Andrew said, trying not to let the urgency of his call keep him from maintaining his cool. "Hey buddy, how are you?" He began taking a deep breath before saying anything else. "How's Edna?" he asked, using a code word established between them years earlier, a simple word, it let the other person know the call was probably being monitored and things were not safe for them.

"Edna's," Mark began, surprised to hear the code word being used by his friend. He was only person who knew why Andrew went to Rome, he hadn't expected to get a call until the mission was completed. "Edna's fine, but I guess you aren't" he continued as he placed a scrambler on the phone to keep anyone listening from hearing the conversation. "It's ok now." He assured his friend, "What's up? Are you in trouble? Did something happened to the mission?"

"I don't have enough time to explain everything that's happened, I just need you to find Steven and make sure he is ok."

"Steven, he's fine," Mark said, surprised by the request.

"Listen to me Mark, Steven is not fine, he left school without explaining anything to his friends and no one knows where he is," Andrew snapped. "Templeton was supposed to be watching him and now I learned he was found dead at his apartment." Andrew rambled on, "Was Steven at the apartment too? Did you see him?"

"Templeton, why was he watching Steven?" Mark asked without answering his friend's question.

"I don't have time to explain it now, just go find my son."

"Steven is fine," Mark repeated. "I talked to him earlier at lunch. He left school after getting some information he thought was involving you and once I explained things to him, he was fine about what was going on."

"Thank god, and you're sure he is safe?" Andrew asked again.

"Yes, he is safe." Mark repeated. "Don't worry, I wouldn't let anything happen to Steven, you know that."

"I know," Andrew replied. "Is he there now, can I talk to him?"

"Sorry, he's not here."

"What, where is he?"

"Listen to me, Andrew. The boy is safe. I promise you, he's fine. I have him in a safe place."

"Ok, if you're sure," Andrew replied. "Just promise me when things calm down here, you'll let me talk to Steven."

"Calm down? What happened?" Mark asked.

Explaining he wasn't ready to fill his frien in on what was happening in Rome just yet, Andrew promised to do so as soon as possible.

"Ok, if that is how you want to play it," Mark replied. "And don't worry about Steven, he's fine, and you'll talk to him soon." Mark assured his friend.

As long as his son was safe, Andrew didn't need to talk to Mark any further. They could continue the conversation later when things settled down a little.

"Oh, I promise you'll talk to Steven very soon," Mark whispered into the dead phone as the sound of someone coming from behind alerted him to the presences of an unwelcome guest.

"Who were you talking to?" Steven asked, returning from the cockpit to find his uncle hanging up the phone.

"No one, kid. Just making sure everything is set for our arrival," Mark explained.

He hated lying to the boy but keeping him safe for as long as possible was his top priority. He wanted to be sure everything was in place before exposing the boy to the truth, certain Steven would understand why he lied to him when he did.

"How long till we get there?" Steven asked.

"We are set to leave in about ten minutes, and as long as we don't have too many delays en-route, we should be in Rome in about twelve hours."

"Twelve hours," Steven repeated, realizing by the time they arrived in Rome yet another day would have passed without word on his father.

"Don't worry, kid. Twelve hours isn't that long, and once we get there, I'm sure the ball will start rolling very quickly," Mark assured him. "We should be able to find your father in no time."

"I hope so," Steven replied. "The sooner we find Dad, the sooner we can prove he is innocent of the charges against him."

"Right." Mark sneered.

CHAPTER FIVE

Standing in the security office at the Rome airport, Steven nervously tapped his fingers against the glass window, as his uncle continued his conversation with the officer sitting by the desk. Stuck there for nearly an hour as the two men reminisced about old times, Steven was growing more frustrated with each second that passed. He hadn't traveled half way around the world just to sit around in the airport so they could waste valuable time. His father was out there somewhere in need of help and all he wanted to do was start searching for him before it was too late.

"Steven, stop that," Mark ordered. The boy's behavior was getting on his nerves.

"How much longer do we have to wait here?" Steven demanded to know.

"First off, when I tell you to do something, do it," Mark snapped, grabbing Steven by the arm in an attempt to stop the boy from tapping the window glass. "Secondly, I have already explained that we have to be very careful how we proceed from now on. There are a lot of people out there looking for your father and if they get wind of the fact we are here trying to help him things could get screwed up even before they get started."

Mark began again, "I also explained when we arrived why we had to wait here till our ride showed up." He continued moving closer to the boy as he spoke, the tone in his voice growing angrier with each breath he took. "You are not a child, Steven, so I expect you to understand what I told you without giving me a hard time about it."

"You're right, I'm not a child," Steven said, pulling away from his uncle. "And I do understand what you told me, but I don't have to like it."

He understood why the ride they expected never showed up—they were checking out a lead—what he didn't understand was why they needed to wait at the airport for them.

"I've already explained why staying at the airport is the safest place for us," Mark replied as Steven continued to argue with his uncle.

"Why can't we just go to the hotel and wait there?" Steven demanded to know, refusing to yield anything to his uncle as he too became increasing angry over the situation.

"Because, my young friend," Mark said, standing toe to toe with the boy now as he looked him directly in the eyes, "I don't know what arrangements Kirk secured as far as a safe house and I have no intentions of risking the entire mission by roaming around Rome with blinders on." He continued grabbing hold of Steven's arm as he spoke. "Now sit down and wait till Kirk arrives," he ordered, his hold on the boy getting tighter with each word.

"Alright. Fine," Steven uttered, pulling away, rubbing his arm, as he stared at his uncle. "I will sit here in this damned airport and wait for these men to show up."

"I'm glad you concur." Mark laughed. "Now relax," he repeated. "The guard at the front gate will let us know when Kirk and Henry have arrived."

"All right already," Steven uttered, obeying his uncle's orders without saying another word. There was something different about Mark since they arrived in Rome, and whatever was causing the strange behavior, it was beginning to make Steven very nervous.

"Your friends have arrived," the security officer announced, interrupting the conversation after receiving a call from one of his officers . "The car is parked on the southwest corner near the loading zone and he made sure there was no one else in the area as you asked," the officer remarked.

"Thanks, old friend, I appreciate your help," Mark replied.

"Great, now we can go," Steven said, taking his bag from the counter. "Nice meeting you," he shouted to the officer before heading for the door.

"Steven! Wait for me," Mark ordered, taking a moment to wish his friend well before following the impatient boy.

"Ciao my friend," the officer replied. "Whatever you're in the middle of, watch your back," he uttered before returning to the office and the day's work awaiting him.

Following the security officer who was instructed to take them to the car, Steven looked around at everyone he saw. His mind reeling, he could not help but wonder if any of them might be in Rome for the same reason as he: if someone nearby was there in search of his father, watching their every move in hopes they would lead them to Andrew and the mission which brought them to Rome in the first place.

"Gentlemen, glad to see you," Mark uttered as they approached two men standing by a small black car. "Is everything ready?" he asked, tossing his bag at Henry before opening the back door to get in.

"Everything is in place," Kirk replied before his partner could.

"Good," Mark said, ordering Steven into the back seat. "Our driver today is Kirk, and the man sitting next to him is Henry," he began introducing the two strangers to the boy as they made themselves comfortable in the car.

"Kirk and Henry, no last names?" Steven inquired, curious about the identity of the men he was entrusting with his father's safety.

"Last names don't matter, the only thing you need to remember is these men are the only two people you are to trust while we're in Rome," Mark explained as they continued on their way.

"Beside you," Steven joked.

"That goes without saying." Mark laughed before leaning closer the tone in his voice changing once more as he spoke. "You do understand what I am telling you, don't you? No matter what we encounter or how confusing things might seem, you are to trust no one but them."

"Yes, sir, I understand," he replied, staring at his uncle. As much as he wanted to say something sarcastic to Mark for treating him like a child, Steven decided to let it go.

"Don't worry, kid, we will make sure nothing happens to you," Henry remarked while his partner started towards the hotel.

"Thanks," Steven replied, grateful for their assistance. Watching both men in the front seat as they continued to talk among themselves, the words barely audible, Steven could not help but feel a little uneasy about the two strangers. Though they seemed friendly enough and Mark said they could be trusted, there was something about them which made him cautious about putting too much of his faith in them. If everyone at the agency believed Andrew was guilty as Mark implied, then their motives for helping out had to be questioned.

"Do you know my father?" Steven asked, hoping the answer would help him better determine their motives.

"Know him? Why everyone at the agency knows the legendary Andrew McCormick," Henry sniped.

"Legendary?" Steven repeated, the animosity in Henry's voice apparent as he spoke. "What do you mean by that?" Steven demanded to know, becoming more concerned about the men as he listened to Henry talk about his father.

"Never mind, kid," Kirk interrupted, trying to avoid a confrontation between the boy and his partner. "Henry is just teasing you, he has a warped sense of humor," he uttered. "We worked with your father in the past and just want to help him out."

"Yea, that's what I meant." Henry chuckled, looking over at Kirk as he did.

"You don't believe he's guilty, do you?" Steven questioned.

"Your father a traitor? Hell no, not GI Joe." Henry laughed.

"All right, what is it with you?" Steven asked, growing angrier with Henry for his words. "I thought you were trying to help, but you're acting like you hate my father or something. So why are you here if that is the case?"

"Sorry, kid, I didn't mean anything by it, just a bad joke," Henry replied.

"I hope that was all it was," Steven said, still not satisfied by the response.

"Enough already," Mark interrupted. "We're all here for the same reason and that is to get your father."

"Sure," Henry echoed. "We're here to get Andrew."

"Get Dad!" Steven whispered beneath his breath, wondering what they meant by those words.

"He means we are here to help your father," Kirk remarked, looking in the rearview mirror as he spoke, catching the look on Steven's face as Henry spoke.

"Exactly," Henry echoed. "That's what I meant," he repeated, as Kirk headed for a small villa about forty miles from the airport.

"I guess if Mark trusts you, I do too," Steven began wishing he could shake the feeling something was wrong.

"Thanks, kid," Kirk replied, before pulling into the hotel parking lot.

"What's our next move?" Steven asked, standing next to his uncle at the entrance to the hotel.

"Our next move is to get you settled in," Mark began, while Kirk went to the front desk to get the room keys. "Once that is taken care of, I have to go meet an informant in town to see what he's learned about your father."

"You mean we, don't you?" Steven objected.

"No, I mean me," Mark reiterated. "This guy is shaky enough without having an audience. He'll talk to me and me alone."

"But—" Steven argued. He didn't want to sit around in a hotel room while his uncle was out getting information on Andrew. "I didn't come to Rome to do nothing but wait. I want to do something to help."

"You are doing something, you're following my orders," he remarked, reminding the boy of the earlier promise to follow his orders without question.

"But I—"

"Look, Steven, I know you want to help, and once I have a solid lead we can use, I promise I will come back and get you."

"You swear you'll be back and you won't leave me stuck here at the hotel with these guys?" Steven asked.

"I promise," Mark assured him. "When things kick off, you'll be right by my side."

"All right," Steven said, reluctantly agreeing to remain at the hotel with the others until he heard from his uncle. Though he hated the idea, he knew obeying Mark's orders was the only way he could ensure not being sent home before they found his father.

"Ok then, let's get to our room and get the ball rolling," Mark instructed as the four men headed for the elevator.

The room, small but elegant, was one of twenty suites in the secluded hotel situated in the hills miles away from the city. The Villa, once the private estate of a local nobleman, was converted into an exclusively resort reserved for tourists of wealth and power that could afford the luxuries it provided.

Perched along a mountain's edge, each window was like a panoramic view, an odyssey of the beauty surrounding it, from the deep blue waters below, to the majestic trails leading into the mountains. With three stables of thoroughbreds and heliport nearby, The Villa was the perfect place for someone who wanted to explore the area and its wonders from both land and air.

The rooms inside were as majestic as the area surrounding them and like a warm blanket wrapped around you on a cold night. Two fireplaces in every suite, one in the living room, the other in the master bedroom, filled the air with the sounds and smells of crackling wood burning continuously from their hearths.

Handing the valet a tip before closing the door, Kirk sighed, relieved they were finally in the safety of their room. Taking the boy out in public where anyone could see him was an unnecessary risk and the mission was too important to take such chances.

Turning towards the others as they made themselves comfortable in the living room, Steven sat down quietly in a nearby chair. As much as he wanted to question his uncle about their plans, he knew any questions he had would have to wait. Mark was already fixing another drink, the third in less than ten minutes, and Steven knew his uncle was not going to be very receptive to his inquiries.

"I thought you were going to meet your contact," Steven remarked, while Mark accompanied his latest drink with a small white pill he taken from his pocket.

"I will in a few minutes," Mark replied.
"Are you going to meet him drunk?" Steven asked.
"I am not," snapped the angry man as he poured another drink.
"Then maybe you should stop drinking that stuff like it is water."
"Don't push me, kid," Mark shouted. "I know what I am doing."
"Then put that stuff away before you are too drunk to leave the room," Steven argued.

If his uncle was going to meet someone with a lead on his father, the last thing he wanted was for him to do so with the smell of alcohol on his breath.

"What this?" Mark laughed. "Ok, I will put it away," he uttered, swallowing the remains of the glass as the boy continued to watch him. "How's that, happy now?"

"Damn it, Uncle Mark, what are you doing? You don't need that junk," Steven said, growing more frustrated with his uncle with each word he spoke. "What is the matter with you?" he demanded to know, trying to take the bottle from Mark as he spoke.

"There is nothing wrong with me."

"Then give me the bottle before it is too late for me to help you," Steven cried.

"I told you before not to interfere with me about this," Mark shouted, pushing the boy away.

"How can I not interfere when you're killing yourself with that stuff," Steven protested, struggling with his uncle for control of the bottle.

"Leave me alone!" Mark snapped angrily as he struck Steven across the face. The blow was strong enough to send him reeling to the floor. "Oh god, Steven, are you all right?" Mark cried out, realizing what he done.

Looking up, stunned by what just happened, Steven's eyes filled with tears while he stood up and faced his uncle.

"Why?" he uttered, his voice filled with both anger and confusion over what just occurred.

"Steven, I am so sorry, I never meant to hit you," Mark tried to explain, drawing nearer to the boy as he spoke.

"Then why did you? I was only trying to help."

"You have to understand," Mark began, "I am so tired of people telling me the headaches I feel are imaginary, that they aren't tearing me apart with each one I get." He continued as he rambled on, "I am tired of people telling me the pills won't help, telling me I have a problem and I need to get help. The last thing I wanted to hear were those same words of doubt coming from you too." He cried, "The pain is real and I need the pills to get through the day."

"Uncle Mark, I don't doubt the headaches are real, but you have a problem with the booze and pills too," Steven began, hoping his words would reach his uncle. "You have a serious problem and you need to realize that if you're going to get better." He continued, moving closer to his uncle, "I don't understand why Dad or the others haven't tried to you help, but I promise you, I will do whatever is necessary to make things better for you."

"You?" Mark yelled. "You help me? You're nothing more than a snot nosed brat who couldn't find his way out of a paper bag if it were not for me," he shouted, his words hurting Steven almost as much as the earlier slap across the face. "I have taken care of you ever since you were a child, and now you presume to think you are old enough to tell me what is best for me. Is that how you show your respect, by calling me a drunk and an addict?" he shouted, moving towards the boy once more.

"I do respect you," Steven began. "My god, Mark, you are like a father to me," Steven argued trying not to let his uncle's erratic behavior, scare him more than it already had. "That is why I am telling you this, telling you the truth before your actions get you killed," he continued, trying to maintain his resolve. "You keep saying the pills and alcohol haven't changed you, but look at yourself, the things you've done. How can you say you haven't changed?"

"What things have I done?" Mark demanded to know, refusing to listen to the boy.

"What things?" Steven replied in disbelief. "Look at you. You are fighting with me as if we were strangers, behaving like a crazed manic who can't control his temper for more than a few seconds." Steven yelled, "My god, Mark, you slapped me, you never raised a hand to me in my entire life and the only reason you did now is because of that junk you keep putting into your body."

"I hit you because you deserved it," Mark said. "Just like you deserve this," he yelled striking Steven again, this time without any warning. "You've spent your entire life expecting the adults in your life to cater to you because of the past, well no more. You are not a child anymore, and you need to understand things do not always go your way. I am the adult in this family and it is up to me to make sure you start learning that."

Staring at his uncle as he nursed the newest cut to his face, Steven found himself too outraged by his behavior to be afraid of him. He was not the same man who raised him and no matter how much he loved him, he was not about to become Mark's punching bag while he worked through his problems.

"You son of a bitch," Steven yelled, striking back at Mark, his punch sending the man falling against the nearby table. "I don't care what you have been through, you're not going to keep hitting me," he continued as Kirk pulled him away, keeping the boy from exacting another blow.

"Let me go," Steven cried out, struggling with Kirk while his uncle rose to his feet.

"It's over, boy." Kirk began, his words interrupted by a sucker punch catching both Steven and himself off guard. "Was that necessary?" he snapped angrily at Mark, who'd struck the boy once more.

"Yes," Mark announced, staring at the others. "He has to understand who is in charge."

"In charge?" Steven replied. "We're supposed to be here working together to help Dad, not fighting about who is in charge. This is not some damned assignment you have been sent on by the agency and I am not one of your flunkies."

"You're right, Steven, please forgive me for what happened earlier." Mark pleaded as he held the boy tightly as the tone in his voice changed once more.

"Whatever." Steven squirmed, his uncle's arms still around him. "Now let me go."

"Good, then everything is all right between us," Mark rambled on.

"Yea, sure everything is fine," Steven replied, staring at his uncle as he spoke.

"Good, then I have to go now and meet with my contact," Mark said, behaving as if the last few minutes hadn't occurred. "When I get back, we will have a nice dinner and discuss your graduation," Mark announced, rambling from one subject to another. "Then we will settle everything here in Rome and before you know it everything will be back to normal." Mark began heading for the door as he spoke. "Take care of my boy for me and make sure nothing happens to him until I get back," he instructed his men before slamming the door shut.

"Yea you want to save that privilege for yourself," Kirk whispered under his breath. Despite the fact Mark trained him as a rookie and he considered the man his friend, his loyalties towards him were beginning to waiver. He too was disgusted with Mark's bizarre behavior and his violence towards the boy he calmed to love.

"I'll be in my room," Steven said timidly before turning to head down the hall, still smarting from the last blow he received. "Let me know when my uncle returns."

"Yes, oh master," Henry snickered, turning his attentions to the television set and the soccer game about to begin. "Finally something interesting to watch," he mumbled before making himself comfort.

"Leave the kid alone," Kirk ordered, after Steven retreated down the hall. "Fine."

"That's all you have to say," Kirk protested. "Mark is losing it more and more and if we're not careful he will blow our entire plan."

"No, he won't," Henry assured him. "Since he is not necessary for our plan to work, we can proceed without him and if Mark gets in the way well, we'll just take care of it for him too."

"Great, I am stuck in a hotel with a kid who is starting to resemble a punching bag and an idiot who thinks eliminating both Mark and Andrew at the same time is going to be the answer to all his problems. What did I do to deserve this miss?" Kirk whispered before heading for the kitchen in hopes of finding something to eat.

Finding Steven asleep in his room, Henry stood over the bed for a few minutes, staring at the unsuspecting boy. It was time to put the next step of the plan into action and he was looking forward to it.

"Steven, wake up," he shouted, shaking the boy several times in hopes the sudden outburst would confuse him even further. "Come on, boy, wake up," he repeated again as Steven looked up still dazed by the deep sleep he was awaken from.

"It sure was a good thing Mark told us to wait here, you fell asleep the minute your head hit the pillow."

"What! What do you mean?' the boy asked, trying to shake the dopiness of sleep from his head.

"It's almost seven," Henry announced. "You've been asleep for six hours and Mark just called, he wants us to meet him at a little chateau about twenty miles from here."

"What Mark called?" Steven began. "I didn't hear the phone," he argued, still fighting the sleep which seemed to overpower him even as he tried to shake it off.

"Why am I so sleepy?"

"Time change," Henry said, smiling slightly as he thought about the pill he slipped into Steven's drink before he went to bed. As long as the drug continued to affect him the way it was, keeping the boy under control would be easy. "You'll be alright in a little while," he lied, handing the boy his shirt as he spoke. "Now hurry up, we have to get moving."

"What time did you say it was?" Steven asked again.

"It is a little after seven, and you have been sleeping for almost six hours."

"Six hours!" Steven cried, trying to get out of the bed. "Why didn't you call me earlier? Where is Uncle Mark?"

"I told you he just called and we're supposed to meet him, so stop stalling and get ready."

"I'll...I'll be ready in a few minutes," Steven promised, still confused as to what was going on around him.

"You better be," Henry remarked. "Here, drink this tea, it will help you wake up," he instructed the unsuspecting boy, the contents containing another pill.

"Thanks," Steven said, obeying Henry's orders as he finished the cup of tea.

"Where are we going?"

"Don't worry, kid, we are going to see your uncle and that's all you need to know for now," Henry replied before leaving the room.

"Is he up?" Kirk asked Henry as he walked back into the living room.

"Yup he's up and asking a lot of questions?"

"Well, the sooner we get him to the safe house, the better I'll feel," Kirk said. He didn't like being put in the position of dealing with the boy and his questions. Nor did he appreciate being so exposed at the hotel where the chances of being caught were much greater. If it hadn't been for Mark, he would've taken Steven directly to the hideout and secured him there before things kicked off. "Did you give him the sleeping pill?" Kirk asked as he finished his sandwich.

"Yup put it in his tea," Henry replied. "The little brat will be a lot easier to handle in a few minutes, but you realize the pill will only make him dopey, it won't keep him quiet should he start to figure things out."

"I know what you are suggesting, but the sleeping pill is enough for now," Kirk argued. "We are not going to use your damned syringe unless we have to."

"Just one shot from my syringe along with the sleeping pill and the kid won't be able to talk to anyone," Henry argued.

"I said no," Kirk repeated. "We can keep him away from anyone else and as long as he's drugged, he won't be any problem," Kirk continued to argue.

"And if he figures it out," Henry said, waving the syringe.

"We will cross that bridge when we have too," he announced. "In the mean time, put the syringe away before he walks out here and sees it."

"You know as well as I do the kid is more like his father than anyone wants to admit, sooner or later he's going to figure out we're not here to help and when he does things are going to get really complicated," Henry insisted. "It would be a lot easier just to drug him now before he catches on."

"I told you no, not unless we have to," Kirk reiterated.

"Alright!" Henry finally agreed. He didn't understand Kirk's reluctance to use the syringe on the boy. Though still experimental, it was harmless drug and would leave no permit effects on Steven. Designed to render the victim unable to speak for up to an hour, the drug made transporting a prisoner, or uncooperative target without gagging them a lot easier and Henry had no qualms about using it. Though still banned by most government agencies including his own, he believed in the drug's promise and wanted to prove to everyone once and for all the value of having it on every mission.

"For the kind of money we're making on this deal I hope you're not making a mistake by letting the boy off the hook so easily," Henry said. "If he figures things out and ruins the plan, it will be your responsibility."

"Fine, I will take the responsibility, but I will not let you use an experimental drug on the kid unless it is the last resort," Kirk argued.

"Whatever you say, you are the senior operative on this mission," Henry answered, putting the syringe in his pocket. "I just hope the sleeping pill is enough to get him out of here."

"It will be," Kirk insisted.

"And you are willing to risk the mission on that fact?" asked Henry.

"Stop arguing with me. We are not going to use the drug on the kid, is that clear?" Kirk insisted.

"Drug?" Steven blurted out. Standing behind a statue in the hallway as he listened to the two men talking, he'd gone unnoticed by them until that moment.

"Steven," Henry shouted upon hearing the boy. "Steven, is that you?" he asked again, signaling for Kirk to move along the other side of the hall entrance to keep the boy from getting away from them.

"Steven, come out here," Kirk ordered, standing a few feet away from the boy, who was still standing at the other end of the hallway.

Staring at the two men, still unsure of what was going on, Steven raced towards his room. He needed to figure things out before he confronted them about what he heard. Slamming the door shut before securing the lock, Steven leaned against the door, listening to the two men ordering him to let them in.

"No, I won't," he replied, refusing to heed their orders.

Checking around the room for another avenue of escape, Steven felt the panic inside growing. He was trapped inside a hotel room miles from home, with two men who he thought he could trust and no help in sight. It was up to him to find his own way out and he didn't like the options before him. The only avenue of escape left open to him was a second floor window. Afraid of heights, the thought of jumping from there did not sit too well with him.

"Steven! Open the damned door," Henry ordered, trying not to let his voice carry out into the hallway. The last thing they needed to do was draw more attention to themselves, especially with Steven still on the loose.

"Not till you tell me what's going." Steven shouted, the effects of the pills he was given starting to make him drowsy. "What did you give me?"

"Nothing. I told you it was just jet lag," Henry replied, trying to convince the boy he was wrong about them.

"You're lying," Steven blurted out. "I heard you talk about some kind of drug you wanted to give me and about the sleeping pills too. Why would you give me those pills? What are you trying to do to me?"

"Steven, I'm warning you if I have to force this door open, the beating you received from your uncle earlier will seem like a love tap compared to what I will do to you, now open this door," Henry ordered angrily.

"No!"

"All right, Steven, you asked for it," Henry announced, kicking in the door.

"Stay away from me!" Steven replied, standing on the window ledge.

"Steven! Whatever you think you heard it was a mistake, just let me talk to you and explain," Kirk began as Henry moved from the door entrance and slowly back out of the room. "As soon as Mark gets back, we'll sit down and straighten this mess out."

"Yea right, you expect me to believe anything you say," Steven shouted as Kirk drew nearer. "If you come any closer, I will jump," Steven declared. "Just how will that help your plan if I end up dead?" he uttered sarcastically. Though there was a small trestle below to help break his fall, Steven did not want to make the jump and hoped Kirk did not call his bluff. Looking down to see if anyone was around, Steven realized he was completely alone, there wasn't a soul around, no one to help him.

"Steven!" Kirk began, afraid to move too close to the boy in case he did try to jump. As long as he kept him talking, the drug would continue to work and Kirk hoped it would be only moments before Steven would be too weak from its effects to do anything but comply with his orders. "Steven, you have to trust me, whatever you thought you heard was a mistake. I want you to get down from the window ledge and come back into the room."

"No! I can't trust you," Steven cried, the effects of the drug making it harder for him to keep his balance. "Where is Uncle Mark? What have you done to him?"

"Steven, please come down from there before you fall," Kirk repeated without answering his questions.

"Stay away or I'll jump!" the boy vowed, his anger getting the best of him as he lost his balance, falling to the ground below.

"Steven!" Kirk shouted as the boy fell. "Damn!" he snapped, racing towards the ledge to find Steven lying on the ground after hitting the trestle first. Grateful to see he was still alive. "Hang on, kid, it will be alright," Kirk yelled, smiling slightly as he saw a figure drawing closer to the injured boy. Relieved to see Henry standing next to Steven, Kirk waved at his partner. "Take care of him. I'll be right down," he yelled, realizing the accident was already beginning to draw a crowd.

"Oh I will," Henry snickered, pulling the syringe from his pocket, careful not to let the others who were beginning to move closer to them see what he was about to do.

Still dazed by the fall, Steven let out a cry as he tried to move his right arm. Not sure how badly he was injured, the pain was enough to keep him from noticing the needle Henry had stuck into his arm.

"You'll be alright, son," a voice from behind said while Steven continued to fight both the effects of the pain he was experiencing and the drugs he had been given earlier.

"I..." he started to say as he turned toward the male's voice with relief only to see Henry leaning next to him. "Henry!"

"Don't do anything stupid," Henry warned him as the area filled with hotel guests. "Unless you want someone's blood on your hands."

"I won't do anything," Steven replied, the sight of Henry's weapon inside his jacket alerting him to the danger the others were in as well. If he tried to get help from anyone, they too could end up caught in the same nightmare he was.

"I'll do what you say, just don't hurt anyone," Steven begged as it became more difficult for him to speak. "Oh god, you gave me the drug, didn't you?" he uttered, realizing what was happening to him.

"Just stay put," Henry ordered, pushing him back to the ground as Steven tried to stand up. "We will be out of here in a few minutes and everyone else will be safe," Henry whispered to keep the others from hearing his words.

"What happened to him?" one of the guests asked.
"He fell from the window," Henry began.
"Are you all right, son?" the man asked.
"I don't think he can talk," Henry replied. "I'm a doctor, and I will take care of him."
"Thank god you were here to help," the guest said before relinquishing the care of the boy to him.
"Let me through," the hotel manager yelled, trying to get past the guests which now filled the garden. "What happened to the boy? Is he all right?"
"He fell and I believe he will be fine," Henry continued, wishing Kirk would hurry up and get there so they could leave with their hostage.
"The man is a doctor," the guest who had been questioning the events earlier said as Henry continued to keep them from the boy while the drug took effect.
"A doctor. Didn't you come with the boy?" the manager questioned, remembering seeing the two of them together when they checked in.
"Yes, I am a friend of the family," Henry began. "I travel with them whenever they leave the country because the boy has seizures and his father likes to keep a doctor on hand just in case."
"Is that what happened now? Did he have a seizure?" the manager asked. The last thing he wanted on his hands was a lawsuit because of some faulty equipment which might have contributed to the boy's fall.
"Yes, I believe so. He was leaning out the window and had a seizure. I tried to help but I couldn't get to the window in time to keep him from falling," Henry lied as he kept up the premise of being a friend.
"Are you all right now?" the manager asked, directing his question to Steven this time.
Nodding he was fine, afraid to disagree with what Henry was saying, he watched helplessly while his captor continued to lie to the others about what happened.
"The boy doesn't speak, he hasn't in years," Henry said.
"Oh, I am sorry," the manager replied, his words of concerned interrupted by a member of his staff.
"The ambulance is here," the bellhop announced.
"Ambulance!" Henry replied. "He doesn't need an ambulance."
"Are you his father?" a police officer asked, walking towards the crowd as he ordered everyone to move on.
"Well no, I'm his family doctor, and we are traveling together."

"Family doctor? Why does the boy need a doctor to travel with him?" he questioned.

"The boy suffers from seizures and his father likes to have a doctor on hand just in case of an emergency," the manager interrupted, repeating what he'd been told a few minutes earlier.

"Where is his father?"

"At a business meeting," Henry explained, "Look, Officer, there is no reason to tie up one your ambulances, I can take care of the boy and if he needs to go to the hospital, I'll see to it he gets there."

"Is there any reason you don't want him examined by the medical personnel?" the officer asked, as he continued to question the others about Steven's accident.

"No, of course not," Henry replied, backing off a little with his protest as he spoke.

If he weren't careful there would be more questions then he could answer, and with the police now involved, everything was on hold. "Go ahead and examine him, you will see he has an injury to his arm and that is about all," he continued, still playing the concerned doctor for the others.

Watching as the medics examined Steven, Henry looked around nervously for Kirk, hoping his delay did not mean another problem. If the medics checked the boy too closely and realized he was drugged, they would have to fight their way out this mess and he wanted Kirk as close by as possible before he took the policeman out.

"Son, can you tell me what happened?" the officer asked while the paramedic checked his injuries.

"I told you he couldn't talk," Henry interrupted, growing increasingly angry by the presence of the officer.

"Is that true? Do you understand me?" the officer asked, instructing Steven to nod if he understood what he was saying.

Looking over at captor for a moment, Steven nodded that he did and motioned he could not speak as Henry indicated.

"Is what this man saying true?" the officer asked, "Did you have a seizure and fall from the window?"

Nodding once more, Steven felt his freedom slowly slipping away while Henry continued to watch his every move.

"You there!" the officer said, turning to the hotel manager. "Do you know this boy or that man? Are they guests at the hotel?"

"Well yes, I believe so," the manager said reluctantly.

"What do you mean you believe so?" questioned the officer.

"A man signed in at the desk for himself and his three friends. I could see them by the door," the manager continued, "and the boy with them."

"Why so many questions?" Henry balked. "I told you I am his doctor and I can take care of him."

"I don't know how you handle these things where you come from, but in Italy we don't take the injury of children lightly," the officer said. "Until I am sure why he fell, I am going to ask questions, is that understood?"

"Fine, whatever," Henry replied.

"Let me through," a voice from the crowd yelled. "I'm his father."

Turning towards the voice in desperation, Steven prayed it was indeed his father coming towards them. But as he looked up at the man, he realized any hopes of rescue were nothing more than a pipe dream.

"Please let me through, I'm his father," Kirk lied, pushing his way to the front where the boy was being treated.

"You're the boy's father?" the officer asked, "I thought you were at a meeting?" he asked, repeating Henry's earlier statement.

"I was, I just came back and heard what happened."

"And you are?" the officer continued.

"My name is Albert Hewitt and this is my son Albert junior, we call him AJ," Kirk continued as he wove his lies to suit his purpose. "Is my son all right?"

"Well, he appears to have a broken arm," the medic began. "Mr. Hewitt, is your son on some kind of medication?" he asked.

"Why?" Kirk began.

"There appears to be evidence of some kind of sedative in his system."

"Yes, AJ is on sedatives, prescribed by his doctor to help him sleep when we do a lot of traveling."

"Well you should be more careful about how much you let him take," the medic said. "The boy is really out of it," he remarked as Steven fought to stay awake.

"We have to take him to the hospital to make sure he doesn't have a concussion, and the drug in his system is making it very difficult to get a proper diagnosis as to his condition."

"Do you think he has a concussion?" Kirk asked, looking over at the boy who was obviously under the influence of both drugs given to him.

"Won't know for sure till we run some x-rays," he said before he turned to help his partner put the injured boy on the gurney.

"Is it necessary to take him by ambulance?" Kirk asked.

"What is it with you and this doctor?" the officer demanded to know. "Why don't you want the boy to ride with the medics to the hospital?"

"I didn't say that, I just meant we could take him to the clinic just outside of town. My friend owns it, and he could take the x-rays needed."

"I think we will let the medics take him," the officer announced.. He did not like the strange feeling he was getting from both men and wanted to be sure there wasn't more going on with them, and he did not want to let the boy leave until he was sure his suspicions were unfounded.

"Can I talk to you for a minute?" the medic said to the officer as he pulled him aside.

"Sure."

"I don't know what's going on, but the kid has a couple of bruises on his face he didn't get from the fall," the medic explained.

"Are you sure?" the officer replied.

"They're old bruises."

"That's what I figured," he said before turning back to Kirk. "Mr. Hewitt, we will be taking your son to the hospital, and if you have any objections, you can take it up with my supervisors later."

"Great!" Henry interrupted angrily. "Then as his doctor I am going to ride along with him," he announced.

"Afraid not," the medic interrupted. "You may be his doctor back home, but not here in Rome," he announced trying to come up with a reason to keep the boy separated from the two men. If he were the victim of child abuse, he wanted to talk to him alone far away from the prying eyes of his suspects. "The hospital is only a few miles down the road, you and Mr. Hewitt can follow in your car," the medic said before closing the ambulance door, with his patient safely inside.

"All right!" Kirk snapped, before walking towards the car. There were too many witnesses around to take the boy from them now, they'd have to wait until they were on the road.

Sitting in the ambulance as it started to pull away, Steven looked through the window watching as his kidnapers racing towards the car in order to follow them.

Now is my chance, he thought to himself, grabbing the paper the medic was writing on. Still shaky from the drugs, Steven held the pen tightly with both hands as he tried to write down a few words.

Help Me, Kidnaped! he wrote, exhausted from the effort.

"What?" the medic echoed. "Are you kidding?" He expected the boy to tell him his father beat him and that was how he fell, but he never expected to see the word *kidnaped* as the reason the men were trying to keep him away from everyone. "Is this for real?" he questioned once more to be certain the words he saw were true.

"Ok, kid, I believe you," he replied as Steven pointed to the note several times. "I don't understand what is going on, but you're safe now," he uttered before turning to the driver. "Radio base tell them to have the police waiting for us we when get to the hospital and make sure you give them a description of the car those two men are driving," he ordered.

"Why? What's up?" the driver asked.

"This!" the medic replied, showing him the note.

"Damn!" he answered, grabbing the mic as they continued towards the hospital.

"I better let the officer behind us know what is going on too," the driver said after informing the hospital of their situaion. "Oh my god!" he shouted, looking in his rear view mirror as the car following them turned its attention towards the motorcycle officer. "They just ran him off the road—the officer behind us—they just killed him," he screamed, horrified by what he witnessed.

"What!" the medic echoed, looking out the window to see the vehicle drawing closer to them, the officer no longer in sight.

"Hang on!" the driver ordered, speeding up in an attempt to get away from the car. "This is unit 423!" he yelled into the mic. "We need help, the kidnapers are after us, and they just killed the policeman escorting us," he explained. "We're—" he tried to say but never completed as he swerved once more in an attempt to keep the car from overtaking them, his actions causing them to slide off the road onto an embankment.

"Is everyone ok?" the medic asked after regaining his composure.

"I think so," the driver replied, "What about the boy?"

"Are you ok?" the medic asked again as he started to check his patient out.

"I..." Steven began, surprised to find his voice slowing coming back. Henry gave him the drug, but its effects were not lasting as long as they said. Not even twenty minutes since he fell, the effects were already wearing off.

"You can talk?" the medic uttered surprised to find his patient could indeed talk.

"Yes, I was drugged," Steven said. The words though difficult to get out, were becoming easier with each moment which passed.

"Get out!" Henry ordered, opening the back of the ambulance, his gun drawn as he stared at the men inside.

"The boy is hurt," the medic announced. "He can't be moved."

"I don't give a damn, " Henry snapped, grabbing Steven by the arm, forcing him out of the vehicle as he spoke. "What the hell?" he said, hearing the radio transmission as they stood by the ambulance. "Damn it!" he shouted, tearing the speaker from the console.

"What is it?" Kirk asked, standing by the three hostages.

"The cops are on their way, they know about the kidnaping," Henry said, glaring over at Steven.

"Please!" Steven began, moving towards Kirk. "Do not hurt them."

"I thought you gave him the drug, why is he talking?" Kirk asked, looking over at Henry as he spoke.

"I only had time to give him a partial injection before the crowd showed up, so I guess the effects didn't last as long as I would have liked."

"You think!" Kirk uttered sarcastically, angry with his partner for not revealing this information sooner.

"Please, don't hurt them, I'll go with you, I won't do anything else, I promise, just don't hurt anyone else," Steven pleaded, still a little drowsy from the sedative.

"Sorry, kid, we're well past that option," Kirk replied, looking over at Henry as he spoke.

"Please!" Steven repeated as gunfire echoed around him before he could finish his plea. "No!" he cried, staring at the bodies of the men who tried to help him laying in a pool of blood.

"Sorry kid," Henry began, "but this was your fault. If you hadn't tried to get away at the hotel, these men would still be alive."

"I hate you!" Steven shouted. Despite his anger, he knew Henry was right.

Three men were dead because of him. Three men dead whose only crime was trying to help him and Steven knew he'd have to live with that fact forever. "Why are you doing this?" he cried. "I thought you were supposed to be friends of my father."

"Well, kid, to tell you the truth, friendship has no baring here," Henry began as he put his gun away. "The only thing we're concerned with is the five million dollars we are going to get for this little caper," Henry replied, grabbing Steven by the arm. Steven let out a cry of pain. "And you, my little pest, are the key to getting it. Oops! Forgot about the arm." He laughed. "Now move it."

"My uncle, what did you do to Mark? Did you kill him too?" Steven asked, struggling with Henry as they headed for the car. He hadn't seen Mark since they arrived at the hotel, and with everything happening around him, he was certain his uncle had to be dead.

"Who Mark?" Kirk began. "No, he's not dead, at least I don't think he is."

"But you might wish he was before this is over," Henry replied.

"What is that supposed to mean?" Steven shouted, confused by the statement.

"Not now!" Kirk said, interrupting Henry before he could answer Steven.

"Where to?" Henry asked, while the three men headed down the road away from the ambulance and the dead men lying nearby.

"Unfortunately, we still have to get his arm checked so take him to Doc Hughes' clinic," Kirk replied. Known for not asking too many questions, the doctor's office was the only safe place they could take the boy without arousing too much suspicion.

"We could just leave him the way he is," Henry balked, still angry with the boy for causing the mess in the first place.

"And would you like to explain to the man why his precious cargo is damaged?" asked Kirk as he tied Steven's hands together. "This will keep you out of trouble till we get where we are going," he remarked before turning his attentions back to Henry.

"Guess not," Henry replied. "That psychopath would kill me just to make a point."

"Who are you talking about?" Steven asked. "Who is this man you keep referring to?"

"You'll find out soon enough," Kirk replied as they pulled into the clinic parking lot. "Now remember, kid, if you do anything stupid you can add the doctor to the list of casualties," Kirk declared as he untied the boy's hands. "Got it?"

"Yes," Steven said. He did not want anyone else hurt because of him and would do whatever it took to make sure of it.

Walking into the clinic, Steven was relieved to see the only person inside was the doctor. At least there would not be anyone else involved in this nightmare if things took a deadly turn for them.

"Please, this way," the doctor said as he led the men into the examining room.

"I'll take some x-rays of the arm, and if there is a break, I can set it right here; I have all the equipment I need in the clinic."

"How long do you think it will take?" Henry asked, eager to get the matter over with.

"It should only take about an hour or so," the doctor replied as he asked both Henry and Kirk to leave the room while he took the x-rays of Steven's arm.

"Fine, just make it quick," Henry snapped, reminding the boy what would happen if he tried anything before leaving him alone with the doctor.

"So what is your name?" the doctor asked as he tended to his patient.

"AJ," Steven lied. He hoped by using the same name as the one Kirk did at the hotel, it might help the police figure out the next move in the investigation. My name is AJ Hewitt," he repeated, praying the doctor would reveal the name to the police once he learned of the other deaths. Even if the man avoided the police when it came to his clients, Steven hoped he would realize talking to them now would be safer for him in the long run.

"AJ. Ok, AJ, how did you hurt yourself?"

"I fell," Steven replied, continuing the ruse.

"Well, son, don't worry I'll have you fixed up in no time at all," the man promised, signally for the others to return to the room as he headed for the door. "Be back in a few minutes," he explained. "As soon as the film develops, I'll check on the x-rays and we can get the arm set."

"Thanks, Doc," Steven replied as Henry moved towards him.

"So far so good, kid," he whispered in Steven's ear as he grabbed the injured boy again. "Now let's keep it that way."

"I won't do anything, I promise, just do not hurt the man," Steven said. He would continue to do as he was instructed, but somehow he would find a chance to escape and he was going to take it.

"Is everything ok?" the doctor asked, walking into the room.

"Fine, Doc," Henry remarked. "What about the x-rays?"

"They show what I expected them to, there is a break in AJ's arm, but it looks like a clean break," he said while he placed the items he needed to set the arm next to his patient. "I'll set the arm in a simple cast, and once I give him a shot for the pain, AJ should be ready to go."

"Shot? No shots!" Steven remarked, the last thing he wanted to was another shot given to him.

"Son, the shot is just to help you with the pain," the doctor continued.

"No, I'm fine really, the pain is not that bad," Steven insisted.

"But by tomorrow your entire body is going to ache from the fall you took."

"No shot," Steven repeated.

"All right, son, how about if I give you some pills, and then in the morning if you need them, you can take a couple," the doctor finally suggested.

"Ok," Steven relented, taking the pills from him.

"Can we go now?" Henry asked, watching as the doctor finally finished working on Steven's arm.

"Just as soon as I write up the bill, you can be on our way," the doctor replied, heading for the door once more.

"Where are you going?" Kirk asked.

"To my office to get the paperwork for you. I'll be back in a minute," he said before leaving the room.

"Hello, this is Doctor Hughes." He began phoning the police; he didn't like turning people in normally, but his instincts told him this time was different. "Yes, down at the clinic," he continued trying not to talk too loud, so as not to reveal to the others what he was doing. "Listen, this might not be anything at all but I have two men here at the clinic, they're traveling with a teenage boy and he's injured—" His words were cut off by a question from the officer on the other end. "Yes, they all appear to be Americans," he replied as the questions continued. "Yes, two men and a boy, like I said," he repeated. "Well, to tell you the truth, he seems more afraid of them than anything else," the man answered, surprised by the question. But the boy did appear frightened more by the man he was with than by his injuries. He'd noticed the boy looking over at his companions several times before answering any questions as if he were waiting for them to give their consent before he said or did anything.

"What's going on?" he finally demanded to know checking the door. The last thing he wanted was to have one of them walk in while he was on the phone with the police. It was obvious from the conversation he was having with the officer, something big was going on. "What! Kidnapers?" he uttered. "Are you sure they are the same people?" he inquired. He'd helped many criminals in the past but drew the line with people who used or hurt kids to accomplish their goals. "Yes, the boy is about seventeen or eighteen," he replied. "Damn, you really think they are the same ones?" he asked again. "What! Yes, I guess I can keep them here a little longer, but you better hurry, I already set the boy's arm and there really isn't any reason to delay them," He explained before hanging up the phone.

"Big mistake, Doc," Kirk remarked, standing in the doorway, "You should have stayed out of it."

"No wait," the doctor cried out.

Startled by the sound of gunfire, Steven jumped from the examining table as he rushed towards the door.

"You killed him," he shouted, fighting with Kirk as he met them at the door.

"Why? I did what you told me to," he cried, tears streaming from his face as yet another person laid dead because of him. "I did what you told me to!"

"What the hell happened?" Henry asked, while Kirk tried to restrain the boy.

"Had no choice, I found the good doctor on the phone with the police."

"Then let's get the hell out of here," Henry said, grabbing Steven. "You know, kid, you're more trouble than you're worth," he declared pulling his gun from his pocket as he pointed it towards Steven's head.

"Henry, put that thing down," Kirk ordered.

"The mission is a bust anyway so why not cut our losses now and get out of here before it's too late," he argued as Steven stood motionless, the gun pressed against his temple.

"Because as long as we have the kid the mission is not a bust," Kirk maintained, pushing the gun away. " The police have no idea who he really is and as long as we have him we can still force Andrew to do what we want."

"Alright," Henry replied, slapping Steven in the back of the head as he spoke. "You're one lucky little brat, but do anything else to mess this up and I will use you for target practice, do you understand?"

"Yes, I understand," Steven said, taking a deep breath as he tried to shake the sensation of the gun against his temple from his mind.

"Good, then let's go," Henry ordered, pushing Steven towards the door.

CHAPTER SIX

The church, perched deep within the mountain walls still possessed the elegance of the past that made it famous even today. Built long before the turn of the century, its ivory towers, marble floors, and handcrafted statues illuminated every corner as it continued to bring countless guests, seeking refuge from the world, to its doors year after year.

Sitting outside its doors, watching as the sun brought yet another day to rest, Mark thought about the boy he left at the hotel and dangers they were both facing. If he did not take great care in his next step, he could lose more than just Steven's love before the entire mess was over. Despite how the boy would feel when he learned the truth, Mark knew in his heart it had to be done, and he prayed once Steven understood his motives they could rebuild the relationship they once shared without seeing the look of anger in his eyes that he had seen at the hotel. Steven was upset with him now but in time everything would be back to normal. Checking his watch again realizing his contact was late, Mark slammed his fist into a nearby pillar as the booze and pills which raced through his veins made him immune to the pain.

"Where the hell are you?" he shouted angrily. He had been waiting hours for the man to arrive and despite the necessity of the information, Mark had no intentions of remaining much longer. He didn't like the way he left things with Steven and wanted to return to him before his men could put any more ideas in the boy's head. Kirk, the better of the two, still gave Mark reason to fear him. With his uncontrollable desire to escape the world, he would do whatever it took to get away, and Henry, a man he did not trust, would be just as ruthless for the money he felt he was entitled to. If he were not careful, Mark knew he would end up losing the battle before it was ever fought if either man let their agendas interfere with his.

Sighing, as his thoughts drifted from the son to the father and the friendship they shared, Mark felt regret for the possible loss of that bound. Best friends for nearly forty years, the actions they had both taken now would change that forever. Wondering, as he took another puff from his cigarette, if Andrew felt any regrets, Mark began pacing around the pillar as if he were playing a child's game. Wishing, as he circled it several times, that there wasanother way to complete his mission. He hated having his hands tied by the measures he must take to secure the mission.

Moving away from the pillar along the church edge, Mark hurried past the statue of the Madonna, making his way past the cleaning lady diligently preparing it for evening mass as he sought the man he had come to see.

"I'm glad to see you," a voice from behind the confessional said as Mark drew closer.

"What the hell took you so long? I've been here for hours," Mark snapped, trying not to let the anger in his voice draw attention to himself. The last thing he wanted was for some noisy parishioners, who were slowing starting to file into the church to attend mass, to overhear the conversation.

"I really don't care how long you have been waiting," the man replied, sounding as if he were in charge, rather than simply someone there to relay information. "I told you I would get here when I could and that is what I did."

"Fine, whatever. You're here now so tell me what you have," Mark replied, too tired to get into a fight with him. "What was so important we had to risk meeting before the scheduled time?" Mark demanded to know. Things were precarious enough without taking unnecessary chances by meeting out in the open. There were too many factors working against them and he was not about to lose the only edge he possessed because of someone else's stupid moves.

"Andrew is becoming more of a problem than we anticipated," the man began.

"How so?" Mark asked, not surprised to hear those words about his friend. Andrew never did what was expected of him and that was one of the reasons he survived so long in a world that did not treat its members fairly.

"He's refusing to make any decisions despite the information he has been given, and if he doesn't decide which side he is on soon, then everything will be lost," the man explained, as the tension in his voice grew. "Unless we put a leash on him before it is too late, nothing we do will save my people."

"Save your people." Mark laughed. "We both know that is not the only motivation behind what you are doing now," he announced, taking a cigarette from his pocket. "As for Andrew, he will be on a short leash soon and after that he will be in jail for his crimes."

"You really believe that, don't you?" the man said, moving closer. "You really believe Andrew is going to pay for everything he has done."

"I wish I didn't," Mark replied.

"Feeling sorry for the man?" the shadowy figure questioned.

"He is my friend and I don't have to like what has to be done," Mark snapped as his contact handed him a piece of paper. "Amateurs," Mark whispered, tearing the paper into small pieces. "Whatever you have to tell me, say it in person, never leave any evidence behind," he balked.

"You fool, that was the conference schedule for the next few days," the man uttered as he wrote done the times once more on a small pad. "Andrew will turn over to the counsel and if he does…"

"I thought you said the files were useless," Mark protested.

"There is not enough proof alone to be of any real damage to my people, but Andrew could obtain the rest of the information somewhere else and learn the truth." He continued, "He is growing more distrustful with each passing day and we do not have much time left."

"Yea, yea, whatever," Mark balked, not really interested in the problems of the man he came to see. His only concern was Andrew and he would take care of that.

"Is that all you are going to say?" the man yelled, growing angrier with each breath he took.

"Ah, no!" Mark laughed. "Oh you mean about Andrew, yes that is all I have to say about him, but I have another question to ask you," he continued moving closer.

"Why the delay on the conference? You have been here long enough to have everything over by now."

"That fool president has decided to take time off to see Rome before he allows the conference to continue. He believes time away from the table will give everyone a fresh prospective on the situation and a better chance at a more fair vote in the end," the shadowy figure said, trying to keep from being noticed by the others in the church as the procession for the evening mass began.

"Great," Mark replied. He could use the extra time to further his cause with Steven before everything broke wide open. He needed to make him understand everything he was doing was to protect him, and it would not be easy. Despite the past and the problems between them, Steven loved his father, turning him against the man would not be as simple a matter as he earlier thought.

"Will you have everything ready in time?" the man asked, distracting Mark from his thoughts.

"You worry about your end and I'll take care of mine," Mark snapped. "I know what has to be done and once I prove to Steven that his father is not the man he thinks he is, I'll make sure you get everything you want."

"Your obsession with the boy is going to get you killed," he protested, afraid the teenage boy might compromise the mission. Andrew needed to be stopped, and if Mark didn't put his feelings for the boy aside and concentrate on the problem at hand, it would fail.

"I told you before never to mention his name to me in any of our conversations!" Mark shouted, turning towards his cohort for the first time. "The boy was off limits to everyone and if you can not keep that straight, then the alliance between us is over."

"Alright!" he replied, Mark's tone sending a chill down his spin. He tried several times to get him to put his feelings for the boy aside so they could concentrate on the mission and knew by his reaction discussing it with him now would not be a very good idea. "You do what you want to, as long as you stop Andrew before he destroys my country," he whispered as he moved toward the rear door. "I will contact you when it is time," were his last words before hurrying from the church, afraid Mark's outburst would draw unnecessary attention to them.

"Till then." Mark laughed, waving as he watched the man leave in such a rush.

The fear in the man's voice very apparent, it gave Mark a sense of power and he enjoyed the adrenaline high it gave him. "Fool, no matter what you think, I am in charge and in the end you will all pay for underestimating me," he whispered to himself before leaving the church a few minutes after his contact.

Rushing towards the hotel to meet with Andrew, Mark smiled as he pulled into the parking lot. Though the seriousness of his mission made things a little more difficult than he anticipated, seeing Andrew again would be fun. Like his old friend, he enjoyed playing the game and soon it would be getting very interesting. Mark could not help savoring every minute of the hand he had finally been dealt. No longer the second banana to the all mighty Andrew McCormick, he would finally be able to prove to everyone, including Steven, that he was the better man.

Sitting in his car for a moment before heading towards the hotel lobby, Mark checked his watch to make sure everything was going as planned. He told Andrew he would be arriving in Rome a little after nine that evening and he wanted to make sure everything appeared as natural as possible. Andrew was the guilty party in this mess, and Mark did not want to tip his hand too soon.

Standing by the entrance to the hotel, Mark turned towards the lobby as he noticed a small crowd gathered around the TV set, apparently enthralled by something very important coming from news report. Walking closer as he stopped to see what was going on, Mark listened to the bulletin that kept repeating itself over and over. His Italian was a little rusty but was good enough for him to realize his men had screwed up and the mission was now in danger of being exposed.

"What the—" he uttered, listening to the report again.

Early this evening the police responded to a chateau outside of Rome for what appeared to be nothing more than an accidental fall involving a young man from America. It seemed he fell from the 2nd floor veranda and was taken by ambulance by medical personnel. However, police soon learned this was anything but an accidental fall. According to our sources, the boy, an apparent kidnap victim was trying to escape when he fell. He managed to tell the medical personnel what was going on. However, before they could get the boy to safety, they were overpowered by the kidnapers. The police found the ambulance along with the two attendants and the motorcycle police officer who was following them just miles from the hospital. All three men had been killed and the boy was missing, apparently once more in the kidnapers' hands. The police have not revealed what leads they are working on nor have they confirmed the identity of boy. This station has learned that a boy matching the missing teen's description was seen earlier today with three men checking into the hotel as guest. It is not certain if these same men are involved or if they too have become victims of the kidnapers.

This news station has also learned of another death which occurred less than an hour after the first killings: a local doctor found murdered in his office. The police are investigating the possible connection between the two crimes. This station will continue to keep updating on this story and give you whatever information we obtain as soon as possible. Stay tuned to this station for further details.

The reporter concluded as the people standing around the lobby began to discuss what they had just heard.

"What happened?" Mark whispered under his breath as he tried to reach Kirk by cell phone. Even as he listened to the reports and realized there was no specific evidence to indicate Steven's involvement, Mark knew in his gut the boy they were talking about was his young charge.

How could they let this happen? he wondered, trying the cell phone several times, each attempt yielding the same negative results, he entrusted the boy's safety with them and did not understand how things took such a dangerous turn.

"Why don't you answer?" he snapped, the sound of the ringing phone echoing like a sledgehammer as his head began to ache from the pain coming from it.

"Mark," a voice from behind said as he turned to find Andrew standing in the lobby beside him. "What the hell is happening?"

"Andrew," he uttered, putting the phone away. Whatever was going on with his people would have to wait until later, for now his attentions had to be focused on the man he came to see. "Nice to see you, too," he remarked, pulling him away from the crowd room. "You might not want to talk so loud in a room filled with people listening to news bulletins about four murders," he joked.

"Four murders, what the hell are you talking about?" Andrew asked. He'd been so wrapped up in his own world since he called home that he hadn't been paying attention to anything going on around him.

"You didn't hear the news?" Mark asked, a little concerned as to how he was going to tell him what he suspected.

"All right, so I have been a little edgy since you told me Steven showed up at the apartment and I have not bothered to watch the local news, big deal, it is not like it will affect me in any way," Andrew began. "Did you know they found Templeton dead the same day I spoke to you?" he continued as he still changed the subject of the television report to the matters he wanted to discuss. "He was killed in my apartment building, and if Steven heard an unidentified man was killed there, he would freak out."

"Steven is a big boy and he could have handled it," Mark insisted, "besides he was gone before that happened."

"Are you sure he is safe?"

"What tape were you referring to?" Mark asked without answering Andrew's question as he asked his own questions.

"The surveillance tape from the file room," Andrew began. "I spoke to Annie and she said they had a tape of the robbery. I thought you rigged the system so it would wipe everything clean?" he asked as they walked over to the bar. "If they do have a tape and it was working at the time of the robbery, it will show me as the thief and, as far as the agency is concerned, the person responisble for killing Peter, as well."

"Don't worry about the tape, I've taken care of it," Mark insisted. He had taken the tape before the others could see it and replaced it with a blank. He would decide later how he was going to use it or if he had to, but that decision would depend on Andrew and his next move.

"Do you have any idea who killed Pete or Templeton for that matter?" Andrew asked.

"Well, if the agency heads get hold of the real tape, they are going to think it was you," Mark joked.

"Glad my problems are making you so happy." Andrew laughed.

"Sorry, it's just in all the years we have known each other this is the first time you are in trouble instead of me."

"Happy to oblige," Andrew uttered. "What is our next move?"

"Well, first off we have to prove that even though you did steal the files, you didn't kill the kid, after that we have to prove you never planned to sell the information to anyone, you didn't did you?"

"Funny," Andrew uttered, taking a drink from his glass, "I need the information in the Vega file and that was why I took it."

"The Vega file? That is a name from the past." Mark said. "Why didn't you tell me that was the reason you stole all those important files."

"All those files, I only took a couple from the same cabinet to keep the agency guessing but the only real important file I took was the Vega," Andrew insisted.

"Andrew, there were several files, very important ones taken that day."

"What files are you talking about?" Andrew asked, confused by what he was hearing.

"The De'Pacy file, the Clark file, and a few others," Mark announced.

"But I never took those files," Andrew insisted. Both of those files were highly sensitive and classified, he would never risk taking them anywhere, let alone leave them in the lab back at the agency as he had done with the files he did take.

"I never took those files, and the ones I did take I hid in the lab for the boys to find later."

"Oh, they found those files, but not the others," Mark said.

"But I didn't take them," Andrew repeated.

"Ok, friend, I believe you," Mark replied. Andrew had entrusted him alone with the information on the plan to break into the file room for the information he needed for an important mission, and he did not believe he would lie to him now about what he took.

"Why didn't you tell me the Vegas were involved in this mission?" he questioned.

"Because, my friend, I knew what you would say," Andrew began. "If you knew the mission I took at the last minute involved Philippe and Antonio you would have told me to let it go and not to get involved."

"You got that right," Mark answered. "You should have left the past in the past and let them deal with their own problems."

"You know I can't do that," Andrew replied.

"Why because of that damned promise you made to Jose Vega over twenty years ago?"

"I gave my word and I have to keep it," Andrew insisted.

"You are the only person I know who still believes in honoring one's word," Mark snapped as he finished his fourth drink.

"I hope not," Andrew said.

"So you broke into the file room to get an update on the Vegas. Why didn't you just ask Stewart for them?"

"Because he would have said no," Andrew said. "Not only would he have refused to give me the latest surveillance information on San Sebastian and its people, but he would have found a way to keep me from coming here." Andrew continued, "I couldn't let him or anyone else interfere with what I had to do."

"So you're saying no one back home but me knows you're here in Rome or the reason for the visit?" Mark asked.

"Pretty much," Andrew answered. "That is why I am so glad you are here, you can watch my back."

"Always!" Mark insisted. "What is our next step?"

"Well, while I continue my mission here in Rome, you can return home and try to find out who killed those men and why?" Andrew instructed.

"I'm afraid things are not going to be that easy," Mark said, glancing over at the TV set as he spoke.

"What do you mean?"

"That!" he replied, pointing to the news bulletin as the story about the kidnaped American boy came on once more.

"What does that have to do with me?" Andrew asked, "You don't think I am involved in that, too?"

"No!" Mark hesitated. "But I think Steven is."

"Steven!" Andrew shouted. "What the hell does he have to do with that?"

"Sit down and be quiet," Mark ordered. "You are just damned lucky most of the people in this bar either don't speak English or they were listening to the news and didn't hear you mention Steven's name in connection to the report," he said. The words causing Andrew to comply with the orders to sit down.

"All right I am sitting down and I am calm," Andrew said as he moved closer to Mark to keep the conversation from being overheard by anyone else.

"I am not sure yet, but there is a chance the missing boy is Steven!"

"What makes you think that?" Andrew asked, trying to remain calm as he listened to his friend's words. "I thought you said Steven was safe at school."

"He was, but the last time I talked to him he knew I was coming to Rome, and I haven't been able to reach him since I heard the report."

"Just because you can't reach Steven doesn't mean he came to Rome to find me and just because the kidnaped boy is American doesn't mean it is him either," Andrew insisted. "Unless there is something else going on I don't know about."

"Steven followed me to Rome, and the last time I saw him was at the airport; he was with a couple of my men," Mark explained, waiting for the explosion as he spoke. But Andrew did not exploded as he expected, instead he sat quietly waiting for more information on what was going on. "I left Steven with a couple of men I could trust, and I haven't been able to reach them either since I heard the news report."

"You let Steven come to Rome knowing I might be suspected of murder and treason, and you left him alone after you let him come here," Andrew said, his voice though low, held a rage inside he could barely control.

"You know your son, I did not let him do anything. He would have found a way to Rome no matter what and I thought he would be safe with the others."

"Maybe he still is," Andrew said as the report came on again. "Maybe the boy in the story has nothing to do with Steven."

"Then why can't I reach my men?" Mark asked.

"I don't know," Andrew replied. "Damn you, Mark, I trusted you to keep him safe."

"I know and I will do whatever it takes to make sure he will be safe from now on, but before we can do anything, we have to figure out if the boy is Steven and why he was taken."

"Well, if someone is setting me up for the theft of the files, maybe they have even bigger plans and Steven is the key," Andrew began.

"I was thinking the same thing," replied Mark. "Before we can figure out who has Steven we have to figure out why?"

"So you are convinced the missing boy is Steven?" Andrew asked, praying that his friend was wrong.

"I am now," Mark said, pointing to the TV as a artist sketch of the missing boy flashed across the screen.

"Oh god!" Andrew cried, while Mark held on to his arm to keep him from moving towards the crowd. "I never wanted my work to touch him again."

"We'll figure this mess out, don't worry," Mark assured him as they walked away from the bar towards the elevator. "Whoever set you up had to throw around a lot of money to get to you in two continents," he continued. "And despite your well known clientele, there aren't too many people who would spend that kind of money just to set you up, so that should narrow our list of suspects down to just a few."

"I hope so," Andrew said as they stepped into the elevator. "Mark, I can't lose my son too," he said, trying not to let his own fears cloud his judgment any more than they already were. His son needed him to be strong and able to handle whatever came his way without fail, and he would do his best to be everything Steven needed if that was the only way he could bring him home safely.

"You won't lose him," Mark insisted. "I give you my word before this mess is over, Steven will finally understand what kind of man his father is and he will get a chance to rebuild a life with him."

"Thanks, Mark. I am glad you are here to cover my back."

"Me too. So what is our next move?"

"I will wait for the kidnapers to call and see what they want. After that I guess I will play it by ear and do whatever is necessary to get my son back."

"Sounds like a plan to me," Mark replied, taking another drink as he spoke.

"I thought you were going to give up the stuff," Andrew began.

"I will," Mark assured him. "But for now let's concentrate on Steven and worry about me later.

"If we work together to get him back we might be able to stop those bastards," Andrew said as they walked up to his suite.

"Just like the old days." Mark laughed.

"Just like the old days," Andrew repeated. "Only this time the prize is going to be Steven."

"You got that right, the prize in this game is Steven," Mark concurred as he stood in front of Andrew's hotel door. "Now, you get in that room and try to figure out which one of the counsel could be involved and I will hit the streets and see if I can locate my men."

"You know who the main suspects are in this, don't you?" Andrew said as he unlocked the door to his room. "Philippe and Antonio are my only suspects at this time."

"Mine, too," Mark replied. "You came here because of them and if they have someone at the agency working with them, then stealing the files and taking Steven might only be the beginning."

"But I saw the file, there isn't anything inside worth kidnaping Steven for," Andrew argued. He read the contents and they did not contain anything of real value.

"They might not be of value to you or me, but maybe there is something inside that neither one of us are aware of that could mean a lot to the kidnapers," Mark insisted.

"Then I better start reading the file over again and see what I missed," Andrew concurred. Like many files, pieces of information they came in contact with often had hidden meanings, maybe this one too held something inside that could help him figure out which one of his old friends had betrayed him.

"I will talk to you later," Mark began as he walked towards the elevator once more. "And don't worry, Steven is a fighter, and he will give those kidnapers hell."

"That is what I am afraid of," Andrew admitted. His son was a lot like his mother in many aspects, including his refusal to give in when cornered. If he tried to fight the kidnapers, he could end up risking his life in the process.

Sitting in his car, Mark took a photo out of his pocket and he stared at the picture of his beloved. It had been ten years since her death and now he finally had a chance to make the people responsible for it pay, he felt the life come slowly into his soul.

I'm sorry, my love, he thought to himself as he thought about the pain Steven would face when he learned the truth. "I tried to protect him but I failed. I never meant for this to happen. I just wanted to get him away before it was too late," he continued as he thought about the boy.

He should have been mine, he thought, staring at the picture of his beloved, *and he would have been if Andrew had not gotten in the way. Everything would have been different if it were not for Andrew.*

FIRST LOVE

Paris, one of the most beautiful cities in the world, held a special meaning to Mark as he made his way to the park. He had seen the girl he would one day marry and soon she too would feel the same way about him.

Smiling at the irony of the situation, Mark looked around for his mysterious lady. He came to Paris to meet Andrew and his fiancée and because of a last minute assignment that sent Andrew away, he had been forced to fend for himself for nearly a week and if his friend hadn't left, Mark never would have seen the woman of his dreams and would have missed the chance to have someone in his life as well.

Skating across the pathway as he made his way to the place, she normally sat with her friends, he was determined to get up enough courage this time to talk to her.

Certainly, she noticed him each morning too as he skated past during his regular exercise regiment. Mark knew it was time they finally got together.

"There she is," he whispered as the woman walked towards a nearby bench and sat down. *It is perfect*, he thought, *the timing is just right*. She was alone today, no friends to distract her. "Mind if I join you?" he asked, skating up to the bench.

"No, not at all," she replied, trying not to be amused by the young man. She noticed him watching her for several days now and found herself intrigued by the mysterious man.

"Nice day isn't it?" he started.

"Yes, very nice," she replied.

"Are you American? " he asked, noting she did not have a French accent.

"Yes. You?"

"Yes. Just here on a short visit."

"Oh I see," she continued as she found herself attracted to the stranger. "I work in Paris."

"How nice," he uttered, feeling like a teenager as he spoke. "Would you like to get some coffee?" he asked. "Oh yea," he replied, as she reminded him of the cup in her hand. "Sorry! How about just a walk or something?" he continued, trying not to let the set back of the coffee remarks deter him from his goal of asking her out.

"Thanks, but I don't normally go walking with strangers, especially ones who try to pick me up wearing roller skates," she remarked. Though she did not intend to let it go any further than the simple flirtation, she was pleased to see someone found her attractive. Her fiancé had been so wrapped up in his career lately, he had not taken notice of her in weeks.

"Sorry again," Mark replied as he skated off without saying anything else.

A little disappointed he did not pursue it any further, the young lady tossed her cup in a nearby trash bin and headed back to work.

"Would you go for a walk with someone who can't darn their own socks?" Mark asked, stepping out from behind a tree holding his skates in his hands, the toes on his right foot exposed by a hole in the seam.

Laughing, finding herself pleased to see the young man again, she finally agreed to go to the café at the end of the park to talk with him.

"So you are here on business?" she asked as they made themselves comfortable at one of the tables.

"Actually I'm here to meet with my best friend and his fiancée," Mark confessed. "He went and got himself engaged while on assignment and now he needs me to be his best man."

"Isn't that nice?" she said. "When is the wedding?

"Don't know yet," Mark confessed. "As soon as I got here my friend had to leave and I am just killing time until he returns. I haven't even met the girl I came to see," he explained.

"Your friend got called away?" she repeated as a sick feeling came over her. "What is your friend's name?"

"Why Andrew McCormick," he replied, curious as to why she wanted to know.

"Oh my god. You're Mark, aren't you?" she uttered, realizing she had been flirting with her fiancé's best friend.

"I'm…" Mark started to say as he realized who he was with. "Sophia?

Acknowledging she was in fact Sophia, the young woman apologized for her behavior as the two embarrassed people remained at the table not sure what to do next.

"Not to worry, I knew who you were all along," Mark lied as he tried to make the situation a little easier for her.

"You did?" she questioned.

"Sure. When Andrew told me he had to leave, I figured I'd check you out on my own and you passed the test. You were polite but not tease, and now I know my friend picked the right girl," he explained, his heart breaking as he spoke to her. Once again, he came in second where Andrew was concerned. The one woman he found attracted to him, found interesting, had to be the same woman Andrew intended to marry. No matter what he did, he was always the loser next to his friend.

"You set me up?" she uttered angrily.

"Listen I'm sorry, I just wanted to make sure Andrew made the right choice," Mark continued as he tried to maintain the ruse.

"How dare you!" she shouted.

"I'm sorry, I didn't intend to hurt your feelings," Mark began. "Can we start over?"

Staring at the man for a few minutes, Sophia finally agreed to his request. Though she didn't like what he'd done, he was Andrew's best friend and the last thing she wanted to do was get between the two men.

"We can just forget the whole thing and not tell Andrew anything," Mark announced.

"I don't think so," she said, explaining she didn't intend to start her marriage with a lie between her and Andrew. "If this was just a test as you said, then telling Andrew shouldn't be a problem."

"No problem at all, if you are ok with it," Mark replied. "As long as we can remain friends I have no problem with anything you do."

~

"I'm sorry, my love!" Mark said staring at the picture. "I could not tell you then how much I loved you because of Andrew and we never had a chance," he continued. "I prayed you would finally see through him and realize I was the better man for you, but we never got a chance for that to happen, did we!" he said talking to the photograph of his lost love as if she were sitting in the car next to him. "Steven should have been my son and he would have been if it weren't for Andrew," he repeated several times as the tears flowed down his cheek. "If it weren't for him, everything would've been different."

CHAPTER SEVEN

Stirring slowly from his drug induced sleep, the sounds of voices in the distance awakening him, Steven found himself handcuffed to the bed as he tried to move. Staring at the door, afraid his moans might have alerted his captors, he let out a sigh of relief as he realized they were still unaware he had come too. Having already endured several injections from Henry's bag of tricks, the last thing he wanted was to feel the sting of yet another needle in his arm.

Listening to the sound of his heart pounding as he laid silently in the bed, Steven wondered how long he had been unconscious. The last thing he remembered was leaving the clinic, after that everything was a blur to him, between the drugs and constant moving from place to place, things were so confused in his mind that he was not sure of anything anymore.

How much time has past? he wondered, was it even the same week as when he left Washington in search of his father or had it been longer? Whatever was going on now, Steven knew for sure the nightmare was only beginning. His captors had no intentions of letting him go after everything he had seen and he could not let them force his father to commit a crime on his behalf.

Staring at the sun from his window, its shimmering glow at least letting him know it was still daylight, Steven's thoughts turned to Uncle Mark. He could not help but imagine the worst, imagine that he too had subscribed to the same fate as the others and he would never see them again.

Struggling to free his arm from the handcuffs that secured him to the bed, Steven tried to figure out a way to gain his freedom. Despite the threat from Henry of yet another beating should he do anything else to escape them, he could not just lie there and do nothing. If his uncle were still alive, he would join forces with Andrew to find Steven and he wanted to help them as much as possible before it was too late.

Closing his eyes, the sounds of footsteps drawing nearer to the door, Steven tried to fool his captors into believing he were still unconscious.

"He's fine," Kirk assured the person on the other end of phone as he stood at the foot of the bed. "When can we expect things to start moving?" he inquired. He had grown tired of the assignment, of the battles between Henry and the boy as well as his own, and wanted the entire matter to be over. The mission, which appeared simple at the beginning, had become one of the most unprofessional jobs he ever encountered, and the sooner it was over, the better he would feel. "Great," he replied, upon hearing an answer which seemed to please him as he continued his conversation on the phone. "Relax will you, Steven's fine," Kirk repeated once more before concluding his conversation.

"Aren't you, kid?" he asked, tapping Steven on the forehead. "If you're going to pretend to be unconscious, try not to flicker your eyes so much, it's a dead give away."

"Fine! I'm awake!" Steven replied in defiance, pulling away from Kirk as he spoke. "Does that mean Henry's going to be in here any minute to drug me again?"

"That's up to you, kid," Kirk answered. "If you plan on giving us anymore trouble, then I'm sure he'll be happy to oblige." He continued checking the handcuff which kept the boy his prisoner. "But you won't do that will you?" he asked, yanking at the cuff as he spoke.

"Me, trouble! No way," Steven lied, trying not let on Kirk's actions were causing him pain.

"Good! Let's just hope you mean that."

"How long have I been asleep?" Steven asked, trying to get a sense of time.

"For about twenty-four hours," Kirk replied.

"Twenty-four hours," Steven echoed relieved that no more than a day had passed since, they left the clinic. "My father, is he…"

"He's fine as far as I know," Kirk said.

"As far as you know?" the surprised boy replied.

"We're on a schedule, kid, and as far as daddy dearest is concerned, he still isn't aware of what kind of trouble you've gotten yourself in," Kirk announced, his words surprising Steven even more.

"You haven't contacted my father yet? Why? What are you waiting for?"

"The right time and place," were the only words, Kirk would reveal to the boy.

"Time and place for what?" Steven demanded to know.

"Why, for the plan to work," Kirk said, teasing the boy with each word as he spoke only enough to induce more questions.

"Plan, what plan?" Steven asked, sitting up in the bed as he spoke to his captor.

"Let's just say your father is a very important man and he going to help me earn several million dollars as a result of that."

"Several million dollars," Steven said, once more stunned by what he was hearing. "Please, tell me what you're going to make him do?"

"Sorry, kid, no can do," Kirk announced. "But if your father loves you half as much as I suspect he does, he will do whatever it takes to get you back alive."

"Why are you doing this? For the money?"

"That pretty much covers it, kid."

"But I thought you were friends of my father and Uncle Mark, how could you have turned on them like this?"

"What makes you think I have turned against anyone?" Kirk said with a teasing tone in his voice.

"What do you mean by that?"

"Sorry, kid, can't tell you anything else right now." Kirk laughed.

"What the hell is going on?" Steven shouted, no longer afraid of the man who held his life in his hands. Kirk had implied several times that either his father or uncle were somehow involved in what was happening to him, yet he refused to tell him what he meant by his critical words. "Why don't you just tell me who you are working for and stop with these damned games," he cried out.

"But the games are half the fun."

"Damn it, Kirk, tell me what is going on."

"Maybe later," Kirk announced as he headed for the door.

"Wait!" Steven shouted.

"Now what?"

"Can, you..." Steven started, hesitating to finish the conversation.

"Can I what?"

"Can you take the cuffs off for a little while?" Steven pleaded, his arm aching from being confined for so long.

"Now why should I do that?" asked Kirk. "You've already tried to escape once, and if I set you free, you might try again."

"I swear I won't," Steven begged. "Please, my wrist is numb from the cuffs."

"All right, kid," Kirk said. "Just remember if you pull anything, I'll stick Henry on you again."

"I'll remember," Steven replied. The threat scared him more than he cared to admit.

Thanking Kirk for allowing him some freedom, Steven's excitement at being able to move around was quickly diminished as his captor explained the windows were nailed shut.

"Can you leave the door open, so I can hear the TV?" Steven asked. "It's so lonely in here and at least the sounds coming from the other room will make it seem like I am not completely alone."

"Fine!" Kirk snapped, not wanting to do anything else for the boy. The last thing he needed was to see his captive as a human being, someone with feelings. The assignment was too important to allow personal feelings to get in the way.

"Thanks," Steven said as he watched Kirk leave the room without saying another word. Waiting silently with the door opened, Steven hoped his own fears of retaliation would not be a deterrent in his plans. If he were going to escape, he needed to do something soon or it would be too late. Slipping off the bed, his eyes fixed on the door and the voices he could hear from the distance, Steven moved towards the door.

Taking his time, careful of each move he took, he moved past the door into the hallway, hoping he would find another room to use as an escape route. Praying as he made his way down the hall that Kirk did not nail the other windows shut as well.

Pausing for a moment, the sound of Henry's voice sending a chill through him, Steven thought about the threats Kirk made earlier. As frightened as he was of what might happen should he be caught trying to escape again, he knew he had to take the risk. Taking a deep breath, he moved his hand along the rim of a nearby door and slowly turned the knob. Sighing, relieved to find it was unlocked, he hoped the rest of his quest would be just as easy. Checking once more to make sure he had not been discovered before moving into the room, he carefully closed the door before rushing towards the window. *I am going to make it*, he thought to himself, finding the path free from any security devices. He was going to find a way to help his father.

Crawling through, grateful this time his avenue of escape was on the first floor and not a hotel balcony, Steven made his way down a small roadway leading to the woods surrounding the house. Turning back once more, the frightened boy started running towards the woods. Though he did not know where he was or how to get off the property, Steven did not care. Freedom was within his grasp and he was savoring every minute of it.

Hurrying towards the woods as he searched for a way out, he suddenly felt the hairs on the back of his neck stand on end, as he heard Kirk's voice. Though off in the distance, it was loud enough to let him know his escape had been discovered.

"Steven, don't be stupid," the man yelled angrily, firing a warning shot at the boy.

"Oh god!" he cried out, running for cover as another shot rang out. No longer confident of his escape, Steven wondered if maybe he should surrender before he found himself in more trouble. It was obvious Kirk would do anything, including shooting him, to keep him from escaping and this terrified the boy.

"No! Damn it," he shouted, as he got up from behind the tree he was using as cover. He was not going to let them win. He was free and there was a chance he could still get away. Running faster, as he tried not to let the sound of Kirk's voice weaken his resolve, Steven stumbled over a small branch in his path as it sent him tumbling down a nearby hill.

"Dad!" he moaned. The pain from his injured arm was agitated by the new injuries he felt as he laid at the bottom of the hill. "Please Dad, help me," he continued, struggling to his feet. He could not give up, not now, no matter how much pain he was in. "Which way? Which way?" he cried, looking around at the vast estate he was on. He did not know the way out, and if he were not careful, he could end up running right back into his captor's hands.

"There!" The sight of a large steel gate a few yards ahead of him gave him renewed hope. "Damn! No!" he snapped. The gate was double bolted shut. "Please, someone help me," he uttered, leaning against the gate, the feeling of defeat overpowering him. No matter what he did, which way he turned, something was always there to stop him.

"Hold it," a voice behind him ordered, as Steven turned to see a guard pointing a gun at him. "Where do you think you are going?" the guard asked, radioing he'd captured the prisoner.

"Please, don't turn me over to them," Steven said, moving slightly closer. "You have no idea what they will do to me."

"Not my problem, kid," the man replied, as Steven's sudden actions caught him as well as the boy himself off guard.

Striking the guard with a kick he learned in Karate class, Steven was grateful his father insisted he take the class as a child. Another blow sending the man reeling to the ground in pain, Steven looked at the man struggling to get out. "Sorry," he remarked as his final blow incapacitated the man completely. "On second thought," Steven said, tossing the unconscious man's gun into the woods, "I'm not sorry." It felt good to strike back for a change, and he was not sorry for his actions at all.

"Damn it! No!" Steven snapped, after searching the man for a key to the locked gate.

It was like a conspiracy, every step he took he found another obstacle awaiting him. The guard did not have the key to unlock the gate and Steven found himself still searching for a way out. "Great! Now what do I do," he said, pulling at the gate once more in frustration. His captors would be there any moment thanks to the earlier report from the guard, and if he did not figure something out soon, everything would be lost.

Distracted for a moment by a sound from beyond the gate, Steven's eyes lit up as he saw a car making its way down the mountain path towards the house. If he could get the car to stop to help him before the others arrived, then maybe he could escape.

"Stop! Please stop," he yelled waving his arms as the car drew closer.

"What the hell?" the driver said, slamming on the brakes as she pulled up to the gate. "What is it? What's wrong?" she asked running from her car.

"Please help me, they're trying to kill me," Steven tried to explain, relieved to find the young Italian woman spoke English.

"Kill you? What! Who?" the young woman repeated, looking over Steven's shoulder as she noticed two men drawing nearer. "Are they the ones trying to kill you?"

"Yes!" Steven announced. "Please, you have to help me before it's too late."

"But how?" she asked, realizing the gate was bolted.

"No wait!" he shouted in desperation as she turned and ran back to her car without saying a word to the young man standing there. "Please don't go."

"Get out of the way," she yelled, shifting the gears into drive as she floored the gas pedal in an attempt to break through the gate. If she was going to help the boy, the first thing she needed to do was get the gate opened and using her car was the only thing she could think of. "Get in," she ordered, her actions surprising not only her but the boy too as he jumped into the car obeying her orders. "Damn and I just bought this car," she said, looking over at the boy as she yelled at him about the damage done to her vehicle. "You owe me a new car."

"Fine, I'll get you one just as soon as we get out of here, now move," he shouted as the men drew near enough now to see faces.

"Hang on," she ordered before looking back at the men approaching them. The expressions reflected in her rear view mirror were enough to send chills down her spine.

"I'll get the car and go after them," Henry began, as he turned to head back to the house.

"Don't bother," Kirk replied, putting his gun away as he spoke. As far as he was concerned following them was unnecessary, the boy was still within their reach and a few phone calls would secure him for them once more.

"What?" a stunned Henry replied. "Are you nuts? The boy is getting away, and if the man finds out we lost him, we are as dead as those medics."

"Trust me, no one is going to know about this little mishap, and we will have the boy back in our hands in a matter of hours," Kirk assured him, as he walked towards the house.

"Whatever you say," Henry finally conceded, not sure what his partner was up to, he had little choice but to follow his instructions. It was obvious Kirk knew something about the driver he did not and felt confident in time they would be able to use that fact to their advantage.

Leaning back in the front seat as they drove further and further away from the house, Steven closed his eyes for a moment as he felt a sense of ease coming over him. It was the first time since the nightmare began he felt safe, felt things might actually work out for him and his father.

"Thank you," Steven remarked, turning to the young woman who had just risked her life to help him.

"No sweat," she uttered, "I always wanted to come to the rescue just like in a Mel Gibson movie," she joked with her young companion, as they continued up the mountain pass.

"Mel Gibson huh?" Steven laughed.

"He's a babe, and if anyone can make you feel safe, it's him," she said, her admiration for the actor apparent.

"Well, Mel, thanks for helping me get away from those men," Steven repeated.

"Like I said, no sweat, who where those guys anyway?" she asked.

"My kidnapers," Steven replied, his words causing her to slam on the brakes of the car as she pulled off the road.

"Your what?"

"Those men kidnaped me, and I was escaping when you showed up," Steven explained.

"They kidnaped you and you were escaping?" she began. "Boy, do I know how to step in it."

"Sorry!" Steven said.

"What the hell? What's life without stepping into a little shit now and then." She laughed.

"Right," Steven replied, staring at the amazing woman sitting next to him. She just risked her life for a total stranger and was joking as if they'd taken a walk through the park.

"Well, you are safe now," she remarked, shifting the car into gear as she spoke. "Mel to the rescue."

"I wish," Steven said under his breath. Until the men after him were caught and their employer exposed, Steven knew he would never be safe again. "Look, I appreciate the help and your company, but I need to talk to the cops right away," Steven explained as the young woman listened to him without saying a word. "I need you to take me to the nearest police station right away."

"Sorry, I can't do that," the young woman announced as she headed away from the road through a side path leading into the hills.

"What! What do you mean you can't take me to the police?" Steven protested. "Don't you understand those men are kidnapers, killers and they are after us?"

"Yes, I understand more than you know, but I still can't take you," she tried to explain as Steven looked at her in disbelief. "But relax mi a'more, I know a place where you'll be safe."

"Safe! I'll be safe at the police station!" Steven said. "Why did you risk your life to help me if you weren't going to take me to the police?"

"Look, I don't have a choice, but I promise you'll be safe at my cottage."

"Your cottage! I do not want to go to your cottage! I want to go the police station," Steven continued, as he tried to open the door while the car was still moving.

"Are you insane?" the woman snapped, slamming on the brakes to keep the boy from falling out.

"Well, if you aren't going to help me, then I'll find another way," Steven began stepping out of the car as he spoke.

"Listen to me," she said, running after him. "I can help you. I have friends who will make sure you're safe, but I can't take you to the police."

"Why?" Steven demanded to know.

"Because," she hesitated, "because I'm wanted by the police."

"You're wanted? For what?" Steven said, wondering what he had gotten himself into this time.

"It is not like I killed anyone or anything like that," she began, noticing the look of apprehension on his face.

"Glad to hear that," Steven replied.

"It's just I grew up in this area and my uncle is the local constable, and well, I just can't let him be the one to put be behind bars," she continued. "It would kill my family if that happened."

"Look, I'm sorry you're wanted and your uncle lives nearby, but I don't have time for this." Steven reiterated, "I have to get to the police and find my father before those men have a chance to hurt him too. I'm sure once the police realize you risked everything to help me, they'll do whatever they can to help you too."

"Listen, why don't we do this?" she said as they sat in the car. "I'll take you to my cottage and call a friend and they can come get you."

"And then?" Steven questioned.

"And then they can take you to the police."

"You promise to call someone to come get me?"

"Yes, I promise," she replied.

"How long will it take?" he asked.

"My cottage is about thirty minutes or so from here," she began. "Once I get hold of my friend, you should be at the police station within an hour or so," she promised, as the look in Steven's eyes convinced her he was contemplating her plan as an option he could live with.

"All right." He finally agreed. Whether he liked it or not she was his only hope. They were almost twenty miles from the local police and he could not risk being caught on his own by the man pursuing him. At least with the plan his rescuer was suggesting, he would have a chance. She knew the area and would be able to hide him from Kirk and Henry until he could talk to the police.

"Great," she replied. "So, handsome, do you have a name?"

"Name!" Steven repeated.

"Yes, a name, I can't go on calling you handsome." She laughed.

"Steven, Steven McCormick," he answered, embarrassed until that moment he had not realized he did not know his savior's name either.

"Well, Mr. McCormick, I'm Helena Royster. Nice to meet you."

"You, too," he answered, shaking hands with the young woman.

"The house is right up this hill," she said to him, "and you'll see once we're there, everything will be all right."

"I hope so!" Steven began as they pulled into a little cottage hidden away by the trees. "Nice place," Steven said as they pulled up to the house.

"Thanks, it belongs to my uncle." She laughed.

"Your uncle the cop? I thought you said the cops were looking for you?"

"They are but that doesn't mean I can't use his place when I'm in town."

"You like to take risks, don't you?" Steven inquired finding himself more and more intrigued by the woman he was with.

"You better believe it," she replied. "Besides he only uses the cottage once a year for vacation and the rest of the time it's empty."

"And when is vacation time?" Steven asked.

"Oh, I don't know, I think it's normally around this time."

"Like I said, you like taking risks," he repeated as they both laughed. "By the way, exactly what are you wanted for?"

"For taking risks," she replied, explaining her offenses though criminal, had never been violent in any way.

"Glad to hear that," Steven replied.

"I am what a lot of people call a working girl and that tends to get me into trouble with the police."

"A working girl?"

"Yes," she said, looking at her young friend as they stood in front of the door. "Does that change your mind about going inside with me?"

"Should it?" Steven said. He did not care about her past or the fact the police were after her. The only thing he knew was she risked her life to save him and he trusted her. "What you do with your life is none of my business."

"Thanks," she replied. "A lot of people wouldn't feel that way."

"Well, a lot of people would not have risked their freedom or their lives to help a stranger, and that holds more with me than what is considered proper in society's eyes," he assured her as they walked in the cottage.

The house situated miles from civilization was the kind of place you expect to find in a vacation brochure. Hidden by a field of trees, close to a small to a stream, it was the perfect picture of a tranquility.

Looking around as Helen told him to make himself comfortable, Steven felt safe within the walls of the home, he had just entered. Whether it was the because he knew the home belonged to a police officer or because the old antiques and cozy little knickknacks touched his soul, Steven felt as if he was home and it was a good feeling.

"Can I get you anything?" Helena asked as she tossed her purse on the nearby couch.

"No thanks," Steven answered.

"Well, you make yourself comfortable while I change," she said, walking towards the bedroom.

"You have clothes here too?" Steven asked.

"Of course. What fun it would be to stay here if I didn't have anything to wear?"

"I know it's part of the game, the risk taking right," Steven uttered. "You leave your own clothes mixed in with your uncle and his family's."

"Of course," she replied. "Between cousins and aunts, there are so many of us that Uncle Hans would never notice my things."

"Uncle Hans, that doesn't sound Italian."

"It's not, he's from Switzerland. My aunt is the Italian half of that family."

"Oh, I see," Steven shouted as Helena continued to tell him about her family from the bedroom.

Helena Royster, in her mid-twenties was your typical free spirit with her own ideas about life and what she wanted from it. A raven-haired beauty, she stood picturesque in her manner with her long slender legs and petite frame. Raised by her parents to believe life was a game, she lived each day as if it were her last, determined not to let the restraints of the world's morality keep her from enjoying what all it had to give her.

"Can you call your friend?" Steven said, reminding her of the promise she had made earlier.

"I'm doing that right now," she yelled, still in the bedroom. "Hello! Yes, it is me," she began, trying not to talk loud enough for her young friend to hear her. "I'm at the cottage and I need you to come here right away," she continued. "Yes, I understand but just hurry will you," she concluded before walking back into the room to find Steven sitting on the couch staring out the window. "Help is on the way."

"Thanks," Steven said, turning to face her, stunned by what he saw.

"Now you can relax," she remarked, smiling at Steven reaction to her attire.

Dressed only in a man's shirt which barely covered her thighs, Helena pulled the pin from hair as it fell below her waist.

Staring at the woman standing before him, Steven had not realized until that moment how beautiful she was.

"Thanks," she replied, his eyes revealing she had gotten the reaction she wanted from him. "Are you sure you don't want a drink?'

"I'm only seventeen," Steven said, regretting the words which just came from him. The last thing he wanted was to appear like a child in this woman's eyes.

She was beautiful, and he found himself very attracted to her.

"I won't tell if you don't." Helena laughed, giving him a glass of wine.

"Thanks," Steven replied as he took a sip of the drink. "You are beautiful."

Helena laughed, as he started to choke from the effects of the alcohol. "I guess you don't drink too much Italian wine at home," she started to say as Steven finally joined in with her laughing at himself in the process.

"Not really," he said.

"Why don't you take your shirt off?" she uttered, her words causing him to choke once more.

"My what?"

"You're covered in cuts," Helena explained, still amused by the innocence of her new friend. "I want to clean those cuts before they get infected."

"Oh, ok, " Steven replied removing his shirt, exposing the many bruises on his body.

"Boy, someone really worked you over, didn't they?" she whispered before gently rubbing the warm cloth along his shoulders.

"Reminders from my kidnapers as to who was in charge," Steven explained the warmth of the cloth and her touch causing him to shiver.

"I'm sorry you were put through this," she began, ushering him to lay back on the couch as she continued to clean his wounds. "Why were you kidnaped?" she asked. "Is your father someone famous?"

"Someone famous? I guess he could be considered someone famous," Steven said, recalling the story his uncle told him in Washington about his father's past.

"My father is a diplomat, and the kidnapers are trying to force him to do something illegal," Steven continued, stirring as he felt Helena's hand on his belt buckle. "I was the bargaining chip." He began looking at her as she undid the belt first and then his pants.

"It's ok," she giggled as she unbuckled his belt. "I just want to make you more comfortable."

"Comfortable, yea right!" Steven stumbled with his words. He was feeling a lot of things with each touch, but comfortable was not one of them.

"Rest," she ordered, as she moved her fingers along his chest, no longer holding the cloth in her hand as she did.

"I…" Steven said, her touch growing more sensuous with each moment.

"You what?" she whispered before kissing the startled man.

Pushing her away for a moment, Steven stared at the woman sitting next to him on the couch.

"Why are you doing this? You don't even know me," Steven asked, curious as to why she was willing to get so intimate with him.

"Do you want me to stop?" she asked, taking her hands away from his inner thigh.

"I… No! " he answered. He didn't want her to stop. No matter what her reasons were, he did not want the moment to end.

"I was hoping you'd say that," she replied.

"You're not doing this because you feel sorry for me?" Steven asked.

"Not in a thousand years," she said before kissing him.

"You're not doing this because I am a hooker?" she asked, kissing him once more as her fingers moved slowly down his chest.

"No, I would never," Steven tried to say without sounding more naïve.

"Then relax," she instructed her young man as she took her shirt off, standing before him completely naked. Though he were neither a friend or client, Helena felt herself drawn to him and wanted him to know just what she was feeling. "I promise not to do anything to make you sorry for coming here," she said as she bent down kissing him once more while she moved her hand gently along his inner thigh.

Responding to her every touch, Steven no longer felt scared or alone as the two strangers finally made love.

Lying next to her lover on the floor, Helena moved her hand along his shoulder as they remained in each other's arms. It had been along time since someone made love to her with such passion and she found herself overwhelmed by it.

"Are you all right?" she asked, touching the cast on his arm as he stirred a little.

"I'm fine," he replied. He had forgotten about the pain and found his thoughts were only her. Everything was perfect; he was safe and in the arms of a beautiful woman, and for a little while the nightmare was over.

"Hi, honey, I'm home!" a voice from behind them shouted as the door busted opened.

"Henry, but how?" cried Steven as he jumped from the floor without realizing he was still naked.

"Well, glad to see you found something to amuse yourself till we got here," Henry joked, tossing Steven his pants as he spoke.

"But how?"

"How did we find you?" Henry laughed, looking over at Helena as he spoke. "You can thank lover over there for that, she called us," he replied.

"What!" the stunned boy answered, looking over at the woman he just made love to. "That's a lie. What would she call you? She doesn't even know you."

"Wrong!" Henry laughed, striking Steven in the stomach as his blow sent him falling into the couch crying out in pain. "You see, you little punk, Helena and Kirk are old friends and he recognized her at the house," Henry continued, grabbing Steven by the hair, this time striking him in the face.

"Stop it! " Helena shouted, "Leave him alone."

"Now, lover, you really didn't think when we arrived it would be a happy reunion, did you?" Henry balked, turning back to strike Steven again. "This little brat has embarrassed me twice already with his actions and he has to understand it is not going to happen again."

"I said stop it," she yelled once more before turning to the second man standing before them. "Kirk, don't let him hurt the boy like that, do something to stop him," she ordered.

Her words caused Steven more pain than the blows he received. It was obvious from the way she addressed Kirk that Henry was telling the truth, and she did know the man.

"Why should I help the brat?" Kirk replied. "I agree with him." Kirk answered without intervening, still smarting from the boy's ability to trick him into undoing the handcuffs in the first place with his innocent victim act.

"Damn it, Kirk, stop him," Helena shouted angrily, lunging towards the man.

"Alright," he finally agreed as he instructed his partner to leave the boy alone. "I think he got the message," he remarked.

"Well, I don't," Henry snapped, grabbing Steven once more.

"Henry, enough!" Kirk yelled, no longer interested in the boy or Helena, only in making sure his orders were obeyed. "Unless, of course, you want to explain to the man how his prize possession got so many bruises."

"Alright," Henry agreed, releasing Steven as he fell against the couch still reeling from everything happening around him.

"You set me up. This whole time you promised to help me you were setting me up to be captured again," he uttered, trying to stand as he moved towards Helena.

"No, I swear, it wasn't like that," Helena vowed, moving closer to him.

"Did you figure I was worth more to them than to the cops, is that why you called and told them where we were?" he argued. "Is that why you insisted on bringing me here? You figured they'd pay more."

"No! That's not why I did it," Helena cried.

"Then why?" Steven screamed, grabbing the woman he just made love to. "Why did you do it?"

"I never meant for this to happen, I didn't have a choice. I had to call them," she tried to explain.

"Yea right," Steven balked. "Were they holding a gun to your head that I didn't see while we were making love?" Steven asked sarcastically. "Or are you and Kirk still lovers and you want to keep him happy by turning me over to him?"

"Steven, I swear that is not it."

"Then why? Why did you do it?"

"Go on, sweetheart, tell the brat the truth!" Henry joked.

"Damn you, Henry, leave it alone," Helena ordered. She did not want to cause Steven anymore pain and knew learning the truth would do just that.

"Tell me," Steven shouted. "I have the right to know what is going on."

"Why don't you ask her again? Maybe she will tell you what she has been doing for the last few weeks." Henry laughed, finding himself enjoying the torment in the boy's eyes more than he did giving him the earlier beating.

"Leave it alone," Kirk ordered. He was not interested in listening to this battle of words, the boy was secured again and that was the only thing that mattered.

"Oh come on," Henry argued, "the kid deserves to know his lover was hired to help set up his father in this little game we are playing," Henry announced.

"My father!" Steven mumbled. "What does my father have to do with this?"

"Don't you get it, kid?" Henry began. "Why do you think she was on that road by the estate in the first place? She was on her way to meet with Kirk."

"Kirk!" Steven repeated. "But you helped me get away. If you were going to see Kirk, then why would you help me?"

"I didn't know you were running from Kirk till I saw him approach the car," Helena finally confessed. "I just saw someone in trouble and I wanted to help."

"You knew I was on the estate where Kirk was supposed to be, didn't you wonder about that?" Steven demanded to know still finding her story hard to believe. "Or was that the plan the whole time, you figured if I went with you, I would not be able to find help somewhere else. Was that it, were you just pretending even then to be helping me?"

"He's on to you now." Henry laughed.

"Oh shut up," Helena ordered. "I didn't know you were their captive, I figured you worked for Kirk and something went wrong at the house." She tried to explain as the three men looked on. "It wasn't until you said you were kidnaped that I realized just how deep I had gotten myself into this mess. I didn't know what else to do but get you to the cottage."

"So you helped me escape and called Kirk just so you could turn me back over to him?" Steven asked as another thought came to him. "My god, is that why you made love to me, to keep me here till he arrived?"

"No, Steven, that is not why I made love to you," Helena argued. "I wanted to make love; it had nothing to do with the job."

"You lying whore, do you expect me to believe that now?" he replied, refusing to listen to anything she had to say.

"I never meant to hurt you, Steven, I swear." She wept, her words falling on deaf ears as Steven pushed her away several times.

"And what about my father, what about him? What did you mean to do to him?" Steven yelled, feeling the rage in him growing with each breath he took.

"That was just a job," she tried to explain.

"A job?" Steven replied, "What did you do to my father?"

"Let me tell him," Henry said, interrupting the conversation so he too could have some fun with the distraught boy. "In order to make the crime your father is going to commit look more genuine, Helena was hired to make it appear as they were lovers and have been for years," Henry continued as he moved closer to the boy. "You see, kid, nothing makes a man look guiltier than a working woman on the side who he's willing to do anything for, including treason and murder."

"What!" was the only word Steven could get out as he felt like he wanted to throw up. He just made love to someone plotting to destroy his father and he was sickened by the very thought of it.

"Steven!" Helena tried to say as he turned away from her.

"What was she supposed to do to my father?" he finally asked. His question was directed at Henry this time as Steve desperately searched for answers from his tormentors.

"Sorry, can't tell you that," his tormentor announced.

"The only way she could have convinced the police of my father's involvement with her was if he wasn't around to argue the point," Steven began as another thought came to him. "You...you were going to kill my father too, weren't you?"

"No, Steven, that wasn't part of my plan," Helena said. She was willing to do a lot of unspeakable things for money but murder wasn't one of them.

"Maybe it wasn't a part of your plan." Henry laughed.

"I never wanted anything to do with murder," she insisted as she took Steven's hand. "I swear, I never knew about any murder."

"And you think that matters?" Steven shouted, pulling away again. "You were willing to set my father up, willing to make it look like he was capable of murder and you think anything else you did mattered."

"Steven, I am sorry."

"Just get away from me," he ordered, moving towards the door.

"Is that anyway to talk to your lover?" Henry laughed.

"You bastard," Helena said.

"As much as I enjoy this game, it's time to go," Henry announced as he threw a kiss in Helena's direction. "Come on, kid, let's get out of here," he ordered as he cuffed Steven's hands together again.

"Whatever!" Steven replied, the fight going out of him. His kidnapers had already revealed enough for him to know things were only going to get worse. Mark had to be dead, his father didn't even know he was missing, and the one friend he thought he found was just another lie in the nightmare he found himself in. He had no where to turn and suddenly freedom felt farther from his reach than ever before.

"Steven, please," Helena began, trying one last desperate bid to make him understand.

"I didn't know the man I was hired to set up was your father, it was just another job, and I needed the money."

"And that's supposed to make it all right," Steven shouted. "You were willing to destroy an innocent man's life, and you didn't care about that till you found out who he was?"

"Steven, please!" Helen tried.

"Leave me alone," Steven repeated, walking out the door with Henry while Kirk remained behind.

"The plan is still a go, do you understand?" Kirk said, "Don't blow it, or the boy will suffer even more."

"Please don't hurt him."

"That is up to you," Kirk replied before heading out the door to join the others.

CHAPTER EIGHT

Awakened by the ringing of the phone, Andrew shook the drowsiness of sleep from his system as he reached over the night stand to answer the phone.

"Hello," he began, praying whoever was on the other end had news of his son. It had been several days since he learned that Steven left the safety of the school only to end up the victim of a kidnaping, yet he still had not received any word from the people responsible for taking his son. It was obvious to him from the lack of communication from the kidnapers that they were playing some type of game with him and his son was just a pawn in the deadly match.

"Hello," he repeated, still waiting for someone on the other end to respond.

"What? Yes, this is Andrew McCormick. Who is this?" he questioned, the voice on the other end slightly familiar to him. "Who? Hans. Hans Ferrier," Andrew replied upon learning it was his old friend from the local police department.

"Hans, how are you?" he began, trying not to give himself away as he hoped the call from his friend had nothing to do with his son. Whenever he visited Rome, the two men made it a point to get together and Andrew hoped the reason for his friend's call now was nothing more than an attempt now for them to meet during this trip as well. "Your office, what for?" he asked, his heart breaking as his worst fears that his friend had learned the truth about Steven and was calling him on the carpet for his betrayal. "Sure, I guess I can come down, say in about forty minutes or so," Andrew replied as he continued to question his friend. "Can you at least tell me what this is all about?"

"When you get here," Hans replied.

"Fine," Andrew whispered to himself after Hans hung up abruptly.

Did he know about Steven? Andrew wondered as he finished the cup of cold coffee he had left on the table and hurried to meet with his friend. If he had discovered the identity of the kidnaped boy and knew it was Steven, then asking him to meet at the office rather than talk over the phone would make a lot of sense to him.

Grabbing his gun, Andrew felt a sense of what was to come looming over him as he secured it in its holster. Even though he kept the weapon in his suitcase whenever he traveled, this was the first time in nearly ten years that he would actually be carrying it with him on a mission. Surprised to find as he put his jacket back on how comfort the holster felt strapped to his shoulder as something about being armed again gave him a sense of ease he had not felt in days. Like an old friend who had come home, the weapon was finally back where it belonged. Rushing towards the police station nearly twenty-five minutes from Rome, Andrew hoped whatever Hans had waiting for him would not necessitate the use of the weapon. Despite how normal it felt, he was not sure he could use it if he had to.

Staring at the pictures of the dead men as he waited for Andrew to arrive, Hans hoped the final body count would not get any higher before he found the people responsible for turning his small town upside down with the rash of violence surrounding it. In a matter of days four men had been killed and their deaths were somehow connected to the botched kidnaping. Yet, as he stared at the artist's sketches of the three men involved with the boy, he could not help but sense he recognized at least one of the men and this bothered him. If he knew the kidnaper, he wondered if he knew the victim of the crime as well.

"Who are you?" he said aloud, this time looking at the sketch of the boy. "Why are you so important these men would kill four people to keep you from escaping?" he asked, talking to the photograph of the boy as if he were sitting in a chair next to him.

"Lieutenant," a young officer said, walking in on Hans as he continued to stare at the composite sketch of the boy.

"What is it? Have you found anything?" Hans asked.

"Not much," the officer confessed as he sat down to discuss the case with his superior. "We are still waiting for the prints to come back from the hotel room but so far nothing more definite on the boy's identity. The hotel register had a name of a father and son staying in suite 22, but we have already determined the names were bogus and they will lead us nowhere."

"We should be able to come up with more at the hotel," Hans said, lighting himself a cigar as he spoke. "It is obvious from the events which occurred at the hotel the kidnapers did not have time to cover their tracks. There has to be more than just a few prints."

"I agree, sir, but there doesn't seem to be," Knoff confessed. "The items left behind in the room were just some clothes and toiletries, there was nothing personal, no passports or IDs of any kind."

"Has anyone figured out what happened at the hotel?" Hans asked, though he had his own theory.

"From what we've learned so far, it looks like the boy was trying to escape his kidnapers when he fell from the veranda," Knoff explained, fixing himself a cup of coffee as he spoke. "What really worries me is the kidnapers," he continued, sitting back down at the desk. "They had to be amateurs, I mean look at the mess they made of everything so far."

"Maybe," Hans replied as he took a couple of puffs from his cigar, "I've seen a lot of strange things in the old days before I came to work here, and this scam might just be what we used to call blindfold."

"Blindfold?" Knoff repeated, curious as to what his supervisor was describing to him.

"Kidnaping someone without him ever knowing he has been kidnaped and this fits the profile," Hans explained. "From what we learned, the kid showed up at the hotel with the suspects and he didn't seem to be in any type of distress, right?"

"Right," Knoff answered.

"So maybe he didn't know he had been kidnaped in the first place. Maybe he went to the hotel believing the men with him were friends, allies."

"Say what?" the confused detective replied.

"Look at it from another point of view," Hans continued. "One of the best ways to keep your opponent off balance is to keep him guessing. If the boy assumed he was traveling with friends, anything they did would seem normal to him including staying at the hotel."

"But if he figured out the truth..." Knoff replied.

"Exactly," Hans said.

"That would explain why he jumped from the veranda," Knoff said, as he became more intrigued with the lieutenant's theory.

"Right," Hans answered his young friend as he continued with his thoughts. "Somehow he learned the truth, that he wasn't traveling with friends, and once he did, he tried to get away," Hans explained. "If the plan was to keep him in plain sight till the right time and then use him as bait in whatever game they were playing, that would explain a lot of other things too."

"Like what?" Knoff asked.

"If this was just a kidnaping for ransom and the plan was exposed the way it has been, do you think they would risk being caught by dealing with both the police and the ambulance crew the way they did at the hotel?" Hans asked his detective.

"Not me," Knoff admitted aloud. "I think I would have bolted the minute he fell and called the mission a bust."

"That's what any kidnaper working for the money payoff would do, but if he were working for a bigger payoff."

"Like?" Knoff asked, curious as to what the payoff could be.

"Well, my friend, that depends on who the boy is and who his parents are," Hans declared. "The payoff could be anything from top government secrets to names and dates of agents working abroad to just about anything worthy of any good agent's pension plan."

"That's why you believe the boy is somehow connected to the diplomatic core," Knoff balked. "If the boy is bait like you said, then one parent or both are being forced to do something other than pay to get him back and that would explain why he is so important to the two men holding him."

"Now you got it."

"That is a little far fetched, isn't it?" Knoff asked, realizing even as he did the answer would be no.

"My young friend, I have seen this scam work on many occasions and it would explain a lot."

"You've seen it or you've participated in it?" Knoff asked jokingly, though he did not expect Hans to reply.

"Let's just say it's part of the job," Hans replied without further explanation. "So is the rest of it," he said, the tone in his voice growing very sober.

"The rest?" Knoff echoed.

"As long as the victim did not know he was just that, a victim, the odds of him getting out alive were in his favor but with this boy…"

"He not only knows about the kidnaping but is a witness to four murders," Knoff answered, this time no doubt in his mind as to what Hans was referring to.

"If we don't figure out who the boy is and find him before it is too late, he is going to end up another victim on our causality list."

"The kid took a big chance trying to get away from his kidnapers," Hans remarked in admiration. "The least we can do is try to make sure he doesn't end up on that list."

"You do have to admit the kid has guts," Knoff agreed. "I don't know if I would have the stuff to do what he did."

"Me either," Hans remarked, "but his actions tell me one thing for sure."

"What's that?" Knoff asked, curious as to what his boss was implying.

"The kid is a fighter and if there is any way he can help us find him, he will," Hans said. "He's been taught by someone who knows the game and he is willing to do whatever it takes to survive."

"Let's just hope he doesn't get himself killed in the process," Knoff remarked as he changed the subject. "Did you reach Andrew yet?"

"Yes, he should be on his way by now."

"How did you know he was in town?" Knoff asked. "Normally, Andrew stops in or calls when he is in Rome, and I haven't seen him, have you?"

"Nope."

"Do you have any idea how long he's been Rome or why?"

"About two weeks from what I've learned," Hans replied as he thought about his friend. Whatever brought Andrew to Rome, it was apparent he did not want his friends at the department to know about it and this worried Hans. His hands were full enough without Andrew bringing more trouble to his town than he already had.

"Well, whatever he's up to, I'm sure it will make things more interesting than they already are." Knoff laughed. "Do you really think he can identify the boy or the sketch we have of the kidnapers?"

"If everyone involved is American as it seems, maybe," Hans replied. Andrew had been in the agency along time and hopefully he would recognize the boy or the others as someone he crossed paths with in the past. If the boy or his parents were somehow connected to the U.S. diplomat agency, then Andrew might be the only hope of identifying them before it was too late.

"And you really think Andrew can help?" Knoff asked.

"Yea, I hope so. I have this terrible feeling we are running out of time."

"Me too," Knoff replied, admitting they needed any lead they could get if the investigation was going to go any further. Even if they did identify the kidnapers through their prints, without an ID on the boy, their hands were tied. "Oh yea," he said as he walked towards the door to go back to his desk, "I almost forgot to tell you, there was a message that came in for you while you were at the coroner's office."

"From who?" Hans asked.

"From Helena."

"Helena!" Hans said with surprise. He heard of the latest warrant put out for her arrest and knew she would never call him unless she was in over her head again in something else. "Did she say what she wanted?"

"No, just said it was urgent," Knoff replied, "and she left a number for you to call."

"Thanks," Hans replied, taking the paper from him. Though he loved his niece dearly, he was not up for one of her dramas at the moment and whatever she was into would have to wait till another time.

"I'll try her later," he said to himself, placing the note in his pocket before turning his attentions back to the investigation on hand. "Why don't you drive over to the forensics office in Rome and see if you can push those guys, along with those prints," Hans began. The results were too important to let anything slip through the cracks. "Make sure you sit on them till it is done and bring me the results as soon as you get them."

"Got it," Knoff replied, "and you?"

"I am going to head back to the house and take a quick shower. Between the accident investigation from yesterday, the kidnaping of this boy, and the meeting with mayor, I need a long hot bath and a cold drink before I start to tackle anything else," Hans admitted.

"What about Andrew?" Knoff asked. "He should be here soon."

"Damn!" Hans uttered. He'd asked Andrew to meet him, but if he didn't take some time to clean up and grab a meal, he would be no good to anyone. "See if you can reach him and have him meet me later. Tell him to make it about a four o'clock, that will give me an hour or so to go home and change."

"Ok, I'll take care of it," Knoff promised. "In the mean time, I baby-sit the guys in forensics."

"If you get anything on the IDs, you call me right away," Hans said before heading to his car in the parking lot.

Hurrying down the road towards his home, Hans berated himself when he realized he had forgotten to call his niece. "Damn!" he uttered, pulling the paper from his pocket with Helena's cell phone number on it. Glancing at his watch, Hans returned the paper to his pocket, he was pressed for time and hoped she would understand the delay when he tried her later.

The house quiet with his wife and kids away, Hans walked over to the answering machine pleased to see the light indicating he had several messages waiting. The kids, away on the same trip with their mother, promised to call him and he looked forward to hearing from them as they filled him in on their adventures each day.

What little story will I find today? he wondered, pushing the button anxious to hear the sound of his children's voices.

Hello Uncle Hans, it's me, Helena. God, I really did it this time. I am in big trouble. I mean big trouble. I swear when I took his job I just figured it was an easy way to make some money. I did not know they were going to kidnap someone and kill all those people. Oh god, Hans, I am so scared and I need your help. I am staying at your cottage! Please come! Uncle Hans, please hurry.

Turning the machine off without listening to the rest of the messages, Hans stood over the table stunned by what he heard. His niece was not calling him for another favor like he thought, but instead for help, desperate help. Somehow she had gotten involved in the very case he was working on and now she too was in danger.

Racing toward the cottage, Hans prayed his delay in contacting Helena would not prove to be a fatal mistake. He adored her as if she were his own, and if anything happened to her because of his behavior, he would never forgive himself.

Moving towards the door, his gun drawn, Hans called out Helena's name several times as he moved past the front entrance into the house. "Helena, it's Uncle Hans. Are you here?" he continued, fearing the worst as his calls continued to go unanswered. "Oh Helena!" he cried, finding his niece lying on the floor next to the couch.

"What did you get yourself into?" he mumbled, leaning down next to her body, the fact of her death very apparent with the blood flowing from the back of her head.

"I'm sorry, my love," he uttered, taking the blanket from the couch as he covered her lifeless body.

"Lieutenant, are you here?" Knoff shouted. He entered the house with his gun drawn, wondering as he moved cautiously past the front door, what he was going to find.

Contacted by his superior to meet him there, Knoff could tell by the tension in Hans' call that Helena had gotten herself into more trouble than usual.

"In here," Hans shouted, as he stood up to and face his officer.

"Lieutenant," the officer said, upon finding his boss leaning over the body of his dead niece. "Helena. But why would anyone kill her?" he mumbled, stunned to find the girl he had had a crush on since grade school lying dead on the floor.

"I don't know," Hans replied. "All I know is somehow Helena got herself caught up in this damned kidnaping mess and it cost her life as well," Hans said, still staring at his niece.

"The kidnaping, the boy, the kidnaping of the boy?" Knoff repeated several times. The words spoken by Hans were the last thing he expected to hear. "But how? Why?"

"I don't know," Han said, turning back to his detective growing agitated with his questions. "Just check the rest of the house and make sure it is secured, then set up a perimeter and contact Rome for the forensics team," he ordered, reverting to investigator mode without saying another word to him about the dead girl lying there.

Determined not to let his niece be another in a long list of murders facing him, Hans was going to put whatever personal feelings he had aside so that he could do his job before that list grew any longer.

"Yes, sir, but what about..." Knoff began.

"It will take the forensics team at least an hour to get here from Rome," Hans replied, cutting Knoff's words off before he could finish. "Until then, we have a job to do and I don't want any mistakes."

"Yes, sir," Knoff replied, turning to walk away. "Lieutenant, I contacted Andrew McCormick after we spoke and asked him to stop here instead of the office," Knoff announced. He assumed Helena's newest problems would tie Hans up for a while and figured the distraction of the kidnaping case would keep the man from tearing into his wayward niece too much. "Do you want me to call him and cancel?" the detective asked.

"No thanks," Hans said, grateful his detective had taken the initiative and contacted Andrew. They would need his help more now than before, and maybe his old friend would be able to provide them with the answers they sought.

"What have we here?" Hans mumbled to himself as he continued to search the living room while his detective checked the rest of the house. *Could we finally be getting a break?* he wondered, carefully taking the glass from under the couch as he placed it in a plastic bag. Maybe if they were lucky the prints on the glass would not be that of his niece but maybe the person responsible for her death.

Arriving at the cottage to find it swarming with police and forensics personnel, Andrew prayed whatever Hans wanted with him, it would not take too long. He still hadn't confirmed one way or another the kidnaped boy was his son and he hated wasting time on anything else without knowing for sure where Steven was.

"Hans," he said, walking in to find the room filled with police as they scoured the house for clues. "What the hell happened here?"

"Andrew," Knoff began, "glad you could make it."

"Nice to see you too," Andrew joked, walking past the young man towards his friend. "Another homicide?" he asked, looking first at Hans and then the dead woman.

"Yes," was the only thing Hans could say.

"Working girl by the looks of her," he began.

"Watch your mouth," Knoff snapped, shoving Andrew. "Helena was his niece."

"His what?" Andrew repeated. Knoff's words the last thing he expected to hear.

He knew about Helena from his relationship with Hans but never met her, she was always off on some adventure or another. The last thing he ever expected was to finally meet her like this. "I'm sorry," he said to his friend as he tried to offer him comfort. "Are you all right?"

"I'll be fine once we find out who killed her," Hans responded.

"Is that why you asked to see me?" Andrew asked, curious as to why they were meeting in the home of a dead girl, no matter who that girl was.

"Not unless you know something about her death," Hans replied.

"Nope, not a thing, sorry," Andrew said. "So why did you want to meet with me?"

"When I called you, it was about the kidnaping case I was working on, I was hoping you could help," he began looking over at the body lying on the floor. "I didn't realize at the time Helena was going to become a part of it too."

"Kidnaping? What kidnaping?" Andrew replied, trying to feign confusion as to what his friend was talking about.

"Come on, even a busy diplomat like yourself takes time to listen to the television," Knoff snipped as he walked back into the living room just in time to hear Andrew's remark. "Surely you've heard about the four men killed yesterday and the teenage boy we believe was kidnaped by the killers."

"That, sure I heard about it," Andrew began. "But I still don't know what it has to do with me?" Andrew replied, relieved his friend hadn't called him there to announce the missing boy too was dead.

"The lieutenant thinks you can help us figure out who the kidnapers are," Knoff began.

"Me? How?"

"The boy and his kidnapers were Americans and you might have better access to finding out who they are then we do," Knoff continued.

"What makes you think that?" Andrew asked.

"Because I think I know them," Hans replied. "And if I do then the connection is the US embassy," he continued as he handed the sketch of the boy to Andrew. "There is something familiar to me about the boy, and I can't figure out why. I thought maybe you might be able to put a name with the face."

Staring at them the drawing of the kidnaped boy, Andrew tried not to let his emotions get the better of him. Until that moment, despite what he believed to be true, he was holding out hope that the boy was not Steven, yet as he looked at the sketch, that last hope slowly slipped away. There was no doubt even as he looked at the drawing, the boy who had been kidnaped and taken from the hotel, was indeed his son.

"I need to talk to you alone," he said, taking his friend's arm as he led him away from Knoff and the other officers in the house. If he was going to let Hans in on his secret, the last thing he wanted was an audience.

"What is it? Do you recognize the boy?" Hans asked as they stood alone by the car.

"Yes, I do, it's Steven," Andrew said. The words choked him as he spoke them.

"Steven who?" Hans replied, not getting the connection between the victims and his friend.

"Steven, my son."

"Your what!" Hans blurted out. He contacted Andrew for help in identifying the kidnaped boy because of his suspicions he was connected to the embassy, but he never expected the identity of his victim would hit so close to home. "The boy in the sketch is Steven. Your Steven," he repeated still finding it hard to believe.

"Yes," Andrew replied. "The boy from the hotel was my son."

"But how? Why?" a confused Hans asked as the case took yet another bizarre twist.

"I wish I knew," Andrew said. "All I know for sure is Steven was the boy at the hotel and now he is in the hands of those murdering bastards," he uttered angrily. "And I have no idea if he is dead or alive."

"Have they made contact with you yet?" Hans' next question.

"No, I haven't heard from anyone."

"Then how do you know it was him?" he asked.

"Mark told me."

"Mark McCormick was at the hotel too?" Hans blurted out, surprised the kidnapers were able to get the boy away from him if Mark were at the hotel at the time of the kidnaping.

"No, he wasn't at the hotel when it happened, he was on his way to see me," Andrew continued. "Mark told me Steven followed him to Rome because he thought I was in trouble," Andrew explained. "They were together at the airport, and he sent Steven to the hotel with the two men he was traveling with for his own safety till he could talk to me."

"Well, he did a bang up job with that, didn't he?" Hans balked. "The two men who were with Steven, what happened to them?"

"They're probably dead too," Andrew replied.

"Great, just what I need more dead bodies," Hans said. "So Mark sent Steven to the hotel and someone kidnaped him, how convenient," he uttered, finding the coincidence of the crime a little too hard to believe.

"I'm not sure what you are implying, but Mark is not to blame. Steven came to Rome to find me after he received word back home that I was in a lot of trouble. The kidnapers must have planted the information to get him here so they could grab him later and things went wrong at the hotel."

"The two men with Mark, do you trust them, could they be involved?"

"I don't know them that well, but Mark trusted them enough to send put Steven in their care so I have to believe they are not involved."

"Great, this damned case gets more complicated by the minute, I now have five confirmed deaths connected to it and maybe two more bodies out there I have not found yet."

"That's the way it looks," Andrew said. "Whatever they want, they are willing to kill anyone who gets in their way without hesitation."

"Including my niece," Hans remarked.

"Including your niece," Andrew echoed, realizing he was not the only one suffering. "How is she connected to this?" he asked, curious as to why Helena would be involved in such a scheme.

"I don't know for sure, but knowing my niece, I figure she got involved for the money thinking it was one thing and when she learned what she was really into, she tried to back out so they killed her."

"Did you find anything in the house to connect her to the kidnaping? Anything that will tell us where my son is being held?"

"No, nothing," Hans admitted. If it had not been for the message on his machine, there would be no evidence linking Helena to the crimes at all.

"Damn. Then I'm right back where I started," Andrew snapped. No matter how hard he fought to keep the professional edge, he needed to fight the men responsible for the nightmare his son was caught up in, the longer they delayed in telling him their demands, the harder it was to keep his emotions in check.

"Do you know have any idea what the kidnapers want?" Hans asked several times before Andrew finally answered him.

"I have no idea what they want or even if my son is alive," Andrew admitted as he began pacing back and forth in front of the car they stood by.

"It has to be connected to the mission that brought you here to Rome," Hans said, hoping Andrew would give him a hint as to what that mission was.

"I can't believe that," Andrew replied. "The mission is a dangerous one but it involves old friends too, I cannot believe they would risk my son's life like this no matter what the stakes."

"What kind of assignment is it?" Hans asked, persisting in his desire to learn what brought Andrew to Rome in the first place.

"I am here to help with the negotiations between President Vega of San Sebastian and his brother Philippe," Andrew finally revealed.

"What kind of negotiations?"

"Philippe has challenged the leadership of his brother claiming he has broken the law by turning the country back into some kind of dictatorial rule, and I am part of a committee who is here to vote on whether the president should be impeached and replaced by Philippe," Andrew explained.

"So both men would have a motive to force your hand," Hans argued, "one brother to keep his power and one brother to gain his."

"I told you they are old friends, and even if they are fighting among themselves, they would never involve my son," Andrew protested.

"We both know when the game is important enough there are no rules and there are no innocent players, just pawns on a chess board."

"I know, but when the rules change and even your friends are your opponents, then it's time to hang up the towel and concede the game before it's too late," Andrew declared.

"Maybe it's time to change the rules," Hans remarked, handing his friend the sketches of the men at the hotel. "These are the photographs of the men at the hotel with Steven, maybe you can see if you recognize them and give us a lead we can finally use," he continued. "I am waiting for some prints from Interpol but maybe you can speed up the process for us."

"That would be nice, a break in this mess for all of us," Andrew replied as he stared at the first of the three sketches Hans gave him.

"By the way, where is Mark now?" Hans asked, curious as to what the man was up to since he left Steven at the hotel.

"He's out looking for leads on Steven and his men," Andrew said as he placed the sketch on the hood of the car. "He has some contacts here in Italy he hopes will be able to help us," he continued staring at the sketch. "This one looks familiar but I am not sure."

"And the other two?" Hans asked.

"Well this one looks like…" Andrew began as he stopped in the middle of his sentence.

"Is everything ok?" Knoff interrupted as he walked towards the two men.

"Fine," Hans said, upset Knoff interrupted Andrew's train of thought as to whom the kidnapers might be. "Did you come up with anything?'

"We found a few things, sir," he announced, before returning to his work. "I'll tag everything and send it back to the office," he said before leaving the two men alone again. Whatever they were discussing was intense, he could feel that, and the sooner he left, the better off he would feel himself.

"What did you see in that sketch?" Hans asked, returning to the question at hand, while he pointed to the one picture that seemed to catch Andrew's eye.

"Is this sketch a joke?" Andrew asked, "I thought you said you didn't know Mark was in town."

"Mark? That sketch reminds you of Mark," Hans echoed several times as he took another look at the face in the picture. "No wonder he looked so familiar to me, it is Mark. He was at the hotel with the kidnapers."

"But that doesn't make any sense, he told me he never made it to the hotel. He said he left the others before then went into the hotel," Andrew argued. "There is no way he would lie to me about that."

"Well, it looks like he did," Hans announced. "According to the people we talked to at the hotel yesterday, Mark was not only in the hotel, but he was in the suite with the others for at least two hours before he left," Hans declared, his words sending chills down Andrew's spine.

"It couldn't have been him," Andrew repeated. "He told me he never made it there. There has to be some kind of mistake. Maybe the witness who gave you this sketch saw him outside the hotel and just assumed he was in the suite."

"I have several witnesses who confirmed this man was in the hotel room, including a maid who was called in to clean up a mess he made after he busted some bottles on the floor," Hans said, filling his friend in on what he knew. "And if he lied about being at the hotel, what else did he lie about?"

"I don't know," Andrew remarked, still to stunned to say much more.

"Andrew, could he be involved in the kidnaping somehow?" Hans asked reluctantly. Though he never liked the man, he found it a little difficult to believe Mark could have turned on his friend and taken the boy.

"I don't know," Andrew repeated. He was not sure about Mark anymore, was not sure about the man who had changed before his very eyes over the years. The man he knew as a child would never be a part of this nightmare, but the man he knew now, he could be a part of anything if it meant the winning edge was on his side.

"I just don't know," Andrew said, once more staring at the picture of his friend.

"Was Steven hurt badly in the fall?" Andrew asked, turning his thoughts back to his son and the events which occurred at the hotel as he continued to look at the sketch.

"From what we learned from the doctor's chart at the clinic, Steven had a broken arm and a few bruises, other than that, he was fine," Hans said.

"He must be so scared," Andrew remarked, thinking about what his son had endured for days at the hands of his kidnapers.

"Strange, don't you think, that two men who did not hesitate to kill so easily, would take the time to make sure Steven was all right," Hans began. "Maybe they are receiving orders from someone else, someone who cares enough about the boy to make sure he did not suffer too much."

"You mean Mark, don't you?" Andrew protested. "But what would be his motive? Why would he turn on not only me but Steven too?"

"That is the sixty-four million dollar question, isn't it?" Hans remarked.

"I'll call you as soon as I hear from Mark," Andrew said, walking towards his car. He did not want to discuss the possibility of his betrayal any further. He needed some time, some space to figure things out, but he knew one thing for certain, even as he fought with his conscience over the news he learned about his friend. If Mark was somehow involved, even the lifetime they shared together would not keep Andrew from killing him. If he endangered his son by bringing the boy back into their world for any reason, Mark would have to pay.

Calling Mark from his cell phone, Andrew needed to know in his own mind his friend was not involved in any way with his son's kidnaping.

"Mark, it's me," he began. "I just wanted to check in and see if you found anything," he said trying to work in a single question, which would alleviate his suspicions.

"Nothing," Mark replied.

"Well, keep in touch with me, and if you learn anything, no matter how small, you let me know," he continued.

"Of course," Mark said, curious as to why his friend was calling him. "Andrew, is there something else wrong?"

"No, it's...Mark, you said you left Steven with Kirk and Henry and you never went to the hotel right?"

"That's right, when we arrived, they took Steven to the hotel and I went to meet with you. Why?"

"The police said there may have been a third man in the hotel and I was just trying to make sure it wasn't you before I try to figure out who the third man was," Andrew lied, listening to his friend on the phone.

"It wasn't me, I never made it there," Mark repeated.

"Thanks. Have you heard from your men yet?"

"Nope, I guess they are dead too," Mark replied with no emotion in his voice as he spoke.

"I'm sorry, I know they were your friends."

"They were incompetents," Mark snapped. "They let what happened at the hotel occur in the first place and they messed everything up for all of us."

"I guess," Andrew said before hanging up with his friend. It was apparent Mark was lying to him, and this was the second time now he had done so. The first lie was when he said Steven was safely at school and he knew he was on his way to Rome and now about being at the hotel. Whatever was going on with his old friend, he knew from now on, he had to be on his guard.

Pulling off to the side of the road as he tried to put the pieces of the puzzle together, Andrew thought about the past he shared not only with Mark but also with the Vega brothers as well. He already suspected one of his former brother-in-laws of some kind of involvement in Steven's kidnaping and it seemed Mark too was connected to it as well. Despite the betrayal he felt surging through him, Andrew could not help but feel a sense of loss as well. He loved all three men, cared for them as brothers and now one or all of them had destroyed that love, the memories they shared, and turned his world upside down.

Rushing towards the police station after a cell phone call from Hans summoned him once more to meet with his friend, Andrew wondered what the urgency of this call meant as far as the kidnaping case. It had not been more than two hours since he left the cottage, and he hoped the news awaiting him now was not bad. There had not been enough time to develop to any new leads and that could only mean one thing as far as Steven fate was concerned.

"Ok, Hans, what's going on?" Andrew asked, walking into the office to find not only his friend but Knoff sitting they are waiting for him.

"Come in and shut the door," Hans said with a tone implying whatever he needed to discuss was very important.

"It's not Steven, is it?" Andrew asked with panic in his voice.

"No!" Hans uttered before turning his attention back to the phone and the conversation he was having on the other end with his supervisor in Rome. "Yes, sir! No, sir. I do not feel it is enough to make an arrest. No, sir, my friendship with the suspect has nothing to do with it. The evidence is still circumstantial and I want to be sure the case sticks before I make any arrests," he continued. "No, sir, I am not letting my personal feelings for Helena cloud my judgment that is why I am trying to wait till there is enough proof to convict. Yes, sir, just as soon as I'm sure," he concluded before hanging up the phone.

"So what's up and why is the brass on your ass already about the case?" Andrew joked. "And just who is this friend you're referring to?" he asked, wondering if Mark might somehow become involved in another mess.

"You know, Knoff is right, you never pay attention to anything more than you want to hear, do you?"

"I found when I don't like what I hear, it is better not to listen. Besides," Andrew said, pouring a cup of coffee as he spoke, "if I listen to what everyone has to say, I would be totally convinced my best friend is guilty of murder and kidnaping and I'm not."

"Yea, that is almost as ridiculous as accusing you of killing Helena, right?" Knoff interrupted.

"Of what!" Andrew replied, looking over at Hans. "Ok, friend, what is boy wonder talking about?" Andrew asked, uncertain if Knoff was teasing him with his words. "I didn't even know Helena, so why would I want to kill her?"

"Is that so, you didn't even know her?" Knoff repeated. "Then can you explain why your name is among her client list."

"Her what?" Andrew repeated. "My name is in her little black book?"

"That's what he said," Hans interjected. "Can you explain why?"

"Got me," Andrew said sitting down in a nearby chair. "Maybe someone else used my name when they visited her."

"Well, then maybe you can explain why your prints were found on the glass we recovered at the cottage?" Knoff sneered, pulling a file from off of Hans's desk as he spoke. "Your prints were positively identified," he continued, tossing the file at his suspect.

"My prints!" a surprised Andrew uttered. "How did my prints get on it?"

"Well, now that is the question we want you to answer, isn't it?" Knoff replied. "So why don't you? How did you prints get on a glass in Helena's cottage?"

"Good question," Andrew remarked, looking at the two men questioning him and the expressions on their faces. "Oh, hold it a minute, you two are serious about this, aren't you?" he argued. "I did not kill Helena. Why would I?"

"Because you had a relationship with her and you found out she was using you to get to your son," Knoff remarked.

"Not bad," Andrew said as Knoff continued to explain his theory to them. "Not bad at all, except for one thing, I did not have a relationship with Helena and I did not kill her," he argued looking over at Hans as he spoke. "You believe me, don't you?" he asked, a little disappointed in his friend not only for suspecting him in the murder but for betraying his confidence and telling Knoff about his son. "I thought you were going to keep what I told you between us," he said as Hans stood up finally ready to say something to both men.

"You know I couldn't do that. I have five maybe seven dead people on my hands and I can't keep anything from my detectives if it is going to help us catch the killers."

"Even if it cost my son his life," Andrew argued.

"We are not fools," Knoff protested. "We will not do anything to endanger the boy; he is our first priority."

"I am glad to see we agree on one thing at least., Andrew said before returning to his seat. "As for Helena, I did not kill her, I give you my word on that."

"And that is supposed to be enough," Knoff replied.

"Enough, Knoff, for now it will have to be," Hans said, not wanting to argue with either of his friends at this point. He wanted Helena's killer found, but just as he told his supervisor earlier on the phone he was not going to jump to any conclusions until all the evidence was in. For now he would assume

Andrew was innocent and work with him on the premise he did not know his niece.

"You said Helena was connected to the kidnaping how?" Andrew asked, after thanking his friend for giving him the benefit of the doubt as far as her death was concerned.

"All we have so far are her own words on my answering machine confessing to being a part of it," Hans revealed. He saved the message earlier and for now it was safely tucked away with the rest of the evidence the case was accumulating.

"Nothing else, she didn't say where they were holding Steven or if he was all right?" the disappointed father asked though he already knew the answer.

"Nothing, I'm sorry," Hans said, trying to console his friend.

"So we are right back where we started."

"Not quite, we still have the prints on the glass," Knoff remarked, refusing to give up on that piece of evidence just yet.

"Again wonder boy, why?" Andrew asked. "If I did find out she was involved in the kidnaping as you say, I would want her alive to answer some questions."

"Maybe it was an accident or maybe self defense, but the way I figure it you found out she was involved and went to see her," Knoff continued. "After all she was your lover, and to learn she helped kidnap your son, well you lost it and in the end killed her."

"That would be great theory except for the fact I did not know Helena in any sense of the word," Andrew argued. "I do not know how my prints got on that glass."

"How about her client list, do you know how your name got there?" Knoff asked, reminding his suspect of the book they found hidden in Helena's house.

"No, I don't," Andrew replied. "Come on, Hans, you know me, you can't believe the way wonder boy does that I killed her."

"That's the problem, Andrew, I do know you," Hans replied. "I know your past and what you are capable of and I know how much you love your son. Whether you and my niece were lovers does not matter, but if you learned she was part of Steven's kidnaping, you would do what had to be done to learn the truth and with the mounting evidence it looks as if you had the motive to do just that."

"I did not kill her," Andrew insisted. "Maybe it was the men that kidnaped Steven, maybe they killed her and set me up to take the fall."

"Not bad," Knoff said, "Except why would they do that?"

"I don't know, more leverage to use against me," Andrew said, grabbing at any slim threat he could for an alibi the others would buy from him.

"That would work except for the prints. How did they get your prints on the glass?" Knoff asked, playing the devil's advocate as he spoke.

"I have no damned idea," Andrew finally snapped.

"Well, that leads us back to you then, doesn't it?"

"Hans, call him off or I swear, friend or not, I will make him sorry he started this," Andrew argued as he moved closer to Knoff

"Like you made Helena sorry," Knoff shouted, refusing to back down.

"Enough!" Hans said, ordering both men to sit down before he had his officers handcuff them both. "I don't need to listen to you two fools carry on like children so sit down and shut up the both of you," he ordered as they complied. "I have enough to deal with, so for now we are going to concentrate on finding Steven first and Helena's killer after that," he announced.

"No matter where we find that killer?" Knoff questioned.

"No matter where," Hans replied, looking at his friend.

"Agreed," Andrew finally said.

"Excuse me, sir," an officer said, walking into the room with a folder. "We found these behind the stove in the victim's cottage," he explained, leaving the evidence with Knoff before closing the door as he left the room.

"And these," Knoff said with anger, throwing the pictures he had just been given on the desk. "Can you explain these?"

"Explain what?" Andrew snapped, looking at the pictures. "I can't," he admitted, staring at photos of himself and Helena in various sexual positions.

"That is you in the photos, isn't it?" Knoff demanded to know.

"I'll be damned!" were Andrew's only words as he continued to look at himself in the pictures.

"Not yet!" Knoff said, retrieving the pictures from his prime suspect. "But from the looks of these you're about to be," Knoff announced.

"I don't know anything about them," Andrew insisted. "Come on, Hans, you can't really believe these photos are for real, can you?" he asked, looking at his friend who remained silent while the verbal battle with the young officer continued. "Obviously, someone is setting me up and they went to a lot of trouble to doctor these pictures."

"So you are insisting you never had an affair with Helena and that isn't you in the pictures?" Knoff asked once more.

"Yes, I am insisting I had never even met Helena before, and as for the pictures, you both know in my world making something look real is very easy to do."

"Maybe so, but why would someone go to so much trouble?" Knoff asked.

"I don't know," Andrew replied. "Just like I don't know why someone would kidnap my son," he continued, growing more angry with the men he spoke to with each breath he took. "Maybe Helena's death had nothing to do with the kidnaping, maybe it was just a client who decided she was too much of liability," Andrew blurted out, wishing he had not as the pain in Hans' eyes grew stronger. "I'm sorry, my friend, I know we are talking about your niece, but I had to say it."

"I know," Hans replied, assuring him they were looking into all the possibilities surrounding Helena's murder.

"Then I am not your only suspect?" Andrew said in relief.

"Just our prime suspect," Knoff interjected.

"Well, wonder boy, you better go back to the drawing board because I did not kill Helena and you still have a murderer running loose in your town."

"And maybe that won't be a problem for long," Knoff argued.

"Great, now I not only have to worry about the Vegas and their mess, the kidnaping of my only child, but also of super cop there trying to nail me to the wall for a murder I didn't commit," Andrew balked. "Damn it, I knew I never should have gotten out of bed this morning."

"Joke all you want, Andrew, but if you did have something to do with Helena's death, none of your quick quips will get you out of this mess," Knoff assured him.

"Look, I am telling you for the last time I did not have an affair with Helena and I didn't kill her," Andrew protested, warning Knoff to back off as he spoke. "Hans, keep junior out of my face before I have to hurt him," Andrew finally said to his friend.

"Quite a temper you have, isn't it?" Knoff laughed. "Easy to see why you killed Helena. She probably pushed the wrong buttons for you too."

"Damn it, don't you listen or are you just so eager to find a killer you don't care who you frame for the crime?" Andrew asked, deciding it was his turn to goat Knoff a little with his own accusations.

"I don't need to frame anyone," Knoff announced. "With all the evidence stacking up against you, it won't be long before I get a warrant for your arrest."

"Evidence, what evidence?"

"Oh, let's see, your prints on the glass, your name in her diary, and oh yea, the photographs, and the fact you don't have an alibi for the time she was killed."

"I was in my hotel room, I told you that," Andrew said.

"Alone right?" Knoff snickered.

"Right, smart ass," Andrew echoed.

"I might be a smart ass, but I think I have enough to take the case to the judge and get a warrant, or at least make sure you don't leave the country for any reason."

"Hans! Do something with this," Andrew said, pointing at Knoff as he spoke. "I have too many things to worry about without being put in a jail cell by an over eager detective trying to make a name for himself," Andrew argued.

"Enough!" Hans shouted. " Whether we have enough circumstantial evidence or not we can't go to the judge till Steven has been found, is that understood?" he announced, looking at his detective when he spoke.

"But what about Helena and the person responsible for her death?" Knoff protested.

"I loved my niece and will do whatever it takes to find her killer, but I will not sacrifice a teenage boy to do it."

"Thank you," Andrew said before sitting back down in his chair.

"Fine, we will hold on the arrest of Helena's murderer till Steven McCormick is found but after that all bets are off," Knoff finally agreed.

"After that, you will finally have the name of the real killer and it won't be me," Andrew said before heading for the door. It was after three o'clock and he was running late for his meeting. "Right now I have a meeting to get to with the Vega brothers. Maybe there I can learn something we can use to find my son," he uttered before heading for his car.

Pulling a bracelet from his jacket pocket, Andrew thought about the day he gave it to his son. A present his mother intended to give him when he turned sixteen, it now bore her name on it as a reminder to the boy of the parent he lost. Never off his wrist, the fact Andrew found it only made things seem so much more final in his heart.

"Damn it," he shouted, slamming his fist against the steering wheel as he drove towards his destination. Why did he let his temper get the better of him? Why did he behave like such an amateur? All he wanted was some answers and now because of his actions Steven was in more danger than before. If he did not start behaving like a professional and instead of a distraught father, his actions could cost more than he was willing to give.

CHAPTER NINE

Making himself comfortable as he sat in the hotel bar, Andrew stared at the glass of whiskey sitting on the table. His mind cluttered with thoughts of his son, he prayed Steven was alright. Nearly forty-eight hours had passed since the incident at the hotel and except for the initial call he received telling him not to contact the police, he had not heard from them in all that time. Whatever the kidnapers wanted from him, they were taking their good old time in letting him know and this worried Andrew more than the constant delays from the president in completing the final summit meeting.

Antonio rescheduled the meeting twice already and Andrew couldn't help but wonder about the connection between his son's disappearance and the delays in his mission.

"Andrew," a voice said several times before he finally looked up to see Mark standing before him. "Are you all right?"

"Mark, what are you doing here?" Andrew asked, still fighting his own doubts about his friend as he stared at the man.

"Where else would I be?" Mark replied. "Have you heard anything from the kidnapers?"

"No!" Andrew snapped, pouring himself another drink "Where have you been for the last two days?"

"Looking for Steven," Mark said, confused by his friend's tone. "Did something happen I should know about?"

"Oh, let me see, I have been accused of murder by the local police, a suspect in murder back home and my son is missing, other than that, nothing much," Andrew remarked sarcastically.

"Ok, fill me in," Mark began. "Who are you supposed to have killed here?"

"A local girl by the name of Helena Royster," Andrew said. "The police found her dead and found my prints in her house."

"Did you know her?"

"Nope, and I told them that."

"So why do they think you killed her?"

"Oh, I don't know maybe the fact my name was in her trick book, or the police found photographs of us together, or maybe just the prints on the glass, take your pick."

"Ouch." Mark laughed. "Did you say her trick book?"

"Yea, she was a local hooker."

"You know how to pick them, don't you?"

"I told you I didn't know her."

"Ok, so tell me who you were supposed to have killed back home?"

"The kid in the records office. Seems he was killed the same night I took the files."

"The kid from records," Mark said, hesitating for a moment. "That is news to me."

"What do you mean, you didn't know?" Andrew questioned, remembering Annie's words that Mark had been put in charge of the investigation as a way of helping him ease back into the field. "You weren't told about it?"

"Nope, Stewart thinks I am still to unstable from by ordeal at the prison camp and I am stuck on medical till he approves my returning to the field."

"Sorry, I thought you were already cleared," Andrew remarked, trying not to let his anger seem apparent to Mark. This was the third lie now he'd caught him in and his apprehensions in believing Mark was involved in Steven's kidnaping was growing weaker with each new lie he faced.

"Sounds like someone is setting you up, my friend," Mark said as he finished his third drink.

"You think," Andrew uttered.

"The questions is by who?"

"I have my suspicions," Andrew replied, staring at his friend as he spoke.

"Who?"

"I'll let you know as soon as I am sure," Andrew replied.

"Fine, in the mean time I will hit the streets again to see what I can find."

"Did you learn anything in the last forty-eight hours?"

"Well, I have my suspicions too, and soon as I am sure, I will get back to you," Mark said as he stood up to leave. "If you hear from the kidnapers, will you contact me?"

"Count on it," Andrew said as he watched Mark leave the bar.

"Sir, the president is ready to start the meeting," John, the president's aide, said to Andrew as he walked past Mark and headed towards the table.

"Fine, I will be there in a few minutes," Andrew advised him as the young man headed back out the door to join the others in the conference room.

"Thanks," Andrew remarked as the waiter handed him the phone. "Hello? This is Andrew McCormick," he began, surprised someone was calling him on the house phone instead of the cellular. "Who is this?" he asked as the person on the other end started to give him instructions. "No, you listen," he argued, "I don't intend to do anything till I speak to my son." He wanted to be sure before he compromised himself any further that they hadn't decided to cut their losses and already killed his son.

"Hello," a shaky but familiar voice said as Andrew held his breath in anticipation. "Steven! Steven, is that you?" he began, trying not to raise his voice and draw any unwanted attention to himself. "Are you all right?"

"Dad!" Steven replied, relieved to finally hear his father's voice. "Dad, you're alive, I thought they killed you too," he cried as his father tried to comfort him.

"I'm fine, son, don't worry," Andrew uttered, the tears flowing down his face as he spoke. "Are you ok?" he repeated.

"I'm fine, Dad," Steven cried, though his body ached from the beatings, he did not want to give his father anything else to worry about by revealing that fact to him.

"Are you sure? I know about the fall at the hotel," Andrew continued.

"Really, Dad, I'm fine," Steven lied as he looked over at one of his captors. "Dad, I'm sorry, I was trying to help and I walked right into their hands and all I did was make things worse for you now than ever before," he explained, ashamed he had been so easily tricked.

"Steven, son, it's not your fault. None of this mess is your fault," Andrew assured him as he tried to keep the boy calm. "Listen to me, Steven, I know you were trying to escape at the hotel when you fell and I want you to promise me no more heroics," Andrew ordered, listening to the sobs of his son on the other end. "Steven, do you understand me, do not do anything else to make these people any more dangerous than they already are."

"But Dad!" Steven argued, without letting on to the others what his father was saying to him.

"Steven, I promise to get you out of this but you have to stop trying to get away from these men," Andrew continued. "Give me your word, you won't do anything else," he pleaded with his son. Andrew would find a way to free him, but his efforts would be worthless if in the end the only thing he found was another causality waiting for him. "Steven, I will get you home safe so just do what I say."

"Ok, Dad," Steven replied, sensing his father needed to promise though he was not sure if he could keep it. "I will do whatever you say, Dad."

"Give me your word," Andrew repeated again.

"Ok, Dad. I swear." Steven began, "Dad—"

"Yes, son, what is it?" Andrew asked.

"Dad, I just wanted to tell you no matter what happens I am sorry about all the time we wasted," Steven began. "I do love you, Dad, really I do."

"I know, son, I feel the same way," Andrew began, but his words were interrupted by the sound of the kidnaper's voice as they took the phone from the boy. "All right you bastards, what do you want me to do?" Andrew snapped, angry once again his chance to talk to his son about their true feelings was taken away from them. "That's it? After making me wait for days, the only thing you want me to do is be at the park just north of the hotel at 3 o'clock," he repeated, growing angrier at each breath he took. "No! Wait!" he shouted as the kidnaper threatened to hang up on him. "I'll follow your instructions and go to the park at the time you want me to and I will wait there till I hear from you. Can I talk to my son again, please?" he asked. "Damn," Andrew whispered to himself as he realized the kidnapers were no longer on the line.

Sitting by the bar now as he thought about the sound of Steven's voice and the pain coming from every word he spoke, Andrew slammed his fist against the counter. He would make them all pay for what they did to his son and if Mark was part of it, he too would be taken care of. It had been a long time since Andrew felt the surge of violence ragging through him, but with each breath he took, he knew killing the men responsible for Steven's pain would be the only way, he could put his life back together again.

"What is it?" he jumped, turning to find Antonio's aide John tapping him on the shoulder.

"They're waiting, sir," John replied.

"Fine, let's go then."

Walking into the conference room to find the rest of the committee already there and in their seats, Andrew moved towards the table as he glanced over at the men he came to see. One or more of them was somehow involved with his son's kidnaping and he intended to figure out who it was.

Great, Andrew thought to himself as the arguing between the men started up again without warning. It was nearly 2:30 and all the delegates were doing was fighting among themselves again.

"Is everything all right?" Antonio asked, leaning closer to Andrew as he ignored his brother's ramblings. "Have you heard from the kidnapers yet?"

"Excuse me?" Andrew replied, stunned to hear that particular question.

"Have you heard from the kidnapers yet?" Antonio repeated.

"How did you find out about the kidnaping?" Andrew demanded to know.

"Mark told me," Antonio said, surprised his friend did not know he was privy to the information. "He said you would feel better if I knew what was going on."

"Better?" Andrew replied. Antonio was one of his suspects, why would he want Mark to tell him anything?

"Yes," Antonio explained. "Mark said you believed one of the delegates might be involved and if I knew what was going on, I could help you figure it out which one."

"Is that what he said?" Andrew replied, wondering if Mark actually told his friend of the kidnaping or if Antonio was just using that as an excuse to find out what he already knew.

"I got a call a few minutes ago, they want me to meet them in the park at three o'clock," Andrew said.

"Is that all they said?" Antonio questioned.

"So far."

"Well as soon as you learn what they want, we will work together to figure out who is responsible for this nightmare and stop them," Antonio assured him. "No matter what the battle is you do not involve family," he said, his own code of ethnics explaining how he worked.

"My feelings too," Andrew said. "Do you have any suspects in this bunch?"

"Maybe one, but I pray I am wrong," Antonio replied without explaining himself.

"Do you two want to join in on the discussion?" Philippe interrupted. "Or are you talking about something I should know about too?"

"We were simply discussing Steven, Andrew's son," Antonio explained, his words worrying Andrew as he spoke. He did not want his second suspect to know what was going on and if Antonio told him, then getting them to admit to any involvement in the crime would be nearly impossible. "Unlike you, my brother, I did not forget about Andrew after the death of our sister. I kept in contact with mutual friends and kept up with his life."

"And?" Philippe asked impatiently.

"And the boy turned eighteen recently. I was just asking Andrew about it and how they plan to celebrate the occasion once he returns home."

"Oh god," Andrew said beneath his breath, with everything happening he hadn't realized till Antonio mentioned it that the date was Sept 5th, his son's birthday.

"Fine," Philippe replied, not completely satisfied with the answer. "Tell your son happy birthday for me and let's get on with the meeting," he ordered before returning to the conference table to speak to the others.

"You really knew it was Steven's birthday," Andrew whispered to his friend once more as they continued the meeting again.

"Yes, I knew," Antonio replied. "As I told Philippe, the death of our sister did not mean you were no longer a part of the family. I have tried to keep tabs on you over the years without interfering in your life."

"I'm sorry," Andrew said, feeling a little ashamed of his own actions. He had turned away from the Vega family after Paulina died, and he returned to the States and never expected to find out Antonio or anyone else from San Sebastian was still keeping an eye on him.

"I understood why you turned away from us but that did not mean you were not thought of often," Antonio revealed.

"Thanks," Andrew said. "And thank you for thinking about Steven," he remarked, praying as he spoke to his old friend, that Antonio would not turn out to be the traitor in their midst.

Sitting at the table as Philippe called for another vote on his referendum that Antonio be impeached for his behavior towards the people of San Sebastian, Andrew waited for the results in hopes his vote would not be necessary. Chosen as the tie breaker, should the vote reach that point, he still did not feel there was enough proof either way for him to make a decision. As the final member of the board, it would be his vote which would make the difference.

"I told you before," he finally remarked as the voting deadlock fell in his lap after all. "I will not vote until I see hard evidence one way or the other of the accusations made against Antonio," Andrew repeated. "If he has been abusing his power, then I want to see it in writing," Andrew said, as Philippe argued with him for his indecision.

"Do you really think your vote has the power to end this?" Philippe snapped. "With one phone call I could chance even that," he said.

"Just what do you mean by that?" Andrew demanded to know as yet another cryptic statement implicated someone else in Steven's kidnaping. "Are you threatening me?"

"I am simply relaying the facts to you. Your vote maybe important at this point but you will not have the final say."

"And just how do you intend on keeping me from that?" Andrew demanded to know.

"I have my ways," Philippe replied.

"It was you, wasn't it?" Andrew shouted as he moved towards the man in anger.

"Enough!" Antonio intervened before Andrew's outburst caused more problems.

The last thing his friend needed was to tip his hand, and if Philippe was involved, attacking him now could do just that. "I too want to see the evidence. If you can not produce it now, then the meeting is over as Andrew stated. I have a country to run and can no longer remain here to listen to your unfounded accusations."

"Very well," Philippe replied, turning to his aide. "Go to my room and retrieve the data we have. It's time to put the matter to rest and show the world my brother's true colors," he declared. As much as he hated defaming his brother and the reputation of the Vega family, he could not longer postpone what had to be done. The evidence would show Antonio was no longer the man they elected to run the country. He'd allowed the power and prestige to cloud his judgments and turned him into the same kind of ruler they once worked to depose.

"If you had the proof, why the hell didn't you bring it with you?" Andrew asked, tired of the games Philippe was playing.

"Because I do not trust anyone but Hector to see to its safety," Philippe began. "Keeping it secured until I was ready was the only way I could be sure the evidence did not mysteriously disappear."

"Are you accusing me of that too?" Antonio protested, angry with his brother already for his accusations of treason.

"I am not accusing anyone of anything. I am simply making sure there are no mistakes in this matter," Philippe argued. "What we are doing here is far too important to rely on chance."

"Are you sure that is the only reason you didn't bring the evidence?" Andrew asked.

"Yes," Philippe began, "I know you prefer believing my brother over me but this time you will have to listen to what I have to say."

"How long will this take?" Andrew asked, looking at his watch.

"Not long."

"Well, I will just have to look at it later," he began, heading for the door as he spoke.

"What are you doing?" Antonio said as Andrew moved to leave the room.

"I have to go," Andrew replied. "And you know why."

"But we have to settle this matter now, if you leave it will only delay it longer," he shouted. He waited almost two weeks to see the proof his brother claimed to have and he did not intend to wait any longer. If Andrew left before they examined it, something else could go wrong before the matter was finally over.

"Sorry, but I have to go, this can wait a few more hours," Andrew repeated, surprised by his friend's attitude. Antonio knew about the meeting and making such a display over his leaving did not make any sense. "I will be back soon, I promise."

"No, you will stay here till this is over," Philippe cried, echoing his brother's contempt over Andrew's sudden need to leave the meeting.

"Just wait for me and when I get back, we will take care of this once and for all," Andrew said before turning to his aide. "You're in charge," Andrew said. "Don't let them do anything stupid till I get back."

"Who me?" the stunned young man replied. "But the president…"

"I'll take care of that later," Andrew promised.

Heading for the lobby as he walked towards the front door, Andrew looked around to see if anyone was waiting for him as the kidnapers said there would be.

"Are you Andrew McCormick?" a taxi driver inquired as he pulled up to the curb.

"Yes."

"Then get in," the driver said as Andrew obeyed him. "I was told to take you to the park and leave you there," the driver explained.

"Were you told anything else?"

"Oh yea, to give you this," the man said, handing Andrew a sealed envelope.

"What is it?" asked Andrew

"Don't know and don't want to," the driver replied. He had been paid extremely well to bring the man to his destination and that was all. Whatever was going on was not his business and he wanted to keep it that way.

"Fine," Andrew replied as he sat back in the seat holding the folder tightly in his hand. Hesitating for a moment, Andrew wondered what he would find inside.

Would it be instructions from the kidnapers? Evidence of his son's capture? Either way he knew whatever it was, it would not be good news.

"You're supposed to wait at those trees," the driver said as they reached the park "No thanks, the fare has been taken care of," he uttered, anxious to get away from whatever was going on.

Sitting on the bench next to the trees, Andrew finally opened the envelope he had been given by the taxi driver. Staring heartbrokenly at the photograph of his son, he felt the rage inside him growing as he looked into the eyes of his child. It was apparent from the bruises Steven had been beaten severely by his captors and the only thing Andrew wanted to do was hold the boy and try to make him forget what he had been through.

"I'm sorry, son," he whispered to himself, touching the face of his son. "I promise when this is over, I will make it up to you," he vowed before checking his watch again.

A little after five he wondered how much longer he would have to wait for the kidnapers to contact him. He not only had to deal with whatever they planned for him next but with the outraged diplomats he left at the hotel, and the sooner he knew what the next step would be in the game, the sooner he could take care of that problem too.

Returning to the conference table still angry with his friend for leaving so abruptly, Philippe began shouting at the other members of the committee. He had endured enough embarrassment at the hands of others and was not going to endure it any longer.

"Please, Mr. Vega," John said, trying to ease the tension in the room. "Andrew will be back shortly and we can continue the meeting. You should try to relax and calm down a little."

"I will not calm down," the frustrated man shouted. "Andrew's departure has already affected these proceedings and I will not stand for this any further," he announced.

"Mr. Vega, please," John repeated, not sure what to do next. He worked for Andrew nearly six years and this was the first time he found his employer so personally involved in the negotiations. The mere fact Andrew possessed a vote, a say in how another country was going to be run was unheard of in their line of work and yet, Andrew treated it no different than any other assignment.

"Mr. President," he began, turning towards Antonio for help in calming his brother down. "Maybe if the two of you talked among yourselves till Andrew comes back, it might make things easier now."

"My brother and I have talked among ourselves, young man, and there is nothing easy about this mess," Antonio announced as he moved towards the windows.

"I don't think that is a very good idea," John said, reminding them of the alert warning Andrew gave me earlier in the day of reports there maybe be trouble during the summit meeting.

"My boy, we are on the eleventh floor, and there are no other buildings around us. I don't think Andrew was talking about an open window as a threat when he gave us the warning," Antonio remarked.

"But sir."

"Enough," Antonio protested refusing to heed anyone's warnings.

"And you wonder why I am trying to prove you are incompetent," Philippe said, moving next to his brother. "Even when someone is trying to do something for your own good, you have to fight with them."

"What can I say, I am a stubborn man." Antonio laughed as the two men stood before the open window.

"Sirs, please for you own safety, you have to move away from the window," John repeated but to no avail. "Gentlemen," he repeated his words drowned out by the sound of a helicopter's propeller drawing closer to the window.

Turning in the direction of the noise, John watched in horror as he saw a man on the edge of the helicopter, a gun in hand.

"Look out!" he shouted, hitting the floor as a barrage of gunfire came streaming through the window. "Mr. President," he uttered still shaken, after the helicopter flew away from the building, the sneak attacks on them finally over. "Mr. President, are you all right?" John asked, moving towards the man he was supposed to protect.

"Yes, I am fine," Antonio replied, brushing off the glass from his body, a few cuts from their jagged edges the only evidence of what just occurred. "You? Are you all right?" he asked the young man who had come to his aid.

"Yes, sir, I think so." John replied.

"Philippe! Where is Philippe?" Antonio cried, realizing he had not seen his brother get up from the floor. "Oh god no! What have I done?" he cried out, kneeling next to the lifeless body of his brother. "Why did I behave like a child and open the window? Why did I allow my pride to put us in danger?" he rambled, berating himself for letting his brother pay for his foolishness.

"Mr. President," John began, hating to interrupt the man in his time of grief. He needed to get him to safety before the assassins returned. "Please, sir, you have to go with the security guards back to your room until the police arrive," John explained. "Please, sir, its for your own safety."

"Yes, yes of course," Antonio replied, wishing he had complied with the young aide's orders earlier as well. "The others are they all right?' Antonio asked concerned for the members of the committee.

"At least one is dead, sir, some of the others are slightly wounded," John said as he continued to take control of the situation. "I already have security taking care of them," he continued before turning to the security guards who began to arrive in the room. "Take the President back to his room and stay with him till you hear from me," he ordered.

"I will avenge your death," Antonio said to his brother before following the guards out of the room.

Looking around at the melee which surrounded him, John wished Andrew were there to take control of the situation. He would know what to do next, how to make things right again. The frightened aide hopped he could handle everything he would soon be facing.

"Who's in charge? " a voice demanded to know as several police officers walked into the room distracting John from his thoughts and worries.

"I guess I am," he replied.

"And you are?"

"John Clark."

"Well, Mr. Clark, I am Detective Knoff from the local police department. Can you tell me what the hell happened here?"

"Oh let me see now. We were just attacked by a man with a machine gun flying in a helicopter outside our window while on the eleventh floor of this hotel," John remarked sarcastically, not sure if his behavior was from fear or the arrogance of the man who just entered the room

"Cute," Knoff replied. "Who are the dead men over there?

"That is President Vega's brother Philippe," John said, deciding not to get caught up in a word game with the officer after all. "The man over there was one of the delegates and that man a security guard," he said, pointing out each of the dead men to the officer.

"Great. Just what I needed, three more bodies to add to my collection," Knoff remarked.

"To your what?" John asked.

"Never mind. Just tell me what happened?"

"We were in a meeting and the helicopter just appeared. Before we could do anything, all hell broke loose."

"Is everyone accounted for from this meeting?" Knoff asked.

"Yes, I mean, no."

"Come on, son, which one is it?"

"Why are you here?" John asked without responding to Knoff's question.

"Excuse me?"

"Shouldn't this be handled by Interpol or someone from that branch of the government? This was a political assassination after all," John said.

"Well, kid, you lucked out. I am not only the local yokel but also a member of a special task force trained to respond to these types of calls," Knoff remarked with venom in his voice. "Now tell me what you meant earlier. Who is missing from here?"

"One of the diplomats," John replied.

"And he is?"

"Andrew McCormick."

"Who?" Knoff repeated as he heard a familiar name.

"Andrew McCormick. He is part of the committee and he left just before the shooting started." John said wishing he hadn't as he heard his words coming back to haunt him by the look on Knoff's face.

"He left before the shooting?'

"Yes. He said he had another meeting to go to and would be back soon."

"Funny, isn't it?" Knoff began.

"What is?" John asked.

"Well, it seems every time I have a dead body these days the name Andrew McCormick is connected to it.

"Every time you have a dead body?" John repeated, unsure what the officer was talking about. "Look, I don't know what is going on but Andrew is not connected to this in any way," he protested. " And I don't like what you are implying."

"And I don't care what you like," Knoff replied. "If Andrew is not responsible for this mess, then who is?"

"I am," Antonio said, stepping out from behind the doors.

"Mr. President you're supposed to be in your room," John protested.

"I had to be with my brother."

"Sir, I am sorry about your loss, but what did you mean you were responsible?" Knoff asked.

"Sir, you don't have to answer that," John said, trying to protect the President from Knoff's interrogation.

"I was upset because Andrew left the meeting so abruptly that I behaved like a spoiled brat. I insisted upon opening the window and I gave the assassin a clear shot at all of us," Antonio said.

"It wasn't your fault, sir," John tried to reassure him.

"The kid is right," Knoff agreed before asking him about Andrew. "Do you know why he left the meeting so suddenly?"

"No, I don't. Why do you ask?" Antonio replied. He had already caused the death of one member of his family with his foolish behavior and he wasn't about to cause another by revealing what he knew of the kidnaping. If he hadn't let his pride get in the way, he would have realized then why Andrew needed to leave so suddenly and maybe his brother in the end would still be alive.

"Well, thank you anyway," Knoff said sarcastically, turning his attention towards the door as Hans walked through. "Lieutenant, what are you doing here?" he asked, curious as to why he was outside his jurisdiction.

"I heard the call on the radio and knew you would be here, so I thought I'd stop by to see what was happening."

"More dead bodies and another connection to your old friend," Knoff said.

"Andrew," Hans replied. " Where is he? Is he ok?"

"Yup. Seems he left just minutes before the shooting started so he is just fine."

"Glad to here that," Hans remarked before heading for the door. "Well, I will leave you to your work."

Heading for the lobby, Hans knew he needed to locate his friend before Knoff did. As bad as it appeared, he had to believe Andrew didn't set the men in the room up to be murdered and wanted to warn him about what was going to happen next.

"Thanks," he replied upon learning from the bellman of Andrew's departure and the cab which picked him up. Getting the address from dispatch, Hans headed for the park praying his friend would still be there. He had given Andrew more than enough rope to try and find his son without interference but if crossed the line, Hans knew it was time put an end to this deadly game.

Nervously pacing around the trees as he continued to wait for the kidnapers to contact him, Andrew looked up with curiosity as several police and ambulance sped past him.

"Andrew," he heard from behind as he turned to see his friend sitting in a nearby car.

"Hans, are you nuts? What are you doing here?"

"Get in," Hans ordered.

"I can't," Andrew said. "The kidnapers finally contacted me, I'm supposed to wait here."

"They're not coming," Hans remarked

"What! How would you know that?" Andrew asked.

"Just get in and I will explain everything."

"Fine," Andrew replied getting into the car. "Now tell me what the hell is going on?"

"You're not going to like it." Han assured him as he filled his friend in on the events at the hotel.

"Damn it," Andrew snapped. "I've been set up again."

"Got that straight," Hans uttered. "Whoever is after you doesn't care what he has to do to get to you, including killing innocent people," Hans said looking over at his friend. "Are you sure you have no idea who it is?"

"Oh, I have ideas but no proof," Andrew explained

"Care to share those ideas with me," Hans asked as they continued to drive around without a real destination.

"Maybe later," Andrew said without explanation.

"Fine, can you at least tell me if you spoke to Mark before or after this latest melee?"

"Mark, yes, I talked to him at the hotel right before the kidnapers called," Andrew replied. "And that is not all," he said filling his friend in on the latest lie he caught Mark in.

"So I guess he is your number one suspect?"

"No matter what lies he has told me, I still find it hard to believe he would hurt Steven this way," Andrew said.

"Well I don't," Hans argued. "I think he is involved and as far as I am concerned you need to forget about your past together and start looking at the evidence."

"Ok, even if he is involved, what is his motive?" Andrew asked. "He has to be working with someone else."

"Someone on the counsel perhaps?" Hans questioned.

"Maybe."

"You know before this mess is over it is only going to get worse," Hans said as they headed back to the hotel.

"I know," Andrew replied.

"There's more and you are not going to like it," Hans remarked.

"Just tell me what you found out," Andrew said.

"I talked to Mark's doctors back in the States and your good friend is in worse shape than you led me to believe."

"What are you talking about?" Andrew questioned. "What did the doctors say?"

"According to the shrinks back home, Mark is suffering from some kind of post traumatic stress."

"I knew that, he's on medical leave because of it," Andrew replied. "What else did they tell you?"

"Well according to the doctors, Mark has turned his own rage into a personal vendetta, a way of coping with his problems by turning it against someone else and holding that person responsible for everything that has gone wrong in his life."

"And let me guess, the doctors told you that person is me, right?" Andrew said.

"Oh yea. Big time," Hans said. "The doctor I talked to told me this in confidence and he assured me that Mark was as close to the edge as you could get. And you, my friend, are the target of all his anger."

"Did he say why?"

"Somewhere in that bastard's sick mind you are responsible for everything wrong in his life from wetting the bed to failing the last mission he was on and the only way he can get his life back is to destroy yours."

"If all this is true, why didn't anyone at the agency tell me about it?"

"I have no idea," Hans admitted.

"Great!" Andrew uttered with disgust in his voice. "I am working blind here and the damned doctors back home are the ones who put the blindfold on me."

"Then we just have to take the blindfold off," Hans said, "starting with the delegates at the hotel. Once we figure out which one is behind Steven's kidnaping, we can find out if Mark is really apart of it or just another patsy."

"Like me."

"Didn't want to say that but yea like you." Hans laughed. "Damn, look at this mess," he remarked as they pulled into the parking lot of the hotel. The place was swarming with police and media personal

"I am not up for this right now," Andrew said, staring at all the people he would have to face if they went any farther onto the hotel property.

"Then why don't we go somewhere we can talk without interruption and maybe figure things out between the two of us."

"Why are you taking such a risk helping me?" Andrew asked. "You know if wonder boy figures out you are helping me, it could cost you your pension."

"Yea I know. But if I do not help you out of this mess, I will never get the fifty bucks you owe me."

"Fifty bucks? I thought it was thirty."

"It was but the interest just keeps getting higher," Hans joked.

"Well ah."

"I know put it on your tab."

"Thanks."

"You owe me," Hans said.

"More than you know, old friend," Andrew replied. "More than you know."

"Remember that when I end up on the unemployment line when this is over," Hans uttered.

"I will," Andrew replied. His friend was putting everything he held dear at risk for him and that was something Andrew would never be able to forget. If it took him the rest of his life, he would do whatever it took to pay him back.

Arriving at a little tavern about four miles away from the hotel, the two men made themselves comfortable as they ordered some drinks. If they were going to figure out who was behind the melee, they needed time alone, time to go through the suspects and weed out the less serious ones.

"Hans, before we get started, there is something else I have to tell you, something I should have told you about earlier," Andrew began. If his friend was going to put his life on the line for him, he wanted him to know all the facts.

"Terrific, more secrets," Hans balked. "Ok, what is it?"

"The reason I came here to Rome for this meeting had to do less with me being a part of the committee and more to do with a promise I made to Jose Vega a long time ago."

"Jose Vega, the old man?"

"Yes. The old man."

"Ok, if you made a promise to him, it had to be back in the old days when you were living in San Sebastian and that was a very long time ago," Hans began, still trying to understand what the promise meant to them now and the situation they found themselves in.

"It was a lifetime ago, but I gave my word and I have to keep it."

"I don't like the sound of that," Hans said. "Ok, what kind of promise was it?"

"First, let me explain how things were back then," Andrew began. "We were fighting the Guillermo family for the freedom of San Sebastian and Jose wanted to be sure in the end his people did not suffer for the actions he took."

"I get that, so what did he make you promise in order to make sure of that?"

"Jose was a very smart man who knew his son Antonio was capable of being a great leader, but he also knew that power and wealth has a way of corrupting even those with the high moral standards he raised his children to have," he explained, pausing long enough for the waiter to leave their drinks before continuing. "Jose wanted to make sure if that ever happened, there would be a way to stop his son before the people suffered too much."

"Right, that is why he formed the committee you told me about, and why he made you a member," Hans interrupted. "Is that the promise you made him, to vote his son out of office should it become necessary?"

"Not exactly."

"Enough already, tell me what it was," Hans ordered, becoming increasingly impatient with his friend's delaying tactics.

"He made me promise should Antonio ever cross the line and become like the man we helped to depose that I would step in and take care of things."

"Ok, you said it wasn't the power of the vote he wanted you to use, so what was it?" Hans asked, hesitating for a minute as he spoke. "Don't tell me he asked you to..." he began. "That old bastard asked you to kill his son if you thought it was necessary?" Hans said in disbelief.

Though he retired from the agency before Andrew became head of the elite squad, he knew all about it and about his friend's involvement in it.

"I promised to make sure if Antonio was proven unfit to run the country any further, I would remove him from office.

"By killing him?" Hans yelled. "I don't want to hear anymore of this. I am a cop for god sakes and you are admitting to me you were hired to kill someone."

"No, I am admitting to my friend that I was considering honoring a promise to another old friend."

"Considering? Then you might not go through with it?"

"I don't know," Andrew confessed. "So far Philippe has not been able to prove any of his accusations and the vote on impeachment has been deadlocked. If I decided to vote in favor of removing Antonio from office, he might have gone without a fight and the promise would have meant nothing in the end."

"And if he did put up a fight?"

"I promised Jose Vega I would not let his country fall into another civil war and both Philippe as well as his brother sounded as if that was one of the options they were considering."

"So let me get this straight. You were going to wait till you found proof one way or the other, and then if you voted and Antonio refused to step down should the evidence prove him guilty, you were going to kill him all because of a promise you made to his father over twenty years ago," Hans argued still trying to comprehend what his friend was telling him.

"Well, if you put it that way, it sounds pretty silly," Andrew joked.

"And just how would you put it?"

"Well, I would," he began, the tone in his voice no longer jokingly, "I would have to put it the same way, I guess."

"And you would have gone through with it?"

"Maybe I shouldn't answer that in the presence of a cop," Andrew replied.

"Maybe not," Hans echoed. "Why didn't you just walk away from it like you did in the past?"

"I tried, but the thought of thousands of people dying in a civil war again kept me from doing that."

"Great, an assassin with a conscious," Hans uttered.

"Life stinks, doesn't it?" Andrew remarked.

"Ok, now listen to me, my friend," Hans uttered, leaning closer to Andrew as he spoke. "I will do everything I can to help you find out what is going on here, but if I find out you were behind the deaths at the hotel, I will nail you myself before I let anyone else die, do you understand?"

"Understood."

"Good, now what is our next move?"

"I am not sure," Andrew replied.

"Tell me did anyone else know about this promise you made to Jose?" Hans asked.

"Just one person."

"Let me guess," he snapped. "Mark, right? Great," Hans said, waving his hand for the waiter to bring another drink to the table. "Any other news you wish to share with me?"

"Nope, I think I covered everything."

"Good, I don't think my stomach could take anything else," Hans remarked as he stood up to leave. "We'll head to my house for now, the family is away visiting relatives so the place is empty, and you should be safe there until we figure something else out."

"Are you sure?"

"Nope, but I am too hungry and tired to worry about it. You'll spend the night and we'll worry about tomorrow when it comes."

"Thanks," Andrew repeated, grateful for the offer. He could use some time away from everything and everyone if only for one night. In the morning he would not only have to face Knoff and the barrage of questions but Antonio as well, and maybe a good night's sleep would help him face the problems ahead of him with a little more ease."

"What about Knoff? He will want to talk to me."

"I will tell him to wait till morning and leave it at that," Hans assured him as they headed for his home.

Awakening the next morning to find himself the recipient of a very sloppy kiss, Andrew awoke to find Hans's dachshund leaning over him.

"Good morning to you too," he remarked, pushing the dog away as he got up from the couch.

"Did you get any sleep?" Hans asked, walking into the room as Andrew continued to play with the dog.

"Oh yea, I love sleeping on a lumpy couch with a horse by my side," Andrew joked as he teased the dog a little more with the bone he'd found.

"You should be honored, Marko doesn't usually let new people in the house, let alone on his couch."

"His couch?" Andrew repeated.

"Would you argue with a dog that big about where he sleeps?"

"Guess not."

"So have you figured out what you intend to do next?" Hans asked, pouring some coffee into his cup.

"The first thing is talk to Antonio, after that I am not sure," Andrew said. "After that I will check on Mark to see what he is up to."

"Fine, I'll check with Knoff and see what he has come up with in the last twelve hours and maybe between the two of us we will get some answers."

"We can meet back at the tavern around lunch time," Andrew suggested.

"Fine, I'll see you then," Hans replied.

CHAPTER TEN

Finding Mark in the hotel bar upon his arrival, Andrew feigned delight at seeing his friend. Maintaining the illusion of ignorance was the only way to convince him the trust between them was still in place.

"I'm glad you are here," Andrew began, playing the game. "We have a lot to talk about," he continued, making himself comfortable at the table where Mark sat, a bottle of scotch sitting in front of him.

"I know we do," Mark began. "I heard about the battle yesterday at the conference, and I am glad to see you looking so healthy."

"Yea, well from what I've been told, it was a sight to see," Andrew replied.

"From what you were told?" Mark said as he played his own game with his friend.

"What do you mean from what you were told? Weren't you there?"

"Not exactly," Andrew explained. "I left a few minutes before the shooting started and missed all the excitement."

"You left, but why? Did something else happen I should know about?" Mark asked as he listened to the steps of his plan fall into place.

"I got a call from the kidnapers and left per their instructions," Andrew continued, wondering as he spoke, how much of this information Mark already knew. "I didn't hear about the shooting till later, and of course the local police think I left because I knew what was going to happen."

"How convenient," Mark uttered, happy that the seeds of doubt were being planted just as he wanted them. Now that the police suspected him in playing a part in the assassination, it would be easy to convince them of the rest too. Before he was done, the precious reputation Andrew cherished would be destroyed, as would the relationship with his son. "Did the kidnapers say what they wanted?" Mark finally asked.

"No," Andrew said, his own thoughts of the next step filling him with rage for the man sitting across the table from him. "They told me to leave and go to a designated spot, once there, I was suppose to wait for them to contact me again."

"And did they? Contact you that is?"

"Nope, I sat there waiting like a fool, while the hotel was being shot to pieces and people I care about were killed," Andrew replied angrily. This time the anger directed at himself for being so gullible.

"The kidnapers never contacted you to tell you what they wanted?" Mark repeated several times, trying to drive the knife deeper into his opponent's soul as he spoke.

"So you still have no idea what they want, or why they are doing this?"

"No," Andrew snapped.

"And you waited at the park for nothing?"

"That's pretty much it," Andrew said, realizing as he stared at his friend that Mark had revealed to him the proof of his involvement. No matter how hard he tried to deny it or tried to believe his friend was being used too, the proof was staring at him in the face and there was no doubt in his mind that Mark was responsible for Steven's kidnaping.

"So they set you up to look like you were apart of the killing spree at the hotel," Mark announced, hoping his words would twist the knife even further.

"What else is new?" Andrew replied. "Seems I am being accused of every crime that occurs these days," he continued.

"What about Steven?" Mark asked, hoping to turn the screws even tighter with his questions.

"They let me talk to him for a few minutes when they called and they left this picture for me with the taxi driver who took me to the park."

"How did he sound?" Mark asked.

"How do you expect him to sound?" Andrew snapped. "Scared and in pain."

"Well, don't worry, once we find the bastards who have him, we will make them pay for every bruise he received," Mark said.

"Oh you can count on that," Andrew assured him as he fought the urge to jump over the table and tear his friend apart.

Looking up with gratitude as the waiter placed another bottle of scotch at the table, Mark quickly fixed himself another drink. Though the plan had not gone as he would have liked it, the fact that Andrew was hurting was enough for him, and when the time was right, he would finish the little game they were playing once and for all.

"Do the police have any leads or other suspects in the shooting at the hotel or with that hooker you mentioned?" Mark asked, changing the subject once more.

"They don't need anyone else, they have me, remember," Andrew replied, finishing the remaining scotch he had left.

"Is that any way to talk?" Mark joked. "I'm sure the police will figure out sooner or later you had nothing to do with any of the deaths."

"The way my luck has been running, it will be later," Andrew replied. "Someone has gone to a lot of trouble to set me up for these crimes and proving I didn't commit them will not be easy."

"I know," Mark said, smiling slightly at the words his friend was saying. That was the way he planned it and at least that part of the plan was going perfectly.

"So what is your next move?"

"I don't know to tell you the truth," Andrew replied. "I guess I wait for the kidnapers to make the next and in the mean time I will try to stay out of Detective Knoff's way."

"Knoff, oh, you mean Hans' man," Mark uttered.

"Yea, the boy wonder is convinced of my guilt and he is doing everything to prove it."

"You don't say," Mark began as another thought came to him. If the rest of the plan was going to work maybe using Knoff as an ally would be his best bet. If he wanted Andrew convicted of the crimes he's been accused of, then using an honest cop like Knoff to do it would be perfect.

"If only I could figure out who is responsible for this mess," Andrew remarked.

He knew of Mark's involvement, but he needed to find out if Antonio was also a part of the conspiracy against him.

"I wish I knew," Mark answered. "I am just as stumped as you are. We both know with the kind of past we have it could be just about anyone."

"Right, just about," Andrew responded, looking at his friend.

"Don't worry, my friend, we will figure it out," Mark assured him as another drink of scotch found its way to his mouth as he reviewed the facts aloud.

"Do the police know about the mess back home?"

"Oh, you mean the dead man there?" Andrew said sarcastically.

"Yup, that's what I mean."

"I have no idea."

"Great, so as far as you know, you are the prime suspect for murder and treason in not one but two countries."

"Thanks for clearing that up for me," Andrew balked. "I would have never been able to figure things out."

"Hey what are friends for?" Mark laughed. "Seriously, Andrew, we have to figure out who is behind this before you end up wanted in every country around the world."

"And just how are we going to do that?'

"Good question," Mark replied, loving every minute of the game as things started to heat up. "We could always go to a fortune teller maybe they could help."

"Glad to see you're so amused to see me in such a mess," Andrew began.

"A little sensitive, aren't we?" Mark laughed as he continued to tease Andrew.

"Just because it is you who is in trouble this time instead of me, doesn't mean we aren't in this together," Mark assured him. "I will do everything in my power to make sure you get what is coming to you," he continued. "You know I always have your back."

"I know. It is just that this time Steven is in the middle of the mess too, and I don't know how to help him," Andrew uttered. The pain in his voice was apparent to Mark as he spoke.

"I'm sorry about that too, but it will be over soon, I'm sure," Mark said.

"I wish I could be as sure as you."

"Trust me, before you know it everything will be over."

"I hope so," Andrew prayed.

"Is there anything else I should know before I head out?" Mark asked.

"Well, there's one more thing I should mention," Andrew announced.

"Which is?"

"Funny," Andrew jeered. "There is one more piece of evidence against me that is going to be a problem as well."

"Great. What is that?" Mark asked amused by the news he was hearing.

"The police found a money trail leading from Helena to me," Andrew began. "According to what Hans' told me, Helena had an account in her name hidden away in Switzerland and somehow yours truly has been connected to it too."

"A money trail," Mark replied, genuinely surprised by this news. He had planned everything very carefully and if the man who recruited him screwed things up by doing something behind his back, he would make him pay dearly.

"Nice isn't it? Someone was willing to shell out thousands of dollars to make it look like I had a hidden bank account and I have no idea who it is."

"Well, whoever is behind this, their plan is working," Mark began, realizing the unscheduled diversion with the money only helped his plan in the end. "If I were the police, I would suspect the money was a payoff for the hotel incident."

"That is exactly what Knoff said to me at our last meeting," Andrew lied. There was no money trail, no fake account, he was only using the story as bait. If Mark thought someone was stepping on his plan, he would react and Andrew hoped that reaction would lead him to the man Mark was working for.

"Well, I better get back out on the street to see what I can find," Mark announced as he finished his drink. "Maybe I can learn more about this money trail you mentioned and hopefully find out who is behind it."

"I knew I could depend on you," Andrew said glancing over at the plain clothes officer standing by the door as he spoke. " You will let me know right away if you come up with anything?"

"Count on it," Mark replied.

"I have no idea what the kidnapers are going to do next so keep in touch every couple of hours and update me with what you have learned."

"No problem," Mark said. "You know you can count on me where Steven is concerned."

"I know and if it weren't for you and Hans helping find my son, I don't know what I would do," Andrew uttered, hoping his words would give Mark more to think about.

"Hans, he knows about Steven?" Mark repeated. "I thought the kidnapers told you not to involve the locals?" he remarked, trying to hold back the anger ragging in him. If his plan was going to work, no one could know that the kidnaped boy was really Steven. Convincing the world that Andrew made up the story about his son to cover his own trail of murder and deceit would not work if someone else was aware of what was really going on. He could not make it appear that Andrew had lost his mind, that he had become a man on the edge if he had someone else to back up his story.

"I had no choice," Andrew began as he made up his story. "They found some prints at the hotel and were able to match them through Inter-pol to the ones on file for Steven."

"Prints?"

"You know as well as I do I had Steven registered with the agency after his mother's death in case something should ever happen, so when they found prints at the hotel and matched them to my son, Hans came to me with the information."

"Does anyone else know?"

"No, he managed to get the results without letting anyone else in on the truth and he came to me."

"Thank god," Mark whispered to himself. It would be easier in the end taking care of one loose end rather than several, and Hans would be handled once the rest of the plan was in effect. "Have they identified the kidnapers too?" he asked keeping up the rouse that his men were dead and the kidnapers unknown to him.

"Not yet, they are still trying to get a match on them, but we both know how difficult that can be if they work for the agency."

"It could be like looking for a needle in a haystack if the prints have been sealed up to protect the agents."

"Exactly," Andrew said. "At this point we are not even sure if the men involved are the two agents who came here with you or if they are dead."

"They were good men," Mark began. "I can only believe they are dead, killed by the kidnapers too."

"Maybe," Andrew replied.

"And you trust Hans not to blow the whistle on you?"

"As long as he believes I haven't crossed the line to get to Steven, I think he will stay quiet about everything," Andrew confessed.

"And with everything that's happened at the hotel and with the girl, does he think that you may have already crossed the line?"

"Not yet," Andrew began." He's not sure what he believes about the shooting at the hotel, and unlike his investigator, he's willing to give me the benefit of the doubt until all the evidence is in," Andrew admitted.

"Hans is a good man, he will try to get all the evidence in before he makes up his mind," Mark declared. "Well, I better get out there and see what I can find out before something else happens," Mark said, standing once more to leave. He wanted to talk to his men about Hans and taking care of him before he let anyone else at the station in on what he knew. "I'll call you as soon as I find out anything," he promised. Though concerned about the newest developments of the case, Mark smiled as he walked past the front desk, pleased by the outcome of his plan, he would soon have everything that should have been his in the first place and Andrew would finally be out of the way. Once Andrew's life was destroyed, everyone including Steven would see for himself what Mark already knew, he was the better man and it was he who deserved to be Steven's father and not his so-called best friend. Everything should have been his from the beginning, loving parents, a loving wife, career filled with honor and respect and a son he could cherish. It was not his fault the fates chose to give him a family who despised him, a stepfather who convinced the authorities he was a sociopath who needed to be locked away and he was tired of paying the price of having those cards dealt to him so long ago. It was time for things to turn in is favor and he was going to make sure they did no matter what he had to do.

"Don't worry, I will take care of Steven," Mark uttered as he walked towards his car. Once he had the boy safely tucked away in their new home, he would find a way to make Steven forget about the father who raised him and get him to realize he was his only real parent, the only one who ever really loved him, and they could finally start a life together as father and son—the way it was meant to be.

Spinning the empty scotch bottle around the table several times, Andrew felt his anger for Mark intensify. The man was not only dangerous to him, but to his son as well, inflicting such pain on an innocent teenage boy he professed to love only served to prove just how unstable Mark really was.

Despite his desire to kill the man on the spot, Andrew knew he needed to be very careful when dealing with him or his son could end up paying for his actions. Proving he was behind the kidnaping would not be easy and finding Steven even harder, but Mark had already made several mistakes and Andrew could only pray he would make just enough mistakes to lead them to his son before it was too late.

Grabbing the hotel phone, Andrew called Antonio's room to see if he was up to visitors. He was a loose end that needed attention and the sooner it was taken care of the better. Whether he was a part of the conspiracy or not, Antonio just lost a brother and Andrew felt he should offer him some support.

"I'll be there in about fifteen minutes," Andrew replied, upon learning Antonio wanted to see him. *First though,* he thought to himself as he headed into a nearby elevator, *I need to stop at my room.* He'd sent another message to his contact in San Sebastian and hoped that when he checked, there would be a response from the man. Even with everything he was facing, the doubts and betrayal, Andrew still had a promise to keep and without the proof he sought to help him, his hands were tied.

Sitting at the computer checking his e-mail to see if there was indeed a response waiting for him, Andrew quickly hit the transmit button after finding he did have something waiting.

Hello love,
Annie here, just wanted to let you know there is nothing new on the Guillermo family. The old man died about six months ago and the two sons are still in their teens. Word has it that they are hiding out, still running from the enemies of their father. So they are not going to be of any help to you. Hope this helps…let me know if you are ok.
Love,
Annie

"Well at least someone is responding to my messages," Andrew remarked. Though not sure if he was pleased with the answers he found waiting for him, he was at least relieved to find his e-mail was indeed working. "Now what?" he whispered to himself.

With the formal dictator dead, the possibility that he was behind the events surrounding them were lost and now his only suspect left was Antonio.

"Why won't you answer me?" he demanded to know. This time his question was directed at the man he had been waiting to hear from. "Where are you?" Andrew wondered, concerned that the man in San Sebastian was not responding because he too was among the casualty list. If everything were ok in San Sebastian, his contact would've replied to all his inquires by now and the fact he had not only led to more unanswered questions.

"Yes, what is it?" Andrew shouted as someone knocked on the door. "Hector," he began, surprised to find Philippe's aide standing before him. "I thought you would be with the escort taking Philippe's body back home."

"I will but we are not leaving till tomorrow," Hector explained. "Besides I needed to complete what he started and getting the evidence to you before the committee leaves is very important to me," Hector remarked, handing Andrew an envelope. "Philippe was a good man. He was trying to save our country and do what was right. His work should be completed."

"Come in," Andrew said as he took the folder. "I am sorry about Philippe," he began.

"He was a good man, but are you sure he would still want me to have this?" Andrew asked. Though a little apprehensive about the contents inside, he already knew the answer to the question even as he asked it. He had to read the contents no matter what the file might say, he had no choice.

"Whether you like it or not you have to complete your mission."

"I know," Andrew replied. "The proof he said he had of Antonio's guilt is in the folder, isn't it?"

"Yes, and if he doesn't agree to resign on his own we both know what has to be done, don't we?"

"Excuse me?" Andrew uttered, surprised by Hector's words.

"Do not act so surprised," Hector said. "I too know about the promise you made to Jose Vega so long ago."

"Promise? What promise?"

"He told me himself."

"Why would he do that?" Andrew asked, still not admitting to anything.

"Jose was a smart man, he knew in your line of work there was a chance something might happen to you so he wanted a backup plan just in case. He wanted someone else he trusted who could fulfill the promise made should you be unable to."

"And that someone was you?"

"Yes."

"So you think I have enough evidence in this folder to complete my assignment?"

"More than enough."

"Great," Andrew remarked sarcastically. He didn't want to believe Philippe's accusations but if the evidence was there. "Why did you wait so long to give it to me if you had the proof?" he asked. "Why did Philippe?"

"As much as he wanted to put an end to his brother's reign of terror, he did not want to believe the evidence he found. Even though they were at odds over the last few years, Philippe still loved Antonio and he wanted to double-check everything before showing it to you and the committee," Hector explained. "On the morning of his death, he went to his brother and showed him the file."

"Antonio knew about this file?" Andrew repeated.

"Yes, Philippe showed it to him first, and despite the way he acted at the meeting, he knew what the evidence was his brother possessed."

"And when did he show it to him?" Andrew asked again.

"Just hours before he was killed," Hector replied. "I too, like you, believe Antonio had his brother killed to keep him from showing anyone else the evidence," Hector continued. "When I went to the room to get the file, I found the room had been broken into and searched, but the intruder did not find where I had hid the file."

"Damn it," Andrew began. Not only was Mark involved but Antonio too. It seemed no matter which way he turned, someone he called a friend was betraying him.

"Antonio killed his brother and needs to be stopped before anyone else is harmed."

"All right I will look at it, and if I think there is enough, I'll do what has to be done," Andrew replied.

"You still don't sound convinced the proof is real," Hector remarked. "Surely you've had a chance to confirm everything with your contact in San Sebastian?"

"How did…?" Andrew began, curious once more how Hector knew about his contact. The fact he still knew people in San Sebastian willing to help him was not supposed to be public knowledge.

"You forget I am also the head of internal security. It is my job to know about everything that happens in my country, including knowing about the man who has been working for you since you left San Sebastian," Hector confessed.

"He is not working for me," Andrew protested. "He was a friend and I hoped he'd be able to help me answer some questions."

"In any case, hasn't he told you what is happening in my country?"

"No, I haven't been able to reach him since my arrival to Rome," Andrew admitted, no longer caring who knew what was going on. "For some reason, my e-mails to him keep going unanswered."

"Well perhaps I can help," Hector remarked. "I will contact my people back home and see if we can locate him."

"Thanks," Andrew replied. "Why are you being so helpful?" Andrew asked. "As far as I remember, we were never the best of friends and the last thing I expected you to do was come to my aid."

"Friendship has nothing to do with this," Hector announced. "Freeing my country from the tyrant ruling it is all I care about and if helping you is the only way, then so be it."

"Fine. Then we are both agreed. We'll work together for the benefit of San Sebastian," Andrew said.

"Agreed! For the benefit of San Sebastian and for no other reason," Hector said.

"Let me know what you decide. If you can't complete the mission, then I will."

"Don't worry, I made the promise to Jose Vega and I will do what has to be done," Andrew balked angrily at Hector before he left the room.

Taking the file he had been given, Andrew turned his attentions to the contents. If there was proof inside, then Antonio betrayed not only his people but him as well.

Hurrying back down to the bar to meet with Antonio after receiving a message he'd be waiting there, Andrew wished he'd had more time to study the contents of the file before confronting his suspect. Surprised to find him sitting alone in the bar when he arrived, Andrew wondered why there weren't guards surrounding him.

"Antonio!" he began as he moved closer, only to find his fears unfounded as several patrons stepped in front of him to keep the president safe. It was apparent they were guarding Antonio as they kept Andrew at arm's length till they received approval for him to draw nearer.

"It is all right," Antonio finally remarked, signaling for his men to allow Andrew to approach.

"How are you?" Andrew began, sitting down at the table with his friend.

"How do you think I am?" Antonio replied sarcastically. "My brother is dead and I have to return home to my family and explain how I allowed this to happen."

"It wasn't your fault," Andrew protested.

"Then who is to blame?" the man asked him. "Philippe would not have been in Rome if it weren't for me and the damned accusations."

"That still doesn't make it your fault," Andrew insisted. "Just like it isn't my fault because I left the hotel before it happened."

"I know what the police think," Antonio said. "I do not believe you set us up nor do I believe you had anything to do with my brother's death."

"Thanks. I appreciate that," Andrew remarked, relieved to hear Antonio's words.

"What will you do now?"

"I will return home, bury my brother and put the ordeal behind me."

"What about the accusations he was making against you?"

"The committed already voted in my favor so it doesn't matter," Antonio insisted.

"My vote wasn't in," Andrew replied, reminding Antonio the vote was not completely in his favor but tied. It was Andrew's vote which would make the difference, and he still had not cast it.

"Whatever it doesn't matter anymore," Antonio insisted. "There was no evidence in the first place and I will no longer remain here playing this game."

"Right, the proof," Andrew echoed.

"Have you learned something else?" Antonio asked, sensing the hesitation in Andrew.

"Nothing," he lied. He was not going to tip his hand. If Antonio was aware of the evidence as Hector suggested, then he needed more time before playing his final card. Until he had a chance to go through the file thoroughly he was not going to let anyone know of its existence.

"Then there's no reason for me to remain is there? " Antonio announced. "I will be leaving in the morning with my brother and as far as I am concerned everything is over."

"In the morning?' Andrew uttered.

"Yes, in the morning. Unless there is a reason I should remain?"

"My son is the reason," Andrew argued. "Everyone involved needs to be where I can find them until my son was free," he explained.

"Very well, my friend," the man replied, agreeing to remain in Rome a little longer. "For the boy's sake, I will remain as long as I can, but I can't promise how long that will be."

"Thanks, any time you can give me will help," Andrew assured him. Not only did he need time to review the file, but he needed to give the officer following Mark enough time to see where he might lead him.

"What will you do now?" Antonio asked.

"I have to go seen Hans at the police station," Andrew began. "From there I am not sure."

"Well as soon as you know anything contact me," Antonio instructed. "Maybe between Hans, myself and you we can figure out what the hell is going on."

"That would be a nice change." Andrew laughed before heading for the door. He was on the move again and still waiting for contact from the kidnapers. Andrew felt like a ping pong ball as he went from place to place, talking to his suspects in hopes one or more of them would give him a much-needed clue as to where his son was. Yet, in the four hours since he started talking to Mark, Hector and Antonio, the only thing he'd been able to accomplish so far was to give himself a headache. Hoping he'd have better luck with Hans, Andrew left the hotel and headed to the police station.

CHAPTER ELEVEN

The room felt as if it were closing in around him as he paced nervously awaiting word from San Sebastian. He received word less than an hour earlier from Hector that they located his missing man and Andrew was eager to learn why he hadn't answered any of his e-mails before this. Even though Hector's people advised him, his friend had not made contact because the government had imprisoned him for his political views, Andrew wanted to hear what really happened from his friend before he made any judgment calls on his next move. However plausible the story was, he found it difficult to believe things in San Sebastian had gotten so bad that they were rounding up political prisoners to keep order.

"Come on, what is taking so long?" he mumbled, turning away from the computer for a few minutes as he fixed himself a drink.

You have mail, finally flashed across the screen as he looked back to see what he'd been waiting for.

Hello, old friend. Are you ok? Andrew eagerly typed into the computer as he awaited a response.

Hello, Andrew. My friend, it is good to hear from you. Thank you for sending Hector's men to get me out of jail.

I wish I'd known about what you were going through sooner, I would have tried to get you help before this. Are you sure you are all right? Andrew typed as he continued to ask questions about his friend the ordeal.

I am fine. I have endured a lot of pain in the last couple of months trying to help my people, but we both know whatever dangers come from the fight for freedom, we cannot be deterred from out battle.

Andrew read over the message several times staring at the response from his friend. Once again he felt something was wrong but could not put his finger on it. The words did not sound like the man he knew and he could not help but wonder why he was behaving so strangely.

Well, my friend, whatever the fight is about, I am glad you are safe, Andrew replied, before continuing with his questions.

So, my friend, I am trying to figure out what is going in San Sebastian. Are the rumors I have heard true about Antonio becoming a dictator like the Guillermos? Has he gone against everything his father believed in for his own personal gains? he asked, not sure of he what kind of response he wanted from his friend this time.

I am sorry to say the rumors are more than true. That is why I ended up in jail. I was writing about the changes in the president and the way he was abusing his power and he did not like it.

"Damn," Andrew uttered as he continued to read the words his friend was sending him.

What can you tell me about Antonio? Andrew typed in.

I am sorry to say he has gone completely mad with power, just as we were afraid of when he took over the country's leadership. Without Philippe there to keep an eye on him and make sure he remained level headed, Antonio lost all sense of pride in his people and became just as bad as the dictators we usurped so long ago. I have documentation, witnesses and victims, and proof of his behavior. That is one of the reasons I was imprisoned, to keep me from publishing the facts in the paper so the rest of the world could see them too.

"Great," another sarcastic response. Just what he wanted to hear. Not only was his contact insisting as Philippe did that Antonio was no longer fit to rule, but he too offered to show him proof and confirm what he was saying. As much as Andrew hated to admit it, Philippe's actions were not out of old jealousies and resentments as he thought, he'd come to Rome to help his people and it was Antonio who had changed so drastically.

Can you fax me a copy of the documents you have? Andrew typed into the computer. If he was going to make a last ditch plea to the committee before he voted, he needed something to backup his accusations.

Of course, I will. Is there anything else you want me to send you? The names of some of the victims of Antonio's abuse perhaps?

Pausing for a minute as he thought about it, Andrew decided the names were not necessary. With both the file Hector gave him earlier and the proof his friend was going to fax him, there was more than enough evidence to vote Antonio out of office.

Turning from the computer, Andrew thought about his next move, he wanted to face Antonio first before presenting the evidence to the committee. To see for himself the reaction he would get and to give his friend a chance to defend him against the charges.

Can you tell me what happened? What turned Antonio into this tyrant you keep speaking of, he asked, returning to the conversation on the computer.

The change was gradual at first. Little things but as time went on he became more and more blatant with his behavior.

Andrew read as he asked once more about the changes and what they were. It was obvious from the conversation, his questions were not really being answered, as if the man on the other end was replying to him without really reading what he was asking him. The words though accusing in nature were nothing more than a smoke screen and Andrew wanted to know why.

Thanks for the information. Send me the fax as soon as you can. And be careful. If Antonio learns you are still helping me, you and your family will be in more danger than you are already. How is the family anyway? Are they safe? Is your wife Louisa ok? he asked.

After a response came across the screen he replied, *Glad to hear that. I better sign off. Take care, my friend.*

Sitting quietly at the desk, Andrew berated himself for being so foolish, for allowing himself to be tricked so easily by everyone in his life. He was supposed to be a professional, an negotiator whose job it was to read people, yet nothing he'd done since the start of this mission showed any signs of those abilities, any signs he knew what the hell he was doing. He'd become an amateur fumbling around in the dark and because of it, everything he cared about in his life was in danger of being destroyed.

"Damn it," he snapped, throwing his glass across the room. He was done living in a vacuum, finished being a wiping boy for everyone he trusted. It was time to get back the edge of the past, time to be as ruthless as his enemies.

"What!" he snapped, the phone interrupting his temper tantrum. "God, not him, too," he uttered as the news about John, the preseident's aide, caught him off guard. "Is he dead?" he asked reluctantly. "Thank god. I'm on my way, should be there shortly," he announced before heading for the door.

He never should have asked for John's help when they talked the day after the shooting. He should have kept him out of the entire mess, yet when they spoke that day, John seemed eager to prove himself once more to his employer and he had done so well during the shooting incident, Andrew felt certain he could handle the simple assignment monitoring things at the hotel in case anything new should come about. There were plenty of police and private security around, he figured John would be safe no matter what happened. The last thing he expected was to receive a call that he too became a victim in this mess.

Rushing to the back of the hotel near the parking area, Andrew found Hans and his staff already at work as they secured the latest crime scene. Watching as the ambulance crew working on the victim lying on the ground, Andrew looked down at his badly beaten aide.

"How is he?" he asked.

"He has a skull fracture among other things," the EMT replied while he continued to work on his patient.

"Will he be all right?"

"Baring any complications, he should be but we won't know for sure till we get him to the hospital."

"Thanks," Andrew said before turning to Hans. "Do you know what happened?"

"Well, let me see, could it be he made the mistake of calling you a friend?" Knoff balked, walking up to the two men as he spoke. "It seems anyone connected to you these days is a target and this kid was no exception."

"Let it alone," Hans ordered before Andrew could respond.

"Why should I, ever since we've learned of his connection to this mess we have had one dead body after another. This kid could have been number six if the person who attacked him had hit him just a little harder."

"Don't you think I know I am responsible for this?" Andrew snapped. "John is my friend, and the last thing I wanted was for him to get hurt."

"Then why did you get him involved in the first place?"

"You have no idea what you are talking about. I did not ask John to get involved, he volunteered when it looked like you were going to railroad me for the shooting incident."

"Which one?" Knoff said sarcastically.

"You bastard," Andrew replied, ready to strike his tormentor, he backed off as Hans stepped between them.

"What's the matter? Does the truth hurt?" Knoff jeered, not ready to give up on his prime suspect.

"Listen you jackass," Andrew began, "I am sick of you and your accusations, either prove I am guilty or get the hell off my back."

"Oh I intend to, prove you are guilty that is," Knoff announced.

"Well, until you do, just stay out of my face," Andrew ordered.

"Enough," Hans argued. He'd grown tired of refereeing between the two men and wanted them both to put an end to the bickering so they could work together and put an end to crime spree which was destroying his town. "I have enough to worry about without you two behaving like children."

"Tell that to wonder boy there," Andrew argued.

"He's guilty as sin and I am tired of pretending differently," Knoff continued.

"Enough!" Hans shouted once more. "We have more immediate problems right now," he began before turning his attentions back to the young man lying in the stretcher. "We found this attached to his jacket and its addressed to you." Hans announced, handing Andrew the note.

"'Next time don't send a boy to do a man's job,'" Andrew read aloud, the same thought running through his mind as he did. John was an inexperienced operative and Andrew should have known better than to involve him.

"He's not a child and he made his own decisions to get involved," Hans argued after Andrew berated himself for letting John gett involved.

"Yea, I know, but it still doesn't make it any easier to deal with seeing him beat up like that," Andrew uttered.

"Just be grateful he's still alive," Hans began.

"I am."

"I'm going to canvass the area for any witnesses," Knoff announced as he walked away without saying anything else to Andrew. For now, he would obey his commander's orders and leave his personal opinions out of the conversation, but as soon as he had enough proof that Andrew was guilty of at least Helena's murder, he would do what had to be done.

"I think that will be a good idea," Hans replied, before turning his attentions back to his friend and the current problems they faced.

"I'm glad he's gone," Andrew remarked. "I have some news for you." He began filling his friend in on the conversation he had just finished with his contact in San Sebastian.

"That's it then," Hans said. With this latest piece of news, there was no doubt who was behind the entire mess engulfing his community. "What do you intend to do?" he questioned.

"First, I'll give him the chance to explain and hopefully give me a reasonable explanation as to what we've learned," Andrew began.

"And if he doesn't?" Hans said. As an officer of the court he could not allow Andrew to carry out his promise to Jose Vega and hoped after everything that happened so far he'd finally realized how unfair the vow was in the first place and give up on it before it was too late.

"I don't know for sure what I am going to do," Andrew confessed. He wanted to give their suspect a chance to prove the evidence against him was wrong but he might not have that opportunity.

"Just out of curiosity," Hans began wondering if the answer to his question might yield another suspect, "who takes over as the ruler of San Sebastian if Antonio agrees to resign? With Philippe dead, there aren't too many options left are there?"

"Well," Andrew began as he thought about it for a minute, " Philippe was next in line so I guess the leadership will fall to Antonio's oldest son."

"But I thought he was only fourteen years old?" Hans uttered, not the suspect he would hoped for.

"He is," Andrew continued. "I figure the committee will pick an regent until he comes of age and then the boy will take over."

"And the people have no say in this?"

"Nope, the revolution did not bring democracy to San Sebastian it just freed them from the Guillermo rule," Andrew explained. "The Vega family took over as its leaders and will remain as such until another civil war challenges that."

"Nice place," Hans remarked.

"Actually it is or was a very nice place," Andrew replied, recalling with fondness his days there. "But like any place you loved, the flaws which surround it seem minuscule compared to the beauty you see in it."

"I guess," Hans began realizing he too felt the same way about his home. "What about Mark and Steven?" Hans asked, changing the subject again. "Have you heard anything more from either of them?"

"I spoke to Mark at the hotel earlier, but other than that I haven't heard anything from anyone." He continued, "If Mark is working for the man we suspect, then we are running out of time."

"You know, even if we prove his guilt in the death of Philippe, without a confession to the contrary, we still can't prove you were set up for the crimes you're accused of," Hans stated.

"I know," Andrew interrupted. "The evidence still points to me in the death of Helena and even Philippe's murder, but there's not much I can do to change that till we resolve the other matter first."

"I'm sorry, my friend, you could still end up on the wrong side of the law when this is all over," Hans confessed. He knew his friend was being framed but proving it could be more difficult than either of them imagined. Even as their list of suspects grew, the evidence against them did not. Able to prove Antonio's involvement in the scandal involving San Sebastian, there was still no hard proof as to connect him to his brother's death. As for Mark, he too was a suspect only. The proof not there for them to use, only the evidence which continued mounting up against Andrew kept hitting them in the face at every turn they took.

"I know but as long as Steven is safe, I can handle it," Andrew said.

"I hope so," Hans remarked, turning away from his friend as Knoff started walking towards them. "Now what?" Hans asked. He could tell something else was going on by the expression on his detective's face.

"We just heard from the magistrate," Knoff began. " He's reviewed the evidence in Helena's case and feels we have enough to make an arrest."

"And let me guess?" Andrew interrupted. "I am the person he wants to arrest?'

"Yup." Knoff uttered, "A warrant will be ready in a few hours and he wants us to take Andrew into custody till it is."

"Damn it, Knoff! I told you not to turn the evidence over to the magistrate yet," Hans protested. "With Andrew behind bars, we have no hope of finding his son."

"I figured you'd have something to say about that," Knoff began, "but it wasn't me who turned the evidence over to the magistrate in the first place. The crime lab sent a copy of the report to the his office and he got the rest of the paperwork from the captain's office."

"Great! Now what?" Andrew demanded to know. He had no intentions of sitting in a jail cell while his son was still in Mark's hands.

"I will talk to magistrate and try to get an extension," Hans promised. "Maybe I can swing at least twenty-four hours before he issues the warrant."

"Will it be enough time?" Knoff asked. Even though he believed Andrew was guilty, he did not want to see the boy harmed anymore because of the quick decision made by the magistrate.

"I guess it'll have to be, won't it?" Andrew snapped. "But you both better understand something from the beginning. I will do whatever it takes to find my son and no one is going to get in my way," he continued.

"So what's next?" Knoff asked, ignoring the remark Andrew just made.

"Now we confront the enemy and set our own trap," Andrew replied as the three men walked towards his car.

"Great! I love confronting the enemy, especially when there seems to be so many of them to choice from," Hans joked.

"Yea, we get to play with all of them."

"It's about time. I'm itching to get into some action," he said. Tired of always one step behind the game, he was glad to finally have the upper hand.

"Me too," Andrew admitted, the adrenaline flowing like never before. As frightened for his son as he was, the excitement of trying to outsmart an enemy gave him a zeal he'd missed for a long time.

"Why don't we go down to this tavern I know and get something to eat?" Hans suggested, after Knoff left the two men at the car to continue his own investigation. It was almost noon and his stomach was letting him know just how hungry he was.

"Sounds good," Andrew replied, feeling a little hungry himself.

Arriving just in time for the lunch rush, the two men walked towards the back of the room after asking for a table away from the other patrons. They needed to discuss the case before confronting their adversaries and did not want to be overheard by the people who now filled the restaurant.

Smiling as the waiter brought a plate filled with hot rolls, Hans helped himself to the treats before them. A regular there, he was familiar with the efforts the chef took in preparing the homemade bread and he was looking forward to enjoying every bit of it.

"The usual, sir?" a waiter asked, returning the table as he turned to Hans first for his order.

"Yea and ask the chef to put a few extra potatoes with the order, will you? I am hungry today," Hans replied. "He makes the best fried potatoes around," he said to Andrew before completing his list. "Also some extra sauce."

"And you, sir?" the waiter asked, turning to Andrew.

"Same as my friend here but skip the extra potatoes," Andrew replied, not even curious as to what he was ordering. He wanted only a hot cup of coffee to start his meal off and anything else would be fine. "Glad to see some things never change," he joked as Hans fixed he another roll with butter and began eating.

"What can I say? Some people need drugs to calm their nerves. Me, I need food," Hans replied. His mouth filled as he spoke. "Ok, what's the plan?" Hans asked in between the bites.

"Are you sure you want to get any more involved in this than you already are?" Andrew questioned as he, too, enjoyed a hot roll. Hans was putting his neck in a noose for him with the magistrate, and if he insisted on being a part of the next step of the mission, he could end up losing everything in the process. If they weren't careful, instead of coming out ahead, they could end up as casualties themselves.

"Andrew," Hans uttered. He put his fork down after starting the salad they received long enough to reply to his friend. "Whatever you're afraid of, let it go. I have no intentions of letting you handle this mess alone," he insisted. "I'm a big boy, too, and whatever the consequences, I can handle them."

"No matter what?" asked Andrew once again.

"No matter what?" Hans repeated, before digging into his meal as he looked eagerly at the plate filled with his favorite foods.

"Thanks," Andrew replied, "I know I keep saying it, but I really do appreciate having you cover my back."

"You're welcome. Now eat. They make the best scampi in town," he declared before turning his attentions back to the plan. "Fill me in on the rest of the conversation you had with this contact of yours," Hans began as Andrew proceeded to give him the run down on the conversation. "Nice to see the old Andrew McCormick is finally back and ready to take care of things," Hans remarked as Andrew revealed his suspicions and the plan he had devised to handle the situation.

"It is about time, don't you think?" Andrew remarked.

"Well, let's just say it's long over due."

"Thought you were on a diet?" Andrew joked as he watched his friend eat.

"I am that's why only one extra potato," Hans protested as he eyed the piece of cake Andrew got for dessert. "Do you mind?" he uttered, taking a bite from the cake. "I promised my wife I wouldn't order any desserts when I eat out."

"Help yourself." Andrew laughed, pushing the plate closer. He was not in the mood anyway to finish his desert and watching Hans eat was always fun. "How long is Maria out of town?" he asked, questioning Hans about his wife.

"Two weeks."

"Well in that case," Andrew said, signaling the waiter to bring another piece of cake, "enjoy and you can honestly tell Maria you never ordered any dessert," Andrew joked.

"Thanks," Hans replied, taking the plate without argument as Andrew stood up to leave.

Agreeing to meet later, the two men hoped once they exposed their suspect to the public, the tide would finally turn their way.

"Sorry, my friend," Andrew whispered to himself as he looked back at the table and at Hans finishing the desert. There was still something he needed to do before it was all over and hoped when he finally faced his friend he did not hate him forever as a result of what he had been forced to do.

Returning to the hotel, Andrew made several calls as he set his plan in motion. "I'll see you there," he uttered into the phone as his final call set up yet another meeting. If he was going to make his plan work, this meeting would be the most important one of his life.

Arriving at the arranged meeting place, Andrew waited for the person he'd contacted to show up as he stared at the picture of his son. *Soon*, he thought to himself, soon he would be able to find Steven and get him home safely and put the entire nightmare behind them.

"Ok I'm here. What was so urgent that you needed to see me right away?" a voice echoed from behind as he turned to find Antonio standing nearby. "Where is everyone else?" he questioned, assuming the rest of the committee would also be present at this meeting.

"They'll be here later," Andrew assured him, explaining he wanted to speak to Antonio alone first.

"Alone. Why? Have you learned something about my brother's murderer?"

"Actually I have," Andrew replied as the two men sat down to talk.

"Mark? Was it him?" Antonio questioned. He had been informed by Andrew earlier of his suspicions against Mark and wondered now if the proof he found would be enough to seal the case against him.

"In a way," Andrew began.

"Mark is your best friend, why would he betray you like this?"

"I wish I knew," Andrew said. "There has to be more to it than I am aware of but I haven't been able to figure it out," Andrew admitted. Despite what the doctors back home told Hans about Mark's obsession with him, Andrew refused to believe their entire friendship of nearly thirty years was a scam. Refused to believe Mark hated him throughout all those years.

"I guess what you said earlier is true." Antonio began trying to comfort his friend. "There really isn't anyone you can trust in this world except for yourself, is there?" Antonio said, offering his sympathies to his friend.

"Does that include you?" Andrew asked

"I hope not, my friend," Antonio replied. "Do you have any idea where they are holding Steven or who Mark is working for?" he asked, also convinced the man was not working alone.

"Funny, you should ask that," Andrew replied angry. "I seem to have enough proof to name one suspect as his accomplice."

"That is wonderful. Who is it?" asked Antonio, pleased things were finally turning around for Andrew.

"Well, everywhere I look, the evidence points keeps coming back to you."

"Me! Are you mad? You cannot believe I would kill my own brother or kidnap your son," Antonio protested, denying the accusations being made against him. Reminding him as they argued of the evidence mounting against Andrew and his insistence of innocence, Antonio hoped his friend would realize the truth. "You claim to be a victim of a set up, well, so am I," the man shouted as he grew angrier with Andrew with each breath he took. "How could you believe I'd turn against my country, my brother with such hatred?" he yelled, "You're supposed to be my friend. My brother! How could you believe such lies about me?"

Staring at him for a moment before replying, Andrew finally tore into his suspect as he began shouting back at him.

"Don't give me that innocent act, Antonio," Andrew finally said. "We both know what you are capable of. I've seen it in the past and you'd do whatever it took to complete your mission then, so I doubt a little thing like diplomacy would stop you now," Andrew argued. He had fought along side Antonio in the past and his guerrilla tactics were as vicious as any he had ever seen.

"That was during war time and I did what had to be done," Antonio protested. "And if the past were an example of what we were capable of, then you too, my friend, would be just as guilty as me," Antonio remarked

"Maybe so, but that doesn't change anything about what I've learned now and the proof I have of your guilt."

"I swear on my family honor and on my brother's honor, I am not guilty of any of the things you're accusing me of," Antonio persisted.

"Honor? What honor?" Andrew finally snapped, grabbing Antonio by the shirt as he yelled at him. "Honor with everything that's happened. You turned against your country, your family, and me. How can you dare talk about honor?"

"I am not guilty," Antonio argued, struggling as the two men continued to battle each other.

"You will step down and let someone with real honor run the country," Andrew ordered as a blow from Antonio sent him reeling to the floor.

"No matter what you say I will not step down," Antonio announced. This time a blow sending him across the room as they continued their fight.

"You will or else I will," Andrew yelled as the two men continued the fight.

"No! I will never," he yelled.

"Then what you're forcing me to do is on your head?" Andrew remarked, pulling his gun from his jacket as he aimed it at the man standing before him. "I have no choice."

"Are you insane?" Antonio cried out, stunned by Andrew's actions. "What do you mean you have no choice? I am still the President of San Sebastian, still your brother. You can not simply kill me so easily?"

"I made a promise to your father and no matter how much I hate it you've left me with no choice but to follow through with it."

"My father," Antonio argued, "What does my father have to do with this?"

"Your father entrusted me with the safety of San Sebastian and its people. Now, because of your betrayal, I am forced to carry out the promise I made him so long ago," Andrew said.

"Then the rumors I heard over the years are true?" Antonio began. "I could not believe my father would instruct someone to murder me."

"Maybe he did because he believed it would never come to that," Andrew began.

"He believed you would always be an honorable man."

"I am an honorable man and I did not betray my father."

"I wish I could believe that," Andrew uttered, pointing the gun. "Please just sign the papers I brought agreeing to resign and we can forget the damned promise," Andrew pleaded.

"I will not sign anything. If you are going to kill me, then go ahead." A defiant Antonio yelled as he refused to yield to his tormentor.

"Please don't make me do it," Andrew pleaded.

"I will not sign," Antonio announced again. "And I will have the satisfaction of knowing you will spend the rest of your life in jail for my murder," he declared.

"Murder! There is not going to be a murder because the world is going to think you killed yourself over the death of your brother," Andrew explained.

"That, too," Antonio said, losing a little of his resolve as he spoke. "You not only intend to kill me, but shame me in the eyes of the church as well by making everyone I know believe I committed a mortal sin."

"Murder is a mortal sin, isn't it?" Andrew argued. "You murdered your brother."

"I did not kill Philippe," Antonio repeated once more.

"Didn't you order the death of your brother to keep him from exposing your corruption?"

"No! Damn it, I didn't," Antonio insisted.

"I wish I could believe you, but in any case it's too late to go back now," Andrew admitted. He had crossed over the line and had to finish what was started.

"Then we shall both lose," Antonio uttered sadly.

"Tell me where my son is?" Andrew demanded, mentioning his son for the first time since they began fighting.

"I can not tell you what I don't know," Antonio argued.

"Then I am sorry for all of us," Andrew declared.

"Please, Andrew."

"I have to," Andrew shouted as he fired the gun at the man standing before him. Killing Antonio was the only way he could save his son.

"Nicely done," Hector uttered, stepping out from behind the pillars.

"Shut the hell up," Andrew balked, distraught over what he had been forced to do. He just killed a good friend and wasn't in the mood to hear anything from the man who'd been a witness to the entire incident. "Are you happy now?" Andrew said. "Now you can go home and tell everyone your country is finally rid of the tyrant."

"You have no idea how happy I am," Hector replied, thanking Andrew for calling him in the first place to be present when he confronted Antonio.

"I wanted to be sure you were here to back me up in case Antonio brought reinforcements."

"Well, obviously he wasn't worried about being harmed with you around," Hector snickered as he moved closer to the body.

"I need some air," Andrew snapped, his words diverting Hector from his actions as he turned to face him.

"You said you intended to make it look like a suicide. Do you?"

"Just give me a minute and I will take care of everything," Andrew announced before walking out the door leaving Hector alone with the dead man.

"Hello. It's me," Hector said as he whispered into his cell phone. "Yes it's over. Andrew killed the president and now there's nothing standing in our way." He continued, "No, I'm the only witness, and when the time comes to accuse Andrew of murder, I will have the videotape I took to back it up," he explained, pleased he been able to film Andrew committing murder. "We've not only rid ourselves of the Vega family for good but their troublesome in-law as well," Hector gloated. His hatred not only for Antonio and his family evident but for Andrew as well. "The man has been a thorn in my side since he came to San Sebastian and convinced everyone he was the great savior of our country. When the people learn he murdered both the president and his brother, I will finally have the pleasure of seeing his great reputation destroyed," he continued.

"No, there's nothing to link you or your family to the deaths," he swore. "The evidence I fabricated will point to Antonio and Andrew as the two people responsible for everything," he explained. "What? The policeman will be no problem either," he said, referring to Hans as he spoke. "I've arranged for him to have an accident in a couple of weeks so there will be no loose ends to interfer with our plans," he promised, checking to make sure Andrew hadn't come back in the building.

"Yes, I told you it was Andrew who killed him just the way you wanted," Hector repeated. "By the time he realizes he killed an innocent man, he'll be behind bars for the rest of his life." He laughed. "No, Mark will not be a problem either. I assure you. All the enemies of your father will finally pay for their betrayal of him," he swore, listening for a few minutes as the person on the other end continued to question him. "The boy? Yes, he is still alive as far as I know," he began. "But I don't understand why you care. Yes, I understand you want him imprisoned in San Sebastian as you're ultimate revenge against his father, but as long as Andrew remains alive, he will keep trying to find a way to free his son and that is more trouble than we need," Hector protested. "It would be better to kill him when we take care of Mark."

Hector wanted his employer to understand keeping Steven alive was a mistake. It entailed too many variables, which could go wrong. Killing him and Mark was the only way they could secure their future. "Very well, sir, I will bring the boy with me when I return and you can do with him whatever you want." He finally relented. "I will be home soon and you'll finally be back on the throne where you belong."

"Don't count on it," a voice uttered as Hector turned to see who was behind him.

Hector was surprised to see Hans standing there with his gun drawn. "Andrew said if we gave you enough rope, you'd hang yourself," Hans said, moving closer as he spoke. "The party's over you bastard," he said to the person on the cell phone as he grabbed it from his prisoner. "Guess he didn't have anything to say," he began, finding the line dead.

"But how?" Hector blurted out, still stunned to find he was caught in his own trap.

"You made one mistake," Hans began. "You assumed everyone involved was too stupid to figure things out. Well guess what? You're wrong. We worked together and before long we had all the answers to our questions right in front of us," Hans gloated. "As for your friend on the other end of the phone. Well Stewart Tibbs was in on our scam the entire time and his people should be arriving at the Guillermo estate any minute now to arrest them for conspiracy," he continued.

"You'll never find them," Hector protested, still trying to defend his leader.

"Wrong again," Andrew shouted walking back into the room. "The minute you helped me locate my man in San Sebastian, I knew the Guillermos were responsible for the entire conspiracy and contacted Tibbs back home." Andrew laughed. "It took a little while to convince him I wasn't insane like Mark suggested to him before he disappeared, but once I did, he was ready to help. His people have been keeping the Guillermos under surveillance since I got that e-mail from San Sebastian yesterday. They should be inside the compound even as we speak arresting the heir apparent and his brother for trying to overthrow Antonio and his leadership."

"But how?" Hector repeated.

"Well, before I answer that, I have another surprise for you," Andrew said, walking over to the body of Antonio. "Wake up, sleepy head," he uttered as Antonio opened his eye and began laughing.

"It's about time. My nose was itching," the man uttered as he stood up.

"I thought you were going to blow it when he kicked you." Hans laughed.

"Me, too! That hurt." Antonio joked as he looked at the vest that protected his body from the gunfire.

"You're dead!" Hector shouted, trying to strike the president as he spoke. Everything he'd worked so hard for, worked to accomplish, was slipping away from him as the men laughed in his face. "Damn you, why aren't you dead?" he yelled as a blow from Antonio sent him falling to his knees.

"Now that felt good," Antonio remarked, rubbing his fists a little.

"Not for him I bet." Hans laughed, helping the injured man back on his feet.

"I am a diplomat; you can not do this to me," Hector protested.

"Tell it to the president," Antonio began. "Oh yea, that's me. Arrest the bastard before I kill him myself."

"Thanks! Think I will, arrest him that is," Hans said.

"Why did you do it?" Antonio demanded to know as Hans handcuffed the prisoner.

"You were my friend, Philippe's friend. Why would you turn against us?"

"Friend! I wasn't his friend or yours. I was simply a pawn in your game," Hector protested.

"A pawn in what game?" Antonio said.

"The game you played all those years ago when you lied to us about the new life we would have if we would overthrow the Guillermo regime, but it was a lie," Hector shouted.

"A lie? How was it a lie? " Antonio asked. "How did I lie? The people have prospered and so has the country. There hasn't been any lies against them."

"You lied when you told the aristocrats like myself life would be better with a community joined together. Well, it wasn't, " Hector yelled. " I was a man of means and I was forced to live like a peon." Hector continued, "There is nothing more humiliating than to be compared to a farmer, a peasant, and to be expected to work along side them. My family is from royal decent and should be shown the proper respect."

"This guy is a real looney tune, isn't he?" Hans said, listening to Hector as he rambled on about his position and stature.

"Why, because I am better than you and those fools who run my country," Hector snapped.

"Pretty much."

"I should have been living like my ancestors, and because of the Vega family, I was denied my rightful place in the world. By having the Guillermo family back in power, I would've been given back my statue."

"And you decided betraying the people who treated you like a friend was the way to accomplish it?" Andrew asked.

"Friendship had nothing to do with it," Hector confessed, "I only wanted what I deserved."

"You can count on that," Hans announced.

"How did you convince my brother I was guilty of treason?" Antonio asked.

"That was easy." Hector laughed. "When Philippe left San Sebastian to start a new life, he was filled with rage. He'd grown tired of living in your shadow and all I had to do was plant the seeds in his mind." Hector continued, "Once I did, I just let his imagination take over. He wanted to believe you were a terrible leader so he could come to the rescue and I just played on that. I sent him fake reports over the years of your corruption and led him to believe you were destroying the very thing your father fought for."

"But why didn't he come to me?"

"Oh, he tried," Hector said. "I set up a meeting between the two of you in Switzerland and when an assassin tried to murder him, he just assumed you had sent the man to eliminate him before he could challenge your rule."

"That's why my brother refused to speak to me in private? He thought I tried to have him killed." Antonio spoke, his voice shaking. "All those months after he challenged my leadership when he refused to have anything to do with me was because you turned him against me and he died believing I betrayed him."

Antonio cried out. "Damn you," he snapped, striking Hector with a blow so strong it sent the man tumbling to the floor.

"Ouch." Andrew sneered as he stood with Antonio over the man lying on the floor. "You had that coming," he began. "Now tell me about my part in this."

Looking up at his attackers, Hector wiped the blood from his face.

"I knew about the promise you made to Jose and used it to my advantage," Hector began.

"Fine, you knew about the promise and decided to use it to get rid of Antonio, but why did you have to involve my son and why did Mark help you?"

"So you know about him, too," Hector remarked.

"Yes, we know about him, too, so tell me why he was involved with this mess and why he let you use Steven?"

"That was Mark's idea," Hector admitted. "He wanted you to suffer and the best way was to take your son." Hector laughed.

"But why?" Andrew asked, still searching for answers as to what turned his friend against him.

"He was never your friend," Hector began. "That was an illusion he invented so he could be apart of your life."

"Say what?" Andrew blurted out.

"You never saw it, did you?" Hector asked. "The envy and jealousy Mark possessed for you and your perfect life."

"My perfect life?"

"The man was insane. He was always angry at life for dealing him such a bad hand and he wanted everything you had. Your parents, your son, and your wife. When he couldn't get any of it, he decided to take them away from you as well."

"By kidnaping my son?"

"By destroying your life piece by piece," Hector remarked. "He not only wanted to see your reputation as an honorable man smashed to pieces but he wanted Steven as well."

"Wanted Steven for what?"

"So he could have his imaginary family. The perfect life he felt he deserved." Hector laughed. "As long as you were caught up in your grief over Sophia's death, he had that life taking care of Steven, but when you started to repair the fences between the two of you, Mark found his world falling apart. So when I came to him for help, he was more than ready to assist me in bringing you down as well."

"What if he'd have said no and came to me with the plan?" Andrew asked, still looking for any glimmer of Mark's innocence.

"I came to him to help me destroy the Vega family because I knew how much he loved to the game. When I heard he'd been taken prisoner and had to be rescued by you, I figured he needed something to help him recover from the embarrassment of once more coming out second best in everyone's eyes. He was eager to help me and didn't care who it involved, but when he learned it was Antonio, he decided to make up his own plan as well."

"He knew about my vow to Jose and was going to watch me kill an innocent man so he could steal my son?" Andrew said, completing Hector's statement as everything finally clicked for him.

"Yes. He wanted you out of the way and turning you into a killer was the perfect answer for both of us."

"Did he know you were working for the Guillermos?"

"He didn't care who I was working with, only that it meant your destruction." Hector continued, "As long as your son was in danger, making you look guilty in the eyes of the world would be easy to do, and Mark played on that. All we needed to do was plant the seeds of doubt and everyone was ready to convict you of the crimes." He laughed looking over at Knoff and the others.

"Nice man," Knoff remarked. "Instead of being happy for his friend, he decided to set him up for murder."

"I have such wonderful friends, don't I?" Andrew joked, trying not to let his own anger overtake him. "Go on tell me the rest," he said, turning back to Hector after hearing there was still more about Mark he didn't know.

"You do not want to hear this, I can tell you that right now," Hector assured him.

"Yea, I do."

"Very well. You asked for it," he said. "The man was possessed by the devil even as a young man," Hector began as he filled in the others on the truth about Mark's nature. "This so called good man was also responsible for many of the things in your life which went wrong. Little things you just assumed were fate or karma. Missions which failed for no reason. Friends who turned against you because of rumor and innuendo. Whatever he could do to make life more miserable for you, he did, including," Hector paused.

"Including what?" Andrew demanded to know.

"Including murdering your wife."

"My wife!" Andrew blurted out. The words he'd just heard were the last he ever expected to hear.

"It was Mark who planted the bomb which killed her so long ago," Hector declared.

"He was trying to kill you but she died instead."

"You're lying," Andrew snapped, grabbing the man as he started to choke him.

"Andrew!" Hans yelled while he tried to pull him off his victim.

Choking from the attack, Hector looked up as Hans pulled Andrew away from him.

"I warned you what I had to say would not be easy," he uttered, still gasping for breath.

"How do you know all this stuff?" Hans asked as he kept an eye on his friend to be sure he did not attack their suspect again.

"Mark has worked for me since he was a young man," Hector explained. "He has been a double agent for years and we know each other very well."

"Working for you, doing what?" was Hans' next question.

"Once I realized Antonio was not the man to lead my people, I recruited Mark to be a teacher to the Guillermo heirs. He has been training them for years in combat and other forms of leadership and at the same time he has been helping me undermine the leadership of President Vega by sabotaging his life as well."

"You bastard," Antonio shouted. His punch reached its target since Hans was not watching for him to attack Hector.

"Mark murdered my wife," Andrew echoed still trying to comprehend what he'd been told as the others looked on realizing he had not heard any other part of the conversation since Hector spoke those words.

"Yes!" Hector laughed, wiping the blood from his face. "And now he has your son and you will never see him again."

"No!" Andrew cried, horrified at the thought of his son in the hands of the lunatic responsible for his mother's death.

"As far as he is concerned, Steven is his son and he has no intentions of releasing him," Hector continued, enjoying turning the tables on the man who'd destroyed his plans.

"Damn you, where is my son? What has Mark done with him?"

"I have no idea where Mark is holding your son," Hector uttered, fighting with his tormentor at the same time. "Even if I did, I wouldn't tell you. My life maybe destroyed but so is yours," Hector said with defiance. "Knowing you'll never see your son alive again will fill my days in prison with such pleasure."

"Get this bastard out of here," Hans ordered his men as he tried to reassure Andrew there was still hope for Steven.

"We have to find him before it's too late," Andrew replied.

"Tell me something," Hector said, struggling with Knoff as he tried to talk to Andrew one more time. "How did you figure it out?" Hector asked. "How did you know I was the one behind everything?"

"I didn't at first," Andrew confessed. "I was convinced Antonio was behind it all and after the death of his brother I felt certain of it," he continued.

"Then how?" Hector repeated.

"You blew it with two very important pieces of evidence," Andrew announced. "First was the folder you gave me. The evidence inside was too pate, even an amateur could see it was not true, that the proof inside had been made up," Andrew explained.

"And the second mistake?" Hector asked, without inquiring on more details on his first. It didn't really matter what the details were, just that he'd failed.

"The second was when my contact in San Sebastian finally reached me," Andrew continued. "Your people should've done more research before trying to pretend they were him on the other end of the computer."

"In what way?"

"When I asked a question, they never gave me a straight answer," Andrew said.

"My friend was a journalist, questions and answers were his forte. He would answer you directly even if it meant asking two more questions himself in exchange for the answers. But the real clincher was when I asked about his wife, Louisa."

"What about her?" Hector asked.

"Louisa is his daughter not his wife," Andrew announced. "I knew I wasn't talking to him and that your people were lying about finding him."

"Those fools," Hector snapped. "I told them not to get to personal with you during the conversation."

"What happened to my friend?" asked Andrew.

"He's dead, of course," Hector announced. "If I was going to convince you Antonio was a traitor, I couldn't have you reach him. He would've informed you that everything was fine in San Sebastian. That Antonio was a wonderful leader and my entire plan would have been destroyed."

"So you killed an innocent man to keep him from talking to me," Andrew yelled, angrier.

"He was not innocent. He was a traitor, just like you and the other rebels, and he got his just punishment."

"So we can add another body to the count," Knoff mumbled before taking Hector out of the room

"I am sorry, my friend, that we did not get the answers you sought," Antonio said as he moved closer to Andrew. "What's the next move?" Antonio asked.

"You are going home," Andrew replied.

"But your son, I can not leave till he has been found," he protested.

"I appreciate you wanting to stay here and help, but we both know it's time for you to go home. Your people need you and so does your family," Andrew began. "They need to say good-bye to Philippe and they need you there when they do."

"I know you are right, but my brother's burial can wait till Steven has been found and Mark captured," Antonio insisted.

"No, it can't," Andrew said as he embraced his friend. "You have to take our brother home," he repeated. "If not for yourself, then for me." Andrew had spent the last couple of weeks angry with Philippe for starting this mess and had forgotten how much he truly loved the man. They had been comrades, friends and brothers, and he owed him for not realizing soon enough that he was just as much a victim as the rest of them.

"Are you sure?" Antonio asked once more.

"Yes, I promise as soon as I find Steven I will send you word."

"But..."

"Please, my friend, go home, and be a good leader," Andrew pleaded.

"Very well," Antonio relented, "but when you find Steven, you will bring him home so that I can see for myself he is all right and I can finally meet my nephew."

"I promise that, too," Andrew replied before instructing the security guards to take Antonio to the airport. "Make sure he is safely on the plane before you leave," he ordered, hugging his friend before watching him leave.

"Ok, now that we have gotten the president safely on his way, what is the our next move?" Hans asked.

"I don't know," Andrew admitted. "My son is in the hands of a madman because I refused to listen or see the signs everyone else saw," Andrew balked, "and I have no idea where he is holding him."

"I wish the officer assigned to Mark hadn't lost his trail so quickly," Hans mumbled.

"Me, too, that might have been our last chance to find them."

"You can't give up now," Hans began sensing the feeling of loss looming over Andrew as he spoke.

"I'll never give up, no matter how long it takes," Andrew announced, assuring his friend he wasn't about to give up on finding his son. "Even if I have to tear Rome down pillar by pillar, I intend to rescue my son from the maniac," he vowed as he followed the others out of the church.

Standing by the front entrance, Knoff signaled for Hans to wait with him as the others headed for their cars. He needed to talk to him alone and this was as good a time as any.

"We have another problem," he whispered so as not to be heard by anyone else.

"What is it?" Hans asked.

"The warrant for Andrew's arrest has been issued, and we are supposed to bring him in."

"What? We know he did not kill anyone," Hans protested.

"Do we," Knoff remarked. "Maybe he didn't have anything to do with Philippe's death but that doesn't mean he didn't kill Helena."

"Knoff, you still can't believe he killed my niece, not after what you just heard?" Hans asked, curious as to why he believed as he did. "It's obvious the evidence was fabricated against him."

"Maybe some, but not all," Knoff insisted. "There is still enough proof there to arrest Andrew.

"What proof?" Hans asked.

"Well, besides the fingerprints we found on the glass, there is also the footprint outside the residence that matches the pair of shoes I took from Andrew's room," Knoff explained. "There is also the button we found near the couch that belongs to his jacket and…"

"Enough already," Hans said. "It is all circumstantial."

"Maybe, but we now have a warrant to arrest him and we have to decide what we are going to do next."

CHAPTER TWELVE

Mark stood nervously outside the safe house as he thought about the phone conversation he had with Hector less than twenty minutes earlier. As pleased as he was to learn about Antonio's death and the fact the police were looking for Andrew, he was still uneasy about his insistence they meet to discuss the situation. The arrangements made before the mission to meet once they safely returned to San Sebastian were the most logical, changing those plans now and risking the police finding a connection between them was an unnecessary risk. A risk Mark was not going to take. Whatever Hector needed to discuss would have to wait until later, no matter how panicked he seemed, Hector's pleas would have to go unanswered.

Maybe, he thought as he took drink from the flask he kept in his jacket pocket, *maybe he just wanted to confirm the next step in the mission and congratulate me for a job well done.*

Smiling as he thought about the pleasure he would have in the last step of the game, Mark envisioned Andrew's face when he killed him. When the moment of his betrayal became real and he finally understood how much he hated him. It would be worth all the failures he'd been forced to endure, all the shame, to finally see Andrew in his grave. Steven still had no idea he was involved in the kidnaping and once Andrew was out of the way, Mark knew he could finally build a life with the boy without anyone else interfering.

"What are you doing here?" Kirk demanded to know as Mark walked into the kitchen unannounced.

"I had to see him, make sure he was all right," Mark explained, pouring a cup of coffee for himself as Kirk filled him in on the boy.

"He's fine," Kirk argued. "What do you mean see him, if he finds out you are here, won't that mess up your perfect plan?"

"He won't see me, I can check on him without him knowing," Mark snapped. "And don't question me or my actions again," he ordered. "You have him secured this time, don't you?"

"Yes," Henry replied as he waved the key to the chain that secured Steven to the bed. "He isn't going anywhere."

"Was it necessary to chain him up like an animal?"

"Look, Mark, you haven't had to deal with that punk, he has caused nothing but trouble."

"So you chained him to the bed?" Mark argued.

"He's got enough room to move around in the room but this time there is no chance he will find a way to escape," Henry declared.

"Are you so sure about that?" Mark laughed. Though he did not reveal the reason behind his remark.

"Why do you insist on taking such a stupid risk when we are so close to finally having this mess over with?" Kirk asked, interrupting the conversation between the two men.

"Because I am in charge and I can do whatever I damn well please, including showing up here without your permission to check on things," Mark snapped, angry his actions were being questioned.

"Whatever," Kirk replied, not willing to get into another fight over the boy. "Have you heard from Hector?" he asked, trying to change the subject to something far more important.

"Yes," Mark replied. "It's almost over. Antonio is dead and the police are looking for Andrew. Once they find him dead by his own hand, the mission will finally be done."

"And you didn't think this bit of information was important enough to tell us the minute you walked in," Kirk argued. He had been waiting to hear this news since the mission started turning sour and did not appreciate Mark's actions in any sense of the word.

"I didn't tell you because until I confirmed everything and I see Andrew dead too, the mission is still in place. I do not want you to get any sloppier than you already have and do something else stupid before I had a chance to take care of things on my end."

"What about our money?" Henry asked.

"We didn't discuss that," Mark announced. "But Hector knows better than to double cross us over something as trivial as the money."

"I hope so," Kirk replied. He had not endured a week of babysitting to have something else goes wrong. All he wanted was to collect his money and get as far way from Mark and his crazy plans as possible.

"You're sure he is ok?" Mark asked, moving towards the door where Steven was being kept.

"He is fine," Henry said, turning towards the direction of Steven's room as he spoke.

Pounding his feet against the wall below the window, Steven stared out at the large oak tree brushing up against the house. His newest prison, though smaller than the estate he had been held in earlier, was still very much an obstacle to him.

Not only did he have to contend with the gates behind the trees, but with the chain that secured him to the bed. He was like a caged animal, trapped by his captors, and unless he could figure something out soon he would remain so.

"Here, kid," a voice from behind remarked as he turned to see Henry standing there with a plate of food.

"Thanks," Steven said, taking the plate, sitting up on the bed as he began eating.

"Can you stay and talk for a little while?" he asked in an almost child like tone. Except for the few times Henry delivered his meals, he had been alone since they arrived at the new safe house and was feeling the need to talk to someone, anyone, even Henry to keep from spending another night just staring out the window of his room.

"You want to talk to me?" Henry laughed. "About what, the weather?"

"Forget it," the defiant boy replied, as his captor turned to walk out. "Wait, can I at least have a radio to listen to. It is so quiet in here and if I do not hear another human voice even from a radio, I am going to go crazy."

"Well, isn't that just too bad," Henry replied before leaving.

"Thanks for nothing," Steven mumbled under his breath as he pulled at the chain on his leg. If he did not find a way to free himself he would go crazy, if not from the silent treatment he was receiving, then from not knowing what was going on in the outside world. It had been a total of five days since he was first kidnaped, five days since the nightmare began and he still had no idea if they had already forced his father to go along with their plan to kill someone or if he too was dead like the others.

"Here," Henry snapped, angry with himself for allowing the boy to get to him. He had been nothing but trouble from the beginning yet there was something about him, something that made Henry pity the boy. If giving him a radio was all he had to do to ease his conscious, there was no harm in it.

"Thanks," Steven said, taking the radio and turning it up loudly as he began fiddling with the chain on his leg. The noise would hopeful hide any noise he might make trying to free himself and keep his captors from learning what he was trying to do.

MATTEA LORETTA

We interrupt our regular radio broadcast to bring you this news story. Local authorities are investigating yet another murder in our area. The body of a young woman was discovered in her home. Helena Royster was found dead in her cottage by her uncle, Police Lieutenant Hans Ferrier. Though local authorities are not saying who is a suspect at this point, this radio station has learned there is at lease one prime suspect in the case who is being questioned by the police. Andrew McCormick, a visiting diplomat, has been named the prime suspect, and though we have yet to confirm this information with the police, our sources at the department tell us the evidence against him is very damaging.

Trying to comprehend what he was hearing, Steven thought about the woman he had made love to only a few days earlier. Like everyone he came in contact with, she too was dead because of him, and if that wasn't difficult enough for him, hearing his father was a suspect in her death only made things worse. They had set Andrew up to take the fall for her death. Helena was just as much a victim as the rest of them; she never knew the men she was working for were going to kill her as part of their warped plan of revenge against his father.

Taking a deep breath as he listened to the rest of the news broadcast, Steven could tell even before he heard the words that things were only going to get worse for all of them.

Our sources have learned that the police are questioning Andrew McCormick about the relationship he was having with the victim. We have also learned that the police have obtained a diary from the victim which names Mr. McCormick not only as her boyfriend but also as one of her paying clients. Ms. Royster, who grew up in the area, was well known for her illegal activities, including prostitution. We have also learned through our sources at the police station that Mr. McCormick's name has also been linked to the assassination of Philippe Vega and the attempted murder of his brother Antonio, the president of San Sebastian. Though the police refuse to comment on either case, saying only that they are looking into every aspect of the case, this station believes Mr. McCormick is the only suspect they are currently investigating. We will continue to bring you any further details the moment we get them. We now return to our local programming.

"Damn it," Steven shouted, turning the radio off. His father was in more danger than he realized, not only was he being accused of murdering Helena, but orchestrating the assassination of a political figure as well.

"I have to do something," he uttered, pulling at the chain which kept him from his goal. "I have to figure out a way to find my father and help him before he is killed by the local police," he continued as his thoughts drifted from his father for a moment to the woman the radio talked about. "Why did they have to kill her?" he mumbled as he took the fork from his plate and began fumbling with it in an attempt to open the lock, which kept him secured to the bed.

Smiling, an almost envious smile, Steven thought about the person who taught him to break into locks in the first place using even a simple thing like a fork. Mark had taught him many strange things over the years, including lock picking and he never thought there would come a time when he would actual need to use such skills.

"See, Uncle Mark, they haven't beaten us yet." He spoke softly, still holding on to the hope that his uncle was still alive.

"Thank you, Uncle Mark," he said, struggling with the lock for about five minutes before he finally pried it open. "I knew in the end you would come to my rescue."

"Hey, Henry!" he shouted out the door as he tried to get the attention of his captor once more.

"What is it now, kid?" Henry replied, leaving the others in the kitchen as he walked into Steven's room to find out what the boy needed.

"This," Steven blurted out, striking Henry in the back of the head with the lamp sitting next to his bed. "Now that felt good," he uttered, checking the man he just attacked to make sure he was not dead, and then the door to be certain his partner did not hear the commotion.

Moving quickly as he walked down the corridor, Steven started towards the front door. Even though he could hear Kirk talking to someone in the kitchen, if he was careful, he could slip past them to the door and make his way out before they figured he was gone.

"What the—?" he uttered, drawing closer to the kitchen. The voice of the man talking to Kirk sounded very familiar to him. "Uncle Mark," he cried out, realizing who the voice belonged to. *Mark was alive and a prisoner too,* he thought to himself as he moved closer to the door. Walking towards the sounds of the voices, Steven knew he could not leave without him, he had to free his uncle no matter the risk.

"The boy must never know the truth, no matter what," he heard come from the kitchen, as he drew nearer. "Steven must never know I was behind the kidnaping."

"Uncle Mark," he cried out, staring at the man as he overheard words that tore his heart to shreds. "You're a part of this?"

"Steven!" Mark blurted out, stunned to see the boy standing by the kitchen door listening to his conversation.

"You're not a prisoner, are you? You're one of them," Steven repeated, reeling in pain as he said the words repeatedly.

"You little brat," a voice from behind said as Henry walked up to the boy and struck him from behind. "I am tired of you and your games," he shouted, continuing to strike him as he ignored Mark's orders to stop. "Let's just finish this now," he declared, pulling his gun from its holster, pointing it at Steven's head, once again threatening to kill the boy.

"Leave him alone," Mark shouted angrily.

"This son of a bitch is more trouble than he's worth," Henry protested. "Let's just put a bullet in his head and get it over it."

"What's the matter? Ashamed to admit a teenage boy got the better of you again," Kirk joked, deferring Henry's attention long enough for Steven to get away from the man threatening him.

"You should know," Henry replied, reminding his partner of Steven's earlier escape attempt.

"That's right, he got both of us, so why don't you stop with the theatrics and put the gun away, we both know you are not going to kill the fatted calf as long as we still have to get paid," Kirk continued. As much as he hated to admit it to himself, they needed Steven in one piece if the mission was going to be completed. "If you kill the kid now, we all lose."

"All right," Henry snapped, putting his gun away. "But if you don't do something about him soon, money or not, I will kill him," he announced, directing his comment to Mark this time.

"Don't worry, I will handle this," Mark declared, taking Steven by the arm. "Come with me now," he ordered as they started towards the kitchen door. "You need to behave from now on, otherwise I can't be responsible for what might happen. Do you understand?"

"I don't understand anything any more," Steven cried out, staring at his uncle. "I thought you were dead, that they killed you and instead I find you alive and part of this entire mess. How could you be apart of it?"

"I am more than just a part of it," Mark announced as he shoved Steven, causing him to fall to the floor next to his bed. "I am the person in charge of this mission."

"Mission. Is that all this is to you?" Steven shouted. "You betrayed me and my father. Helped to kill all those people and you call this a mission."

"Steven, I never wanted you to find out like this," Mark began. His tone changed as he helped the boy to his feet and the two men sat on the bed. "I wanted to explain everything to you when the time was right, to help you understand why I did what had to be done."

"What had to be done? What else did you do?" Steven cried The tears flowed from his eyes. He moved away from his uncle and he stood by the window.

"I told you I did what had to be done."

"Is my father dead?" he asked hesitantly, afraid of what the answer might be. "Did you kill him, too?"

"Not yet," Mark uttered without thinking about what he was saying.

"Not yet," Steven repeated. "You bastard," he snapped, swinging at his uncle as his surprise attack caught the man off guard. "I'm going to kill you," he shouted fighting with his captor as the rage of the last week seeped from his body.

"Steven, I don't want to hurt you," Mark argued, defending himself from the attacks.

"I hate you, I hate you," Steven continued, another swing this time deflected as his opponent returned his own blow instead.

"Steven, calm down, Don't you understand I did all of this for you." Mark tried to explain as he struggled with the distraught boy. "I never wanted you to know about my part in this mess, but now that you do, you have to realize I did it all to protect you."

"Protect me from what?" Steven asked, struggling to his feet after the last blow from Mark sent him to the floor again.

"From your father and his world."

"My father and his world," the confused boy mumbled. "You wanted to protect me from his world by helping those bastards to kidnap me and throwing me to the wolves at the same time."

"I did what was necessary."

"You really believe that, don't you? Steven asked, staring at his uncle. "You really believe what you did was for me?" he repeated, afraid to hear the answer even as he asked the question. It was apparent by the expression on his face that Mark thought what he did was right, and this terrified Steven more than the threat of another attack.

"Yes, I believe that," Mark reiterated. "I am doing what is best for you and that is all I am doing."

"Why? Why would you think that?" he begged. He finally gave in as he sat down on the bed and waited for the man to answer him.

"Oh, Steven," Mark began as he sat next to the boy, putting his arm around him as he spoke. "It was going to be so simple. I would get rid of your father, rescue you from the kidnapers and we would finally live together as father and son, the way it was supposed to be in the first place."

The deranged man began pacing around the room with Steven by his side, his grip on the boy grew stronger making it impossible for him to get away from his tormentor. "I knew once your father was out of the way we could finally have a life together and the only way to make sure of it was to frame him for murder and treason," he continued, still moving around the room.

"And the charges back home? Did you make them up to?" Steven asked, reminding him of the reason they came to Rome in the first place.

"Oh, that was so easy, " Mark continued. "Your father entrusted me with a surveillance tape of the file room and I just doctored it up a little, so when I finally turn it over to Stewart, it will not only prove he broke in to get the files he needed but killed the clerk working that night as well," Mark explained. "Your father told me about his plan to steal the files. He knew Stewart would never give them to him because of the relationship Andrew had in the past with the Vega family, so when he told me about it, I knew it was an opportunity I could not give up," he continued, still holding tightly onto the boy as he spoke. I had planned only to frame your father for murder here in Rome, but once he told me about his plan, I knew I had to make him look guilty back home too. Imagine the great Andrew McCormick accused of murder and treason in two countries, the pain he would feel knowing that his precious reputation would be destroyed forever." He laughed. "It was the perfect plan."

"And me," Steven said, trying not to lose it as he listened to his uncle speak. He needed to understand, needed to figure out what was going on inside the man who was tormenting him.

"I told you I never meant for all this to happen to you," Mark explained. "It was supposed to be so simple. You would be kidnaped and I would rescue you, but by the time I did, your father would already be dead," he said as he faced Steven while they talked. "You would have been so grateful to me for saving you that in the end we would end up moving away from the United States living in a small town in San Sebastian and we would be a family."

"You thought I would live with you as if nothing ever happened, as if you were my hero and pretend I was not kidnaped or Dad wasn't dead?"

"Of course, why not?" asked Mark. "You weren't supposed to know about my part in the kidnaping and I would convince you to come with me."

"And if I didn't want to come with you?" Steven asked, again afraid of what the answer would be.

"Wouldn't come," the deranged man uttered as he walked towards the window away from his captive. "There was no way you wouldn't come, I had it planned. I even had the drugs ready if I needed them to make sure everything went as I wanted them too."

"Drugs?" the horrified boy said, stepping farther away from his uncle.

"They would not hurt you, I promise," Mark assured him as he tried to comfort the boy. "The drugs were just supposed to keep you in line till you came to understand what I did and why."

"I would never understand any of it, and I would never live with you as if we were a family."

"Of course you would," Mark declared. "I had it planned."

"You're insane," Steven cried out.

"I know," Mark finally replied with pride as he moved towards Steven and stood next to him. "I did it all because I wanted to, not because of the past, or my hatred for your father, I did it because I enjoyed the game," he revealed. "I enjoyed killing the man at the apartment, and the others."

"The others?" Steven uttered "What others?"

"My men of course," Mark answered, staring at Steven as he spoke. "I lied about my men dying when we landed at the land zone. They didn't die there, they died in the prison camp after we were captured."

"The what?"

"Yea, we were the prisoners of the rebels and I suddenly realized after they beat me nearly to death that I liked what I was feeling. The pain, the rage, it felt like it was a part of me, so I made a deal with them, " Mark rambled. "I told them I would help them with their battle if they let me escape. It seemed they learned of a team coming in to try a rescue and they had another trap set. So when they agreed to set me free I had to prove myself to them, prove I would give them the money I promised to help their fight."

"Prove yourself by betraying your own men?"

"That was the price, there could be no witnesses to my deal and my men would have told everyone the truth if they ever escaped," Mark announced, "So I did what had to be done."

"Oh my god," Steven cried out. "I thought you were acting this way because of what happened to you, because of the drugs, but you were insane before this happened, I just never saw it before."

"I know, neither did your father." Mark laughed. "He was so convinced I was the victim in everything that happened to me, he never saw the truth, and never saw I wasn't the poor little boy he knew as a child but a man who was in complete control of everything he did."

"Control. You wanted control of everything so you set my father up and kidnaped me, is that the way you get control?"

"Yes, it is," Mark replied.

"Dear god, you are insane."

"I had to kill them, all of them if I was going to get you back," Mark continued, ignoring Steven's remarks. "Even the man at the apartment. He was a friend of your father's, and when he heard us talking, he knew something was wrong. When I confronted him in the living room, he said he'd been sent to guard you and I couldn't let him get in my way, I couldn't let him tell your father I was with you, it would have messed up everything and I couldn't let that happen."

"So you murdered him, too."

"I took care of the problem that was all."

"And the others, did you know about their deaths, too, planned them?"

"You mean Helena and the medics?" Mark asked. "Well that wasn't supposed to happen. No one else was supposed to get killed except for your father and the Vegas," he confessed. "The others were just collateral damage after you tried to escape."

"Collateral damage?" the boy uttered. "You murdered all those people and all you can say is it is collateral damage."

"Yes!"

"And me, am I collateral damage, too?" Steven asked, this time with a defiance in his voice. "Do you intend on killing me now that I know the truth?"

"You, Steven, never. You are my life, my reason for living. You are my son and I love you."

"Love me?" Steven echoed.

"Yes, I love you, and some day you will understand that."

"Never!"

"I will prove my love once your father is dead."

"Please no more," Steven pleaded

"I have to, I have to make it look like your father killed himself over his guilt. I have to make it look like Andrew shot himself in the head after he realized he would be arrested not only for treason but for the murder of Helena and the others."

"But why?"

"Because we will never be happy if he is alive."

"Please, Uncle Mark, no more."

"I am sorry but after I clear up a few loose ends, your father will be next and then we can go to our new home and start over."

"Loose ends," the frightened boy said.

"Yea, that stupid cop, Hans Ferrier, I have to take care of him to now thanks to your father."

"Helena's uncle. Why him?"

"It is your father's fault," Mark began. "He wasn't supposed to tell anyone about the kidnaping and he told Hans."

"So he has to die for that?" Steven shouted.

"Yes. If my plan is going to work and the world is going to believe your father killed himself over his guilt of betraying his country, then there can be no other motive for the police to find. If they learn you were kidnaped they might start to believe Andrew did not kill himself and start looking for you. No one back home knows you are missing, they think we are away on a fishing trip, and Hans is the only one here who is aware of the truth so he has to die too."

"But I'll tell the police the truth when I am free," Steven said, reminding his uncle of his words that he would not kill him no matter what.

"That will be impossible, Steven," Mark explained, taking Steven in his arms once more. "We will be living on a small island off of San Sebastian and you will never see the outside world again."

"I won't let you kill my father or keep me prisoner," Steven shouted as he took a punch at his tormentor in anger.

"Sorry, kid, not this time," Mark echoed as he sent Steven reeling to the floor with a blow of his own. "You will learn in time I am charge and there is nothing you can do to stop it."

"I..." was the only word Steven could muster as he looked up at his uncle. He was at the mercy of a mad man and there was nothing he could do except pray his father would find him in time.

"Enough," Mark said as he began rubbing his temples the pain growing stronger with each word they spoke. The headaches were getting worse and fighting with Steven was making it even worse.

"No matter what you do, I will never be part of your life again," Steven finally declared, refusing to give up. "I hate you and that will never change even if you keep me drugged for the rest of my life."

"No! Steven, don't say that," Mark pleaded, moving towards him in an attempt to comfort the boy. "I know you're upset right now but in time you will understand," he continued, wrapping his arms around the boy once more. "I know in time you will understand everything," he repeated.

"Leave me alone," Steven ordered, pushing him away.

"Steven, please."

"No," Steven cried. "You're not my Uncle Mark, the man I loved all my life," Steven continued. "You are just like your father was, a bastard who enjoys hurting people just for the fun of it."

"Don't say that, I am not like him, I will never be like him," Mark screamed, striking the boy repeatedly with his hand as Steven tried to defend himself from the blows. "Oh god, Steven," Mark cried, realizing as the boy cowered in the corner of the room trying to get away from his attacker, what he had done. "I swear I never meant to hurt you. I am sorry for what happened." He began moving towards the boy as he tried to help him back to his feet.

"Leave me alone," Steven ordered. "Just get the hell out of here and leave me alone."

"All right, Steven." Mark began moving towards the door. "We will talk later and I will make you understand everything I did was for you."

"Not in this lifetime," the boy shouted, still refusing to give in to the tormentor standing before him.

"Steven!" Mark began, his words interrupted by the arrival of Kirk at the bedroom door. "What is it?"

"You might want to come out and listen to the news bulletin," Kirk said. "The kid too."

Following them into the living room, not sure what to expect next, Steven moved into the room as they all stood before the TV screen.

Repeating this latest news bulletin, the man on the screen began as Steven held his breath, terrified by what he was going to hear next.

THE NIGHTMARE'S EDGE

The police are on the scene of a fatal car accident which occurred less than twenty minutes ago. From what we have learned, the police responded to reports that murder suspect Andrew McCormick was in the area of his hotel trying to retrieve something from his personal belongings. We learned the police had just issued a warrant for his arrest and he may have been trying to secure funds to flee the country. Though the police have not confirmed our report at this time, it is believed that Andrew McCormick was about to be arrested when he was spotted by a police officer in the area. Apparently a gun battle ensued during the attempt, and Mr. McCormick was killed as a result. The coroner still on scene confirms at least one fatality and at least one injured officer.

"Dad," Steven said, stumbling into a nearby chair as the announcer on the TV continued to relay the current events.

From what we have learned, the officer who was injured during the assault had fired on Mr. McCormick's car as he tried to escape, and the vehicle crashed into a nearby statue causing the vehicle to explode on impact with the suspect still inside. For those viewers who are not familiar with the case, Mr. McCormick was the prime suspect in several murders in the area and the police were attempting to talk to him at the time of the accident. The police are not making any statements at this time and we have no further details. This station will continue to bring you news reports on this bizarre case and its aftermaths as we get them.

"No," Steven mumbled several times, staring at the TV. The tears were flowing from his face once more. "Dad can't be dead, he can't be."

"Well, I guess that's that," Henry said, unaffected by the boy and his torment.

"Now we can collect our money and be on our way."

"You are an asshole you know that," Kirk said, looking over at Steven. Though the boy had been a pain in the ass from beginning, learning about his father's death in such a manner could not have been easy for the boy. "I am sorry, kid."

"He can't be dead, not like this," Steven repeated, looking at the man trying to offer him comfort. He had lost his mother in a fiery car explosion and now to lose his father the same way—it was more than he could bear.

"Maybe," Mark said as he sat next to the boy, "maybe it is for the best."

Looking up at his uncle, Steven sat quietly unable to say or do anything about what he had just said.

"Kirk, take him back to his room and make sure he is secured," Mark ordered as he helped Steven to his feet. "I don't want any more mistakes. We leave in a few hours and I want everything ready."

"Just relax, kid," Kirk said as he led him away. "It will all be over soon."

"It's already over if my father is dead," Steven uttered, the fight in him dissipating as he sat on the bed. As long as he had his father, had the hope Andrew would find him and rescue him from the nightmare he was in, but if he were dead, then there was no hope of anything anymore ever being the same again.

"Just stay in your room till it's time to go," Kirk said before closing the door, "and don't cause any more trouble." He left Steven in his room as he laid in bed crying for the parent he just lost.

Returning to the living room in time to see Mark and Henry still arguing over the news bulletin, Kirk remained silent as the two men tried to figure out the next move.

"How is he?" Mark asked, turning to Kirk for a moment to find out about the boy.

"How do you think?" he replied.

"I want him ready to leave within the next few hours," Mark announced.

"Excuse me?" Kirk snapped. "You still plan on taking him with you?"

"Of course I do, why wouldn't I?"

"Why not? The boy knows the truth; he knows you were part of his kidnaping and now his father's death, you still can't believe your original plan will work, can you?" Kirk asked, surprised by the depth of Mark's madness where the boy was concerned. "The boy despises you and will never let you control his life now."

"I will find a way to make him understand and in time we will be like we were before," Mark said, still lost in his own fantasies of what the future held for them.

"Whatever," Kirk replied, not wanting to get into it with the madman standing before him. He knew there was no way Steven would ever forgive his uncle for what he did, and in the end one or both of them would end up dead. "It doesn't matter to me as long as I get my money," he remarked before sitting down at the kitchen table. "Have you figured out the next move?"

"Yup," Mark replied. "Henry is going to go the hospital morgue and check out the body. If it is Andrew, then everything is finally over."

"And if it isn't?" Henry balked, not liking the idea of being the bait in this newest game.

"Then make it so, and get the hell out of there when you're done," Mark instructed him. "If Andrew was not dead, then he expected his agent to finish the job they started. He wanted Andrew out of the way forever and he did not care how it was done.

"So you want me to kill the bastard if he is still alive?" Henry said with a gleam in his voice.

"Just make sure it looks like a suicide."

"What difference will that make if it is a trap?" Kirk interrupted. If Andrew was setting a trap to capture his son's kidnapers, then it meant he had more of the answers to the puzzle then any of them thought. Making his death now look like a suicide would be pointless.

"There is still a chance my plan is going the way I wanted it to and Andrew's death needs to look like a suicide just in case," Mark snapped, not willing to give up on his goal of destroying Andrew's reputation with his suicide and the note left behind admitting his guilt. "Here is the letter I wrote explaining everything, make sure you put it on his body no matter what you find at the hospital."

"And you don't think the cops already searched his body if he is dead?" Kirk said, still playing the devil's advocate.

"Andrew has a habit of putting things in the lining of his shoes, put the note there and make sure it is just obvious enough for the forensics team to find it when they begin their work."

"Fine, I will do whatever you want," Henry said. "What about the time? It will take me nearly an hour just to get to the morgue and you want to leave this place in two hours, that will be cutting it very close."

"If you know how to do your job, you will be able to make sure everything is in place at the hospital and still have time to meet us at the airport," Mark began. "If not, then find your own way to San Sebastian, just make sure you do not lead anyone to my door."

"And you?"

"I am going to talk to Steven again while Kirk checks with the pilot to make sure our private plane is ready when we get there," Mark began as he headed towards the hallway. "We leave in two hours with or without you," he announced, before heading down the hall to Steven's room.

Walking up to the bed as he stared at the boy, "Soon we will have it all and finally be a family," he mumbled as he reached down and began stroking his hair. "Steven," he began, "are you awake?"

"Please. Please just leave me alone," Steven begged, no longer having the strength to fight his uncle, all he wanted was to be left alone.

"Steven, we need to talk," Mark uttered, refusing to give up on the boy.

"About what?" Steven cried turning towards the man "About how you betrayed my father and me?" Steven rambled.

"No, Steven, we have to discuss our plans and the future."

"Our plans, our future?" Steven laughed. "We have no future together. You might as well just let Henry kill me and get it over with."

"No, Steven, that is not what I want," Mark uttered, trying to console the boy as he spoke. "We do have a future together, I promise you. No matter how upset you are with me, know in time we will be happy again," he continued. "Once we move into our new home, you will come to understand everything and we will finally have the dream life I have always wanted."

"You mean the nightmare you dreamed of, don't you?" the defiant boy continued. "No matter where you take me, we will never be a family. All I am is your prisoner and that is all I ever will be," he announced, making his feelings very clear to Mark as he spoke.

"Steven, don't you understand you are my son and I am trying to do what is best for you," Mark declared.

"I told you before I am not your son," Steven shouted. "And if you believe I am you are more insane than I ever imagined."

"No, you're wrong. You are my son and not Andrew's," Mark declared. "Your mother loved me and gave me the most beautiful gift one person could give another."

"If that were true, then why did she marry my father and not you?" Steven demanded to know.

"Because she did not want to hurt him, he was my best friend and Sophia did not want to tear that friendship apart," Mark explained. "But she loved me and we had some very precious moments together."

"That's a damned lie," Steven shouted, jumping from the bed in anger as he stood toe to toe with his uncle. "My mother did not have an affair with you, and you are not my father," Steven declared.

"She was my true love and we had you as a result," Mark said refusing to hear the words Steven was speaking.

"I know she never had an affair with you, and the fact you believe she did proves you are more of a psychopath than I ever thought."

"What do you mean you know I never was with your mother?" Mark shouted.

"Don't you remember the diary she used to keep?" Steven argued. "Well, I have that diary, and I have read it repeatedly. I know every word inside it," he began. "My mother hated you, hated the way you treated Dad, and she believed you were crazy."

"That is not true," Mark yelled, growing angrier as the pain in his head grew worse.

"The only reason she tolerated you was because of Dad and the friendship you shared," Steven said.

"That is not true," Mark shouted.

"She said you kept insisting that the two of you should have been married and that one day you would realize it and leave Dad. Well, she never loved you, and if she was not so afraid of the pain finding out the truth would have caused Dad, she would have told him years ago what kind of creep you were," Steven said, realizing at the time he first read the diary he did not believe his mother either. He had known Mark his entire life and never saw any side of him other than the loving friend, and he was certain his mother was wrong, was somehow trying to ease her own conscience about her feelings for the man. "I used to think Mom had feelings for you so she wrote those words to make herself feel better, but now I know the truth," Steven snapped. "She saw you for what you really were, a sick, obsessed madman who needed to be kept as far away from the family as possible."

"That's not true, none of that is true," Mark cried, as he began rubbing his temples again.

"What's the matter? Can't face the truth?" Steven balked as the man moved around like a caged animal. "Do you remember Mom telling you she would never reveal what kind of man you really were as long as you never betrayed my father. Do you remember how much she hated you?" Steven continued as his words sent Mark reeling in pain, his head ready to exploded.

"Damn her," Mark mumbled as he began remember the past and the words Sophia spoke to him shortly before her death. "She lied to me and said you were not my son," he began. "She took you away from me and told me after your birthday party I could never see you again," Mark said. "I could not let that happen. It did not matter if I lost my best friend but I could never lose my son."

"She didn't take anything from you, it was never yours to begin with," Steven snapped.

"If only they had both died that day, then I could have had my son, and no one would ever have taken him away from me," Mark rambled.

"That day," Steven blurred out. "What do you mean?"

"The explosion was supposed to kill Andrew before he found out the truth and teamed up with your mother to take you away, but it killed her instead."

"You? You set the bomb that killed my mother?" Steven wept, realizing what Mark was referring to. "You put the bomb in the car."

"I loved her but she scorned me, " Mark said. "I could not take the chance Andrew would hate me too, so I had to do it, had to make sure our friendship never ended."

"By killing him before he could turn on you?" Steven repeated, trying to comprehend the magnitude of his uncle's madness.

"I did what had to be done," Mark repeated. "I did it for you."

"Stop saying that, nothing you did was for me," Steven argued. "You did it because you were jealous of the life they had and wanted to destroy it."

"No, I wasn't jealous, I…." Mark began, his thoughts becoming more and more confused as he spoke. "It was not my fault my parents hated me and tried to beat the life out of me," he said staring into space as he talked. "It wasn't my fault I had to kill them when I was a child just so I could survive."

"Kill them? Your parents, you killed them too?" Steven blurted out, nearly choking on the words. He heard about the death of Mark's parents, the fire that killed them when he was sixteen years old. Now to find out he murdered them too, been a killer since he was a teenager, sent Steven reeling. "You murdered my mother and your parents," Steven repeated, feeling as he was going to throw up even as he said the words.

Terrified, Steven wanted only to find a place to hide before the madness surrounding him grew stronger. His uncle was insane, a psychopath who tricked everyone he ever knew into believing in him and now everyone was paying the price. "Mom was the only one who saw you for what you really were, wasn't she?"

"She loved me, but she never understood my world or the things I had to do to survive."

"So you murdered her because of that?"

"Yes, I wasn't going to have something else taken from me and I wanted her dead to keep that from happening," Mark shouted. "You are the only person that ever loved me for me, saw me as a good guy and I wasn't going to lose that because of Andrew or Sophia, not anyone."

Afraid to reply as he listened to Mark carry on, Steven felt the hopelessness of his life growing stronger. Even if he managed to escape from the madman who held him prisoner, he would never be able to escape from the knowledge the man he trusted his entire life was responsible for his mother's murder, for the destruction of his family.

CHAPTER THIRTEEN

Anxious about this latest assignment, Henry hurried through the streets of Rome rushing towards the hospital. His own fears of walking into a trap, heightened only by the possibility Andrew was actually dead, made this one of the most important endeavors of his life. If his enemy was indeed gone, then he'd proven to himself that he was the better agent, the better man. He used his skills to set up the almighty Andrew McCormick, to make him appear guilty of not one but several murders and he was very proud of himself. If the rule books were rewritten showing Andrew not to be one of the best agents in the field, it didn't matter to Henry if the truth of his role in destroying that legend was never known, he knew the truth and that was what mattered.

Arriving at the hospital shortly after six in the evening, Henry found himself concerned by security lax surrounding the facility. Even if the prime suspect in several homicides was dead as the news announced, he still expected to see more security around the facility, more press. It was obvious from the lack of both either Andrew's body was not there as he had learned from his contact, or the press was given a different location other than this one to keep them at bay.

Glancing at his watch, Henry balked at the time restraints placed on him in completing the mission. Already thirty minutes into the deadline, he would have to move very quickly if he did not want to get left behind. Staring at a young man dressed in hospital blues as he stepped off the elevator into the parking garage, Henry moved in on him without warning. A single blow to the back of the head made his victim easy to handle as he dragged the man behind a nearby car and began to remove his clothes.

"This is going to be easier than I thought," he said to himself as he adjusted the hospital uniform he now wore and made his way to the elevator.

Why is the morgue always in the basement like some horror movie scene? he wondered as the elevator descended several floors before finally stopping at the level he wanted.

"Afternoon, Officer," he said, walking past the only guard he saw as he flashed the badge on the jacket, exposing just enough of the face to reveal he was a white male with brown hair.

"Sir," the officer replied, straining his eyes to get a better view of the picture, "where are you headed?' he asked.

"Where else would I be heading in the basement?" Henry joked. "The morgue of course."

"Can I see your ID again?" the officer asked. He was given special instructions by the police to make sure no one entered the morgue without their permission.

"Sure thing," Henry said, stepping closer, striking the man with a blow across the jaw as he did. "Next time don't be so curious," he uttered shoving the man under the desk to keep him well hidden, if only for a few minutes. "This is going to be more fun than I thought," he mumbled, realizing he was enjoying himself as he continued to show the locals how inept they really were.

Looking down at the corridor once more as he explored his avenues of escape, Henry examined his options carefully before proceeding. Two exits were his only choices. One at the east end of the hall and one leading to the stairs and the emergency room which a little more risky in that it exposed him to more of the personnel. The elevator he used to come down to the morgue in the first place was safer but would make him more of a target should he be trapped behind the doors when discovered. Neither route was a good option should his trip prove to be nothing more than a trap; Henry decided to play it by ear. He would make his decision when it was time and would worry about the options open to him then.

Walking into the morgue, relieved to find the room empty except for the bodies of the dead, Henry began checking the name tags in search of the man he sought.

"Here we are," he began, a gleam in his eye as he read the name aloud. "Well, hello, Andrew old boy, glad to see you in such terrible shape." He sneered as he looked at the face beneath the blanket. "God," he mumbled. The badly burnt face of his prey was staring back at him. "What a shame, seems that pretty face of yours got some more scars it, doesn't it?" he said, as he took a moment to check both the heartbeat and pause of his target. "Maybe next time you will learn how to handle a car a little better before you try to outrun the cops," he uttered jokingly as he found no sign of life coming from the body. "Oh, I forgot, there will be no next time. Well, at least that psychopath will be happy to know you are dead," he remarked before telephoning Mark with the news. "That's right he is dead, I am standing in front of his body now," Henry said over the phone. "No, no doubt," he continued. "Look, I did as you asked, and now I am on my way back, just make sure you wait for me," he ordered, quickly hanging up before Mark could reply. The sound of someone entering the outer room disrupted his call.

Pulling his weapon from his jacket, Henry hid behind a set of file cabinets as he waited to see who had come into the room.

"I'm sorry, my friend," he heard, as the voice of a man standing near Andrew's body began to speak. "I tried to convince the others to give us more time to prove you were innocent, but without any proof of Steven being the kidnaped boy, there wasn't any way to convince the authorities your story was true," Hans said as he spoke to his old friend. "If only we could have proven the boy was Steven, but when your boss back home insisted he was off on a fishing trip with Mark, it made your entire alibi seem like a phony," he continued as Henry listened to his conversation.

"I'm sorry I couldn't do anything to clear your name. Now, not only do the authorities think you were involved in the death of Antonio Vega and my niece, they are also convinced you had some part in the other deaths because of the things you knew about the kidnaping," he said, turning away for a moment as he looked around, the sense he was not alone causing him concern. "I guess I am getting as paranoid as you were, my friend," he said, turning back to the body of his friend. "I wish I had known about the warrant Knoff issued for your arrest, I could have warned you and maybe you wouldn't have tried to get away from the police the way you did and you might still be alive," he said, covering the body of his friend. "I couldn't stop them from killing you, but I promise I will find your son, no matter how long it takes."

Listening as Hans continued to talk to his friend, Henry found himself amused by what he heard. If the man in front of him expected to find Steven as he vowed, he would have a tough time of it. Only four people knew of the island where Mark planned to take the boy, and the police would never figure it out. Steven was lost to the rest of the world, just as his father was.

"I promise you, my friend, no matter how long it takes, and I will find your son and bring the people responsible for this mess to justice," Hans repeated, his words of grief interrupted by the arrival of another officer.

"Sir, sorry to disturb you, but we have received a report the kidnaped boy was spotted at a villa in Sicily about an hour ago." the officer announced.

"Have we gotten a positive ID on him yet?"

"No, sir, just that two men, and a boy matching the description of our suspects were seen in the villa," the officer replied. "We have a plane waiting for us at the airport."

"Good, then let's go," Hans said before looking back at his friend. "Don't worry, if that boy is Steven, I will bring him home," he whispered before following his officer towards the elevator.

"Yea right." Henry laughed moving from behind the counter. "That dummy has no idea what is going on. Sicily. You go ahead and search the entire island for the kid, knock yourself out," he said as he took his cell phone from his pocket once more. "It's me again, I thought you might want to know those fools are heading for Sicily to look for the boy, and they have no idea who has the boy either," he reported before heading for the door himself. He had done what he came to do and now it was time to get out. So far, the odds had been in his favor and he was not going to push his luck.

Heading for the stairs, Henry tossed the jacket into a nearby trash can before walking past the main desk, he had a little more than twenty minutes to make it to the plane and there was no time to waste.

"He's on the move," Knoff said into his police radio as he stood behind the desk watching their prey walk out the emergency door. "The suspect is wearing a pair of blue jeans, a blue jacket and gray shirt," he continued. "I don't want any mistakes on this, so everyone get ready."

"Knoff, this is Hans. Are you sure it is him?" Hans asked, jumping into his car as he transmitted over the radio.

"It's him all right," Knoff replied, he'd remember the face on the poster for as long as he lived. The man tried to use him to set up an innocent man, and he would never forget the faces of all the parties involved.

"Good," Hans said. "Unit 230 to all units, our man is on the move, I want him guarded at every angle but don't do anything to spook him, he is our only lead to the boy and we need him to take us to him," he instructed as he drove towards the rear entrance leading to the morgue.

"Unit 6 to 230," a voice on the radio said.

"Go ahead," Hans began.

"We found a hospital worker in the parking garage. He is still alive, but he has been badly injured," he began.

"Get him some medical aid and secure the area," Hans ordered. "The rest of the team remains in place till I give the order."

"I've got him in the north tower parking lot," an officer declared nervously over the radio.

"Keep him in sight but don't let him spot you," Hans ordered as he waited at the morgue entrance. "Come on, get in," he said, as a man jumped in the front seat next to him.

"Do we have him?"

"Yes, one of my men has him in the parking lot," Hans replied.

"Then let's go," he said removing the makeup from his face as he spoke.

"I never thought he would fall for that ruse but it sure did look real," Hans confessed as his passenger slowly removed a layer of skin from, his throat and face.

"It's the latest thing in the game," Andrew replied, peeling the burnt skin off as he spoke. "A synthetic fiber designed by one of the boys at the agency," he continued as he started removing the skin from his arms and chest as well. "All you do is apply a thin layer over your body and any signs of life are wiped away," he explained.

"The counter-agent in the fiber acts like a sealant and anyone who checks for a pulse or a heart beat gets nothing, a dead body."

"I'm surprised Henry there didn't think about that when he checked your pulse," Hans remarked, curious as to why someone from the agency did not anticipate the possibility of the fiber being used now.

"That, my friend, is because he does not know about it," Andrew revealed.

"It's fairly new and only a hand full of people, outside the scientists working on the fiber, knew of its existence."

"Guess it pays to be up there in the food chain," Hans remarked.

"Also pays to have a boss who believes in you," Andrew replied, referring to Stewart as he spoke. "He trusted me enough to let me in on the ground floor when it was being tested and even allowed me to keep some with me in case a situation should arise where I might need it."

"And this was definitely that kind of situation," Hans joked as they moved towards the others and their latest position. "Here put this on," he uttered, grabbing a shirt from the back seat of his car. "The last thing you want to do is rescue your son in a shirt covered in blood."

"Thanks," Andrew replied, realizing as he spoke how good the words *rescue your son* sounded to him. "I hope he understands why I had to do it this way." He began thinking about the pain his son must have endured believing his father were dead.

"Your son is a smart boy, and when he realizes why you faked your own death, he will understand," Hans assured him.

"I know you're right, Steven is a smart boy and will understand why I did it, but I still can't help but worry about the effects it will have on him in the end."

"He is your son, remember that he can handle anything that comes his way."

"Thanks," Andrew replied. As much as he hated the ruse of faking his own death it was the only way to flush the others out. Once it became clear Hector was not going to reveal where they were holding Steven, the options left open to them were minimal. Convincing Mark that Andrew was dead seemed the only logical step.

Though he came to realize over the course of days how little he knew about his friend, Andrew was certain about one thing, Mark's ego. He would not make another move until he was certain the enemy was neutralized and this was the best way to convince him of just that.

"I hope this fool can lead us to Steven before it is too late," Hans declared as they moved towards the parking lot.

"He has to," Andrew uttered. They had not gone through all this to lose now. Their prey had to lead them to Steven before it was too late, he had to.

"There he is," Hans said, as they spotted Henry about twenty feet away from them near a row of cars. "All units on your toes, he is getting into his car now." He began instructing his men of their next move as they watched their man move towards his car.

Walking past an approaching ambulance, Henry felt the hair on the back of his neck stand up on edge. Always a signal something was not right, he looked around to see if he could spot anything out of the ordinary.

"Amateurs," he whispered as he got inside his car and started the engine. He spotted two people sitting in a car about two aisles behind him, and though they were trying to make themselves inconspicuous, Henry knew they were cops.

So it was a trap, Henry said to himself as he adjusted the rear view mirror to get a better look at the players in the game. "Well, my friends, if I am going down, I plan to take as many of you with me as I can," he vowed, shifting the car into gear as he started for the main exit ramp.

"He knows," Andrew blurted out as he watched their prey through a pair of binoculars. "Damn it, he knows."

"How?" Hans argued. No one had moved; there was no way he could have known they were watching him.

"I'm telling you he knows," Andrew declared. He could feel it, Henry knew they were watching him and he was getting ready to start the game. "Tell your people to watch their backs, he knows we're here."

"All units move in," Hans ordered.

Trying to get out of the parking lot, each access point blocked by another police car, Henry finally dumped the car in the middle of the road as he ran towards the street in hopes of making it to a nearby marketplace. If he could make it there, getting lost in the crowd would be much easier for him.

Firing at the men as they raced towards him, Henry shoved a nearby tourist into his path to keep the others at bay.

"Freeze! Police!" Knoff ordered, jumping out from behind a small gateway just a few feet ahead of Henry as he drew closer. This was his home, and he knew all the short cuts and avenues to take to make sure the man he sought did not get away. "Freeze or I will shoot," Knoff repeated, standing in front of Henry now as they stood toe to toe. "Give it up, it's over."

"Not in this lifetime," Henry replied, aiming at the man who was in his path.

"No, don't," Andrew cried as the echoing of gunfire filled the air. He needed Henry alive, needed him to help find his son.

"Andrew," Henry balked, his hand pressed against his chest as the blood poured from his injured body, "I should have known you couldn't have been killed that easily." He fell to his knees in pain.

"No, damn you, you can't die, not yet, not till you tell me where my son is," Andrew moaned, grabbing Henry by the shirt collar, as he continued to fall to the ground in pain.

"Get an ambulance," Knoff ordered, as the others drew closer.

"Where is my son?" Andrew screamed. "Where is Steven?"

"You will never find him." Henry sneered, coughing from the blood which now filled his every breath.

"Damn it, tell me where he is."

"Henry, you're dying," Hans began, leaning down next to the two men in hopes he could persuade the injured man to tell them the truth. "Keeping his whereabouts a secret now won't serve any purpose, so tell us where Mark has the boy."

"You knew about Mark too?" Henry uttered.

"We figured it all out," Hans said.

"But not in time." Henry laughed.

"Please tell us where the boy is," the officer repeated.

"What and miss the last thing I will ever see?" Henry balked. "The look on Andrew's face is worth everything. He knows he will never see his son again."

"Tell me where my son is."

"I should have known the local yokels couldn't have killed you in a car crash," Henry said, finding it harder to speak with each breath.

"Where did Mark take him?" Andrew screamed, shaking the dying man as the others looked on without saying a word.

"What time is?" Henry finally asked.

"A little before eight o'clock," Hans replied. "Why?"

"Because, my friend, even if I told you where he was, it's too late," Henry explained. "Mark has already taken him out of the country by now, they were supposed to leave by eight o'clock, and if I know that madman, he probably left early anyway."

"No," Andrew cried. It could not be too late.

"We still have fifteen minutes so why don't you tell us where he is and we will take it from there?" Hans said to Henry.

"Too late," Henry uttered before taking his last breath.

"Damn you, don't die on me without telling me where my son is," Andrew screamed, pulling at the man's shirt as he struggled to get him to respond.

"Andrew, he's gone," Hans shouted, trying to get his friend to let the man go.

"It's all my fault," Andrew began, leaning against the car, his hands still covered in the blood of the dead man. "Everything that has happened is all my fault."

"You can't blame yourself for this," Hans began, trying to console his friend.

"I can't," Andrew snapped. "Mark was after me, he hated me, and in his sick mind taking my son was the only way he could get back at me."

"First off," Hans interrupted, "no matter what those shrinks back home said, Mark is responsible for his own actions. He planned this entire thing out for months and he knew exactly what he was doing. He has been insane most of his life, you and your family just got caught up in the middle of it. No one but Mark is to blame for his actions, and you have to know that no matter how guilty you feel right now."

"I wish I could believe that," Andrew replied.

"Damn those doctors for letting him out of the hospital when they knew he could be dangerous," Hans snapped. "Why didn't they just leave him there and save all of us this pain?"

"What? And have the agency lose out on the perfect killing machine," Andrew said, his tone calming slightly as he spoke. As much as he hated Mark for everything he did, the agency was just as guilty as his friend. They knew of his illness, knew how dangerous he could be, yet they let him out so they could use him as their own personal killing tool. There was nothing better in the field then an operative with no conscience. No false beliefs of right and wrong to hold him back from completing the mission.

"And you work for these animals?" Knoff said.

"Not any more," Andrew replied. He wanted to leave for some time now, and this was the final straw. No matter what happened next, the agency would be out of his life forever. "Taking responsibility for the life I chose so long ago doesn't help the situation now or relinquish any of the guilt I feel for not walking away sooner when I realized just how far they would go to complete the mission. I've done some things in the past I am not very proud of and I will have to live with that, but my son never should have been made to suffer because of it," Andrew said, staring at the dead man. "He is out there alone and in trouble because of me and I have no idea where to start looking for him."

"Maybe I can help with that," Knoff said after examining the body of the dead man a little closer.

"How?" Andrew questioned.

"With this," he replied, holding a cell phone in his hand. "If Henry phoned Mark while he was at the morgue, then the last number called will still be available for us to use to find Steven."

"But even if the number is there, we can't call, it will tip them off," Andrew remarked, not thinking straight, for if he had been, then he would have realized calling Mark back was not part of Knoff's plan.

"Who said we have to call him back?" Knoff began as he looked at the number before radioing headquarters for some assistance. "If the number comes back to a home, or hotel, the information screen at our dispatch center will give us the address," he explained as the three men waited for the operator at the other end to relay the information to them.

"We have an address," the dispatcher finally announced over the radio.

"You have got to be kidding," Hans replied, after everything they went through the crosses and double crosses and now the final answer they sought was a simple phone call away.

"Base to unit 224," the radio echoed out as they waited to hear what they had discovered.

"Go ahead base," Knoff began.

"The number 555-5151 comes back to an estate about five miles from the airport. The address is 623 Loranzo Drive."

"Got it," Knoff began as he signaled his people to get to their cars. "Shall we go?"

"We have less then ten minutes," Andrew shouted.

"Then let's go," Hans yelled as they got in the car. He would have them there in a matter of minutes.

"Things could get pretty hairy if Mark is still there. Are you sure you want to risk your people?" Andrew said. He was ready to risk his own life to save Steven but enough people already died because of this mess without risking the lives of the officers standing before him.

"I don't know about the others, but I am a police officer and taking risks is part of the job, besides, I would like to get my hands on the animals that believe terrorizing a teenage boy is part of any game played in this town," Knoff replied, jumping into the back seat of the car while Hans started the engine of the car.

"You heard my detective, now get in, we are wasting time," Hans yelled as his officers ran for their cars ready to move with the others.

Stopping about a ¼ mile from the gate entrance, the rescue party regrouped by Hans' car as they prepared to for the next move out of the sight of the guards surrounding the estate. From the number of men still there, it was obvious the prize they possessed was still on the grounds and they had not arrived too late to stop Mark from taking Steven out of the country.

"You two take the northeast corner, you the south," Hans instructed. "And don't let anyone leave the estate," he ordered before his men began moving in on their target.

Startled by the sound of gunfire echoing through the grounds, Steven jumped from the bed.

Could the gunfire mean someone had finally come to the rescue? he wondered as he began pounding on the door in desperation.

"I'm in here," he screamed, hoping whoever it was could hear his cries for help. "I'm in here," he repeated, the sound of someone at the door trying to get it opened sending his heart racing. "Help me, I'm in here," he began. The excitement he felt dissipated as he came face to face with the person at the door.

"Sorry, kid," Kirk said, stepping inside as he secured the door behind him.

"Kirk!" Steven cried out, trying not to let his anguish of still being a prisoner take hold of him again. "Who's out there?" he uttered.

"Doesn't matter, kid, it's time to go," Kirk said, tying Steven's hands together in front of him as he spoke.

"Go where?" Steven demanded to know. If the gunfire was indeed someone coming to his rescue, he couldn't allow Kirk to take him away now.

"Look, kid," Kirk shouted, yanking the boy towards him as he spoke, "I do not intend to spend the rest of my life in jail and as long as I have you for bargaining power, there is still a chance I can get out of this nightmare in one piece. Now move it and maybe you might make it out too."

"Please, Kirk, someone is out there looking for me, please let me go," Steven cried, hearing the gunfire once more as they made their way down the hall. "Can you at least tell me who it is?" Steven shouted, pulling away from Kirk as he held tightly onto the ropes around his wrist.

"More than likely, it's your father," Kirk said, his words surprising Steven.

"My father, but the news report…"

"Probably a set up and we walked right into it," Kirk declared. It was obvious from the fact the police were at the estate that the reports of Andrew's death had been nothing more than a ploy to get one of them at the hospital in order to find out where they were holding the boy. "That fool, Henry probably sold us out once he got caught and now the calvary is here trying to free you," Kirk snapped, certain his weak kneed friend was the reason they were under siege.

"Good, you have him," Mark interrupted, as he ran into the others in the hall.

"Take him to the helicopter and wait for me there," he instructed, holding a box tightly in his hand as he spoke.

"Mark, it's over, you have to give yourself up before it's too late," Steven said, trying to make his uncle understand one last time that he needed to surrender.

"It's not over, I still have a little surprise for those bastards." Mark laughed, touching the box slightly as he did.

"What do you mean, a surprise?" Steven asked. "What is in that box?"

"Just a little going away present," Mark uttered. "Actually three little presents."

"What is it?" Steven repeated.

"Three very special bombs designed to destroy this entire estate," Mark said without flinching over the words of yet more murders he was about to commit.

"My god, Uncle Mark, you can't do this," Steven pleaded, terrified by what he just heard.

"Take the boy to the chopper and wait for me. If I am not there in five minutes, leave without me and take him to the island. I will meet you later," he instructed his reluctant accomplice.

"You want me to take him where?" Kirk balked. He was tired of the entire mess and the last thing he wanted was to baby-sit the boy any further.

"If you want the rest of your money, just do as I say," Mark snapped before running off. "I am going to make sure no one, not that damned cop or his men and not even Andrew gets in my way ever again," he shouted before disappearing.

Calling for his uncle to stop, Steven struggled with Kirk desperately to get away. He could not let them kill any more people because of him.

"Please, Kirk, we have to stop him."

"Sorry, kid, too late," Kirk replied, firing his gun as an officer drew near, his actions sending the man to the floor with a bullet in his leg. "Now move it, kid," he ordered, shoving Steven up a small spiral staircase leading to the roof of the building.

The helicopter was less than thirty feet away and there was no way anyone was going to stop them from getting away.

"Freeze! Police!" a voice from behind the helicopter shouted as Hans stepped out his gun drawn.

"Back off or I will kill the boy," Kirk ordered, grabbing Steven as he spoke, his gun aimed at the teen's head.

"You know I can't do that," Hans said moving closer. "It's over, there's no where to go, so drop the gun, and let the boy go."

"Not as long as that helicopter is my way out."

"It's not," Knoff said, as he too moved closer, sneaking up behind them, undetected by the gunman. "I disabled it and you are not going anywhere in that bird. So do as the Lieutenant said and drop the gun."

"Damn you," Kirk snapped, pulling Steven closer to him, "you back off now or the kid is dead."

"There's no where to go," Hans repeated as he looked into Steven's eyes. "Steven," he uttered, trying to calm the fear he saw within them, "son, listen to me, your father is alive and around here somewhere looking for you and everything is going to be alright."

"Dad is alive, he's really alive," Steven repeated, afraid to believe the words he heard could be true.

"Yes, he is alive and kicking," Hans said.

"Look, bright boy, I don't care if Andrew is alive or not, if you don't want to see this kid dead, tell your man over there to drop his gun and back off so I can get down the stairs," Kirk snapped. If he could not get away with the chopper, then a car would have to do.

"All right," Hans said, stepping away as he ordered Knoff to do the same thing.

"Steven, you have to trust me, ok?" he began, hoping the boy would understand it was up to him to make the next move if they were going to stop Kirk.

"I…" Steven started, unsure if he trusted the man standing before him. "I don't know what to do," he said as Kirk pulled him towards the stairs. Realizing as they drew nearer if he did not do something soon, he would forever be a prisoner not only of his uncle but also of his own fears. "No more!" Steven screamed, bolting away from his captor, his actions catching Kirk off guard.

"Now," Hans yelled as Knoff aimed his gun and fired. The kidnaper was no longer beyond their reach as Steven tumbled to the ground after his escape.

Afraid to move, the sound of gunfire erupting, Steven felt a hand touch his shoulder as he looked up to see one of the policemen standing over him.

"It's all over," Hans said, extending his hand to help the boy. "He's dead," he remarked, while his officer checked to be sure the statement he just made to the boy was true.

"Is he really dead?" Steven questioned, afraid to believe the nightmare could finally be over.

"Dead as a door nail," Knoff replied. "Isn't that how you Americans say it?"

"Yup," Steven said, smiling slightly at the officer's use of American slang.

"Are you alright?" Hans asked.

"I think so," Steven began, staring at the body of the man who had been his captor for so long.

"Are you sure you weren't hurt in the fall?" Hans asked once more. "You hit the ground hard."

"I'm fine," Steven uttered. "Can I ask you a question now?"

"Sure, kid, what is it?" the lieutenant said.

"Who are you?"

"It's ok, kid, you're safe now," Hans said.

"But who are you?"

"I'm Hans Ferrier, a friend of your father's."

"So was he," Steven remarked, pointing at the dead man. "Everyone I met this week claimed to be a friend of my father's and they were all trying to kill him," Steven declared, not sure if he could trust the man who just saved his life.

"I promise you, Steven, I am a friend, and your father is alive and here in the house somewhere."

"Then he really is alive," Steven said. He thought those words spoken earlier were just a ploy to trick Kirk into surrendering.

"Yes, son, he is alive." Hans laughed as he untied the boys hands. "And if I know your dad, he is inside that house kicking some butt trying to get answers about where you are."

"He's alive," Steven repeated as he sat on a nearby chair. "He's really alive and inside the house now," he began. "No, the house!" he screamed as the memory of something Mark told him earlier came back like a bolt of lightning.

"What about the house?" Hans said, concerned by the boy's outburst.

"Mark said he was going to blow up the house before we left."

"He was going to do what?" Hans echoed, turning towards his man as he did.

"Get in that house and make sure everyone is out. Tell them not to transmit, we do not want to set the explosives off by accident," he instructed before turning back to Steven.

"Do you know where Mark is now?" he asked as Knoff headed back down the stairs to warn the others.

"No, he said he was going to meet us here in five minutes," Steven replied, revealing what he knew. "What about my father?" he asked. If Andrew were still in the house, he was in as much danger as the others.

"Don't worry, Knoff will get everyone out of the house before anything happens, but you and I have to get off this roof before we end up apart of the skyline," Hans declared, grabbing the boy by the arm as they ran towards the stairs and started back down the pathway. "Come on, Steven, we have one more floor to go and we will be safely out of this mess," Hans announced as they reached the second floor of the estate.

"I can't leave without my father," Steven protested, pulling away from his rescuer.

"Steven, don't be silly, your father is probably out of the house already," Hans said, trying to assure him that everyone including his father was safe.

"No!" Steven cried.

"Steven, wait," Hans shouted as the boy bolted away and ran towards the stairs once more. "Great," Hans quipped as he tried to keep up with the teen, "not only do I have to search the damned house for a bomb but for the kid as well." His attempts to stop Steven failed as the boy out ran him and returned to the house.

"Next time I leave this crap to the younger generation," Hans mumbled to himself as he tried to catch his breath. The strain of running so quickly up the stairs reminded him how out of shape he really was. "If that damned bomb doesn't kill me, all this exercise will," he uttered as he called out Steven's name several times in hopes the boy would reply.

Running towards the pool in a desperate attempt to get away from his pursuer, Mark looked back as he saw the face of the man he tried so hard to destroy. He thought the game was over, thought he had won but now as Andrew drew closer he knew he lost yet again as he came in second in their latest game.

"Mark, stop it's over," Andrew shouted as the two men began to struggle, each one trying to maintain control of the battle they now fought.

"It will never be over," Mark replied. As their fight continued, a blow to the jaw sent him against the nearby patio table.

"Where is my son? What have you done with him?"

"Why won't you die?" Mark screamed without answering his question. "No matter what I do, you just won't die," he echoed. This time his own blow sent Andrew to the ground. "No matter what I do, the fire that killed my parents was supposed to kill you too." Mark began revealing the horrors of the past as he spoke. "I knew you were in the house with them and you should have all died."

"My god, I never realized how much you hated me," Andrew said, struggling to his feet as he listened to the man before him.

"You stole my life from me. I should have had the perfect parents who wanted me and loved me, the perfect wife and career, but instead I got the leftovers while you got the prize. Well not anymore, I have Steven, he is mine now, and you will never see him again. You will never take my son away from me again."

"He's my son, damn it," Andrew yelled, no longer interested in the reasons behind Mark's madness. "Where is he?" Andrew repeated, grabbing his opponent by the shirt collar as he yelled. "Where is my son? You have no right to take him from me."

"I had every right," Mark snapped. "If it wasn't for you taking Sophia away from me, too, he would have been my son."

"I never took her away from you. My god, Mark, I was engaged to Sophia before you even met her."

"She would have loved me if it weren't for you."

"Is that why you killed her too, because she did not love you?" Andrew demanded to know as the two men stopped fighting as stood there yelling at each other.

"She was going to take him away from me," Mark began. "She told me after his birthday I could not come see him any more. Couldn't be a part of the family anymore," Mark rambled as he recalled the day Sophia had told him these words.

"It was a few days before the party, she said she was going to tell you that I was dangerous and she wanted me to stay away from Steven," he continued as he sat down near the patio table. "He was the only good thing in my life, he loved me no matter what and I couldn't let that happen."

"So you put a bomb in my car and killed her," Andrew yelled, lunging at Mark. His attempts to strike him were blocked as Mark delivered his own punch, sending Andrew reeling to the ground in pain.

"That is not all. I didn't just intend to kill Sophia that day; I wanted both of you dead," Mark announced, grabbing his gun which had fallen to the ground during the struggle. "I wanted both of you out of the way, and I figured you would take her to the store when I didn't show up, and Steven would be my son, and I could finally have something good in my life."

"Both of us. You wanted both of us dead," Andrew said, as he stood before the man wielding a gun in his hand refusing to back down.

"If you had taken her like I planned, then none of this would be necessary. Steven would be mine and he never would have suffered so much," Mark yelled. "This is all your fault."

"Why now, after all these years, did you have to involve my son in this again?" Andrew demanded to know. "It has been ten years, why now?"

"That was your fault too," Mark said. "I had it all after Sophia died, you gave up on life, on your job, and your son, and they both fell into my lap," Mark explained as he ordered Andrew to move closer to the pool. "But then you decided to come out of your depression to try and make things right with your son, and suddenly I found myself the odd man out again. After ten years, you were taking my life away from me, so I decided to take yours instead."

He continued pushing Andrew closer to the pool's edge. "When Hector came to me and asked me to help assassinate the president and his brother, I came up with this plan instead. I knew about the promise you made to Jose Vega and I figure I could use it to my advantage," Mark yelled, as he pointed the gun at Andrew. "It would have been prefect, you would be dead, by your own hand and forever remembered by everyone as a murderer and traitor. Then I would have Steven as my son again and we would have the perfect life, just the two of us," Mark screamed as he aimed the gun.

"And it would have all worked out if you hadn't interfered again," he uttered, the sound of the gunfire echoing around them.

"Steven!" Mark cried out, turning to see the boy standing behind him with a gun in his hand. Looking down at the blood coming from his body, Mark smiled at the boy as he called his name out once more before falling to his death.

Unable to move, Steven stared a the man he just killed. Ever since he learned the truth about his uncle, all he wanted was to see him pay, but as he laid there bleeding, all Steven could see was the man who helped raise him, the man he loved like a father.

"Steven. It's all right," Andrew began as he took the gun from his son's hands. "It's all over."

"I had to shoot him; I couldn't let him kill you like he killed Mom," Steven mumbled. "I had to shoot him."

"I know, son," Andrew replied, slowing putting his arms around his son as he tried to comfort the boy. "It's over now and everything is going to be alright."

"Dad." The boy wept as he held tightly onto his father.

"I am glad to see you two are ok," Hans interrupted, running towards them.

"This damned estate is bigger than I thought," he said, still trying to catch his breath as he looked at the dead man floating in the pool. "I see you took care of things."

"Everything is fine now," Andrew replied, still holding onto his son. "What about the rest of the house? Is it secured?"

"Yup."

"The bombs, too? Are they taken care of?" Steven blurted out.

"Not to worry, kid, I took care of it," Hans began, bragging about disarming the bomb he found along the stairwell. "Did you say bombs?" he questioned, realizing what the boy had just uttered.

"Yes. Mark had three of them in his hands when he disappeared earlier."

"Damn, I knew it was too easy," Hans remarked as he looked around at the estate.

"Let me guess you only disarmed two of them right?" Andrew started to ask.

"Well, actually I only found one," Hans protested. "I told you this estate is too large, finding the one was nothing but dumb luck."

"Then might I suggest we get the hell out of here before the house blows up around us," Andrew said.

"Sounds good to me," Hans replied as they raced towards the front gate, reaching it just seconds before the bombs exploded around them.

"See, stick with me and everything works out." Hans began wiping the dirt from his suit after the explosion sent them tumbling to the ground.

"Yea, right." Andrew laughed as he helped his son to his feet. "Steven, are you all right?"

"I never thought I would get out of there alive," Steven began, the tears flowing from his face.

"But you did, son, and that is all that matters," Andrew said, hugging his son once more. "That's all that matters," he repeated.

"What about Uncle Mark?" Steven asked, staring at the rubble.

"Don't worry, kid, as soon as the fire department says it's safe to go back inside we will retrieve his body," Hans assured him.

"Can we make sure he gets a decent burial?" Steven pleaded. Despite everything, he still loved the man and wanted to do right by him.

"Yes, son," Andrew replied. "We will take care of Uncle Mark."

"Thanks," Steven said. "Can we go home now?"

"Not just yet, Steven," Hans answered. "There are a few things that need to be cleared up and in a couple of days, I promise you and your father will be on a plane heading home."

"You know my father didn't have anything to do with those murders, Mark set him up," Steven said, defending his father.

"I know that, Steven, but we have to show proof to the rest of the world before we can finally close the book on this mess."

"Can you show the rest of the world the proof?" Steven asked, afraid now that he found his father, he would be taken away from him again.

"Without a doubt," Hans assured him.

"It will be over soon, son, and then we will go home, I promise," Andrew said before turning towards his friend. "Hans, there is something we need to talk about later."

"No, Andrew, there isn't," Hans said.

"But?"

"But nothing, take your son to your hotel till I call and then take him home."

"Hans," Andrew began to say as his friend stopped him once more.

"I know," Hans replied. "Take care of your son," he ordered as he watched the two of them walk towards the car.

Looking at Hans as Steven got into the car, Andrew nodded to his friend as a silent understanding was established between them. He wanted to tell him the truth, tell him what happened that day but his friend was determined not to let him.

He never meant to kill her. It was an accident. Helena contacted him about his son and he thought his prayers where answered. It was not until after he arrived and saw the bracelet Steven always wore that he realized just how involved she was with the kidnaping. He never meant to kill her, she tripped over the coffee table as they argued and hit her head on the fireplace. If only he had not reacted the way he did when he saw the bracelet, hadn't allowed his instincts as a father overrule his better judgment, she might still be alive.

"Are you sure about this?" Knoff asked, moving next to Hans as they watched Andrew and his son drive off. He had the proof, enough proof to arrest Andrew for the murder of Helena. The broken glass with his fingerprints on it, the blood stain he found on Andrew's jacket in his closet and the button she held in her hand, it was all circumstantial but it was enough.

"Yes, I am sure, all that evidence was planted by Mark and his people," Hans replied.

"Sir," Knoff began, questioning his superior's words.

"It's over, Knoff, let it go," Hans ordered, for he knew the truth too and as much as he loved his niece, he knew she would not want Andrew or his son to suffer any more because of her. The people responsible for her murder were all dead and that was enough for him to bury his niece without guilt.

"Sir," Knoff said one more time in hopes of changing his mind.

"Let it go, for me," Hans said, patting his officer on the back. "It's time for the nightmare to be over for everyone."

"Alright, Hans, for you," Knoff replied. He would falsify the report for his friend. He'd never done that before, lied on a crime report, it would be something he too would have to live with, but Hans was right, it was time for the nightmare to be over for everyone.

Printed in the United States
22318LVS00004B/193-195